Praise for *New York Times* bestselling author

LORI
FOSTER

"Lori Foster delivers the goods."
—*Publishers Weekly*

"This fantasy plays out with sexy innuendos
and steamy love scenes throughout the book."
—*Romantic Times BOOKreviews* on *Jude's Law*

"Filled with Foster's trademark wit, humor, and sensuality."
—*Booklist* on *Jamie*

"Foster supplies good sex and great humor
along the way in a thoroughly enjoyable romance
reminiscent of Susan Elizabeth Phillips' novels."
—*Booklist* on *Causing Havoc*

"Foster executes with skill...convincing, heartfelt family drama."
—*Publishers Weekly* on *Causing Havoc*

"Suspenseful, sexy, and humorous."
—*Booklist* on *Just a Hint—Clint*

"Fans of Foster's sexy romantic comedies...
will find much to like here."
—*Booklist* on *The Secret Life of Bryan*

**Other newly released Buckhorn Brothers classics
from Lori Foster and Harlequin Books**

Sawyer
Morgan
Gabe
Jordan

LORI FOSTER

FOSTER

Enticing

HQN™

HQN™

ISBN-13: 978-0-373-77267-4
ISBN-10: 0-373-77267-X

ENTICING

Copyright © 2007 by Harlequin Books S.A.

The publisher acknowledges the copyright holder of the individual works as follows:

THE BUCKHORN BROTHERS: CASEY
Copyright © 2002 by Lori Foster

CAUGHT IN THE ACT
Copyright © 2001 by Lori Foster

This edition published by arrangement with Harlequin Books S.A.

® and TM are trademarks of the publisher. Trademarks indicated with ® are registered in the United States Patent and Trademark Office, the Canadian Trade Marks Office and in other countries.

www.HQNBooks.com

Printed in U.S.A.

CONTENTS

THE BUCKHORN BROTHERS: CASEY

prologue

THE FAMILY PICNIC had lasted all day, and Casey had a feeling everything that should have been accomplished had been. In fact, even more had developed than he'd expected—like his present uncomfortable situation.

He hadn't exactly meant to pair up with Emma Clark. She had few friends, none of them female, and Casey had just naturally defended her when the others had started sniping.

So now, with nearly every girl in town chasing after him, he found himself behind the garage at the far end of the house with a girl—the one girl he'd been doing his best to avoid—snuggled up to his side. No one else in the yard could see them. They had complete privacy.

How the hell was a guy supposed to deal with that?

His father and his uncles had been the most eligible bachelors in Buckhorn, Kentucky. It had been fun for Casey growing up in an all-male household and watching his uncles and his dad deal with all that female adoration. Casey had been proud of their popularity and amused by it all. And pleased by the situation, since he'd gained his own share of adoration as he'd matured. He'd learned a lot from watching them—but he hadn't learned how to deal with Emma.

Like his father and his uncles, Casey loved and respected women, most especially his grandmother and his new stepmother and aunts. But then, they were all so different from Emma.

And that thought had him frowning.

Emma was…well, she had a reputation that could rival his Uncle Gabe's, and that said something since Gabe had been a complete and total hedonist when it came to his sexuality. By all accounts, Gabe had started young; from what Casey knew, Emma had started even younger.

At seventeen, she flaunted herself with all the jaded expertise of a woman twice her age. Her bleached-blond hair and overdone makeup advertised her status of being on the make.

Lately she'd been on the make for Casey. For the most part, he'd been able to resist her.

For the most part.

Emma's small soft hand began trailing over Casey's chest. His heart thumped hard, his body hardened. Very gently, doing his best to hide his reaction from her, he eased her away. "We should join the others."

In fact, he thought, all too aware of the heat of her young body so close to his own, he never should have been alone with her in the first place. Thanks to his stepmother and her father, he had a great business opportunity coming up. But before he could take advantage of that, he had several years of college to get through. Emma, with her hard-to-resist curves and open sensuality, would be nothing but trouble.

"No." She stroked down his bare chest, but Casey caught

her hand before she reached the fly to his jeans. He liked her more than he should have, and wanted her more than that. Hell, to be truthful, he was crazy nuts with wanting her, not that he'd ever even hinted as much. His plans for the future did not include Emma. They couldn't.

Emma had led a very different life from him. Tangling the two up wouldn't be good for either of them.

His head understood that, but his body did not.

It took more control than he knew he had to turn her away this time.

"Emma," Casey chided, hoping that she couldn't hear the shaking of his voice. He'd only wanted to champion her, but Emma wanted more. She was so blatant about it, so brazen, that it took all his concentration not to give in. Besides, more than anything else, Emma needed a friend not another conquest. And beyond that, Casey didn't share.

"Are you a virgin?" she taunted, not giving a single inch, and Casey laughed outright at her ploy. She was determined, he'd give her that. But then, so was he.

Flicking a finger over her soft cheek, he said, "That's none of your business."

Her incredible brown eyes widened, reflecting the moonlight and a femininity that went bone deep. She shook her head in wonder. "You're the only guy I know who wouldn't have denied it right away."

"I'm not denying or confirming."

"I know," she whispered, still sounding amazed, "but most guys'd lie if they had to, rather than let a girl think—"

"What?" Casey cupped her face and despite his resolve, he kissed her. Damn, it was hard fighting both himself and her. "I don't care what anyone thinks, Emma. You should know that by now. Besides, what I've done or with who isn't the point."

"No," she agreed, her tone suddenly so sad it nearly broke his heart. "It's what I've done, isn't it?"

Thinking about that, about the guys she'd probably been with and the notoriety of her reputation, filled Casey with possessive rage. So many guys had bragged. Too damn many. Ruthlessly, Casey tamped down the urges he refused to acknowledge, and repeated his own thoughts out loud. "I don't share."

"Casey," she said, shyly peeking up at him, her expression tinted with hope, "what if I promised not to—"

"Shh." He couldn't bear for Emma to start pleading, to make promises he doubted she could keep and that wouldn't matter in the long run anyway. He couldn't let them matter. "Don't do that, Emma. Don't make it harder than it already is. Summer break is almost over and I'll be leaving for school. You know that. I won't be around, so there's no point in us even discussing this."

Big tears welled in her eyes, causing his guts to cramp. One of her hands fisted in his shirt. "I'm leaving too, Casey." Her breathing was choppy, the words broken.

Emma leaving? That surprised him. As gently as possible, Casey stroked the tears from her cheeks and then, because he couldn't help himself, he kissed her forehead. "And where do you think to go, Em?" She hadn't finished high school yet, had no real prospects that he knew of, no opportunities. Her home life was crap, and that bothered him too. He wanted…

No, he couldn't even think that way.

"It doesn't matter," she said. "I just wanted you to know."

He didn't like the sound of that, but had no idea what to say. He could see her soft mouth trembling, could smell her hot, sweet scent carried on the evening breeze. Unlike the other girls he knew, Emma didn't wear fragrances. But then, she didn't need to.

Her warm palm touched his jaw. "You're all that matters to me right now, Case. You and the fact that we might not ever see each other again."

Boldly, she took his hand and pressed it to her breast. Casey shuddered. She was so damn soft.

His resolve weakened, then cracked. With a muttered curse, he pulled her closer and kissed her again, this time giving his hunger free rein. Her mouth opened under his, accepted his tongue, gave him her own. It didn't matter, he promised himself, filling his hand with her firm breast, finding her puckered nipple and stroking with his thumb.

She gave a startled, hungry purr of relief, her fingers clenching on his shoulders, her hips snuggling closer to his, stroking his erection, driving him insane.

Casey gave in with a growl of frustration and overwhelming need. He was damned if he did, and damned if he didn't. And sometimes Emma was just too much temptation to resist.

But it wouldn't change anything. He told her so in a muted whisper, and her only reply was a groan.

Two Months Later

CASEY SAT BACK in his seat and watched them all with an indulgent smile. Family gatherings had become a common event now that everyone had married and started families of their own. He missed having everyone so close, but they visited often, and it was obvious his father and uncles had found the perfect women for them.

The girl beside Casey cleared her throat, uncomfortable in the boisterous crowd of his family. It didn't matter because he doubted he'd see her again anyway. Donna was beautiful, sexy and anxious to please him—but she wasn't perfect for him. He knew it was dumb, considering he wasn't quite nineteen yet, but Casey couldn't help wondering if he'd ever meet the perfect girl.

An image of big brown eyes, filled with sexual curiosity, sadness, and finally rejection, formed in his mind. With a niggling dread that wouldn't ease up, Casey wondered if he'd already found the perfect girl—but had sent her away.

Then he heard his aunt talking to Donna, and he pulled himself out of his reverie. No, she wasn't perfect, but she didn't keep him awake nights either. And that was good, because no matter what, no matter how he felt now, he would not let his plans get off track. He decided to forget all about women and the future and simply enjoy the night with his family.

It was late when the family get-together ended and Casey finally got home after dropping off his date. He'd just pulled off his shirt when a fist started pounding on the front door. He and his father, Sawyer, met in the hall, both of them frowning. Sawyer was the town doctor and out of necessity, patients sometimes came this late at night, but as a rule they called first—unless there was an emergency. Casey's step-mother, Honey, pulled on her robe and hustled after them.

When Sawyer got the door open, they found themselves confronted with Emma's father, Dell Clark. Beyond furious,

Dell had a tight grip on his daughter's upper arm. His gaunt face was flushed, his eyes red, the tendons in his neck standing out.

Casey's first startled thought was that even though he hadn't seen her in two months, Emma hadn't gone after all. She was right here in Buckhorn.

Then he got a good look at her ravaged face, and he erupted in rage.

He'd been wrong. His plans were changed after all.

In a big way.

chapter 1

ENRAGED AND UNCERTAIN what he planned to do, Casey started forward. Before he reached Dell, Sawyer caught his arm and drew him up short. "Take it easy, Case."

Emma covered her mouth with a shaking hand, crying while trying not to cry, held tight by her father's grip even as she attempted to inch away from him. She wouldn't look at any of them, her narrow shoulders hunched in embarrassment—and possibly pain.

Casey's heart hurt, and his temper roiled. Emma's pretty brown eyes, usually so warm and sexy, were downcast, circled by ruined makeup and swollen from her tears. There was a bruise on her cheek, just visible in the glow of the porch light.

Casey felt tight enough to break as a kind of animal outrage that he'd never before experienced struggled to break free. Every night he'd thought about seeing Emma again, and every night he'd talked himself out of it.

Not once had he considered that he'd see her like this.

His vision nearly blurred as he heard Emma sniff and watched her wipe her eyes with a shaking hand.

With unnecessary roughness, her father shoved her forward and she stumbled across the wide porch before righting herself and turning her back to Casey. Without a word, she held on to the railing, staring out at the moonlit yard. Her broken breathing was audible over the night sounds of wind and crickets and rustling leaves.

"Do you know what your damn son did?" Dell demanded.

Casey felt Sawyer look at him but he ignored the unasked questions and instead went to Emma, taking her arm and pulling her close. It didn't matter why she was here; he wanted to hold her, to tell her it'd be all right.

Drawn into herself, Emma sidled away from him, whispering a broken apology again and again. She hugged her arms around herself. Casey realized the night was cool, and while Dell wore a jacket, Emma wore only a T-shirt and jeans, as if she'd been pulled away without having time to grab her coat. Since he was shirtless, he couldn't offer her anything. He tried to think, to figure out what to do, but he couldn't get his brain to work. He felt glued to the spot, unable to take his gaze off her.

She needed his help.

Honey came to the same realization. "Why don't we all go inside and talk?"

Looking horrified by that proposition, Emma backed up. "No. That's not—"

"Be quiet, girl!" Her father reached for her again, his anger and his intent obvious.

Casey stepped in front of him, bristling, coiled. "Don't even try it." No way in hell would he let Dell touch her again.

Face mottled with rage, her father shouted, "You think

you get some say-so, boy? You think what you've done to her gives you that right?"

Without moving his gaze from the man in front of him, Casey said, "Honey, will you take Emma inside?"

Honey looked at her husband, who nodded. Casey hadn't had a single doubt what his father would do or say. Not once in his entire life had he ever had to question his father's support.

Never in his life had he been more grateful for it.

Again, Emma tried to back away, moving into the far shadows of the big porch. Casey snapped his gaze to hers, so attuned to her it seemed he felt her every shuddering breath. "Go inside, Emma."

She bit her lip, big tears spilling over her blotchy cheeks and clinging to her long lashes. Her mouth trembled. "Casey, I…"

"It's all right." He struggled to keep his voice soft, comforting, but it wasn't easy—not while he could see the hurt in her eyes and feel her very real distress. "We'll talk in a little bit."

Speaking low and gentle, Honey put her arm around Emma, and reluctantly, Emma allowed herself to be led away. The front door closed quietly behind them.

With his daughter out of sight, Dell seemed more incensed than ever. He took two aggressive steps forward. "You'll do more than talk. You'll damn well marry her."

Casey gave him a cool look of disdain. That Dell could treat a female so callously made him sick to his stomach, but that he'd treat his own daughter that way brought out all Casey's protective instincts. More than anyone else he knew, Emma needed love and understanding. Yet, her own father was throwing her out, deliberately humiliating her.

"You brought her here," Casey growled. "You've delivered her to my doorstep, to *me*. What she or I do now is no concern of yours. Go home and leave us the hell alone."

Though Casey knew it would only complicate things more, he wanted to tear Dell apart. It wouldn't strain him at all. He was taller, stronger, with raw fury adding to his edge. He deliberately provoked Dell, and waited for his reaction.

It came in a lightning flash of curses and motion. The older man erupted, lunging forward. Smiling with intent, anxious for the confrontation, Casey braced himself.

Unfortunately, Sawyer caught Dell by his jacket collar before Casey could throw his first swing.

At well over six feet tall, solid with muscle, Sawyer wasn't a man to be messed with. He slammed Dell hard into the side of the house, and held him there with his forearm braced across his throat. He leaned close enough that their noses nearly touched.

"You come onto my property," Sawyer snarled, looking meaner than Casey had ever seen him look, "treating your only daughter like garbage and threatening my son?" He slammed Dell again, making his head smack back against the wood siding. "Unless you want me to take you apart right now, which I'm more than willing to do, I suggest you get hold of your goddamn temper."

Dell's face turned red from Sawyer's choking hold, but he managed a weak nod. When Sawyer released him, he sagged down, gulping in air. It took him several moments, and Casey was glad that Emma had gone inside so she didn't hear her father's next words.

Wheezing, Dell eyed both Sawyer and Casey. "You're so

worried about Emma, fine. She's yours." He spit as he talked, his face distorted with anger and pain. "You and your son are welcome to her, but don't think you can turn around and send her back home."

"To you?" Casey curled his lip. "Hell no."

Something in the man's eyes didn't make sense. The fury remained, no doubt about that. But Dell also looked...desperate. And a bit relieved. "You swear?"

He should have hit the son of a bitch at least once, Casey thought. He nodded, and forced the next words out from between clenched teeth. "You just make sure you stay the hell away from her."

Glaring one last time, Dell stepped around Sawyer and stomped down off the porch. At the edge of the grass, he stopped, his shoulders stiff, his back expanding with deep breaths, and for a long moment he hesitated. Casey narrowed his eyes, waiting. For Emma's sake, he half hoped her father had a change of heart, that he showed even an ounce of concern or compassion.

Dell looked over his shoulder at Casey. His mouth opened twice but no words were spoken. Finally he shook his head and went to his battered truck. He didn't glance back again. His headlights came on and he left the yard, squealing his tires and spewing gravel.

Casey stood there, breathing hard, his hands curled into fists, his whole body vibrating with tension. The enormity of the situation, of what he'd just taken on, nearly leveled him. He squeezed his eyes shut, trying to think.

Jesus, what had he done?

Sawyer's hand slipped around the back of his neck, comforting, supportive. A heavy, uncomfortable beat of silence passed.

"What do you want to do first, Case?" Sawyer spoke in a nearly soundless murmur, his voice disappearing in the dark night. "Talk to me, or talk to Emma?"

Casey looked at his dad, a man he loved and respected more than anyone else on earth. He swallowed. "Emma."

Nodding, Sawyer turned them both around and headed for the door. Casey hoped a few answers came to him before the morning light began creeping over the lake. Because, at the moment, he had no idea what the hell was going on.

EMMA HEARD the opening and the closing of the front door. She squeezed her eyes shut, horrified, ashamed, scared spitless.

And oddly relieved.

More tears leaked out, choking her, burning her cheeks and throat. What had she done? What choice had she been given?

Honey touched her arm in a motherly way. "Drink your hot chocolate. And Emma, everything will be okay. You'll see."

Shaking down deep in her soul, Emma wiped at her eyes. She felt like a child, and knew she looked more like a barroom whore. Her makeup had long since been ruined and her nose and eyes were red. Her hair was a wild mess and her T-shirt was dirty.

Though the Hudson household was cozy and warm, she still felt chilled from the inside out. In that moment, she wondered if she'd ever be warm again.

Hugging herself in self-conscious dismay, she wished she could just disappear. She didn't belong in this house with these nice respectable people. But disappearing wasn't an option. She'd gotten herself in this mess and now she had to face them all. She had to explain.

She owed Casey at least that much.

At that moment, barefoot and shirtless, Casey came around the corner into the kitchen. His muscled arms crossed over his chest as he stopped in front of the kitchen table where she sat. His light-brown eyes, filled with compassion and confusion, warmed to glittering amber as he looked her over.

Stomach churning in dread, Emma flicked her gaze away.

Casey's father, Sawyer, stood behind him. Honey sat beside her. She felt surrounded, circled by their concern and curiosity, hemmed in by their kindness.

The damn tears welled up again and she felt herself start to shudder. Oh God, if she bawled like a baby now she'd never forgive herself.

His expression solemn, Casey held out his hand. "Let's me and you talk a little, Emma."

She stared at him through a haze of tears.

Sawyer frowned. "Casey…"

"Just a few minutes, Dad. I promise."

Honey sent Sawyer a pointed look, then patted Emma's shoulder. "You can use the family room. Sawyer and I will make sandwiches and join you in just a few minutes."

Keeping her head bowed so she wouldn't have to make eye contact with anyone, Emma left her chair. She didn't want to take Casey's hand, and tried to walk around him, but he caught her and his fingers laced into hers. His hand was big and warm, strong and steady. Reassuring.

Normally, just being near him made her feel more secure. But not this time.

To her amazement, when he reached the family room, Casey sat down and tugged her into his lap. She couldn't remember anyone ever holding her like that before. Emma was so shocked she almost bolted upright, but Casey wrapped both arms around her and pulled her so tightly to him, her head just naturally went to his shoulder. Her shaking increased.

Very gently, Casey stroked one hand up and down her back. "Em? Tell me what's going on."

Despite her resolve, she clutched at him. "I'm so sorry, Casey. So, so sorry."

He pushed her hair away from her face, then reached for a box of tissues on the end table and held them in front of her. Emma blew her nose, but it didn't help. The tears kept coming and she couldn't make them stop. "I didn't mean to get you involved, I swear."

Calmly, as if she hadn't just turned his life upside down, he said, "Involved in what?"

That was the thing about Casey. He was always calm, always so mature and sure of himself that, without thinking, she'd used his name and now... Emma grabbed for three more tissues. This was where she had to be careful. "I told my parents that I'm pregnant."

Casey went very still. Silence hung heavy in the air, broken only by her gasping breaths and awful sniffling. Casey sat there, tall and proud and strong, while she fell apart like a deranged child.

In that moment, Emma hated herself.

His hand began stroking her again. "I take it they weren't too happy about it?"

She laughed, but the humor faded into a wail. "I couldn't think of what else to do."

"So you came to me?"

He didn't seem nearly as outraged as she had expected. But then Casey was so different from any other guy she knew, she didn't know what to expect from him. He had a good handle on everything, on his life, his temper, his future.

"It's not...not what you think." This was even harder than she'd imagined. On the silent drive to his house, with her father fuming beside her, she'd tried to prepare herself, tried to make decisions. But this was the worst thing she'd ever done.

"No?" His thumb carefully smoothed over the bruise on her cheek.

God, she wished he'd say something more, maybe yell at her or throw her out. His calm destroyed what little control she'd been able to hold on to. "No." She shook her head and leaned away from the gentleness of his touch. It took one breath, then another, before she could speak convincingly. "I don't need or want anything from you, Case."

The intensity of his dark gaze seeped into her and she tried to look away.

Gently, Casey brought her face back up to his. "Then why are you here, Em?"

"I just..." *I had to escape.* She drew a shaking breath and attempted to gather herself together. The last few hours had seemed endless, and the night was far from over. "I needed to get away and I couldn't think of anything else."

A rap on the door made her jerk, and she looked up to see Sawyer and Honey standing there, each carrying a tray. Sawyer held sandwiches and Honey held mugs of hot chocolate.

Emma started to groan. God, they were like Leave it to freakin' Beaver or something, so homey and together that nothing shook them for long, not even the neighborhood riffraff dropping in with a bombshell that should have disrupted the rest of their lives.

Envy formed a vise around her heart, but she knew she'd never belong to a family like theirs. They'd never want her.

Her own family didn't.

Sawyer's smile appeared strained but kind. "I think we should all do a little talking now."

He set the tray on the coffee table and settled into a chair. Honey did the same. They both seemed to ignore the fact that she'd ended up perched on Casey's lap, held in his strong arms. But the second Emma realized just how that would look, she shot to her feet. Before she could move too far away, Casey leaned forward and caught her wrist. Unlike her father's grip, his was gentle and warm.

Casey's hold offered comfort not restraint.

He came to his feet beside her, and she had the awful suspicion he wanted to provide a united front to his parents. He faced his father squarely, without an ounce of uncertainty or embarrassment. "Emma is pregnant."

Sawyer's jaw locked, and Honey looked down at her clasped hands, but not fast enough to hide her distress. When Emma started to speak, Casey squeezed her hand, silencing her. She understood what he wanted to do, and this time it was love clenching her heart. Not infatuation, not jealousy for all he had.

Real love.

There didn't exist a better man than Casey Hudson. Emma knew in that moment she'd never forget him, no matter what turns her life took in the morning.

Very slowly, her movements deliberate and unmistakable, Emma pulled herself away from Casey. She took one step, then another and another, until she stood several feet away from him.

It wasn't easy, but she managed to face his parents. This time her gaze never wavered. What she had to say was too important to leave any doubts. "Casey has never touched me."

Sawyer sat up a little straighter, and his eyebrows came down in a dark frown of bewilderment. Honey's gaze darted between them.

"Emma…" Casey took a step toward her.

She shot up a hand to ward him off. His nobility, his willingness to sacrifice himself, amazed her and made her love him that much more. She smiled at him, her first genuine smile in weeks. The time for sniffling and crying and being a fool had ended. She owed this family more than that. She owed Casey so damn much. "Casey, when I told my parents I was pregnant, I lied."

"But…"

Feeling stiff and awkward, she rolled one shoulder in a casual shrug. "I'm sorry." Her words trembled, nearly incoherent, and she cleared her throat. She wanted to beg him not to hate her, but that wouldn't be fair. "I know it was wrong. I had to say something to get away and I couldn't think of anything else."

His gaze locked on her, Sawyer rose from his chair. He looked angry, but Emma had the feeling his anger wasn't directed at her. Still, she couldn't stop herself from backing away at his approach. When she caught Casey's frown, she halted and forced herself to remain still.

With a large gentle hand on her chin, Sawyer tipped her

face this way and that to examine her bruised cheek, then he carefully looked at the rest of her face. He was an imposing man, and she'd always been in awe of him. Now, with him in front of her and Casey close at her side, she almost felt faint.

"What happened to your face, Emma?" Sawyer's tone left no room for evasions. He expected an answer. He expected the truth.

He couldn't have it.

Emma touched the bruise, and winced. "I...I fell, that's all."

Casey snorted.

She cast him a quick worried look, but couldn't meet his piercing gaze for more than a few seconds. They didn't deserve to be lied to, but neither did they deserve to be drawn into her problems. If they knew, they'd never let her get away. She'd done enough to them. From here on out, she would handle things. Alone. She had to.

Sawyer again tipped up her chin, this time to regain her attention. "We can help if you'll let us."

Did every one of them take nobility in stride? Emma wiped her eyes on her crumpled tissue, wondering how to explain without telling too much. Shame bit into her, and she sighed. "Dr. Hudson, I'm so sorry—"

Casey caught her elbow and whirled her around to face him, his anger barely leashed. "Quit apologizing, damn it. It's not necessary."

Emma pulled back. "I've barged in here—"

"Your father barged in, not you." Casey's light-brown eyes burned nearly gold, and his jaw was set. "You're not responsible for what he does, Emma."

"But...this time I am," she explained gently. She was very

aware of his parents' attention. "I told him I was pregnant, and I told him…I told him that you were the father."

She turned to Sawyer and Honey in a rush, stumbling over her words. "Casey hasn't ever touched me, I swear. He wouldn't. He's so much better than that. But I knew if I named any other guy…" She stalled, not sure what else to say. From the time she became a teenager, she'd been with so many boys. And yet, she'd named the only one who hadn't wanted her.

Hands on his hips, Casey dropped his head forward, staring at the floor. He made a rough sound, part growl, part sarcasm. "None of the other guys would have defended you, would have taken you in."

Relief that she hadn't had to explain, after all, made Emma's knees weak. "I used your integrity against you, and I *am* sorry." Twisting her hands together, she faced Sawyer. "Everyone in Buckhorn knows that you and your brothers are good people. I thought that you might help me, so I used Casey's name to get here. It wasn't right and I can understand if you hate me, but it was the only thing I could think of."

"Emma," Honey murmured, her tone filled with sympathy, "no one hates you."

Impatient, Sawyer shook his head. "Why did you need to get here, Emma? That's what I want to know."

And Honey added, "But of course you're more than welcome to stay—"

"Oh, no." Appalled by the conclusions she'd led them to, Emma shook her head. "No, you're not stuck with me or anything like that." She'd made a real muddle of things, she realized. "I have no intention of imposing on you, I swear."

They met her promises with blank stares.

She started trembling again. She'd never felt more unso-phisticated or more trashy than she did right at that moment, standing among them. The comparisons between herself and them made her stomach pitch. She wanted to take off running and never look back.

Soon, she promised herself. Very soon. "I have some money that I've saved up, and I know how to work. I'm going to go to Ohio first thing in the morning."

"What's in Ohio?" Casey asked, and he didn't look so even-tempered now. He looked ready to explode.

A new life, she wanted to tell him, but instead she lied. Again. "I have a…a cousin there. She offered me a place to stay and a job."

Her expression worried, Honey glanced at Sawyer, then Casey, before tilting her head at Emma. "What kind of job?"

What kind of job? Emma blinked, taken aback by the question. She hadn't expected this. She'd thought they'd be glad to see her gone. Oh, she'd known that they would offer to let her stay the night, that they'd be kind. She wouldn't have come to them otherwise. But she figured once she told them she had a place to go they'd send her on her way with no questions asked.

Think, she told herself, and finally mumbled, "I'm not sure, actually. But she said it'd be perfect for me and I assume it'll be something…reasonable."

The way they all looked at her, they knew she was lying. Emma started backing away toward the phone. "I…I'm going to call a cab now." She dared a quick peek at Casey, then wished she hadn't. In all the time she'd known him, she'd never once seen him so enraged. "When…when I get settled, I'll write to you, okay?"

Casey again crossed his arms over his chest. "That won't be necessary."

Her heart sank and she wanted to crumble in on herself. "I understand." Why would he want to hear from her anyway? She'd offered herself to him plenty of times—and every single time he'd turned her away. And still she'd barged into his life.

"You don't understand a damn thing." Casey began striding toward her. "Emma, you're not going anywhere."

His tone frightened her. She felt locked in his gaze, unable to look away, unable to think. "Of course I am."

"No." Sawyer strode toward her too, his movements easy, nonthreatening, which didn't help Emma's panic one bit. "Casey is right. It's damn near the middle of the night and you look exhausted. You need to get some sleep. In the morning we'll all talk and figure out what's to be done."

"No..." She shook her head, dazed by their reactions.

"Yes." Sawyer took her arm, his expression gentle, his intent implacable. "For now, I want you to eat a sandwich and drink some chocolate, then you can take a warm shower and get some sleep."

In a quandary, Emma found herself reseated on the sofa. They weren't throwing her out? After what she'd done, what she'd just admitted to them?

Her own father, despite everything or maybe because of it, had used the opportunity of her supposed pregnancy to rid himself of her. And her mother... No, she wouldn't, *couldn't,* think about that right now.

Honey smiled at her. "Please don't worry so much, Emma. Everything is okay now."

"Nothing is okay." Why couldn't they understand that?

Honey's gentle smile never slipped. "I felt the same way when I first came here, but they're sincere, I swear. We're *all* sincere. We just don't want you rushing off until we know you'll be all right."

Confusion weighed heavy on her brain. She didn't know how to deal with this.

Casey sat down beside her and shoved a peanut butter and jelly sandwich into her hand. Emma stared at it, knowing she wouldn't be able to swallow a single bite without throwing up. She had to do... something. She had to get out of here before their acceptance and understanding weakened her resolve.

She would not become someone else's burden.

Her mind made up, she put the sandwich aside. "I'd really like to just take a shower if that's okay. I know I look a mess."

Using his fingertips, Casey wiped away a lingering tear she hadn't been aware of. He hesitated, but finally nodded. "All right. You can sleep in my room tonight."

Her eyes widened and her mouth fell open. Casey grinned at her, then pinched her chin. "I'll, of course, sleep on the couch."

Mortification washed over her for her asinine assumption. At her blush, Casey's grin widened. She couldn't believe the way he teased her in front of his parents.

"You could have used Morgan's old room, except that Honey's been painting it and everything is a mess in there."

Morgan was his uncle, the town sheriff. Most people thought he was a big, scary guy. He was enormous, but he'd always been kind to Emma, even when he'd caught her getting into trouble, like breaking curfew or being truant from school. Newly wed, Morgan had recently moved into his own house.

"I'll take the couch." Emma thought that would be easier, but Casey wouldn't hear of it.

"You'll take the bed."

His father and stepmother agreed with him. In the end, Emma knew she was no match for them. Exhaustion won out and she nodded. "All right." It would be strange sleeping in Casey's room, in his bed. A secret part of her already looked forward to it. "Thank you."

Casey took her down the hall to the bathroom, then got her one of his large T-shirts to sleep in. She knew it was selfish, but she accepted the shirt, holding it close to her heart. It was big and soft and it held his indescribable scent. Since she couldn't have Casey, it was the next best thing.

Their bathroom was bigger than her whole bedroom. It was clean and stylish and that damn envy threatened to get hold of her again. Emma swore to herself that someday, she'd have a house as nice as this one. Maybe not as big, but just as clean and warm and filled with happiness. Somehow, she'd make it happen.

Knowing it would take forever for it to dry, she didn't bother washing her long hair. When her opportunity arose, she had to be ready, and she didn't want to run away with wet hair. She did brush out all the tangles and tie it back with a rubber band. The shower did a lot to revive her and make her feel less pathetic.

After she'd dried off and donned the shirt, Emma glared at herself in the mirror, and cursed herself for being such a crybaby. Casey wouldn't be a whiner. If something happened in his life, he'd figure out how to deal with it. He'd do what he had to.

And so would she.

With the makeup washed away, her red nose and eyes looked even worse. The bruise showed up more too. It had all been necessary, she reminded herself, but still the thought of change terrified her—just not as much as staying.

She lifted the neckline of the shirt and brushed it against her nose, breathing deeply of Casey's scent. She closed her swollen eyes a moment to compose herself.

Everyone was waiting for her when she left the bathroom, which made her feel like a spectacle. She was used to being ignored, not drawing attention. In a lot of ways, she preferred being ignored to this coddling. They were all just so…*kind.*

Sawyer gave her a cool compress to put over her puffy eyes, along with two over-the-counter pills that he said would help her relax and get some sleep.

Honey fussed over her, occasionally touching her in that mothering way. She told Emma to help herself if she got hungry during the night and to let her know if she needed anything.

She'd rather die than disturb any of them further. Emma knew she could be very quiet when she needed to be; she'd learned that trick early in life. Like a wraith, she could creep in and out without making a sound. No way would she wake anyone up tonight.

Honey kissed Emma on the forehead before she and Sawyer went down the hall, leaving her alone with Casey so he could say good-night. Emma was amazed anew that they'd trust her enough to leave Casey in the room with her, especially now that they had firsthand evidence of her character. She was a liar and a user.

Then she realized it wasn't a matter of trusting her. They trusted Casey, and with good reason.

Casey sat on the edge of the bed and looked at her. After a moment, he even smiled.

Emma remembered how many times she'd done her best to get Casey this close. That last time at his family's picnic, she'd almost succeeded. But in the end, Casey had been too strong-willed, and too moral to get involved with her. She'd decided that night to leave him alone, and for the most part she'd stuck to that conviction. She hadn't seen him in so long.

Now he was right next to her and she was in his bed, and she could see the awful pity in his gaze. That hurt so much, she almost couldn't bear it. She'd make sure this was the last time he ever looked at her that way.

"Are you all right now, Em?"

"I'm fine," she lied, confident that it would be true soon enough. "I just wish I hadn't put your family through all this." She wished she could have thought of another way.

Rather than reply to that, Casey smoothed his hand over her head. "I've never seen your hair in a ponytail."

Her heart started thumping too hard and her breath caught. She stared down at her hands. "That's because it looks dumb, but I figured I looked bad enough tonight that nothing could make it worse."

As if she hadn't intruded in the middle of the night, hadn't dragged him into her problems, hadn't disrupted his life, Casey chuckled. "It does not look dumb. Actually it looks kinda cute." Then, startling her further, he leaned forward and brushed his mouth over her forehead. "I'll be right out on the couch if you need anything, or if you just want to talk."

Emma said nothing to that.

"Promise me, Em." His expression was stern, with that

iron determination that awed her so much in evidence. "If you need me, you'll wake me, okay?"

"Yeah, sure." *Not in a million years.*

Looking unconvinced, Casey straightened. "All right. I know it's not easy, but try not to fret, okay? I'm sure we'll be able to figure everything out."

We. This family kept saying that, as if they each really wanted to help. She'd made herself his problem by using his name, but by tomorrow he wouldn't have to worry about her ever again. "Casey? Thank you for everything."

"I haven't done anything, Em."

She lifted his large, warm hand and kissed his palm. Her heart swelled with love, threatening to break. "You're the finest person I've ever met."

THE RED HAZE OF DAWN streamed through the windows when Honey shook Casey awake early the next morning. He pushed himself up on one elbow and tried to clear away the cobwebs. He'd been in the middle of a dark, intensely erotic dream. About Emma.

His father stood behind Honey and right away Casey knew something was wrong. "What is it?"

"Emma is better than me," Honey said.

Casey frowned at that. "How so?"

"None of us heard her when she left."

Sawyer looked grim. "There's a note on your bed."

Casey threw the sheet aside and bolted upright. He wore only his boxers, but didn't give a damn. His heart threatened to punch out of his chest as he ran to his bedroom. Worry filled him, but also a strange panic.

She couldn't really be gone.

He came to a halt in the middle of his room. The covers had been neatly smoothed over the empty bed, and on the pillow lay a single sheet of paper, folded in half.

Dreading what he would read, Casey dropped onto the mattress and picked up the note. Honey and Sawyer crowded into the doorway, watching, waiting.

Dear Casey,
I know you told me not to say it, but I'm so sorry. For everything. Not just for barging into your life tonight but for trying to corrupt you and trying to interrupt your plans. It was so selfish of me. For a while there, I thought I wanted you more than anything.

Here she had drawn a small smiley face. It nearly choked Casey up, seeing her attempt at humor. He swallowed and firmed his resolve.

But that would have been really unfair to you.
I'm also sorry that I took the money you had on your dresser.

Casey glanced at his dresser. Hell, he'd forgotten all about the money, which, if he remembered right, amounted to about a hundred dollars. Not enough for her to get very far. Emotion swamped him, then tightened like a vise around his chest, making it hard to breathe.

I had some money of my own, too. I've been saving it up for a long time. I promise as soon as I get settled I'll return your money to you. I just needed it to get me away from Buckhorn, and I figured better that I borrow your money and leave tonight than to continue hanging around being a burden.

Damn it, hadn't he told her a dozen times she wasn't a bother? No. He'd told her not to apologize, but he hadn't told her that he wanted her there, that he wanted to help. That he cared about her.

Have a good life, Casey. I'll never, ever forget you.

Love,
Emma Clark

Casey crumpled the letter in his fist. He wanted to punch something, someone. He wanted to rage. It felt as though his chest had just caved in, destroying his heart. For a long moment, he couldn't speak, couldn't get words out around the lump in his throat.

Sawyer sat down beside him with a sigh. "I'll call Morgan and see if he can track her down."

As the town sheriff, Morgan had connections and legal avenues that the others didn't have. Casey looked at his father, struggling for control. "We don't know for sure where she's going."

"To Ohio, to her cousin, she told us," Honey reminded them.

"She never gave us her cousin's name."

"I'll call Dell." Sawyer clapped Casey on the shoulder, offering reassurance. "He'll know."

But half an hour later, after Sawyer had finished his conversation with Emma's surprisingly rattled father, Casey's worst suspicions were confirmed. Emma didn't have a cousin in Ohio. As far as Dell knew, there was no one in Ohio, no relative, no friend. Dell spewed accusations, blaming Casey for his little girl's problems, for her pregnancy, even going so far as to insist he should be compensated for his loss. He said his wife was sick and now his daughter was missing.

Casey suffered a vague sense of relief that Emma had gotten away from her unfeeling father. If only he knew where she'd gone.

If only he knew how to get her back.

Neither he nor Sawyer bothered to explain the full situation to Dell Clark. If Emma had wanted him to know, she would have told him herself. Eventually Dell would know there had never been a baby, that Emma had only used that as an excuse to be thrown out—to escape.

But from what?

Casey hoped she hadn't gone far, that it wouldn't take too long to find her. Damn it, he *wanted* to take care of her, dumb as that seemed.

But hours after Sawyer put in the request to Morgan, he came outside to give Casey the bad news.

Casey had been standing by a fence post, staring out at the endless stretch of wildflowers in the meadow. He'd bored the horses with his melancholy and they'd wandered away to munch grass elsewhere. The sun was hot, the grass sweet smelling and the sky so blue it could blind you. Casey barely noticed any of it.

"Case?"

At his father's voice, Casey jerked around. One look at Sawyer's expression and fear grabbed him. "What is it?"

Sawyer quickly shook his head. "Nothing's happened to Emma. But Morgan checked with highway patrol… They haven't seen her. There've been no reports of anyone fitting her description. It's like she vanished. I'm sorry, Case."

Casey clenched his hands into fists, and repeated aloud the words that had been echoing in his head all morning. "She'll turn up."

"I hope so, but…something else happened last night." Sawyer propped his hands on his hips and his expression hardened. "Late last night, Ceily's diner caught fire."

Slowly, Casey sank back against the rough wooden post. "Ceily…?"

"She wasn't even there. It was way after hours, during a break-in, apparently." Sawyer hesitated. "Morgan's investigating the fire for arson."

"Arson? But that means…"

"Yeah. Someone might have tried to burn her down."

On top of his worry for Emma, it was almost too much to take in. Ceily was a friend to all of them. Everyone in town adored her, and the diner was practically a landmark.

"It's damn strange," Sawyer continued, "but the fire was reported with an anonymous call. Morgan doesn't know who, but when he got on the scene the fire was already out of control. Structurally, the diner is okay, but the inside is pretty much gutted. Whatever isn't burned has smoke damage."

Casey felt numb. Things like arson just didn't happen in Buckhorn.

Of course, girls didn't accuse him of fathering a nonexistent baby very often either. "Morgan's okay?"

"He's raspy from smoke inhalation, but he'll be all right. Ceily's stunned. I told her we'd all help, but it's still going to take a while before she'll be able to get the place all repaired and opened again."

Barefoot, her long blond hair lifted by the breeze, Honey sidled up next to Sawyer. Automatically his father put his arm around her, kissed her temple and murmured, "I just told him."

Honey nodded. "I'm so sorry, Casey. Morgan has his hands full with the investigation now."

"Meaning he doesn't want to waste time looking for Emma?"

Honey didn't take offense at his tone. "You know that's not it." She reached out to touch his shoulder. "He's done what he can, but considering the note she left, there's no reason to consider any foul play."

Sawyer rubbed the back of his neck in agitation. "I know how you feel, Case. I'm not crazy about her being off on her own either. Hell, I've never seen such an emotionally fragile young woman. But Dell doesn't want to file her as a missing minor, so there's nothing more that Morgan can do. She'll come back when she's good and ready, and in the meantime, all we can do is wait."

Honey patted Casey again. "Maybe she'll contact you. Like Sawyer said, we'll wait—and hope."

When Casey turned back to the meadow, both Sawyer and Honey retreated, leaving him alone with his worries. Yes, he thought, she'll contact me. She had to. They shared a special bond, not sexual, yet…still special.

He felt it. So surely she felt it too.

THE DAYS TICKED BY without word from Emma.

The fire at the diner had stolen all the news, and Emma's

disappearance was pretty much skipped by most people. After all, she hadn't made any lasting friendships in the area. The boys had used her, the girls had envied her, and the schools had all but given up on her. Not many people missed her now.

In the next few weeks, the town gradually settled back down to normal, but an edgy nervousness remained because whoever had broken into Ceily's diner and started a fire was never found. Casey went through his days by rote, hurt, angry with himself as much as with Emma.

Three months later, he got a fat envelope filled with the money Emma had taken, and a few dollars more. In her brief note, Emma explained that the extra was for interest. There was no return address and she'd signed the note: *Thanks so much for everything. Emma Clark.*

Frustrated, Casey wondered if she always signed her first and last name because she thought he might forget her, just as the rest of the town had.

At least the return of the money proved she was alive and well. Casey tried to tell himself it was enough, that he'd only wanted her safe, that all he'd ever felt for her was sympathy with a little healthy lust thrown in.

But he'd be a complete fraud if he let himself believe it. The truth burned like acid, because nothing had ever hurt as much as knowing Emma had deliberately walked away from him.

He didn't ever want to hurt like that again.

Since she didn't want to return, didn't want to trust him, *didn't want him,* he couldn't help her. But he could get on with his life.

With nothing else to do, he went off to school as planned. And though he knew it hadn't been Emma's intention, she'd changed his life forever. He wanted her back, damn it, when he'd made a point of never having her in the first place. .

Forget her? There wasn't a chance in hell that would ever happen.

chapter 2

Eight Years Later

THOUGH SHE COULDN'T SEE beyond the raised hood, she heard the very distant rumble of the approaching car and gave a sigh of relief. Damon, who had been about to set a flare on the narrow gravel road, walked back to her with the flare unlit. He stuck his head in the driver's-door window. "I'm going to flag this guy down and maybe he'll give us a hand."

Emma smiled at him. "The way this day is going? We'll be lucky if he doesn't speed on by and blow dust in our faces."

B.B. hung his head over her seat and nuzzled her ear. His doggy breath was hot and impatient. Likely, he wanted out of the car worse than she did. The winding gravel roads opened on both sides to endless stretches of overgrown brush that shielded anything from rabbits to snakes. B.B. heeded her call, so she wasn't really worried about him wandering off. But she also didn't want to take the chance that he'd get distracted with a critter on unfamiliar ground.

The day had already been endless with one hitch after

another. What should have been a six- or seven-hour drive from Chicago to Buckhorn, had turned into eight and a half, and they hadn't even had a chance to stop for a sit-down meal. Even with the occasional breaks they'd taken and her quick stopover at the hospital, they were all beat. The dog wasn't used to being confined for so long, and neither was she.

Damon patted her hand. "Stay put until I see who it is. This late on a Saturday night, and in a strange town, I don't want to take any chances with you."

Emma rolled her eyes. "Damon, I grew up here, remember? This isn't a strange place. It's Buckhorn and believe me, it's so safe it borders on boring."

"You haven't been here in eight long years, doll. Time changes everything."

She scoffed at that ridiculous notion. "Not Buckhorn. Trust me."

In fact, Emma had been amazed at how little it had changed in the time she'd been away. On their way to the one and only motel Buckhorn had to offer, they'd driven through the town proper. Everything looked the same: pristine, friendly, old-fashioned.

The streets were swept clean, the sidewalks uncluttered. There were two small grocery stores at opposite ends of town, each with varying specialties. The same clothing store that had been there for over a hundred years still stood, but painted a new, brighter color. The hairdresser's building had new landscaping; the pharmacy had a new lighted sign.

Lit by stately lampposts, Emma had gazed down a narrow side street at the sheriff's station, situated across the street from a field of cows. Once a farmhouse, the ornate structure still boasted a wraparound porch, white columns in the front, and black shutters. Emma wondered if Morgan Hudson still reigned supreme. He'd be in his mid-forties by now, but Emma would be willing to bet he remained as large, strong and imposing as ever. Morgan wasn't the type of man ever to let himself go soft.

She also saw Gabe Kasper's handyman shop, now expanded into two buildings and looking very sophisticated. Apparently business was good for Gabe, not that she'd ever had any doubts. Women around Buckhorn broke things on purpose just to get Gabe to do repairs.

Then she'd seen Ceily's diner.

Her stomach knotted at the sight of the familiar building, quiet and closed down for the night but with new security lights on the outside. Everyone in town loved that quaint old diner, making it a favorite hangout.

Her heart gave a poignant twinge at the remembrance of it all.

"For once," Damon said with dramatic frustration, drawing her away from the memories, "will you just do as I say without arguing me into the ground?"

B.B. barked in agreement.

"You guys always gang up on me," Emma accused, then waved Damon off. "Your caution is unnecessary, but if it'll make you feel better, I'll just sit here like a good little helpless woman. Maybe I'll even twiddle my thumbs."

"Your sarcasm is showing, doll." He glanced at the dog. "B.B., see that she stays put."

The dog hung his head over her shoulder, mournful at the enormity of the task.

The approaching car finally maneuvered through all the

twists and turns of the stretching road, and drew near. Arms raised, Damon rounded the hood to signal for assistance. It must be a nice vehicle, Emma thought, hearing the nearly melodic purr of the powerful engine. She'd learned a lot about cars while living with the Devaughns.

Unfortunately, she hadn't learned enough to be able to change a water pump without a spare pump on hand.

At first, because of the angle of the road, the swerving headlights slanted partially in through her window, blinding her. When the car stopped right in front of them, the open hood of her Mustang kept her from being able to see the occupants. In a town the size of Buckhorn, the odds weren't too bad that she might recognize their rescuers. Though few people had really befriended her, she'd grown up with them and could still recall many of them clearly.

Beside her, B.B.'s head lifted and he rumbled a low warning growl at the strangers. Emma reached over her shoulder to put her hand on his scruff, calming him, letting him know that everything was okay.

The purring engine turned off, leaving only the night sounds of insects. "Well, hello."

With amusement in his tone, Damon replied, "Good evening."

Emma couldn't see, but she could hear just fine, and the feminine voice responding to Damon was definitely flirtatious. She sighed.

Sometimes Emma thought he was too good-looking for his own good. He wasn't overly tall, maybe an inch shy of six feet, but he had a lean, athletic build and warm, clear blue eyes and the most engaging grin she'd ever witnessed on a grown man. Everywhere he went, women turned their heads to watch him.

"Can we give you a lift?"

"Actually," Damon's deep voice rumbled, "I'd just like to make a call to Triple A. Do you have a cell phone with you? My battery went dead an hour ago."

A car door opened, gravel crunched beneath someone's feet, and the next voice Emma heard almost stopped her heart. "Sorry, I don't carry one when I'm not working. The ringing is too bothersome. But we can take you into town to make the call."

Stunned, Emma pushed her car door open and slowly climbed out. Damon wouldn't leave her alone to go to town and make the call, especially once he realized that he'd just flagged down the only person in Buckhorn that she had serious reservations about seeing again.

B.B. jumped over the seat and climbed out behind her, sticking close to her side. The big German shepherd moved silently across the grass and gravel, his head lifted to scent the air for danger, his body alert.

Emma paused a moment in the deep shadows, sucking in fresh, dewy air and reminding herself that she was now an adult, not a lovesick schoolgirl with more bravado than brains. There was no reason to act silly. No reason to still feel embarrassed.

Casey was nothing to her now. He'd never really been anything to her except a friend—and an adolescent fantasy. After what she'd done to him, and after eight long years, friendship wasn't even an issue.

She had planned to see him, of course. Just not yet. Not when she looked so… Emma stopped that line of thought.

It didn't matter that she wore comfortable jeans and a logo sweatshirt, or that her eyes were shadowed from too little sleep over the past few days.

Smoothing her hair behind her ears and straightening her shoulders, Emma slipped around the front of the Mustang and stepped into the light of the low beams. B.B. stationed himself at her side, well mannered but ready to defend.

Emma took one look at Casey and a strange sort of joy expanded inside her. He looked good. He looked the same, just…more so. With every second of every day, she'd missed him, but she didn't know if he would even remember her.

"Well, I thought I recognized that voice," Emma said, proud that only a slight waver sounded in her words. "Hello, Casey."

Damon twisted around to face her, and Casey's head jerked up in surprise. Emma held herself still while the woman with Casey scooted closer to him, blatantly staking a claim.

Caught between the headlights of both cars, they all stood there. The damp August-evening air drifted over and around them, stirring the leaves and the tension. Moths fluttered into the light and wispy fog hung near the ground, snaking around their feet. Emma heard the chirp of every cricket, the creaking of heavy branches, her own stilted breath.

His body rigid, his thoughts concealed, Casey stared toward Emma. In the darkness, his eyes appeared black as pitch, intensely direct. He explored her face in minute detail, taking his time while Emma did her best not to fidget.

The silence stretched out, painful and taut, until Emma didn't know if she could take it anymore.

Finally, he took a step forward. "Emma?"

Like a warm caress, his familiar deep voice slipped over and around her. He said her name as a question, filled with wonder, surprise, maybe even pleasure. At eighteen, he'd seemed so grown up, but now that he was grown, he could take her breath away.

Her smile felt silly, uncertain. She made an awkward gesture, and shrugged. "That'd be me."

"My God, I'd never have recognized you." He strode forward as if he might embrace her, and Emma automatically drew back. She didn't mean to do it, and she silently cursed herself for the knee-jerk reaction to seeing him again. His physical presence, once so comforting, now seemed as powerful, as dark and turbulent, as a storm. The changes were subtle, but she'd known him so well, been so fixated on him, that they were glaringly obvious to her.

At her retreat, Casey drew to a halt. His smile faltered then became cynical, matching the light in his eyes. He veered his gaze toward Damon, and Emma knew he'd drawn his own conclusions.

When he faced her again, his expression had turned icy. "I'm surprised to see you here, Em."

"My father...he's in the hospital." She hated herself for stammering, but when she'd thought Casey might touch her, her heart, her pulse, even her thoughts had sped up, leaving her a little jumbled. *No, no, no,* she silently swore, wanting to deny the truth. Surely, eight years was long enough. It *had* to be.

But right now, with Casey so close she could feel the beat of his energy and the strength of his presence, it felt as if less than eight days had passed. Long-buried emotions clamored to the surface, and Emma struggled to repress them again.

Oh, it wasn't that she still pined for Casey, or that she carried any fanciful illusions. The time away had been an eternity for her. She'd gone from being an immature, needy girl to a grown, independent woman. She'd learned so much, faced so many realities, and she now considered herself a person to be proud of.

But seeing him, being back in Buckhorn...well, some memories never died and her last ones with Casey were the type that haunted her dreams. She could still blush, remembering that awful night and what she'd put him and his family through. Like old garbage, her father had dumped her on Casey's doorstep—and he'd taken her in.

That wasn't the only thing that made her hot with embarrassment, though. The nights that preceded her eventful departure were worse. She'd thrown herself at Casey again and again, utilizing every female ploy to entice him—and had always been rebuffed. The strongest emotion he'd ever felt for her was pity.

And now he had no reason to feel even that.

"I'd heard your dad was sick. Will he be all right?"

It didn't surprise her that he knew. There were few secrets in Buckhorn, so of course he'd heard.

Renewed worry prodded her, sounding in her tone. "He was asleep when I stopped at the hospital earlier, and I didn't want to disturb him. He needs his rest. But the nurse assures me that he's doing better. They have him out of intensive care, so I guess that's a good sign. I just...I wish I could have talked with him."

"What happened?"

She swallowed hard, still disbelieving how quickly things had changed. The call from her mother had rattled her and she hadn't quite gotten a grip on her emotions yet. She hadn't seen her father in so long, but she'd always known he was there, as cantankerous and hardworking as ever. But now... Emma stared up at Casey and felt the connection of a past lifetime. "He had a stroke."

"Damn, Em. I'm so sorry to hear that."

She nodded.

Casey shifted closer, scrutinizing her as if he couldn't quite believe his eyes. His expression was so probing, she felt stripped bare and strangely raw.

When Casey moved forward, so did the very pretty redhead with him. She plastered herself to his side in a show of possessiveness. "You two have met?"

Casey glanced at her, then draped his arm over her shoulders with negligent regard. There didn't seem to be any real level of intimacy between them.

But then what did Emma know about real intimacy?

"Emma and I practically grew up together." Casey watched her as he said it, his eyes narrowed, taunting. "We were close, real close I thought, but she's been away from town now for..."

"Eight years," Emma supplied, unwilling to hear him say any more. Close? The only closeness had been in her head and in her dreams. Dredging up her manners, Emma held out her hand and prayed the darkness would hide her slight trembling. "I'm Emma Clark, and this is my friend, Damon Devaughn."

With a look of suspicion, the redhead released Casey to shake hands politely with both Emma and Damon. "Kristin Swarth."

"It's delightful to meet you," Damon murmured, and

Kristin's frown lifted to be replaced by a coy smile. Damon had charisma in spades and the ladies always soaked it up.

Though Damon had no problem warming up to Kristin, he didn't treat Casey with the same courtesy. The second she'd first said Casey's name, Damon had gone rigid and he hadn't relaxed again.

Now, at the introduction, Casey eyed Damon anew, then drew the woman a little closer. "Kristin and I work together."

It wasn't easy, but Emma managed another smile. "I hope we're not interrupting your plans?"

"Not really." Casey gave her a lazy look. "I was just about to take Kristin home."

At the word *home*, B.B. let out a friendly *woof*, and Emma laughed. "I'm sorry, I almost forgot. This is my pal, B.B."

With a wide grin, Casey hunkered down in front of the big dog. "Hello, B.B."

Using noticeable caution, the dog sauntered forward, did some sniffing, and then licked Casey's hand. Emma had almost forgotten how good Casey's family was with animals, Casey included. His Uncle Jordan was even a vet, but they all loved animals and were never without a menagerie of pets.

"Where'd you come up with the name B.B.?"

Emma chuckled, her tension easing with the topic. B.B. was her best friend, her comrade in arms when necessary, her confidant. They'd comforted each other when there was no one else, and now it often seemed B.B. could read her mind. "Big Boy," she explained, and B.B. barked in agreement.

"He's a gorgeous dog." Casey stroked along B.B.'s muscled back, then patted his ribs. "How old is he?"

Damon answered for her, his gaze speculative as he

watched man and dog bonding. "We're not sure, but probably about nine or so. He was young when Emma got him, more a ball of fur with nothing big about him, other than his appetite."

Emma quickly elbowed Damon, hard. A history of how she'd gotten the dog was the last thing she wanted discussed. She didn't mean for Casey to witness that prod, but when she glanced down at him, their gazes clashed and held. He didn't say anything, and that was a relief. When she got Damon alone, she'd choke him.

As Casey scratched the dog's head and rubbed his ears, Emma absorbed the sight of him. It seemed impossible, but eight years had only made him better—taller, stronger, more handsome. As a teen, he'd been an unqualified stud. As a grown man—wowza.

The gentle evening breeze ruffled his dark-blond hair, and his brown eyes caught and held the moonlight. He wore dark slacks and a dress shirt that fit his wide shoulders perfectly. Emma forced her gaze away. It was beyond dumb for her to be ogling him.

The car behind him was, amazingly enough, also a Mustang, but surely a much newer, ritzier model. Emma nodded at the car, trying to see it clearly in the shadows of the night. "Black or blue or green?"

Keeping his hand on B.B.'s head, Casey straightened. "What?"

"Your car."

He swiveled his head around and looked at the car as if he'd never seen it before. "Black."

"Mine is red and in desperate need of a water pump. If you're heading into town, do you think you could direct someone this way? Or is there even road service in the area yet?"

Casey shook his head. "Hell no. If you call Triple A it'll take them at least a couple of hours to get out here to you."

Emma groaned. She was dead on her feet and anxious to get settled. All she wanted to do was shower, eat and sleep, in that order. She'd already stopped at the hospital on the way into town. Damon had kept an eye on B.B., letting him walk about on the grounds while she'd spoken briefly with the nurses before visiting her father.

He'd looked so old and frail, and hadn't registered her visit. She'd wanted to touch him, to reassure herself that he was alive, stable. But she'd held back. Since the doctor was due to see him again in the early morning, she planned to be there so she could get a full update on his prognosis.

Casey moved closer to her again. "The garage is closed for the night, too. That hasn't changed. We still roll up the sidewalks by nine. But I can give you both a ride into town if you want."

Emma looked at Damon. He lounged back against the car and smiled his sexiest smile. "We'll be staying at the Cross Roads Motel. Is that too far off?"

Casey cocked one eyebrow and gave Emma an assessing look. "You're not staying with your mother?"

"No." Just the thought of seeing her mother again, of being back in the house where her life had been so miserable, made Emma's stomach churn. Because Casey couldn't possibly understand her reserve, she scrambled for reasons to present to him, but her wits had gone begging. It didn't help that Damon was deliberately provoking Casey, suggesting an intimate relationship that didn't exist. "The house is small, and my mother... Well, I, ah, thought it'd be better if..."

Before she could say any more, Damon was there. "We've been driving for hours," he interjected smoothly, "and we're both exhausted. Just let us grab a few things and we can stop holding you up."

Casey frowned. "You're not holding me up."

"*I* need to be going," Kristin said, clearly miffed by the turn of events and the way everyone ignored her. Her tone turned snide and her eyes narrowed on B.B. "But I have my cat in the car and she doesn't like strangers. She especially doesn't like dogs. Casey, you know she'll have a fit if we try to put another animal in there with her. Besides, there's not room for everyone."

Casey turned to Emma with a shrug. "I'm afraid she's right. Kristin treated me to dinner because I agreed to help her move."

Laying a hand on his chest, Kristin turned her face up to his. "You know that wasn't my only reason."

Casey countered her suggestiveness with an inattentive hug. "We've got the last load in the car now. The floor and the back seat are already packed."

Damon brought Emma a little closer, and no one could have missed the protectiveness of his gesture. Emma refrained from rolling her eyes, but it wasn't easy. She was the last woman on earth in need of protection, but Damon refused to believe that.

"No problem." The baring of Damon's teeth in no way resembled a smile. And if Emma didn't miss her guess, he was relieved to send Casey away. She only wished she felt the same. "Perhaps you could call us a cab, then?"

"No cabs in Buckhorn. Sorry." Reflecting Damon's mood, Casey looked anything but sorry by that fact. "And you know, if you don't get to the Cross Roads soon, you'll get locked out."

"Locked out?"

"Yep." Casey transferred his gaze to Emma—and his eyes glittered with a strange satisfaction. "Emma, you remember Mrs. Reider? She refuses to get out of bed to check people in after midnight." He lifted his wrist to see the illuminated dial on his watch. "That gives you less than fifteen minutes to make it there."

The beginning of a headache throbbed in Emma's temples. She rubbed her forehead, trying to decide what to do. "It was difficult enough convincing her that B.B. wouldn't be a problem."

Casey lifted an eyebrow. "I'm surprised you *could* convince her. She's not big on pets."

"Paying a double rate did the trick. And I just know she'll still charge us if we don't make it there on time. Her cancellation policy is no better than her check-in policy."

Casey's eyes twinkled in amusement. "She's the only motel in town. She can afford to be difficult."

"Damn." Damon started to pace, which truly showed his annoyance, since Damon normally remained cool in any situation.

Casey stopped him with a simple question. "Can you drive stick?"

Somewhat affronted, Damon said, "Of course."

"Great." Casey pulled a set of keys from his pocket and tossed them to Damon, who caught them against his chest. "Why don't you take Kristin on home? The Cross Roads

Motel is on the way. You can stop and check in, get your room keys, and then after you get Kristin unloaded, you can come back for us."

Damon idly rattled the keys in his palm, looking between Casey and Emma. "Us?"

"I'll stay here with Emma and B.B."

Emma nearly strangled on her own startled breath. Seeing Casey so unexpectedly had unnerved her enough. No way did she want to be alone with him. Not yet. "I can drive a stick."

B.B. looked at her anxiously and took an active stance. His muscles quivered as if he might leap after her if she tried to leave.

"Right." Damon sent her a look. "And you really think he'll stay alone with me on an empty street while you ride off with a stranger? He'll have a fit. Hell, he'd probably chase the car all the way into town. It'd be different if we were at the motel and you left, but out here..."

"Okay, okay." Damon was right. B.B. was so defensive of her, she often wondered if he hadn't been a guard dog in another life.

"Besides," Damon added, further prodding her, "the room is held on my credit card." He stared at Emma hard, undecided, then abruptly shook his head. "Hell no. Let's forget this. It's already late, so what's a few more hours? We can wait for Triple A and then find a motel back on the highway to stay in for the night."

Emma gave that idea quick but serious thought, and knew the only reasonable thing to do was to stop acting like a desperate ninny. She couldn't imagine finding another motel that would allow her to bring B.B. inside. Besides, Damon had driven most of the hours, and despite his suggestion, he looked exhausted. B.B. wasn't in much better shape.

She'd stopped being selfish long ago.

"It's all right, Damon." She gave him a smile to reassure him. "I'm beat and so are you. You go on, and B.B. and I'll wait here."

Kristin crossed her arms and struck a petulant pose. "Don't I get a vote on this?"

Casey spared her a glance. "Not this time." Then he added, "And, honey, don't pout." He walked her to the car, his large hand open on the small of her back, urging her along while he spoke quietly in her ear.

Damon used that moment to pull Emma aside. He practically shoved her behind the open driver's door and then bent close. "Dear God," he muttered, holding his head. "I can understand why he became your adolescent hero, Emma. He's testosterone on legs."

Emma couldn't help but laugh at Damon's look of distaste. He wasn't into the whole machismo display. Damon was far too refined for that, a man straight out of *GQ*. He also knew exactly how to lighten her mood. Not that he was wrong, of course. If anything, Casey was more ruggedly masculine now than he'd ever been.

Emma decided to tease him right back. "I hate to break it to you, Damon, but he's obviously into women."

Refusing to take the bait, Damon glanced over at Kristin with critical disdain. "*I'm* into women. He's obviously into twits. There *is* a difference."

Casey and Kristin were still in quiet conversation, their bodies outlined by the reaching glow of the car lights. "You really think so?"

"That she's a twit? Absolutely."

"No, I didn't mean that." She swatted at him and stifled a laugh. "I mean, do you think they're a couple?"

"Worried?"

Damon knew better. She wouldn't be in Buckhorn long enough to get worried about Casey and whom he might or might not be involved with. Probably his girlfriends were too many to count, anyway. Until he'd turned sixteen, Casey had been raised in an all-male household. Sawyer and his three brothers had been the most eligible, respected and adored bachelors in Buckhorn. One by one they'd married off, starting with Casey's father. But Casey had inherited a lot of their appeal and long before Emma had left town, the females had been chasing him. "Only curious. I haven't seen him in so long."

Damon's look plainly said *yeah, right.* "I think he wants to be into her, if you need true accuracy. Whether or not he likes her—who knows?" Then he added with more seriousness, "You know to most men, liking and wanting have nothing in common."

That was Damon's staunchest requirement. He had to genuinely like and respect a woman to decide to sleep with her. Intelligence sat high on his list, as did motivation and kindness. The second a woman got gossipy or catty, he walked away. Unlike many of the men she'd known through the years, Damon wasn't ruled by his libido. Emma respected him for that, even while she knew he'd be a tough man to please.

Again Emma chuckled, but her humor was cut short as Casey called, "You ready to go?"

Damon ignored him as he cupped Emma's face, forcing her to look him in the eyes. "Will you be okay?"

"Yes, of course."

"Too fast, doll. That was nothing more than an automatic answer."

"But true nonetheless."

He waggled her head. "Just be on guard, okay? I don't want to see you hurt."

"I'm not made of glass," she chided.

"No, it's sugar I think." He lifted her hand to his mouth, nipped her knuckles and said, "Yep, sugar."

Emma was well used to that teasing response—he'd been saying it to her since she was seventeen years old, when they'd first met. She'd been backward, afraid, alone. And he'd treated her like a well-loved kid sister.

Laughing, she turned toward the other car, and caught the censure on Casey's face. He didn't say a word, but then he didn't have to. She knew exactly what he thought. And none of it was nice.

Worse, none of it was accurate.

chapter 3

EMMA STOOD in front of her car, watching Damon and Kristin drive away. With their departure, the previously calm evening air suddenly felt charged. She was aware of things she hadn't noticed before, like the warm, subtle scent of Casey's cologne, the nearly tactile touch of his watchfulness. The pulsing rhythm of her own heartbeat resounded everywhere, in her chest, her ears, low in her belly.

B.B. shifted beside her, restless and uncertain with this turn of events and her renewed tension.

Though he didn't make a sound, she knew Casey was now closer behind her. As if he'd touched her, she shivered in reaction, and continued to stare after the car.

"So how've you been, Em?" His voice was low and intimate, a rough whisper of sound somewhere above her right ear.

The twin taillights of the other car faded away, swallowed up by distance and fog, the inky blackness of the night. Left with nothing to stare at, Emma drew a deep breath, took two steps away and turned to him with a bland smile. "Good. And yourself?"

"Good." He visually caressed her face, slowly, thoroughly, as if he'd never seen her before. As if maybe he'd...missed her.

Emma moved to the side of the car, taking herself out of the harsh beams of the headlights. The dog followed and she leaned down to give him a reassuring pat. When she straightened, Casey was even closer than before and he made no attempt to move away. She felt vaguely hunted.

"You look so different, Em."

She wasn't about to back away a second time. Faking a calm that eluded her, she shrugged. "Eight years different."

"It's not your age," he murmured, once again looking her over in that scrutinizing way of his. "Your hair is different."

Emma started to reply, but the words hung in her throat as Casey reached out and caught a shoulder-length tress, rubbing it between fingers and thumb.

Both breathless and a little indignant, she tossed her head so that her hair fell behind her shoulders. That didn't deter Casey. He simply drew it forward again, making her frown. He was bolder than she remembered.... No, that wasn't true. He'd always been bold—with the girls he'd wanted.

He just hadn't ever wanted her.

"I don't bleach it anymore." Despite being annoyed, awareness trembled in her belly, sang through her veins. "This is my real color."

His long fingers tunneled in close to her scalp, warm and gentle, then lifted outward, letting the silky strands drift back into place. "I can't see it that well here in the shadows."

Her breath came too fast. "Light brown."

"I never really understood why you lightened it." He stroked her hair again, totally absorbed in what he did, unmindful or uncaring of her discomfort. "Or why you wore so much makeup."

She refused to apologize for or explain about her past. That was one of the things Damon had taught her—to forget about what she couldn't change and only look forward. "I thought it looked good at the time, but then, I was only seventeen and not overly astute."

Casey stood silent for only a minute. "Why don't we sit in the car? The air is pretty damp tonight."

Being that she was already far too aware of him, she didn't consider that a good idea. But the dog had heard him and, not wanting to be left out, quickly went through the open driver's door and performed an agile leap into the back seat.

Emma gave a mental shrug and scooted inside, leaving Casey to go to the passenger side. The consummate gentleman, he closed her door first before walking around the hood of the car. When he slid into his seat, she had only a moment to appreciate the sharp angles and planes of his face fully lit by the interior light. He closed his door too, and the light clicked off with a sort of symbolic finality that made her senses come alive.

Casey twisted sideways in his seat and spoke in a low vibrating murmur. "Better turn off the headlights, Em, or you'll have a dead battery to go with the busted water pump."

Though Emma knew he was right, she hated to be in utter darkness with him. Her awareness of him as a man defied reason.

He hadn't touched her, but God, she felt as if he had. All over.

"There's a flashlight in the glove box."

Casey opened the small door, moved a few papers aside

and pulled out the black-handled utility light. He didn't hand it to her, didn't turn it on, but instead held it in his lap. She turned off the headlights and inky blackness settled in around them. Emma wondered if he could hear the wild pounding of her heart.

Her reactions irritated her as much as they distressed her. No other man had ever affected her this way. She'd had plenty of relationships since she'd grown up, and she'd assumed her tepid reactions had been mostly due to maturing, to wising up, to learning what was best for her. She'd accepted that sex was pleasurable but not vital. It eased an ache, provided comfort, added to the closeness, and nothing more.

Yet, sitting in a dark car next to Casey Hudson, she felt the biting greed of lust in a way that hadn't touched her since...since the last time she'd been this near him.

"So what have you been doing with yourself?" he asked, and Emma started in surprise.

"What?"

"It's been a long time." His voice held the same easy cadence she remembered from long ago, but there was an edge to it now. An edge to him. "You disappeared without a trace, so I'm just wondering what you've been up to."

Emma didn't want to get into this now. He wouldn't understand and she wasn't up to explaining. In truth, it wasn't any of his business what she did or had done while she'd been away from Buckhorn. But telling him so would have been too ballsy, even for her, and would have made her sound defensive.

Keeping her answer vague, she shrugged. "Working, like most people I guess."

She braced herself for the questions that would follow,

and wondered at the hesitation she felt in explaining her job to him. Damn it, she loved her job and was proud of herself for doing it so well.

But Casey took her off guard by skipping her occupation and going straight to a more difficult topic.

"You and Damon involved?"

Anger flashed through Emma, pushing some of the sexual awareness aside. Regardless of their pasts, she didn't deserve an inquisition.

"Are you and Kristin?" Her voice sounded sharper than she'd intended, but Casey just laughed.

"No." His white teeth gleamed in the darkness. "As I said, she's a co-worker, a friend. No more than that."

Emma shook her head. Men could be so dense. "So you say. My guess is that she wants to be considerably more."

Casey touched her cheek, a casual gesture that felt hotly intimate and made her breath catch. "Yeah, well, I can be stubborn when I want to be."

She almost replied *I remember,* but caught herself in time. His honesty provoked her own. "Damon and I are friends."

"Uh-huh."

She didn't care if he believed her or not. *She didn't.* She turned away to stare out the window, letting Casey know without words that he could think what he wanted.

"If you were homely," Casey teased, "then I could maybe believe it. But Em?" He waited just long enough to make her antsy. "You're far from homely."

She tried to ignore him. The field to her left sounded with a thousand insects: the buzz of mosquitoes, the singing of crickets. Like stars in the sky, fireflies twinkled on and off.

She hadn't forgotten that Buckhorn was beautiful in the

summer, but somehow the clarity of it had been blunted. The colors, the smells, the texture of the air and the lush grass and the velvet sky...

Casey stroked one finger over her cheek, down to her throat, then her shoulder. "Hell, if anything, you're more attractive than ever, and you were plenty attractive at seventeen."

Her heart punched painfully against her rib cage. How had the conversation gotten out of hand so quickly? Her laugh sounded more believable this time. "I'm guessing you must have lowered your standards."

Casey stared at her, not comprehending.

Emma rolled her eyes. "I've been in the car all day, Case. I'm dressed in what can only be called my comfortable clothes—and that's if I'm being generous. No makeup, my hair's windblown..."

"You look sexy as hell to me."

The way he growled that pronouncement robbed Emma of clear thought. She searched her brain for something to say, some way to derail him. "How long will it take Damon to get back, do you think?"

Casey didn't take the hint. He didn't stop touching her either. He smoothed her hair behind her ear and curled his fingers around her head. "Men only pretend to be friends with women to get one thing."

Goaded, Emma shifted around to face him. His hand dropped, but his gaze, glittering in the darkness, remained steady.

Even the gearshift between them didn't hinder Casey's movements. He got so close that Emma inhaled the warmth of his masculine smell on every breath.

"Is that right?" Her voice shook, her hands trembled. "Then I guess we're enemies, because there's never been a single thing you wanted from me."

Beneath the fall of her hair, Casey's hand curved around her neck in a gentle restraint that felt far too unbreakable. Trying to be inconspicuous, she pressed into the car door. It didn't help.

With near-tactile intensity, his gaze stroked her face, then rested on her mouth.

"True." There was a heavy, thrumming beat of silence, and Casey whispered, "Until now."

KNOWING HE PUSHED HER, knowing it was unfair, Casey tried to pull back. But damn it, he wanted her. Seeing her again...it hit him like a ton of bricks, throwing him off balance, making him defensive and fractious and keenly alert. Emma had influenced his life when he hadn't thought that possible. Forgetting her hadn't been easy.

In fact, he'd never managed it.

Just the opposite.

At twenty-seven, his solid position within his stepgrandfather's company should have been enhanced with a wife on his arm and a couple of kids underfoot, just as he'd always intended. Instead, no woman had ever quite measured up.

The bitch of it was, he had no idea what they needed to measure up to. He didn't even know what he was looking for.

Until moments ago, when he saw Emma standing there.

As always, her eyes had been huge and soft, and all his senses had quickened with recognition. He hadn't experienced that rush of pure, white-hot intensity since... *No*, he wouldn't do that, wouldn't give her credit she didn't deserve. She'd run out on him and he wasn't quite ready to forgive her for that. But he was more than ready to take what he'd often regretted missing so many years ago.

Her small hands lifted to press against his chest, burning him, heightening the ache. "Casey..."

The way she said his name was familiar. Did she want him to stop or, like him, was she anxious to feel the flash fire of their unique chemistry? Her appearance, her attitude, were different. But her natural sensuality hadn't waned at all. Instead, it had aged and ripened and gotten better, richer. No woman had ever affected him like Emma did, and now, with no effort at all, she'd gotten him hot.

She wasn't a lonely, insecure child anymore.

She wasn't afraid, wasn't mistreated.

He had no reason to hold back, no reason to still feel protective. *Damn it.*

Without thought, Casey let his fingers stroke the nape of her neck. Just as it always had, her softness drew him, the remembered texture of her skin, her hair and her scent... God, he loved her scent. Heady and warm, it mingled with the damp fog and the gentle evening breeze.

He felt alive. He felt challenged.

"Emma?"

Her thick lashes lifted.

"Are you married?"

She shook her head, causing the silky weight of her hair to glide over his arm.

"Engaged?"

"No." She pulled her head back a little and Casey kissed her throat, nuzzling her fragrant skin, breathing her in. A sound of near desperation slipped past her open lips. "Are you…?"

"Hell no. There's no one." He didn't want to talk about that though. "You feel good, Em. You smell even better."

"Casey."

If she kept saying his name like that, he'd lose it. "You know, since you and Damon aren't involved…" If she had no commitments to anyone, then why not? It didn't matter that he rushed things. They were both grown now, both adults, so Emma could damn well make a rational decision now, rather than one based on fear and insecurity.

"Damon and I are friends." A measure of steel laced her declaration.

Had she misunderstood his suggestion?

Casey drew back so he could see her face. Her heavy lashes half covered her eyes as she watched him warily. She remained guarded, but she didn't push him away. He tried a different tack. "You're staying at the Cross Roads tonight."

"Yes."

Adulthood had provided new dimension to her features. Her cheekbones were more noticeable, her mouth wider, fuller, her jaw firm. She was lovely—and he had to have her. "You'll be sleeping alone?" Which would make it easy for him to join her.

Her gaze flickered away, and his stomach knotted even before she spoke. "That's none of your business, Casey."

Frustration unfurled in his guts, making his tone raw with sarcasm. "Sounds like a *no* to me."

Chin lifted, she faced him squarely and confirmed his suspicions. "No. I won't sleep alone."

Very slowly, doing his best to rein in his seldom-seen

temper, Casey released her and moved back to his own seat. The sexual turbulence remained, gnawing at him, testing him, but now other, darker emotions gripped him too. He didn't want to study them too closely. "I see."

He could feel her turmoil. And he could taste her interest, damn her. It was there, shimmering between them. Yet, she'd be with Damon, her *friend*.

Once long ago, Casey had been her friend. Probably her best friend, if not the only one. He'd told her then that he didn't share. That much hadn't changed. He wanted her, but on his terms.

And that's how he'd have her.

Emma slowly straightened in her seat and stared straight ahead. "I seriously doubt that you see anything."

The dog stuck his head over the seat and whined. Emma shifted enough to pat him, then buried her face in his scruff. "It's okay, B.B."

Casey sat in brooding silence for several moments, watching as she comforted the big dog. Slashes of moonlight silhouetted her body and the slow movements of her stroking hands through thick fur. She ignored him as if he didn't exist, not once looking at him. It didn't matter.

Despite any protest Devaughn might make, Casey knew he'd eventually have her.

By her own admission, she wasn't married, wasn't engaged, so no one, Damon included, had any real claim on her. That left Casey free to do as he pleased. And it would please him a hell of a lot to take care of unfinished business so he could get her out of his system and get on with his life. It felt as if he'd been on hold for eight years. Now, finally, he'd discover what he'd missed so many years ago. Finally, he'd appease the ache.

Because he knew he'd lost ground by letting her see his anger, Casey changed his tack. "I got the money you sent."

Startled, she released the dog. "I'm sorry I took it in the first place. It was wrong."

"You know I'd have given it to you if you'd asked." She nodded without recognizing the outright lie. Hell, if Emma had asked him for money, he'd have known her plans and rather than leave her alone that night, he'd have kept close to her. He'd have stayed with her and everything would have turned out different.

He wouldn't have lost her for so long.

Remembering that night still made Casey tense. So many times over the years, he'd replayed it in his head, thinking of things he should have done, should have said. He'd given up on ever seeing her again.

Now she'd returned, and he'd done nothing but paw her. He wanted to tell her that he'd missed her, that she'd left a void in his life. But, damn it, she'd walked out on him without a backward glance. It still pissed him off.

"Where did you go when you left, Em?"

More silence. She turned her head to stare out the window.

Not bothering to hide his exasperation, Casey said, "C'mon, Emma. Hell, it's been damn near a decade. Does it really matter if you tell me?" He couldn't soften his tone, couldn't soften his reaction to her. Emma had always had the ability to make him feel things he didn't want to feel, to feel things he hadn't felt since she'd left him.

He could see her resistance, her reticence. She didn't trust him, never really had, and that bothered him most of all. "You came to me once, Emma. Why can't you talk to me now?"

"People change over time, Casey."

"Me or you?"

"In eight years? I'd say both." Turning from the window, she looked at him and sighed. "I don't even know you anymore."

In so many ways she knew him better than anyone ever had. But he was glad she didn't realize it. "So where you went is a big secret, huh?" He rubbed his upper lip as he considered her. "Must be something scandalous, right? Let me think. Wait, I know. Did you become a spy?"

She rolled her eyes, looking so much like the old teasing girl he used to know.

"No? Well, let's see. Did you join up with a circus or get sent to prison?"

"No, no, and no."

"Then what?" Unable to help himself, he stretched out his arm and cupped her shoulder. Her nearness made it impossible for him *not* to touch her. The ancient, baggy sweatshirt she wore all but hid her breasts. But Casey knew their softness, their plump weight. How they felt in his palms.

Oh yeah, he remembered that too well.

Emma lifted her face and met his gaze. "There's no reason to rehash old news."

"It's not old for me." He recalled the many nights he'd lain awake worrying about her, imagining every awful scenario that could happen to a girl all alone. It had made him sick with fear—and blind with rage. "I offered you help, Emma, and rather than take it you left me a goddamn note that didn't tell me a thing. You ran out on me. You stole money from me." *You ripped out my heart.*

She bit her lip, her face awash in guilt. "I'm sorry."

Damn it, he didn't want her apology. He thought to take back the words, but instead he drew a deep breath and continued, hoping to cajole her, reassure her. "I worried about you, Emma, especially when I found out you didn't have a relative in Ohio. I worried and I thought about you and wished like hell I'd done something different. I screwed up that night, and I know it."

Her eyes were wide and dark, filled with incredulity. "But…that's nonsense."

"I don't think so. You came to me, and I let you down."

"No." She leaned forward and her cool fingers caressed his jaw. His muscles clenched with her first tentative touch. "Don't ever think that, Casey. You did more than enough. You helped me more than anyone else ever could have."

"Right."

"Casey…" She hesitated, then she whispered, "You were the best thing that ever happened to me. You always made me happy, even after I'd gone away."

Robbed of breath by her words, Casey closed his hand over hers and kept her palm flat against his jaw. It was such a simple touch, and it meant so much to him. "But I don't deserve an accounting? Or do I have to go on wondering what happened to you?"

She tugged her hand free and let it drop to the gearshift. Their gazes were locked together, neither of them able or willing to look away. The dog laid his head on the back of the seat between them, watching closely. He gave a whine of curiosity.

B.B. probably felt Emma's distress, Casey thought, because he sure as hell felt it. He regretted that he'd upset her, but he needed to know where she'd gone and how she'd gotten by. He *had* to know.

"All right." Her whispered words barely reached him,

then she cleared her throat and spoke with new strength. "But it's a boring story."

"Let me be the judge of that."

With a sigh, she dropped back into her seat and folded her hands in her lap. Her hair fell forward to hide her face. Casey wanted to smooth it back so he could better see her, but he didn't want to take a chance on interrupting her confession.

"For the first two weeks I lived in a park. There were plenty of woods so it was easy to hide when they shut the gates. There were outdoor rest rooms and stuff there, places for me to clean up and get a drink and..." She rolled her shoulders. "I had everything I needed. In a way, it was fun, like an adventure."

"Jesus, Em. You don't mean..."

"Yeah." She dredged up a smile that didn't do a damn thing to convince him. "I slept on the ground, using my backpack for a pillow. You know, it reminded me of all those nights we used to stay out late on the lake. You remember how we could hear the leaves and see all the stars and the air was so cool and crisp? We'd get mosquito bites, but it was worth it. Well, it was like that. A little scary at times, but also sort of soothing and peaceful. It'd be so quiet I'd stare up at the sky and think about everyone back in Buckhorn." Her gaze darted away, and she added on a whisper, "I'd think about you."

Pained, his heart aching, Casey closed his eyes. Emma didn't know how her words devastated him, because she wasn't looking at him.

"That's where I found B.B. He was still a puppy, a warm, energetic ball of fur, and when we saw each other, he was so…happy to be with me." She laced her fingers together, waited. "Someone had abandoned him."

Just as her father had abandoned her?

"I picked ticks off him and used my comb to get snarls out of his fur and he played with me and kept me company."

This time her smile was genuine, a small, sweet smile, as she talked about the dog. Casey wanted to crowd her close and put his arms around her and protect her forever. The urge was so strong, he sounded gruff as he asked, "Why did you stay in a park, Emma?"

"There was nowhere else to stay. I used the money I had—and your money—to pay for my bus fare to Chicago, and for food. After I got there, I couldn't get a job because I couldn't give a place of residence, and I couldn't get a place of residence without a job reference. I was afraid if I went to any of the shelters, they'd contact my family and…send me back home."

Casey scrubbed at his face. Emma was twenty-five now, but he saw her as she'd been when she left—young, bruised, scared and lonely. What she'd gone through was worse than he'd suspected, worse than he'd ever imagined. He'd held on to the belief that she knew someone, that she'd had someone to take care of her. But she'd been all alone. Vulnerable. And it hurt to know that.

"I'm not sure what would have eventually happened. But then one day B.B. got really sick. He'd eaten something bad and he was dehydrated, weak. He could barely walk. I was so afraid that I'd lose him, I chanced going to the vet clinic that I'd seen not far from the park. That's where I met Parker Devaughn and his son, Damon."

She turned to B.B. and hugged him close. Several seconds passed, and Casey knew she was weighing her words. "It took almost a week before B.B. was healthy again. I hung out there, staying by his side as much as they'd let me."

The images flooding his mind were too agonizing to bear. "What happened?"

"They…figured out my situation when I couldn't pay the bill and offered to let me work it off instead."

"They realized that you were homeless?" Casey wanted to hear all the details about where she'd slept, how she'd stayed safe. When the dog was sick, she'd been alone more than ever.

But one thought kept overriding all others. How bad had it been for her in Buckhorn that she'd rather sleep alone in a park with no one for company except an abandoned dog? What the hell had happened to make her run away?

Emma gave a small nod. "I couldn't leave B.B. and they wouldn't let me have him without explaining. I was afraid they'd turn me in and send me back home. But when I told them everything, they surprised me."

"Everything?"

She glanced at him, then away. Skipping his question, she said, "They took me in and they've treated me like family ever since. Parker even helped me to get my G.E.D. and to find a job I love. Life now is…great."

She'd left out everything painful, either to spare him or because she couldn't bear to talk about it. Casey didn't know which, and neither was acceptable. He suddenly wanted her to be his friend again, that young girl with the enormous soft eyes always filled with invitation. The girl who always came to him with open admiration and her heart on her sleeve. The girl who'd wanted him—and only him.

His decisions, his feelings for her back then, had seemed

so simple and straightforward. He'd liked controlling things, only letting her so close, giving her only as much as he wanted and holding back everything else.

Or so he'd thought.

But somehow Emma had crawled under his skin and into his head, his heart. He hadn't known until she was gone that she'd taken more than he'd ever meant to give her. He hadn't known until she was gone, and a big piece of him was missing. Being apart from her while becoming a man hadn't changed how he felt. It had only complicated it.

Disturbed by his reaction to her, he teased her by tugging on a lock of her hair. "That story is so full of holes I could use it for a sieve."

"No, I've told you everything that's important."

"Em…"

"Thanks to Parker and Damon, I did fine," she insisted. She smiled a little, and her eyes glinted with humor. "In fact, I might owe them even more than I owe you."

Annoyance fought with tenderness, making his voice gruff. "You don't owe me a damn thing and you know it."

"I knew you probably felt that way." She shook her head, still smiling in that small, tantalizing way that made him want to lick her mouth. "That's one of the things that always made you so special, Casey."

Hearing her say such a thing took some of the edge off his urgency. He liked thinking that he'd been special to her, because she'd certainly been special to him. He just hadn't known it until it was too late.

Acting on impulse, he took her hand. "Have breakfast with me tomorrow. We can catch up on old times and you can fill me in on the pieces you're leaving out right now."

She gave a shrug of apology. "I can't. I'm going to the hospital first thing."

He'd almost forgotten about her father and felt like an ass because of it. It surprised him that she'd return to see the man who'd run her off, but he supposed time could heal those wounds. And Dell wasn't in the best of health. "We can make it dinner."

She closed her eyes on a sigh of weariness. "I don't think so, Casey."

Her rejection struck him like a blow. "I'm special," he asked, "but not special enough to share a meal with?"

She swiveled her head toward him. "I'm sorry—"

In an instant, his temper snapped. "Will you quit saying that!"

She flipped her hair back and her eyes flashed. "Don't yell at me."

"Then quit apologizing." And in a mumble, "You always did apologize too much."

B.B. let out a low warning growl, breaking the flow of anger. Emma turned to the big dog and rubbed his muzzle. In a calmer tone, she said, "I can't make any plans because I don't know what my schedule will be, or how much free time I'll have."

And she wasn't sleeping alone.

Casey cursed softly, but he couldn't blame Devaughn. If he had Emma warming his bed, no way would he let her out with another man.

He wouldn't give up, but he would slow it down. He'd been her friend once, maybe her only friend in Buckhorn. He'd build on that. He'd give her time to breathe, to get used to him again.

Until Emma got the water pump fixed, she'd need transportation to the hospital. He'd be happy to oblige, to give her a helping hand.

One thing was certain, before she took off this time he'd have all his questions answered. He'd be damned if he'd let her sneak out on him a second time.

chapter 4

As IF FROM A DISTANCE, Emma heard the knock on the thin motel-room door. She forced her head from the flat, overstarched pillow and glanced at the glowing face of the clock. It was barely six-thirty and her body remained limp with the heaviness of sleep. She'd only been in bed five hours.

After Damon had finally returned and they'd transferred everything from her car to Casey's and gotten to the Cross Roads Motel, it had been well past one o'clock. She hadn't unpacked, had only pulled off her shoes, jeans, bra and sweatshirt, and dropped into the bed in a tee and panties. She'd been so exhausted, both in body and spirit, that thoughts of food or a shower disintegrated beneath tiredness.

Why would anyone be calling on her this early?

B.B. snuffled around and let out a warning *woof,* but Emma patted him and he resettled with a modicum of grumbling and growling. Stretched on his side, he took up more than his fair share of the bed. "It's okay, boy. I'll be right back."

Probably Mrs. Reider, she thought, ready with a complaint of some kind, though Emma couldn't imagine what it might be. They'd kept very quiet coming in last night and hadn't disturbed anyone as far as she knew.

B.B. was atop the covers, so Emma grabbed the bedspread that had gotten pushed to the bottom of the bed. She halfheartedly wrapped it around herself and let it drag on the floor.

Without turning on a light, she padded barefoot to the door, turned the cheap lock, and swung it open. The room had been dark with the heavy drapes drawn, but now she had to lift a hand to shield her eyes against the red glow of a rising sun. She blinked twice before her bleary eyes could focus.

And there stood Casey.

His powerful body lounged against the door frame, silhouetted by a golden halo. In the daylight, he looked more devastatingly handsome than ever. Confusion washed over Emma and she stared, starting at Casey's feet and working her way up.

Laced-up, scuffed brown boots showed beneath well-worn jeans that rode low on his lean hips and were faded white in stress spots, like his knees, the pocket where he kept his keys. His fly.

Emma blinked at that, then shook her head and continued upward. With the casual clothing, he'd forgone a belt. In fact, two belt loops were missing from the ancient jeans.

In deference to the heat, he wore a sleeveless, battered white cotton shirt that left his muscular arms and tanned shoulders on display. Mirrored sunglasses shielded his eyes, and his mouth curled in a lopsided, wicked grin. "Morning, Emma."

Her tongue stuck to the roof of her mouth, making speech difficult. "What are you doing here?"

Lifting one hand, which caused all kinds of interesting muscles to flex in his arm, he showed her the smallest of her suitcases. "You forgot this in the trunk of my car. I thought you might need it today."

"Oh." She looked around, not sure what to do next. She did need the case, seeing that it held her toiletries and makeup. But she could hardly invite him in when she wasn't dressed. Loosening her hold on the bedspread, she reached for the case. "Thank you…"

Casey removed the decision from her. Lifting the case out of reach, he stepped inside just in time to see B.B. bound off the bed and lunge forward with a growl. When he recognized Casey, he slowed and the growl turned into a tail-wagging hello. Casey greeted the dog while eyeing the bed he'd vacated. Being a double, it provided just enough room for one woman—and her pet.

He quirked an eyebrow at Emma as realization dawned. She hadn't slept alone, so he couldn't accuse her of lying. But she hadn't slept with a man either, which had been his assumption.

Casey grinned and reached down to pat the dog. "You've sure got the cushy life, don't you, B.B.?"

The dog jumped up, putting his paws on Casey's shoulders. Casey laughed. "Yeah, sleeping with a gorgeous woman would put any guy in a good mood."

Left standing in the open doorway, Emma hadn't quite gathered her wits yet. Too little sleep combined with Casey Hudson in the morning could rattle anyone. She certainly wasn't up to bantering with him. "He's always slept with me. It's one reason I bring him along everywhere I go."

"Gotcha." Casey looked around again, and his grin widened. "So. Where's Damon?"

He tried to sound innocent, but failed. Knowing the jig was up, Emma scowled at him. Would he now consider her fair game, since she wasn't involved? What would she say to dissuade him if he did?

Did she really want to dissuade him?

The connecting door opened and Damon stuck his dark head out. With only one eye opened, he demanded, "What the hell's going on?" Then he saw Casey, and that one eye widened. "Oh, it's you. I should have known."

In his boxers and nothing more, Damon pulled the door wider. Emma wasn't uncomfortable with his lack of dress. More often than not, Damon acted like her brother.

Casey took in the separate rooms with a look of deep satisfaction. "Morning, Devaughn."

"Yeah, whatever." Damon yawned, leaned in the doorway, and crossed his arms over his naked chest. His blue eyes were heavy, his jaw shadowed with stubble, and his silky black hair stuck out in funny disarray. "You country boys like to get up early, I take it?"

"Country boys?" Casey didn't sound amused by that description.

Undisturbed by Casey's pique, Damon lazily eyed him with both eyes this time, taking in the old snug jeans and the muscle shirt. "Brought it up another notch, I see."

Casey's scowl darkened. "What?"

Damon just shook his head and glanced at Emma. "Give me a minute to get dressed."

She didn't want to turn this into a social gathering, and besides, both men were bristling, which didn't bode well. "That's not necessary."

"No?"

"No." Emma saw Damon's surprise and rubbed her forehead. He looked as tired as she felt, so why didn't he just go on back to bed so she could deal with Casey in private? She moderated her tone. "It's fine, Damon. Get some more sleep."

He didn't budge. "You turned willing overnight?"

Her moderation shot to hell, Emma ground her teeth together. "Damon…"

"Was it the macho clothes that turned the trick?"

Casey shifted his stance but Emma growled, causing both B.B. and Damon to watch her warily.

Damon straightened in the doorway with dawning suspicion. "Have you had your coffee?"

Emma slowly looked up at him. A long rope of tangled hair hung over her bloodshot, puffy eyes. She wore only her T-shirt and a bedspread. Curling her lip, she asked, "Do I look to you like I've had coffee?"

"Shit." He turned to Casey with accusation. "So where is it?"

Casey blinked in incomprehension. "Where is what?"

As if speaking to an idiot, Damon enunciated each word. "The coffee?"

Casey shrugged, but offered helpfully, "They keep a pot brewing in the lobby."

"Right. In the lobby. And here I had the impression you knew something about women." Shaking his head at Casey in a pitying way, Damon turned to Emma. "Just hang on, doll. I'll run down and snag you a cup."

On a normal day Emma would have thanked him and dropped back into bed. But this wasn't a normal day. Today, Casey stood in her temporary bedroom looking and smelling too sexy for a sane woman's health and she wasn't properly dressed. "It's okay. B.B. needs to go out too, so I might as well get the coffee myself." And then she wouldn't be left closed up in the motel room with Casey.

Apparently stunned, Damon blinked at her. "Are you sure?"

"I'm sure I'm going to smack you if you don't stop pushing me."

"All right, all right." Damon held up both hands, which should have been comical given that he wore only print boxers. "Hey, what do I know about a woman's needs? They're ever shifting and changing, right? One day coffee is a necessity before she can open her eyes. The next, no problem, she'll get it herself."

Emma turned away and stomped to the dresser to snatch up her jeans. Ignoring both men, she trailed into the bathroom and shut the door. She didn't exactly slam it, but her irritation definitely showed.

She heard Casey whistle low. "Wow. Is she always like that in the morning?"

"Be warned—*yes*."

Casey chuckled, but Damon, clearly disgruntled, said, "I wouldn't if I was you. What you just saw is nothing compared to how grouchy she'll get if she doesn't get a cup of coffee real soon."

"I'll keep that in mind."

"You do that."

Emma brushed her teeth while praying that Damon would now go back to bed. He did, but not without a parting shot.

"I usually fetch her a cup before I wake her up, especially when she hasn't had enough sleep. But since you did the deed this morning, and at such an ungodly hour at that, you can deal with the consequences all alone."

She heard Damon's door close, then heard Casey mutter to B.B., "You won't let her hurt me, will you, buddy?"

B.B. whined.

Emma exited the bathroom. She slipped her feet into her sneakers, latched B.B.'s leash to his collar and stepped around Casey to head out the door. Obedient whenever it suited him, B.B. followed, and, without a word, Casey fell into step behind him. She'd only gone down three steps, her destination the lobby where fresh coffee waited, when she heard Casey begin humming some tune that she didn't recognize.

He knew she slept without a man. Emma wondered what he intended to do with that knowledge, because she knew Casey too well to mistake him now. He was up to something, and she dreaded the coming battle.

It was herself she'd have to fight, of course. She'd never been able to resist Casey, not then, and not now. Damn.

BEFORE SHE COULD HEAD for the lobby, Casey caught Emma's arm. "Take B.B. to the bushes, then park yourself at the picnic table. I'll get the coffee."

She looked ready to argue, so Casey reasoned with her. "You can't take the dog inside, and he's starting to look desperate. Really, fetching you a cup of coffee won't tax me. I'll even get one for myself. Okay?"

She glanced at the dog, who did indeed appear urgent, then nodded. "All right. Lots of sugar and a smidgen of cream."

"Got it." Casey sauntered away with a smile on his face. He'd spent the night thinking about Emma, and being sexually frustrated as a result. He couldn't say what he'd expected this morning when he'd knocked on her door, but the picture she'd presented had taken him by surprise.

Soft. That was the word that most often came to mind when he thought of Emma. Soft eyes, soft heart, soft breasts and hips and thighs…

This morning, still sleepy and wrapped in a bedspread, she'd been so soft she'd damn near melted his heart on the spot, along with all the plans he'd so meticulously devised throughout the long night. He'd taken one look at her and wanted to lead her right back to bed.

It had been doubly hard to give up that idea once he knew Damon had a separate room.

Seeing her sleek, silky hair tangled around her shoulders, her cheeks flushed, her eyes a little dazed had made him think of a woman's expression right before she came. Emma's very kissable mouth had been slightly puffy, and her lips had parted in surprise when she saw him at the door, adding to the fantasy.

Her legs…well, Emma had always had a killer ass and gorgeous legs. That hadn't changed. As a perpetually horny teen, resisting her had been his biggest struggle. As an adult, it wasn't much easier. In fact, he had no intention of resisting her now.

Unfortunately, she'd pulled on jeans rather than the ultrashort shorts he remembered in their youth, and her legs were now well hidden. But she hadn't bothered with a bra yet. With each step she took, her breasts moved gently beneath the cotton of her T-shirt, and the faintest outline of her nipples showed through.

Casey's muscles tightened in anticipation of seeing her again and he snapped lids on three disposable cups of coffee then plucked up several packets of sugar, two stirrers and some little tubs of creamer. He stuffed them in his pockets.

Balancing the hot cups between his hands, he shouldered the door open and started back to Emma.

In limp exhaustion, she rested at one of the aged wooden picnic tables that had always served as part of Mrs. Reider's small lot. Guests used the tables often, but this early in the day no one else intruded. Casey didn't make a sound as he approached, and Emma remained unaware of him.

She'd kicked off her shoes, and her legs were stretched out in front of her with her bare toes wiggling. Sunlight through elm leaves, shifting and changing with the careless breeze, dappled her upturned face.

The air this time of morning remained heavy with dew, rich with scents of the earth and trees. Emma sighed and her expression bespoke a peacefulness that made Casey smile from the inside out. He liked seeing Emma at peace. When she'd been younger, so often what he'd seen in her eyes was uncertainty, loneliness, even fear.

She spoke a moment to B.B., who sprawled out in the lush grass at her feet, then she reached up and lifted her hair off her nape. Casey stalled in appreciation of her feminine gesture. Even from her early teens, Emma had displayed an innate sensuality that drove every guy around her wild. She stretched her arms high, and her hair drifted free to resettle over her shoulders.

Damn. He absolutely could not get a boner in Mrs. Reider's motel lot.

Neither could he allow Emma to affect him this strongly. He had to remember that despite her appeal and everything he'd once felt—still felt—she'd walked out on him and hadn't bothered to get in touch in eight long years. And she hadn't come back for him now. If her father wasn't so sick, she wouldn't be here.

"Here's your coffee." His emotions in check, Casey took the last few remaining steps to her and set the cups on the tabletop. "I hope you haven't chewed off any tree bark or anything." He scattered the sugar packets and creamer beside the cups.

Eyes scrunched up because of the sun, Emma turned to him with a frown. "Damon exaggerated. I'm not that bad."

"If you say so." He smiled at her. "But remember, I witnessed you firsthand. For a minute there I expected to see smoke come out of your ears."

She looked ready to growl again, but restrained herself. "I hadn't had much sleep."

"I'm sorry I woke you."

"You don't look sorry."

Casey shrugged and continued to smile.

Emma considered him a long moment, then took the coffee and quickly doctored it to her specifications. The second she tipped the cup to her mouth, she moaned in bliss. "Oh God, I needed that." She took another long drink. "Perfect. Thank you."

Casey sipped his own coffee, prepared much like hers. "Not a morning person, huh?"

She shook her head. "I'm barely civil in the morning. I've always been more a night owl."

He remembered that—and a whole lot more.

She didn't say anything else, made no effort toward casual conversation, which annoyed him. She sat with him, drank the coffee he'd brought to her, but kept him shut out.

To regain her attention, he touched the back of her

hand with one fingertip. "I still think waking up with you would be fun."

Surprised by that comment, Emma froze for a good five seconds. Abruptly, she drained the rest of her cup and stood. She didn't look at him. "Thanks again...for everything." She started to step away.

Casey moved so fast, she gasped. In less than a heartbeat he'd reached over the table and snatched her narrow wrists, shackling them in his hands. He stared into her mesmerizing, antagonistic brown eyes until the air around them fairly crackled.

"Don't go." Two simple words, but his heart pounded as he waited.

She looked undecided.

"I brought you another cup." Casey stroked the insides of her wrists with his thumbs, kept his tone easy, persuasive. "Sit with me, Emma. Talk to me."

He ignored the rise of her breasts as she slowly inhaled. Her hesitation was palpable, forcing him to think of more arguments, other stratagems, until she said, "Why?"

Sensing that she'd just relented, Casey relaxed. "Sit down and I'll tell you why."

With enough grumbling to wake the squirrels, she dropped into the seat. This time she slid her legs under the table and faced him with both elbows propped on the tabletop to hold her chin. "I'm waiting."

Casey took in her belligerent expression and swallowed his amusement. Not once in all the time he'd known her had Emma ever shown him disgruntlement. She'd shown him adolescent lust, feminine need, a few flirting smiles and occasionally her vulnerability.

It didn't make any sense, but he felt as if he'd just gained three giant steps forward. "Yeah. You know, I think I'll feel more secure if you drink the other cup of coffee first." He prepared it as he spoke, and handed it to her with a flourish.

She slanted him a look through her thick lashes. "With the way you've acted so far, you're probably right." She accepted the coffee and sipped. "You've been deliberately provoking."

Casey waited until she swallowed before he spoke. "There's still something between us, Emma."

She promptly choked, then glared at him before searching in vain for a napkin. Casey offered her his clean hankie. "You okay?"

She brushed away his concern. "Something, huh?" Her voice was still raspy as she wheezed for air. "Well, I can tell you exactly what that *something* is."

Casey tilted back. "That right?"

"Sure." She finally regained her breath. "I'm not dead. I felt it too."

Her mood was so uncertain, he couldn't decide how to handle her. "You know, you're a lot more candid when you're crabby."

Without another word, she dropped her head to her folded arms. He didn't know if she was laughing, but he was certain she wasn't crying.

Casey wanted to touch her, wanted to feel the warmth of her skin. Her light-brown hair lay fanned out around her, spilling onto the table. The sun had kissed it near her temples, along her forehead, framing her face with natural golden streaks. Her hair looked heavy and soft and shiny. The length of her spine was graceful, feminine. Her wrists, crisscrossed under her head, were narrow, delicate.

Everything about her turned him on. At the first hint of her scent, the natural perfume of warm woman fresh from her bed, he got excited. Around her, he felt things more acutely than he had for years.

Making an abrupt decision, he stroked one large hand over her head, down to her nape. "I want you, Emma."

Her silent laughter morphed into a groan.

Casey waited, content to smooth her hair and rub her shoulder. Content just to touch her in this innocent way. For now.

When she lifted her head, she was smiling and her eyes twinkled with teasing devilment.

Dazzled, Casey let his hand drop to the table. He couldn't pull his gaze away from her. "You are so pretty when you smile."

That made her laugh again. "Casey Hudson, you're as shameless as your uncles ever were, and God knows they were nigh infamous for their ways with women."

"Until they married, maybe." Her infectious smile soon had him grinning too. "Now they've taken to family life with as much gusto as they relished bachelorhood. I have a passel of nieces and nephews to prove it."

"Yeah, well, they were bachelors long enough for you to pick up their habits, I see. I've barely been in town a single night."

"But it feels like old times, doesn't it?" To him, it was as if she'd never gone away, they'd fallen into such an easy familiarity.

"Maybe, but it's still only one night, and already you're hitting on me."

"Tell me you don't want me."

Her smile disappeared, replaced with chagrin. "I wish I could."

His heart swelled and thumped. "Then…"

"No." The shake of her head seemed all too final. "Based on our pasts, I can understand why you think I'd just jump into bed with you. We both know I tried hard enough to get you there before I left. And I won't claim I've been a nun since leaving."

That made him wince. The thought of her with other men shouldn't have mattered, but it did. It always had.

"I'm only going to be in town for a short while and having a brief fling for old time's sake isn't on the agenda."

"Why not?" Though he didn't like what he wanted called a fling, he'd take what he could get for now. He wanted her that much.

She wrinkled her nose at him. "C'mon, Case. We're both older and wiser and more mature."

"Which only means we can damn well take advantage of the chemistry." He tipped his head, studying her. "The second I recognized you, Emma, I felt it. Again." Hell, it had nearly knocked him on his ass.

She stared at him a moment, then turned to look out over the street. "You know, I'd forgotten how wonderful it was to be in Buckhorn in the morning. In my apartment in Chicago, I don't hear birds first thing or see black squirrels running up a tree. The air I breathe isn't so fresh it has almost the same kick as my coffee. I'd forgotten the scents and the sights."

As hard as he'd tried, he hadn't forgotten a damn thing. He felt nettled—until she spoke again.

"I'd almost forgotten your effect on me." Emma's smile was a little sad, her dark eyes a little wistful. She picked a fat clover blossom from the ground and twirled it between her fingers. "I kept your shirt, did you know that?"

Watching Emma enjoy her surroundings, hearing the catch in her voice stirred him as much as being stroked by another woman would have. Casey felt primed enough that he would happily take her deeper into the trees and skim off her jeans right now—if she'd been at all willing.

But she wasn't.

Her old vulnerability, which had kept his baser instincts at bay as a teenager, was now gone. But in its place was something just as compelling to his heart. He took her hand. "What shirt?"

"The one you gave me the night I left."

"The night you snuck away."

"Semantics." Her crooked smile charmed him. "It smelled of you, so even when you weren't with me, you were. Do you know what I mean?"

He nodded. "It was something familiar."

"It was you. I still have it, though after all this time the scent is gone."

The idea of her hugging his shirt to her body night after night burned him. "Spend the night with me," he offered in a low rasp, "and you can have my whole damn wardrobe."

Her mouth curled, but the humor didn't spread to her eyes. "If I spent the night with you, Casey, I'm afraid I wouldn't want to go."

Her honesty surprised him, and it must have showed. She squeezed his hand and then pulled away.

"I don't mean to put you on the spot, I really don't. I'm not asking you for anything, because I don't need anything. I got my life together and I'm happy with it. But you were always my ultimate fantasy, and I have a feeling that indulging a real-life fantasy wouldn't be a good idea."

He discounted all that fantasy nonsense to ask, "Why?" A little indulgence sounded like a hell of an idea to him.

"It'd complicate things, when I won't be around long enough to deal with anything complicated."

Most of what she said seemed too difficult to understand. Her fantasy? He didn't want to be anyone's fantasy, but he did want to be her reality. In bed.

Anything more than that…well, he doubted he could ever trust Emma again. He'd wanted to be her savior, her protector, and instead she'd walked. And hadn't contacted him even once through all the long, lonely days that had followed. He'd gone from worried sick to angry to bitter.

Now she was back and all the other emotions faded behind the sexual greed, because that at least was easy enough to understand. "You just got here and you're already talking about leaving. How long do you plan to stay?"

She shrugged. "Damon's on a self-assigned sabbatical. He's rethinking his life, so he's able to stay as long as I want."

"A sabbatical from what?" Damon Devaughn seemed like a very real complication. He was close to Emma, no two ways about that. How close—that's what Casey wanted to find out.

"He's an architect, but he's tired of commercial design… you know, putting up shopping centers and parking lots. He wants to go into residential design and do single-family housing instead, because it's more personal. The thing is, starting over will mean realigning his life along with a huge cut in pay. Not that he can't afford it, but he's thinking things through."

It surprised Casey that he and Damon might have something in common—discontent with their current careers.

For months, Casey had been rethinking his future plans, and wondering if he'd made a mistake in being lured by his stepgrandfather into a position of money and influence. The job provided a challenge and drew a lot of respect, but because his office was in Cincinnati, it also took him away from his home. At first his big corner office had seemed impressive, but he'd quickly realized that he didn't like sitting behind a desk and answering to others, working for strangers instead of neighbors and friends. Dealing with computers and electronic programs was so impersonal, it left Casey feeling empty.

Unlike Damon, he hadn't yet made up his mind to do anything about it. He wanted a change, but instigating it would stir things up a lot.

"What about you, Emma? How much time do you have off work?" She hesitated so long, Casey's irritation resurfaced. "Is it such a big deal telling me one little thing about your life?"

She pushed her hair off her forehead, thoughtful for a moment before she smiled and shrugged. "I've already spilled my guts, so what difference does it make?"

Another cryptic comment that he couldn't understand. "It doesn't."

"All right." She made up her mind and nodded. "I suppose I can stay as long as I like too. I have my own business. It's small, but I like it that way, and since I'm the boss, I don't have to answer to anyone. But, unlike Damon, I can't afford to stay off indefinitely. How long I stay depends on how my father does, but I'm thinking that if I want to have a business to go back to, I shouldn't stay more than a few weeks."

Her obvious enthusiasm added to his curiosity, and he asked, "What kind of business is it?"

She chewed on her smile, then rolled her eyes. "I'm a massage therapist."

"A...?"

"Yeah, a massage therapist. And I'm good." She went on in a rush, as if to convince him. "My shop is called The Soothing Touch and I've got a really dedicated clientele. When I told them all I'd be gone for a while, they wished me well and told me they'd be waiting for me when I got back."

Casey stared. Not a single intelligent comment came to mind.

At his continued silence, Emma's smile faded and she gave him a defiant look. "I started by working in the Tremont Hotel fitness center, then branched out on my own. Now I work from my own shop throughout the week, but I also do house or office calls over the weekend and in the evening. And once a month I teach sensual-massage classes to couples."

The images that leaped to Casey's mind left him numb: Emma rubbing oil over a man's naked back, his thighs. Emma visiting some corporate asshole in his office. Emma *enjoying* her damn job.

Doing his best to keep the cynicism out of his tone, Casey repeated, "Office calls, huh?"

She nodded. "A lot of executives have high-stress jobs. They'll pay big bucks to have me come to the office and relax them during their lunch hour or before a big meeting."

He absolutely hated the way she put that.

"I have portable equipment that I use. It's not the same as

coming to the shop, but I carry special music and oils with me. Sometimes, if it's allowed in the offices, I'll light candles too."

"Candles?"

"Mmm." She looked displeased with his continued, short questions. "You surround the client with soothing ambience. Incense or scented candles, soft music, low lights. I can make a body go boneless in a one-hour session."

Casey's eyebrows pulled down in a suspicious frown. "I just bet you can."

She frowned right back. "You can stop right there, Casey Hudson. I know assumptions run wild and believe me, I've heard every stupid joke there is, so don't bother. Massage therapist is not a euphemism for call girl, you know. I'm not ashamed of what I do. In fact, I'm proud that I do it so well."

This new facet to Emma's personality fascinated Casey. He liked the way she stood up to him, how she defended herself. And because he knew he had jumped to some hasty conclusions, he relaxed enough to tease. "And here I was going to ask what you charge."

Her nose lifted. "Thirty-five an hour at my shop, fifty if it's a house or office call."

Casey considered her, and then had to ask, "I bet most of your clients are men, right?"

"What do you want to bet?"

Keeping the grin off his face wasn't easy. "A kiss?"

"Doesn't matter because you lose. Most are women in their mid-forties, early fifties."

"Really?" That relieved him, until she continued.

"But like I said, some are execs—male and female—with seventy-hour-a-week jobs. And some are athletes with sports injuries that still bother them."

"Athletes?"

"I treated one of the Chicago Cubs for a while early in the season."

New jealousy flared. "What the hell for?"

"He was in a slump and so every time he went to bat, he got tense." She spoke candidly and knowledgeably, using her hands to emphasize. "Massage can help loosen contracted, shortened muscles and at the same time, stimulate flaccid muscles."

Casey grunted at that. "With you touching him, I find it hard to believe there was anything flaccid on the guy." Sure as hell wasn't anything flaccid on him, and he was just *thinking* about her touch, not experiencing it. But he would. Oh yeah, he most definitely would.

Rather than get angry, she got exasperated. "Now you're just being nasty."

"I want you," he reiterated, as if it explained everything. And to his mind, it did.

Her mouth fell open. "I can't believe how pushy you've gotten. You know, you're the only man ever to say such a thing to me."

Casey examined her face, from her sexy mouth and stubborn chin, up to her hair gently teased by the morning breeze. When he locked onto her dark bedroom eyes, she fidgeted in a way that had Casey's insides clenching. "Sorry, Em, but no way in hell can I believe that."

She smirked. "Hey, I've heard other, more crude come-ons. But not an outright statement like *I want you*."

Never in his life had Casey sat with a woman and had such a discussion. In the normal way of things, if he wanted to get intimate, he made a move and she either reciprocated or not. He didn't spell out his intent and give her a chance to rebuff him. This was unique, exhilarating—and so was Emma. "Well, I do. Want you, I mean. So why shouldn't I be honest about it?"

"Oh, by all means, be honest. Just know that it's not going anywhere."

He didn't like hearing that, and he sure wouldn't accept it, so he changed the subject. "When can I get a massage?"

Her eyes widened. "Never."

"Why not?"

"Because…" She got flustered, and a blush rose all the way to her eyebrows. "I just know you too well. I'd be uncomfortable."

With his eyes holding hers, his body warm with memories, he said, "You've touched me before, Em. Plenty of times, in fact."

"That was a long time ago."

"You don't like touching anymore?"

She groaned and covered her face. "It's not that."

So she did like touching? Anyone, or him specifically? It made Casey nuts wondering what she'd done and who she'd been with…and how much she might have enjoyed it. "Then what, Em?"

She dropped her hands. Her gaze landed first on his face, then dipped to his chest, shoulders. She looked away to the parking lot. "I'll, um, give it some thought, okay? That's all I'll promise for now."

"Yeah, you do that." In the meantime, Casey knew damn good and well that he'd think of little else.

chapter 5

THE IDEA OF GETTING her hands on Casey's bare flesh left Emma jittery. She'd given too many massages to count, and she'd always been friendly, talkative, but detached. She could never be detached with Casey.

She decided it was past time to go. Standing, she slipped her feet back into her shoes and avoided his astute gaze. "The coffee's gone and I've got a full day ahead. I should get on my way."

Casey stood with her and to her extreme relief, he dropped the topic of a massage. "What's on the agenda?"

"I have to get the car fixed first, then I want to take Damon into town so he can explore while I make the drive to the hospital." Both Casey and B.B. fell into step behind her when she started back toward the room.

"Several questions come to mind."

The day was already warming, and Emma knew that by ten o'clock, it would be sticky with humidity and heat. "Yeah? Like?"

"How're you going to get your car fixed when you're here, the car is on the road, and the garage is in town?"

"I figured I'd call a tow truck." She stopped right outside her door. She didn't want Casey in her room again. "I can do the work myself, but it's not easy without my tools."

"No kidding? You really know how to work on cars?"

Her feminist core insulted, Emma glared at him. "Do you know how to change a water pump?"

"Sure. But that's because I helped Gabe work on our cars and trucks often enough. I learned, but I wouldn't say it's something I'd choose to do."

Casey's uncle, Gabe Kasper, was known as a handy-man extraordinaire. He could build, repair or remodel just about anything. It made sense that Casey would have learned alongside him. "I helped Damon and his father work on cars, and they helped me with my Mustang. I like it. Besides, I've done all the restoration myself, so I don't trust many other people to touch it."

The smile he gave her looked almost...proud. Emma shook her head to clear it, refusing to disillusion herself.

"You baby your car."

Emma's chin lifted. "She's a seventy Boss in cherry condition. I rebuilt the 429 engine. Front and rear took me four years. After all that, of course I baby her."

"Damn." Casey laughed, but his expression was warm, amused. "Massage therapist, mechanic and beautiful to boot. A woman to steal a man's heart." He touched her nose with a dose of playfulness. "It was so dark, I didn't see your car that well last night, so I didn't notice..." He stopped, touched her cheek and sighed. "Okay, truth is, it wasn't your car that held my attention."

Emma had no idea what to say to that, so she just watched him and waited.

"Of course, now that I know it's a classic Boss, I can understand why you'd want to oversee the work. One problem, though."

"What?"

"It's the weekend and the garage won't open till Monday."

Eyes closed, Emma dropped back against the door. "Damn. I forgot about that."

"Around here, almost all the trade businesses still close on the weekends. Only the grocery stores and restaurants stay open. Buckhorn never changes, Emma. No one really wants it to."

"I told Damon as much when we drove in." Now what could she do? Wait another day to see her father? She might not have any choice.

"Can I offer a solution?"

Emma opened one eye. "What?"

"I'll give Gabe a call. He's got a tow truck and he can replace your water pump—I promise you can trust him. He'll treat your car with kid gloves. While he does that, I'll drive you to the hospital."

"No."

Casey crowded closer, blocking the sun with his wide hard shoulders, lowering his head closer to hers. "Why not?"

With him invading her space, Emma found it difficult to speak, but more difficult to move away. "I might be at the hospital for a while. I don't want you to have to wait."

"I've nothing else planned for the day."

She widened her eyes in disbelief. "It's Saturday and you have nothing to do?" *No dates with beautiful women?*

"Nothing important."

She found that very hard to swallow, knowing firsthand of Casey's popularity. "Then you should just relax, not spend your time hanging out in a hospital."

"You can pay me back by going boating with me. Do you still remember how to ski?"

Longing swelled up inside her. She missed being on the lake, missed the peacefulness of the water, the joy of skiing, the fresh air and sunshine. As a kid, she'd often escaped to the water, staying there late until it was safe to go home again. Sometimes Casey would hang out with her and they'd listen to the frogs croaking and the splash of gentle waves on the shore.

She'd also met plenty of other boys on the lake, and none of them had been interested in the frogs. In those days, sex in a quiet cove had been as much of an escape for Emma as anything else. "I haven't skied since I left here."

"No kidding? The Devaughns weren't much for water?"

"It's not that. I was just...busy."

Casey looked very unconvinced. "It's like riding a bike—you never forget how. And I bet B.B. will love being in the boat too. I haven't met a dog yet who doesn't."

"What about Damon?"

Casey lowered his lashes, hiding his expression. "I thought he wanted to explore the town a little."

"He might, but I'm not going to abandon him on his first day in town."

Rubbing the back of his neck, Casey muttered, "So he'll come along—" he narrowed his eyes at her "—if you insist."

It was so tempting to give in to him, on all counts. She had missed the exhilaration of boating, the wind in her hair, the sun on her face. And accepting Casey's assistance would save her from the hassle of finding another ride to the hospital. "Gabe doesn't mind working on a Saturday?"

"He wouldn't schedule work, no. But this is different. He's always willing to help out. I doubt it'll take him that long."

"Why would he want to help me out?"

Casey's voice gentled in reproach. "You've forgotten how my family is if you have to ask that."

She gave a short laugh. "No one in her right mind would ever forget your family. I half wondered if Buckhorn would have sainted the bunch of them by now."

Casey's unselfconscious smile made him more handsome than ever. "We like to lend a helping hand. Most everyone in Buckhorn does."

Emma didn't reply to that. She remembered all too well how most of the locals felt about her. She'd been shunned at best, a pariah at worst. But his family had been wonderful.

"Let me be helpful, Em."

Oh, she could imagine that husky voice seducing any number of women. That is, if they needed to be seduced. She'd be willing to bet the women had been chasing Casey most diligently. "It'll take me a little time to get ready. I haven't even showered yet."

His gaze warmed, then moved over her with slow deliberation. "Take your time. While you do that, I'll come in and give Gabe a call. We can grab a bite to eat on the way to the hospital. How's that sound?"

B.B. scratched at the door, indicating he'd had enough of idle conversation. He wasn't much of a morning creature either. "All right." She opened the door and watched B.B. head straight for the bed. With one agile leap he hit the mattress, circled once, twice, then dropped with a doggy sigh, his nose tucked close to his tail.

As she entered, she realized just how small and crowded the room was. The second Casey stepped in and closed the door behind him, it became even smaller. Emma laced her fingers together. "Promise me that if Gabe has other plans, you won't push him. I'm sure I could figure something else out."

"Absolutely."

She wasn't sure if she believed him or not. Resigned, she went to the connecting door and tapped on it, then stuck her head inside. Damon was on his stomach, his face turned toward her, snoring. Ignoring Casey for the moment, she crept in and touched Damon's bare shoulder.

Immediately his eyes opened, but otherwise he didn't move. "Hey, doll," he said in a rumbling, still half-asleep voice.

"You awake enough to catch an explanation?"

"Depends." He stretched, then pushed up to his elbows. "Is Romeo gone?"

From his hovering position in the doorway, Casey said, "If you mean me, no."

Damon dropped his head forward. "Persistent, isn't he?"

Casey showed his teeth in a false smile. "Afraid so."

"All right. I'm awake." Damon pushed into a sitting position on the side of the bed and ran his hand through his hair. "What's up?"

"The garage is closed on weekends. Casey's uncle is a handyman and we're going to see if he'll fix the car while I go to the hospital."

"Wait." Damon held up a hand, got sidetracked by a huge yawn, then eyed her. "You're saying you'll let someone else touch your car?"

"I know Gabe, or at least his reputation with cars. He's good."

"Yeah, yeah. I remember the stories. All the holy men of Buckhorn—"

Emma felt like throttling him, especially when she heard Casey chuckle rather than take offense. Through her teeth, she said, "You can either sleep in—"

"Nope, I'm awake now."

"—join us—"

He laughed and spared a glance for Casey. "Does *he* get a vote on that one?"

"—or go exploring."

"So many options. Let's see." He slapped his knees. "I choose C. That is, unless you want me to go to the hospital with you." His voice dropped and he caught her hand. "How do you feel about seeing your dad? You okay?"

Emma glanced at Casey and found him listening intently. Though her stomach was in knots at the idea of facing her father after so many years, she mustered a smile to relieve both men of worry. "I'll be fine, really."

"It's been a long time, doll."

"Exactly. Past time I visited."

Damon didn't look convinced, but he knew her well enough to let it go. "What about B.B.?"

"He'll be happy to sleep until I get back. Then I'm going to take him boating with me."

"Boating?"

Without turning to face Casey, Emma flapped a hand toward him. "He, uh, he has a boat."

"Of course he does."

Casey spoke up, his tone dry. "We have several boats,

actually. A speedboat for skiing, a pontoon, couple of fishing boats. The biggest recreational draw for Buckhorn is the three-hundred-and-five-acre water reservoir."

"A man-made lake?"

"Exactly. Around here, everyone considers a boat as important as a car."

Emma cleared her throat and tried to sound enthusiastic. "I thought you might like to go along, Damon."

"Not I, thank you. I can already hear the awkward squeaking of that third wheel."

By his very silence, Casey agreed, but Emma rushed to convince him otherwise. "You wouldn't be a third wheel! And I'd love to show you the lake, Damon. It's beautiful and so peaceful. You could see some of the vacation homes built along there."

"I remember everything you've told me about it." He yawned again, stood, and scratched his belly. "How about we go check it out after the car is fixed and you've had a chance to visit and get reacquainted? Maybe in a day or two?"

"Are you sure?"

"Most positive." Damon strolled to his open suitcase resting on the dresser. He pulled out chinos, a black polo shirt and clean boxers. "I'm heading to the shower. I'll be ready in half an hour."

The second the bathroom door closed, Casey walked over to Emma and took her arm. "Why don't you go ahead and get ready too while I call Gabe? You don't want to miss the doctor at the hospital."

The town's small hospital, Buckhorn Memorial, was efficient and well run, but it wasn't equipped for anything life or death. She'd been reassured when she found out her father was staying there, rather than at one of the larger neighboring hospitals in the next city. It told her that a full recovery was expected.

Still, the idea of seeing him left her nervous, anxious and wary. She'd spoken to him regularly over the years, but because of how they'd parted, the mutual ruse they'd pulled off, their conversations always felt superficial. Despite everything, despite how she'd left him—how he'd *helped* her to leave—Emma knew he loved her.

Just not enough.

"All right." Putting off going wouldn't make it easier. She'd made her decision and now she'd follow through. "I won't be long."

Casey watched her as she riffled through her suitcase to locate a sundress, panties and sandals. The dress, a fitted chambray sheath with embroidered scallop edging, was casual and cool enough for the summer sun, but also dressy enough for the hospital. It always packed well, but the white cotton blouse she'd brought along as a jacket was wrinkled. Hopefully the steam from her shower would help. As she headed for the bathroom, Casey stretched out on the bed with B.B., propping his back on the headboard and reaching for the only phone, situated on the nightstand.

Emma's mouth went dry, not only because he was in her bed, where she'd slept, and he looked right at home there. But because B.B. rolled to his back and waited for Casey to scratch his chest—and Casey did, as if they'd been longtime friends. B.B. was always polite unless provoked, but he didn't warm up to strangers easily. Yet he already treated Casey like a pal.

Emma sighed and went on into the bathroom before she

did something stupid, like join Casey on the bed. She felt melancholy, and with good reason. Like her, it seemed her dog had a fondness for Buckhorn's golden son. Well, they'd both just have to get over it, because once her business was finished in Buckhorn, Emma fully intended to return to her old life, the life where she'd found contentment.

Her life—without Casey Hudson.

OF COURSE, Gabe agreed to help out, just as Casey had known he would. He hadn't yet told his uncle who he was helping, just a lady friend. Casey wondered if Gabe would recognize Emma. The others had known her better. His father because of Emma's trip to their house. His Uncle Morgan because, as sheriff, he'd had occasion to check up on Emma for skipping school and breaking curfew. And his Uncle Jordan would probably recall her from the hospital, the night Georgia's mother had taken ill and he and Emma had dropped in to help out. Granted, Jordan had been mightily distracted with Georgia and her two children. Casey was convinced that Jordan had fallen in love with Georgia that night. But he'd surely at least noticed Emma.

His youngest uncle, Gabe, had only met her a few times, interspersed with all the other girls that Casey had dated. Casey didn't want any of his relatives looking at him with speculation, wondering about his feelings. It was better that Gabe be the only one to know about Emma. At least for now.

Still idly rubbing the dog's neck, Casey listened as B.B.'s breathing drifted into a doggy snore. He grinned. B.B. was a beautiful, well-groomed, healthy animal, testament to the care Emma had given him. He obviously had a regular sleeping spot in the bed, too.

Lucky dog.

Casey wouldn't have minded a little of Emma's care directed his way, yet she seemed determined to keep their involvement platonic. He'd have her alone this afternoon and he'd begin working on her.

Knowing Gabe would be there soon, Casey got up to stroll the room, peeking out the window to the parking lot every so often. As he paced, he noted Emma's open suitcase, stuffed mostly with casual clothes. He also saw her bra on the only chair in the room, strung over the arm. He stopped to stare, impressed with her feminine choice.

He absolutely loved lingerie, the sexier the better.

The discarded bra, likely removed the night before, appealed in a big way. Made of ice-blue transparent lace, it looked sheer, but had an underwire. The reason she would require an underwire tormented his libido with visions of her full breasts free, or held only by his hands. Casey picked up the bra, rubbing the delicate material between his fingers.

"That surely has to be illegal."

Disgusted at being caught, Casey dropped the bra and turned to face Damon Devaughn. "What's that?"

"Molesting a woman's clothing." Devaughn lazily moved into the room, propped his hip on the dresser and crossed his ankles. He wore pressed tan chinos, a black designer polo and casual loafers. "Does Emma know that you have these kinky tendencies?"

Casey narrowed his eyes. Around Emma, Damon acted casual but proprietary, intimate yet not sexual. Casey couldn't quite figure him out. Then he decided *what the hell?* and just blurted out his biggest question. "Are you gay?"

Damon blinked at him and a smile twitched on his mouth. Somewhat demure, he said, "Why do you ask?"

Stumped as to how to reply, Casey scowled. "It seemed pertinent to the situation."

"Ah, let me guess. It's my fashion sense, isn't it?" He smoothed his hands over his shirt. "No? My neatly trimmed hair?"

When Casey didn't bother to reply, Damon's eyes narrowed. He crossed his arms over his chest, and Casey couldn't help but notice that muscles bulged. He didn't understand Devaughn, but he had to admit that the man was no wimp.

"Or," Damon asked, dragging out the word until Casey wanted to throttle him, "is it because I like Emma, even though I'm not screwing her?"

Casey took an aggressive step forward before he could stop himself. He felt like smashing Damon and wasn't even sure why. No, that was a lie. He knew he disliked Damon because the man was close to Emma. "It was a simple question, Devaughn."

"No."

"No *what?*"

"No, I'm not gay." Damon shrugged. "A simple answer."

Striving for control, Casey drew a slow deep breath, then another. They both heard the shower stop, and the telltale sounds of Emma moving around in the bathroom. Naked.

Casey swallowed, distracted by images of her toweling off. Staring toward the bathroom door, he muttered, "I didn't mean to offend you, Devaughn. I have nothing against—"

"Yeah, yeah, whatever. No offense taken." Suddenly the

bathroom door squeaked open and Damon, too, turned to stare.

Emma, her hair wrapped in a towel, stuck her head out. She looked startled to find that she already had both men's attention. She glanced first at Casey, then at Damon. "I need a blow-dryer. Who has a motel without blow-dryers in the bathroom?"

She sounded very disgruntled, then answered her own question. "Obviously Mrs. Reider, which I should have guessed, but I stupidly assumed that she'd gotten a little with the times over the past decade."

Damon laughed. "I'll get mine. Hang on."

Casey mouthed silently, *I'll get mine,* then realized Emma was watching him. He pasted on a leering smile. "You need any help?"

Eyes wide, Emma asked, "With what?"

"Drying off?"

"Uh, no." She looked toward the connecting door as if willing Damon to reappear. He did, curse him.

"Here you go. Don't electrocute yourself."

Emma snatched the dryer out of his hand, cast another quick look at Casey, and shut the door. Seconds later, a loud hum reverberated throughout the room, ensuring Damon and Casey some privacy.

Damon took immediate advantage. Steely-eyed, he advanced on Casey until he stood a mere foot in front of him. "I haven't had many occasions to issue these hairy-chested, testosterone-drowned warnings, but I hope you'll listen despite my inexperience in these things, because I'm dead serious."

Casey drew back and it took him a moment to figure out what the hell Damon had just said. When his meaning sunk in, Casey shook his head. Damon was about the oddest damn duck he'd ever run across. "Yeah, I'm listening, Devaughn. Wouldn't miss it, in fact."

"I love Emma like a sister—a younger sister whom I feel very protective of."

That suited Casey just fine. As long as Damon didn't lust after her, he could love her all he wanted. "I'm glad to hear it."

"You crushed her once."

Casey scowled. How much had Emma told him? *What* had she told him? "If that's true, it wasn't on purpose." Hell, Emma had run out on him, not the other way around.

"Yeah, well, you were a kid." Damon's voice dropped to a harsh whisper when the blow-dryer got turned off. "But you're not a kid anymore. Don't hurt her."

Nettled at being chastised, Casey turned away to the window. "I wasn't planning on it." No, he planned on making love to her until they were both exhausted.

Damon followed. "Bullshit. You're on the prowl and we all three know it."

"All three?"

"Emma isn't a stupid woman and she's well acquainted with come-ons. In case you've failed to notice, she's got this natural sexuality about her that turns normal men into wildebeests in heat."

Casey's hands curled into fists. Was it his imagination, or was Damon getting stranger by the moment? "I noticed."

Damon's expression lightened, and he even grinned. "It was a facetious statement, man. Believe me, I noticed you noticing."

"Is there a point to this, Devaughn?"

"Yeah. If you're half as honorable as Emma claimed, you'll leave her alone."

Half as honorable? He again wondered exactly what Emma might have said about him. "I can't do that."

Angered, Damon stepped toward him—and Emma came out of the bathroom. She looked…astounding.

Casey immediately forgot all about Damon and his half-baked warnings. Emma's hair, loose and soft and feminine, bounced gently around her shoulders and caught the reflection of every light. She wore only a touch of makeup, which made her eyes even larger, darker. But it was the gloss on her lips that really got to Casey. Damn, he wanted to lick it off her mouth, then taste her, only her. Her mouth drove him nuts it was so sexy.

The chambray dress fit her and emphasized every womanly curve without seeming too obvious. She carried a blouse in one hand, her sandals in the other. Without looking at him, she bent and slipped on one sandal, then the other. Enthralled, both he and Damon watched in silence until she was ready.

"Is Gabe here yet?"

Casey shook himself out of his stupor. He moved the utilitarian curtain aside and looked out the window. "Just pulled in. I told him I'd watch for him, so we should go on down."

She nodded and went to sit on the side of the bed next to B.B. The big dog raised up in silent query. "I'll be back soon, bud. You sleep."

The dog's tail smacked hard against the mattress in agreement, and Casey could have sworn he grinned. Then he resettled his head and went back to sleep.

"He understands you?"

"He knows a lot of phrases, and he's smarter than most people I know." Emma picked up her purse. "Besides, he's used to dozing the day away when I work. He'll be fine."

Damon held the door open and they all went out to the parking lot together. Gabe stood lounging against the side of his tow truck in dark sunglasses, a backward ball cap, ragged cutoffs and an unbuttoned shirt that showed his tanned chest. All in all, typical weekend wear for Gabe.

Emma smiled when she saw him and said in an aside to Casey, "He hasn't changed a bit." Then Gabe's youngest daughter, five-year-old Briana, stepped out from behind him and Emma laughed. "Well now, that's new!"

Casey grinned. "We wondered if there'd be any girl babies born into the family since the dominant gene appears to be male. But Gabe surprised everyone, including his wife, by fathering not one, but three daughters. They're five, seven and nine years old. All with blond hair and blue eyes. This is Briana, the youngest."

With twinkling eyes, the little girl scooted to Casey and held up her arms, obliging Casey to lift her. He hefted her to his hip, kissed her golden head, and gave her a fierce hug. "Hey, squirt."

"She's beautiful," Emma said, and stroked Briana's little shoulder. Briana beamed at her for the compliment.

"All three of his daughters are."

Emma laughed again. "Actually, she looks like a small feminine version of Gabe."

"Exactly. Makes him nuts, too."

Damon stepped forward with an outstretched hand. "Damon Devaughn. Thank you for coming out on a weekend."

Gabe, always jovial, shrugged off the remark. "Not a

problem. Casey said you have a Mustang Boss. Can't very well leave a sweet car like that on the side of the road, not even here in Buckhorn."

"It's not my car. It's Emma's."

"Emma?" His uncle didn't seem to remember her at all, until he went to shake her hand, which caused him to look at her more closely. "You look familiar." He glanced at Casey. "Have we been introduced before?"

Casey wanted to groan. He sent Gabe a look, but his uncle was distracted trying to recall where and when he'd met Emma.

"I'm from here originally," Emma said. "And really, Mr. Kasper, we do appreciate the help."

"Good God, girl, no one calls me mister. Gabe will do, if you don't want to make me feel old." Gabe stared at her a moment more while attempting to recall her. A smile appeared. "That's right, I remember now. You're that girl who…"

He drew up short on his verbal faux pas, and Casey hurried to fill in the awkward silence. "Emma's been away for eight years."

"S'that right?" Gabe lifted the cap from his head, scratched his right ear and then replaced his hat, all the while grinning. "Welcome home, Emma."

Scrupulously polite, Emma said, "I'm just here for a visit."

Gabe took his daughter from Casey. "Don't be silly. You don't *visit* home, because you can't ever really leave it." Before anyone could argue that point, Gabe turned to Damon. "You're coming with me, right?"

Damon pulled his concerned gaze from Emma. "Yes. I have the keys to the Mustang. I was hoping to explore the town while you repaired the car."

"Have you had breakfast?"

"Not yet."

"Then I'll drop you at Ceily's diner. You'll get the best ham and eggs in three counties."

Damon and Emma shared a look of mutual wariness. Not understanding, Casey took Emma's arm. "You remember Ceily, don't you, Em?"

She looked stricken only a moment, and in the next instant her face was blank of any expression. She pulled sunglasses from her purse and slipped them on. Casey noted that her hand shook and her tone was clipped when she finally said, "Yes. I remember her." Her smile appeared forced. "You'll enjoy the food, Damon."

Casey didn't know what had upset her, but he decided it was past time to get on the road. "Damon, we'll see you later." Much, much later. "Gabe, thanks again." He waved to Briana. "Be good to Damon, sweetie."

When Damon slid into the seat next to her, Briana beamed at him and said, "You smell good."

"Why, thank you," Damon said with a chuckle.

Gabe groaned. "This is the penance I pay for my misspent youth. Three flirting daughters will definitely be the death of me."

Emma smiled at the exchange as Casey led her to his car. Her moods changed quicker than the breeze, but eventually he'd understand her. Once they finished the visit to the hospital, he'd have her alone on the lake. He'd get some answers, make some headway—and reestablish old bonds.

He could hardly wait.

chapter 6

DAMON FELT as if he'd stepped into another world, or at least taken a step back in time. "We're not in Kansas anymore, Toto," he murmured to himself.

Gabe Kasper, a very friendly, laid-back fellow with the absolute worst fashion sense Damon had ever witnessed firsthand, had dropped him off in the middle of the town—if you could call such a small, old-fashioned gathering of buildings a town. But the architecture was impressive, ornate yet sturdy, able to withstand the passing of time.

Prior to letting him out of the truck, Gabe had pointed in the direction of the diner and admonished Damon to stay out of the sun.

True enough, he wasn't much for tanning, and a ball cap, especially one worn backward as Gabe preferred, was out of the question. While looking around, Damon noticed that nearly every person he saw was dressed in a similar fashion. It was like being at Palm Beach during spring break. He wondered how many people constituted the local denizens and how many were vacationers visiting the lake.

Women paraded up and down the sidewalks in shorts and bathing-suit tops. Adolescent boys were shirtless. Some children were barefoot. Every doorway spawned several loiterers and damned if there weren't two grizzled old men in coveralls playing checkers under the shade of the barbershop awning. It was like landing in Mayberry, but with color. Lots and lots of color.

Enormous, lush oak trees lined the side of the road and provided some shade to most of the storefronts. The sky was so blue it dazzled. Flowers grew from every nook and cranny, and birds of every size and song flitted about.

Damon drew a deep breath and felt his lungs expand with fresh, humid air. Jesus, he liked it. A lot.

He strolled along the sidewalk, soaking in the atmosphere and acclimating himself. A few minutes later, he smelled the luscious scents from the diner even before he saw it.

When they'd driven through the night before, Emma had pointed the place out, but other than noting the location, he'd paid little attention. He'd been too worried about Emma, watching her to see how she took her return to Buckhorn.

As an architect, he now studied the simple but unique lines of each structure. The diner was spacious, in the same design as the other buildings around it, but modern windows and roofing materials had been added, making it somewhat unique. He knew that eight years ago it had been gutted by fire, which probably accounted for the improvements. Damon shook his head. Emma had retold the story so many times that he knew it by heart.

He continued along, nodding to the people who gave

him cautious looks until he reached the diner. Up close, the modern materials were even more noticeable. Still, the re-construction was a quality job, nicely executed.

The walkway had been swept clean, the windows were spotless, and the ornate oak front door stood propped open by a large clay flowerpot filled to overflowing with purple, yellow and red flowers. The quiet buzz of conversation mingled with the sounds of dishes clacking, food sizzling on the grill and a jukebox playing.

Damon peered inside, making note of the tidy rows of booths and tables, the immaculate floor, the utilization of every available space. Apparently Ceily did an efficient job of running the diner, and in hiring good help. He wondered if he'd be able to meet her. Based on everything Emma had told him about her, he was curious. He'd already formed an image of her in his mind and he wondered if she'd look as he pictured her—work-worn, tired, frumpy. As he was glancing around, a waitress moved into his view, drawing his attention.

The second Damon's gaze landed on her, everything and everyone else faded into the background. Lord have mercy, they grew the girls healthy in Buckhorn. He leaned into the doorway to watch her, and felt intrigued.

Damon had always considered Emma to be a luscious woman, healthy and earthy and sensual. The woman now bent to a booth picking up dishes was just as luscious, maybe more so because, damn, he didn't view her in any familial way.

He did a visual sweep of her body, taking in every detail and noting the lack of a ring on her left hand, as well as the delicate bracelet circling her slim ankle. He also noted that she appeared busy but happy, rushed but energized.

Tight, faded jean shorts made her rump look especially round—a deliberate effort on her part, no doubt. A red cotton crop top hugged her breasts and showed off her trim, lightly tanned midriff. A sturdy utility apron with only a few spots on it had been tied loosely around her hips, looking more like decoration than protection against stains. Sun-streaked, sandy-brown hair hung to the middle of her back, contained in a loose ponytail that added to the country-girl charm. She wore snowy-white canvas sneakers on her feet. Cute.

He'd known, admired and sexually enjoyed a lot of polished, sophisticated women. Not once had he ever gotten involved with a country bumpkin. The idea appealed to his sense of adventure and variety. Would she romp with him in the hay? Make him biscuits and gravy the morning after? He grinned to himself, wondering at the possibilities and feeling a tad whimsical.

Someone at the table behind her spoke, and she laughed as she turned—and caught Damon's speculative stare. As if the meeting of their eyes snared her physically, she went still. Her wide smile faded but her green eyes remained bright. Damon estimated her to be in her early thirties. Their gazes locked for a long moment before the customers regained her attention. She dismissed Damon with a quick, curious smile and got back to work.

Miss Ceily had done all right in hiring that one, Damon decided. Not only was she a conscientious worker, but she provided some very nice scenery.

Propelled forward by his own curiosity, Damon stepped inside. He watched her a moment more to judge which tables were hers then he seated himself. And he waited. He didn't stare at her again; that would have been too obvious. But his awareness of her was so keen he always knew just where she was within the diner. He listened to her as she visited with the other customers, and decided her laugh was nice. Her voice had the same pleasant country twang he'd noticed the first time he'd met Emma.

Satisfaction oozed through him as he sensed her approach. It'd be interesting to see if she suited him. And if she did, well, this visit might turn out more stimulating than he'd anticipated.

She set a glass of ice water in front of him. "Hi there." Without blinking, she leaned her hip on the edge of his booth and met his bold gaze.

Damon allowed a small smile. Checking for her name, he glanced at her breasts, but she wore no name tag, so he couldn't look as long—or as thoroughly—as he'd have liked. Glancing back at her face, he kept his gaze fixed, his voice low and heavy in a way that he knew would indicate his interest. "Hello."

The second he spoke, her slim eyebrows lifted. "A visitor, huh?"

Her easy, friendly familiarity pleased him. "Guilty. My lack of accent gave me away?"

"That it did, but don't worry. You won't stand out too much. This time of year we have a lot of vacationers around." She looked him over, then asked, "You staying at the lake?"

"No." Damon continued to smile without offering further explanations. He waited to see if she'd push him or back off.

She did neither. "I didn't think so. You don't look much like a fisherman."

Startled by that disclosure—and a little relieved, because, really, who would *want* to look like a fisherman?—he said, "No?"

Her smile quirked. "Too tidy."

"You have sloppy fishermen in the area, do you?"

"Not sloppy. Relaxed." She straightened away from the table. "Fishing requires a lot of patience and time spent in the weather. You don't look all that patient, and you don't look like you hang outdoors much."

Now *that* sounded vaguely like an insult, causing him to frown. So he didn't have a tan. Hadn't she heard that too much exposure to the sun wasn't healthy for you?

With a look of innocence, as if she hadn't just deliberately riled him, she tapped the menu. "You had a chance to decide what you want, yet?"

Oh, he knew exactly what he wanted. Damon pushed the plastic printed menu aside without interest. "What do you recommend?"

Her smile widened and her lashes lowered in a coy, rather effective manner. "That'd depend. Whatcha in the mood for?"

Damn, her flirting stirred him. It had been far too long since he'd had the relief of sex. "I somehow doubt it's listed on the menu."

"We're not that backward." She shifted, and deftly managed to draw his attention to her legs again. "Why don't you give us a try?"

"All right." He eyed her shapely hips, not lingeringly, but with enough intent that she couldn't miss it. "How about something…hearty."

Suddenly she laughed in delight, tipping her head back

and showing a seductive length of throat. She had a husky laugh, and it turned him on. But then, at that particular moment, everything appeared to be turning him on.

"Hearty, huh?"

"That's right."

Smoothing a wisp of tawny hair behind her ear, she said, "All right. We have a sinful egg and ham casserole that'll stick to your ribs till dinnertime."

"Sinful, you say? Interesting. And who prepared it?"

She looked at him beneath her lashes. "Me."

"Ah." He tilted his head to study her. Her lashes were long and thick, her eyes smoky, with small crinkles at the corners that showed her to be a woman used to laughing, a woman who lived her life with enthusiasm. Her nose turned up slightly on the end, giving her an elfin appearance in direct contrast to her earthy sensuality. And her body...he'd love to see her naked. He was fair sick of skinny women on a perpetual diet, honed so tightly that nothing ever jiggled. With a long, leisurely ride, this woman would jiggle—her breasts, her behind...

Feeling the heat expand inside him, Damon stuck out his hand, anxious to touch her. "I'm Damon Devaughn, by the way. I'll be in the area for a little while."

"S'that so?" She took his hand, but didn't perform the customary shake. Instead, she just held on to him, giving her own brazen show of interest. "I'm Ceily."

Surprise momentarily made him mute. Damn, he hadn't seen that coming. To be sure, he asked, "Ceily, as in the owner of the diner?"

"One and the same." She smiled down at their clasped hands, one eyebrow raised, but she didn't pull away from him. And Damon didn't release her. She had a firm hold, her hand slim, warm, a little rough from work.

For whatever reason, he'd expected Ceily to be older, more timeworn, tired. Emma's memories of her had been of a grown woman, yet Ceily must have had responsibility for the diner at an early age because by his count, she was still young.

Beyond his sexual interest, Damon felt... impressed.

Knowing who she was slanted things though, made them a tad more difficult, but not impossible. He decided to test her before he got any more involved. "I'm here with a friend."

Disappointment made her green eyes darken. "Female friend?"

"Yes." He released her hand and leaned back in his seat, watching for her reaction. "You might remember her. Emma Clark?"

A brief moment of confusion crossed her features, then she brightened. "No kidding? I remember Emma. She's Casey Hudson's age, right?"

Damon scowled. Why the hell would she mention Casey? "That's right. In fact, she's with Casey today, visiting her father in the hospital."

Ceily turned and hollered toward the kitchen. "Hey, I need a casserole and—" She looked back at Damon. "What do you want to drink?"

"Do you have sweet tea?"

Nodding, she yelled, "And an iced tea."

A dark-haired man in a hair net poked his face into an opening visible behind the bar that led into the kitchen. "Be ready in a sec."

"Thanks." Without being invited, Ceily sat down in the

booth opposite Damon. "So Casey's already hooked up with her, huh?" Dimples showed in her cheeks when she grinned. "Doesn't surprise me much. From what I remember, she always did like him. And he's just like his uncles, meaning he's not one to waste time."

"How…reassuring."

Ceily laughed, then crossed her arms on the tabletop and leaned toward him. It was a toss-up what fascinated him more—her mouth or her cleavage. "You with her, or just friends?"

"Friends." She wasn't wearing any lipstick, but her naked mouth looked very appealing. Her bottom lip was plump, her upper lip well defined. "If it was more, I wouldn't be flirting with you."

That sexy mouth tilted up. "So you are flirting, huh?"

"Of course." He stared into her eyes without smiling. "And you're flirting back."

She shrugged. "Around here, that might mean something—and then again, it might mean nothing."

"Around here?"

"We're all real sociable and quick to tease."

"I see. So which is it this time?"

She pondered her reply before answering. "I reckon it means I wouldn't mind showing you around the area, if you're interested."

Uncertainty made her offer casual, yet Damon noted her anticipation, the way she held herself hopeful. Oh yes, the trip had become quite intriguing.

"My interest has already been established." His body hummed with that interest as he began considering what the night might bring. The irony of it amused him. Emma might not like it, but then there was no reason she had to know right off.

He reached across the table and took her hand again. "So tell me, Ceily. What time do you get off work, and how late do you want to stay out?"

CASEY WATCHED EMMA grow increasingly subdued the farther they got from town. The ride to the hospital took her back along the way she'd come in, to the outskirts of the city proper. The twenty-minute trip had been mostly silent, yet not uncomfortable. From the drive-through, they'd picked up two bottles of orange juice and breakfast sandwiches to eat along the way. Emma had also downed another cup of coffee.

After gathering the sandwich wrappers and empty bottles together, Emma had spent the remainder of the ride looking around with a mixture of awe, recollection and melancholy. She'd missed Buckhorn, that much was plain.

So why had she waited so long to return?

Casey didn't mind her silence as she reacquainted herself with the area. But the closer they got to the hospital, the more she retreated until he could feel her agitation. Was she worried about seeing her father again?

Old habits were indeed hard to break, and Casey found himself wishing he could shield her from the unknown. Would her father be happy to see her again? Or would he treat her with the same callous disregard he'd shown so long ago?

For the rest of his life, Casey knew he'd remember the look on her bruised, tear-streaked face the night her father had jerked her forward, presenting her as a problem, ridding himself of her.

It still infuriated him, so how must it make *her* feel to face Dell again?

The roads here were smooth, open, with no need to shift from fifth gear. Though the temperature had reached eighty already, with high humidity, Emma had been all for skipping the air-conditioning in favor of leaving the convertible top down. Casey glanced toward her, watching her hair dance behind her, seeing the concentrated, determined expression on her face.

He tightened his hands on the steering wheel, fighting the urge to reach for her. "Hey."

She started, then glanced at him. "What?"

"You okay?"

"Sure, I'm fine." She clutched at her purse in her lap, giving away her unease. "Just thinking."

"About what?"

"I don't know. Everything. Nothing." She turned toward him, folding one leg onto the seat. She had to hold her hair out of her face with her hand. "Buckhorn hasn't changed at all."

Her position exposed more of her thigh—something Casey made immediate note of. As a teenager, she'd kept a golden tan. Now she looked fair, with only a faint kiss from the sun. He had to clear his throat. "Not much, no."

"Everything seems exactly the same, maybe aged a little more. But still…the same."

"That bothers you?"

She leaned back in her seat and stared up at the sky. "No." She spoke so low her voice almost got carried away on the wind. Casey strained to hear her. "It's just that I've changed so much, and yet I still feel like I don't belong here."

A vague panic took Casey by surprise. "This is your home." He sounded far too gruff, almost angry. "Of course you belong."

Silence hung between them, pressing down on him, until she swiveled her head toward him. "If you have anything you need to do today, you can just drop me at the hospital."

It bugged the hell out of him how she kept trying to shove him away. "I'll wait for you."

"Dad's probably not up to a long visit, but it still might be an hour."

"I'll wait."

She stared at him, so Casey gave her a smile to counter his insistent tone and then, because he *had* to touch her, he opened his hand over the gearshift in invitation. She hesitated only a moment before reaching across and lacing her fingers in his. Like old times.

Now, that felt right—Emma reaching for him, accepting him. The touch of her hand to his, palm to palm, fingers intertwined, filled him with a sense of well-being.

Two minutes later, he parked in the crowded visitors' section of the hospital lot. Emma, now utterly silent, flipped down her visor to quickly comb her hair and reapply lip gloss. He'd seen the feminine routine performed by numerous women. But this was Emma, and she fascinated him.

He went around to her side of the car and held her door open. "You look beautiful, Emma."

She sent him a look of tolerance. "I'll settle for passable, thank you."

"Very passable, then." Casey took her arm as they crossed the scorching lot. Damp heat lifted off the pavement in waves. "Do you remember the last time we were here together?"

Nodding, she said, "With your Uncle Jordan and his wife. But that was before they'd gotten married."

"The night they met, actually. Georgia's mother, Ruth, was sick, and Jordan had brought them, along with Georgia's two kids, to the hospital." While driving to the hospital to lend a helping hand, Casey had found Emma walking on the side of the road. As if the picture had been painted on his brain, he recalled exactly how she'd looked that night in ultrashort shorts, a hot-pink halter, and her skin dewy from the humidity as she'd sashayed down the roadway. *All alone.*

He'd been worried about her, as usual, and had insisted on giving her a ride. She'd climbed into his car, then made him sweat even more with wanting her.

Shaking his head, Casey wondered why the hell he hadn't taken what she'd offered. If he had, maybe he wouldn't feel as he did now. And maybe he wouldn't have felt this way for most of his adult life.

Putting himself back on track, he continued with the family discussion. "Ruth still has some problems with her lungs, but now she's hooked up with Misty and Honey's dad, and he pampers her. She's doing pretty good."

"Do you mean your grandfather? Do you work for him now?"

"Stepgrandfather officially, but yeah. I've been working with him since I finished college. I'm the executive vice president of sales and marketing."

"Wow." Emma sounded genuinely impressed. "That sounds like an important position."

Self-conscious about the rapid and consistent promotions, Casey grumbled, "My grandfather has shoved me right up the ladder. He takes every opportunity to give me a bigger office, a better parking spot, more perks. It's his goal that I'll eventually run the company for him."

"What exactly is his company?"

"Electronics, computer hardware. You know, very high-tech, state-of-the-art stuff for businesses. Boring stuff." He laughed at himself. "Very boring."

"I see." Her look was filled with comprehension in a way exclusive to Emma. She understood him, which made long explanations unnecessary. "So you don't like your job, or is it your grandfather you don't like?"

He avoided giving her a direct answer by saying, "I like him fine. He's loosened up a lot, especially since he and Ruth married."

That disclosure diverted her. "Wow, everyone is getting married."

Casey stared ahead, strangely annoyed. "Nope, not everyone."

Emma did a double take, probably trying to judge his mood. When she saw his sour expression, she went a little quiet. "Like everyone else, Casey, you'll eventually find the right woman and swear love everlasting."

She didn't sound overly thrilled with that prospect, which pretty much mirrored his own feelings on the matter. Marriage? Just the thought of it left him tight and uncertain in a way he refused to accept. "We'll see."

Emma bit her lip, feeling the new tension just as he did. In an obvious effort to lighten the mood, she said, "Georgia had two really cute little kids, right?"

"Yeah, but they're not so little anymore. Lisa is fifteen and a real heartbreaker, though she doesn't know it, or else doesn't care." He glanced down at Emma, saw her pensive frown, and regretted adding to her uneasiness. She had her hands full with the coming confrontation. "Lisa's more into her studies than boys, and she's so smart she scares me."

Emma relaxed enough to grin at that. "As I recall, nothing scares you—especially a female."

That was far from the truth, but Casey just shook his head. "Adam's thirteen, a helluva football player and real interested in becoming a vet like Jordan. He's even got the soothing voice down pat. They're great kids."

She gave a wistful sigh. "You've got a lot of nieces and nephews now, don't you?"

He shrugged. To Emma, it probably seemed like a lot. She had only her mother and father, and had been estranged from them for a long time. "Jordan has those two; Morgan has Amber, now eleven, and Garrett who's nine. And Gabe has the three daughters." Casey grinned. "By the way, they not only look like Gabe, but they all take after him, too."

"Natural-born flirts, huh?"

"Yep. And it makes him crazy. Gabe's about the most doting father you'll ever meet, and he shakes whenever he talks about his girls growing old enough to date."

Emma snorted. "He's probably remembering his own un-restrained youth."

"Gabe was rather unrestrained, wasn't he? Not that any of the women complained."

"'Course not."

Casey admired the way her eyes glowed, her cheeks dimpled when she was amused. Hearing Emma laugh was a treat. "I have a little brother too, you know. Shohn, who's almost ten now. He's a hyper little pug, never still, and he knows no fear." Knowing he bragged and not caring, Casey added, "He learned to water-ski when he was only five. Now he's like a damn pro out there."

"Uh-huh. And who taught him to ski?"

Casey pushed the glass doors open and ushered her inside. "Me."

Air-conditioning rolled over them as they stepped into the hospital and headed for the elevator. Casey transferred his hand to the small of Emma's back, and just that simple touch stirred him. Her waist dipped in, taut and graceful, then flared out to her hips. Standing next to her emphasized the differences in their sizes. He told himself that was why he felt protective. Then. Now.

Always.

Naturally, he cared about her. They'd been friends for a long time, and that, combined with the sexual chemistry, heightened his awareness of her. It wasn't anything more complicated than that.

But even he had to admit that talking with Emma came pretty easy. He couldn't remember the last time he'd shared stories about his family. When he was with a woman, he remained polite, attentive, but everything felt very...surface. There wasn't room for personal stuff. Yet with Emma, he'd just run down his whole damn lineage—and enjoyed it too much.

He was disturbed with his own realizations on that, when he heard someone say his name. He looked down the hallway and saw Ms. Potter, the librarian, being pushed in a wheelchair by a nurse, followed by her daughter, Ann. Casey drew Emma to a halt. "Just a second, okay?"

He went to Ms. Potter and bent to kiss her cheek, which warmed her with a blush. "Getting out today, huh?"

"Finally."

"You were only here two days," the nurse teased, then added, "And you were a wonderful patient."

Ms. Potter fussed with the elaborate bouquet of spring flowers in her lap. "Even so, these will look much better on my desk than on the windowsill here."

Casey gave her a mock frown. "Your desk? Now don't tell me you're rushing right back to work."

"Monday morning, and it's none too soon. I can just imagine what a mess my books are in. No one ever puts them away properly."

Ann stepped up to the side of the wheelchair. Her brown eyes twinkled and her dark hair fell in a soft wave to her shoulders when she nodded down at her mother. "The flowers are gorgeous, Casey. Thanks for bringing them to her."

"My pleasure." He saw Ann look beyond him to Emma, so he drew her forward. "Ann, Ms. Potter, do you remember Emma Clark?"

Ms. Potter, always sharp as a tack, said, "I do. It was a rare thing for you to come to the library, young lady."

Embarrassed, Emma stammered, "I—I've never been much of a reader."

"You only need to find the right books for you. Come and see me next week and we'll get you set up."

Emma blushed. "Yes, ma'am."

Casey did his best not to laugh. Ms. Potter had a way of putting everyone on the spot, but always with good intentions. She genuinely cared about people and it showed.

Ann stared hard at Emma before her eyes widened with

recognition. "Now I remember. You went to school with me, didn't you?"

"A long time ago, yes. I think we were in the same English class."

"That's right. Didn't you move away before your senior year?"

"Yes." To avoid going into details, Emma grinned down at Ms. Potter. "That's a doozy of a cast you have on your leg. And very art deco, too."

Ms. Potter reached out and patted Casey's hand. "You can blame this rascal right here. I was all set to keep it snowy white, as is appropriate for a librarian and a widow my age. But Casey showed up with colored markers." She pointed to the awkward rendition of a flower vine twining around her ankle in bright colors of red and blue and yellow. "Before I could find something to smack him with, Casey had flowers drawn all over me. After that, everyone else had to take a turn."

The nurse shook her head. "She loved it. She wouldn't let me move those markers and she made sure everyone who came in left their signature behind."

"Tattletale," Ms. Potter muttered with a smile.

Emma bent to look more closely and laughed. Casey had signed his name to his artwork with a flourish. Others had added a sun and birds and even a rainbow. "It looks lovely."

"I think so—now that I'm used to it."

Laughing, Ann said, "Mom is insisting on going back to work, but she'll only be there part-time and with limited duties. Your dad is stopping in later today to see her, to make sure it'll be okay, and he'll keep tabs on her."

Casey shook his finger at Ms. Potter. "I know Dad won't want you overdoing it."

Ann said, "That's what I told her, which is why I got two student employees to promise to stay with her and follow her directions. They'll be doing most of the lifting and storing of books." Ann winked at Casey. "Mom'll have the library back in order in no time."

"I'll be checking in on you with Dad," Casey warned, "so you better follow doctor's orders. That was a nasty break you had." He took Ann's hand. "If you need anything, let me know."

Ann pulled him toward her for a hug. "We'll be fine, but thank you. And, please, thank Morgan again for us. If he hadn't found her car that night…"

Casey explained to Emma, "Ms. Potter ran her car off the road, and because of the broken leg, she couldn't get out to flag anyone down. Morgan was doing his nightly check and noticed the skid marks in the road. He found her over the berm and halfway down the hill."

"If you're going to tell it, tell it right. The deer ran me off the road." Ms. Potter sniffed. "The silly thing jumped out right in front of me. Of course, he escaped without a scratch."

"Thank God for Morgan. I thought she was at bingo and wouldn't have worried until she didn't come home. She might have been there for hours if it hadn't been for him."

"It's his job," Casey commented.

Ann turned to Emma, and her dark eyes were sincere but cautious. "I should get Mom home. Emma, it was nice to see you again."

Casey slipped his arm around Emma as she said, "Thank you. You too."

"Have you moved back home?" Ann asked.

"No, just visiting my father."

"He's here at the hospital too," Casey explained. But because he didn't want Ms. Potter or Ann to ask Emma too many questions, he gave their farewells. Ann had been as nice as always, but anyone could blunder onto uncomfortable ground. He kissed Ms. Potter on the cheek again, and drew Emma away.

They moved inside the elevator and Emma pressed the button for the fifth floor. "Is Ann married?"

She asked that casually, but she looked and sounded stiff. Casey wanted to hug her close, but he had no idea why. "Not yet, but she and Nate—you remember Morgan's deputy?—are getting real friendly, especially since this happened with her mom. On top of the broken leg, she had more scrapes and bruises than I can count. Nate was the one who went to get Ann while Morgan took Ms. Potter to the hospital."

"They seem nice."

"Ms. Potter's a sweetheart, and Ann's just like her."

"Pretty too."

Casey shrugged. Ann had dark hair and eyes, and a gentle smile. He supposed she was an attractive woman. What he noticed most about her though was that she didn't judge others. She had a generous heart, and he liked that about her. "She's thanked Morgan about a dozen times now. She and her mom are really close."

Emma actually winced. If he hadn't been watching her so closely, he wouldn't have seen it. Emma quickly tried to cover up her reaction. "As big and bulky as he is, Morgan can be really gentle. He's a perfect sheriff."

Casey wasn't fooled. "I think so."

"Your dad's the same way." She spoke fast, almost chattered. "I remember when most every female in Buckhorn mooned over him and your uncles. Even the girls my age used to eye them and fantasize."

Casey put his hands in his pockets and leaned against the elevator wall. "You too?"

She cast him a quick, flustered look. "No. Of course not."

"How come?"

"I had my sights set on a different target." Her attempt at humor fell flat, even though she lightly elbowed him. "I was embarrassingly obvious."

Something in her tone got to Casey. Nothing new in that. Emma had always touched him in ways no one else could. "You never embarrassed me, Em."

She appeared rattled by the seriousness he'd injected, and quickly turned her attention to the advancing floor numbers. Casey crowded closer to her and inhaled the subtle aroma of her hair and skin. It was the same as and yet different from what he remembered. Would she taste the same?

The elevator door hissed open and Emma all but leaped out. He had to take big steps to keep up with her headlong flight down the hallway toward her father's room. Her nervousness had returned in a crushing wave. He could feel it, but was helpless as to how to help her.

When she reached the right door, she gave Casey an uncertain look. "There's a waiting room at the end of the hall if you want to watch a little television or get some coffee." She pushed her hair behind her ear with a trembling hand.

He glanced down the hall. It was empty. Not that it mattered. In that particular moment, he had to hold her. He pulled Emma against his chest and gently enfolded her in his arms. She resisted him for a moment before giving up and relaxing into him.

God, it felt good, having her so close again. He lowered his mouth to her ear, felt her warmth and the silk of her hair against his jaw. "I'll be waiting if you need me."

She lifted her head to stare up at him, embarrassed, confused, a little flushed. "I'm fine, Casey. Really."

The softness of her cheek drew his hand. He wanted to stroke her all over, find all her soft spots. Her hot spots.

Taking her—and himself—by surprise, he bent and kissed her. Her lips parted on a gasp, an unconscious invitation that was hard to resist. But Casey kept the kiss light, contenting himself with one small stroke of his tongue just inside her bottom lip. He leaned back, hazy with need, not just lust but so many roiling emotions he nearly groaned.

Using just her fingertips, Emma touched her mouth, drew a breath, and then laughed shakily. "Well, okay then." Bemused, she shook her head, turned and opened her father's door to peer inside.

Casey watched as she entered the room. Damn it, he'd rattled her when all he'd meant to do was offer comfort.

He heard her whisper, "Dad?" with a lot of uncertainty and something more, some deep yearning that came from her soul. Then the door shut and he couldn't hear anything else.

Humming with frustration, Casey stalked into the waiting room. There was no one else there, yet empty foam cups were left everywhere and magazines had been scattered about. He occupied himself by picking up the garbage, re-arranging the magazines and generally tidying things up.

It didn't help. Pent-up energy kept him pacing. All he really wanted to do was barge into that room with Emma to make sure her father didn't do or say anything to hurt her. Again.

He hated feeling this way—helpless, at loose ends. Emma was a grown woman now, independent, strong. She neither wanted nor needed his help. There was no reason for him to want to shield her, not anymore.

Moving around didn't help his mood, not when his imagination kept dredging up the sight of her bruised face eight years ago.

After about ten minutes, he gave up. Telling himself that he had every right to check on her, Casey strode across the hallway and silently opened the door to Dell Clark's room. The first bed, made up with stiff sheets and folded back at one corner, was empty. A separation curtain had been drawn next to it so that he couldn't see the second bed where Dell rested. But he could hear Emma softly speaking and he drew up short at the sound of her pleading voice.

Without a single speck of guilt, Casey took a muted step in and listened.

chapter 7

DELL'S VOICE sounded weak and somewhat slurred, from the stroke or the medication, Casey wasn't sure which. But he could understand him, and he heard his determination. "See yer mama."

"Dad." Weariness, and a vague acceptance, tinged Emma's soft denial, making Casey want to march to her side. "You know I can't do that. Besides, I doubt she even wants to see me. And if I did go, we'd just fight."

Casey realized that Emma hadn't yet seen her mother. She hadn't even been to her home, choosing instead to stay in a motel. He frowned with confusion and doubt.

"She'szer mother."

"Dad, please don't upset yourself. You need your rest."

Shaken by the desolation in Emma's words, Casey didn't dare even breathe. Their conversation didn't make sense to him. Why would Emma make a point of coming to see her father, the man who'd run her off, but not want to visit her mother?

"*Damn it.*" Dell managed to curse clearly enough, but

before he spoke further, he began wheezing and thrashing around. Casey heard the rustling of fast movement, heard Emma shushing him, soothing him.

"Calm down, Dad, please. You'll pull your IV out."

In his upset, his words became even more slurred, almost incomprehensible. "Hate this…damn arm…"

"The nurse says you'll get control of your arm again soon. It's just a temporary side effect of the stroke. You've already made so much progress—"

"'Mnot a baby."

A moment of silence. "I know you're not. I'm sorry that I'm upsetting you. It's just that I want to help."

"Go 'way."

There was so much tension in the small room, Casey couldn't breathe. Then Emma whispered, "Maybe this was a bad idea, maybe I shouldn't have come home…"

Casey's heart skipped a beat, then dropped like a stone to the bottom of his stomach. If she hadn't come home, he wouldn't have ever gotten the chance to see her again.

Dell didn't relent, but a new weariness softened his words. "She neez you."

As Emma reseated herself in the creaky plastic chair, she brushed the curtain, causing it to rustle. "Dad, she doesn't even like me. She never has. When she called to tell me about you, she made it clear that nothing's changed. I've tried to help her, and it's only made things worse."

"Can't help 'erself," Dell insisted.

Even before she spoke, Casey could feel Emma's pain. It sounded in her words, weary and hoarse and bordering on desperate. "You have to stop making excuses for her—for her sake, as well as your own."

"Love 'er."

Sounding so sad, Emma murmured, "I know you do." Then softly, she added, "More than anything."

"Emma…"

Images from the past whirled through Casey's mind. Emma hurt. Emma wandering the streets at night. Emma with no money for new clothes or schoolbooks.

Emma needy for love.

He fisted his hands until his knuckles turned white. *I know you do,* she'd said. *More than anything.*

Or anyone?

With sudden clarity, Casey knew that Emma wasn't estranged from her father.

No, as he remembered it, Dell Clark had been genuinely worried when Emma had run off. He'd blustered and grumped and cast blame, yet there'd been no mistaking the fear and regret in his eyes.

But her mother…not once had she asked about Emma, or shown any concern at all. Casey had all but forgotten about the woman because folks scarcely saw her anymore. She stayed hidden away, seldom going out.

Now Emma was in town, but staying at a motel rather than her home. And despite her father's pleas, she resisted even a visit with her mother.

In rapid order, Casey rearranged the things he knew, the things he'd always believed, and decided he'd come to some very wrong assumptions. Just as Emma had fled to his house for protection, perhaps Dell had gone along with that plan for the same reason.

Because she needed a way out.

Jesus. He propped his hands on his hips and dropped his head forward, trying to decide what to do, what to believe.

The door swung open behind him, making him jump out of the way, and Dell's doctor entered, trailed by a nurse. Recognizing Casey from his association with Sawyer, the doctor bellowed a jovial greeting. "Casey! Well, this is a surprise."

In good humor, he thwacked Casey on the shoulder. There was nothing Casey could do now but take his hand. "Dr. Wagner. Good to see you again."

"But what are you doing here?" Concern replaced Dr. Wagner's smile. "The family's okay?"

Emma stepped around the curtain, rigid, appalled, her attention glued to Casey. Her big dark eyes were accusing, her mouth pinched.

Casey got his first look at Dell and realized that he looked like death. His face was white, his eyes red-rimmed and vague from medication, one more open than the other. His mouth was a grim line, drooping on one side, and his graying hair stuck out around an oxygen tube that hooked over his ears and ran across his cheeks to his nostrils. More tubes fed into his arm through an IV. Machinery hummed around him.

Aw hell. Casey watched Emma for a moment, hoping to make her understand that everything would be okay now, that it didn't matter what he'd heard or what had happened in the past. But she turned away from him.

"The family's fine," Casey said without looking away from her. "I'm here with Emma."

The doc apparently sensed the heavy unease in the room and glanced from one person to the next. "I take it you two know each other then?"

"Yeah." Accepting that everything had changed—the past, his feelings, his motivations—Casey moved toward her. "Emma and I go way back." His attention shifted to Dell. Damn it, the man was too sick to deal with Casey's anger right now. He drew a breath and collected himself. "Hello, Mr. Clark."

Dell gripped the sheet with one gnarled hand while the other flailed before resting at his side. "Sneakin' 'round."

"Of course I wasn't." He reached Emma and looped his arm around her stiff shoulders. She didn't look at him and, if anything, her expression was more shuttered now that he touched her. "I just stepped in to check on Emma."

Emma ducked away from him. "Dr. Wagner, I'd like to speak to you privately."

"Yes, yes, of course." The good doctor looked stymied.

Casey nodded to him. "We'll wait outside until you finish your checkup with Dell."

"Use the waiting room. I'll come for you there."

Emma shoved the door open and strode out. She'd only made it three steps when Casey caught her. His long fingers wrapped around her upper arm in a secure yet gentle hold. "Oh no you don't."

She whirled on him, equal parts furious, indignant and, if Casey didn't miss his bet, afraid. *You had no right.*

Still holding her with one hand, Casey brushed the backs of his knuckles over her cheek with the other. "Now there's where you're wrong, sweetheart. You gave me the right eight years ago when you came to me. And this time, it won't be so easy for you to run off. This time you're going to tell me the truth." He touched the corner of her mouth. "You can count on it."

EMMA STRUGGLED to get enough air into her starved lungs, but the panic set in quickly. Nothing had really changed, she knew that now. Her reaction to Casey, his protective instincts, her smothering fear…it was all still there. It had only taken one day back in Buckhorn to make it all resurface.

Just like his father and uncles, Casey had a soft spot for anyone in need. She hadn't wanted him to see her that way. Not this time. Not now. But given what he'd just overheard, she knew damn well he'd be doling out the pity again. God, she couldn't bear it.

She licked dry lips and cautiously tried to free her arm. He didn't let go.

"Why are you doing this, Casey?"

All his attention remained on her mouth, unnerving her further. "Doing what?"

She rolled her shoulder to indicate his hold. "This…overwhelming bombardment. You insist on coffee, insist on giving me a ride, insist you have to know everything even though it's none of your business. Why nose in where I don't want you?"

"Where is it you don't want me, sweetheart?"

Oh, that soft, coaxing voice. She couldn't let him do this to her. She'd come home because she had to, and all along she'd expected to see Casey again. This time, however, she'd wanted his respect. "What's between me and my father doesn't concern you."

Filled with conviction, Casey started to lead her into the waiting room.

"Casey!"

They both looked up to see the young nurse who'd accompanied the doctor into her father's room. She'd slipped out the door and she had her sights set on Casey. As she bore down on them with a proprietary air, Emma tried to retreat.

She heard Casey's annoyed sigh as he tugged her closer and draped his arm over her shoulders. Emma didn't know if he did it as a sign of support, or to make damn sure she couldn't slip away. Whatever his purpose, it didn't matter. She couldn't let it matter.

But being tucked that close to him shook her on every level. He was so hard, so tall and strong and masculine. Heat and a wonderful deep scent seemed a part of him, encompassing her and filling her up in places she'd forgotten were empty. With every pore of her being, she was aware of him. He was her living, breathing fantasy, and he kept touching her in that man/woman way, just as she used to dream of him doing.

Only the timing was all wrong now. Or she wasn't right for him—and never would be.

She had to get away.

The nurse halted in front of them, her smile bold, her posturing plain. Unlike Ann, who had been cordial, not by so much as a flicker of an eyelash did this woman acknowledge Emma. "Casey, I had such a nice time last weekend." She spoke with a heavy dose of suggestion. "I sort of expected you to call."

While Emma went stiff enough to crackle, Casey was loose and casual and relaxed, as if he didn't hold Emma prisoner at his side, forcing her through this awkward come-on.

"I've been busy." And then to Emma, "Lois and I were both at the same party last weekend."

Lois? Forgetting her own discomfort for a moment,

Emma took in the bouncing brown hair and heavy hazel eyes. Recognition dawned. "Lois Banker?"

With an effort, Lois pulled her gaze from Casey. She lifted perfectly plucked eyebrows. "That's right. And you are…?"

Unbelievable, Emma thought in wonder. At least the maturity had shown on Ann. Her dark hair was shorter now, and there'd been a few laugh lines around her eyes. But Lois…she looked just as she had in high school. She was still pretty, perky, stacked.

She still had a thing for Casey.

Emma dredged up a smile even as she lifted her chin, preparing for the worst. "You don't remember me, but we went to school together." She held out a hand. "Emma Clark."

Lois scowled as she scrutinized Emma, and then slowly, with the jogging of her memory, her lip curled. "Emma Clark. Yes, I remember you." She shifted away from Emma's hand as if fearing contamination.

Emma found the petty attitude ridiculous, but not unexpected. Lois had never hid her dislike of her. But Casey pulled Emma a little closer and his fingers on her shoulder contracted, gently massaging her in a manner far too familiar. Of course, Lois made note of it, and her expression darkened even more.

Casey said, "Emma is back for a visit."

"A brief visit?"

You wish, Emma thought, and then was appalled at herself. Good God, she had no claim on Casey, and Lois certainly had no reason to be jealous of her. "Until my father is well."

Lois's eyes narrowed. "I hadn't made the connection." She glanced at Casey's hand on Emma. "Mr. Clark… He's the one who was drunk when he had a stroke, isn't he?"

Emma took the well-planned words like a punch on the chin. They dazed her. And they hurt.

"My father doesn't drink." Defensive and a little numb, Emma retreated. "Excuse me, please."

Casey released her as she pushed away. "Emma?"

On wobbly legs, Emma wandered into the waiting room and headed for a plastic padded seat, praying she wouldn't embarrass herself by tearing up.

Why would Lois say her father had been drinking? Emma knew for a fact that he never touched alcohol. Like her, he'd made other choices.

In order to find answers, would she have to go see her mother, after all? Memories fell over her in a suffocating wave.

Then Lois's voice reached her, offering a much-needed distraction.

"Casey, what in the world are you doing with that nasty girl?"

In response to the slur, Casey became terse. "Nasty girl, Lois? Just what the hell does that mean?"

"Oh come on, Case." Lois's laugh of disbelief grated along Emma's nerves until she shivered. "She was the biggest slut around and everyone knows it. Besides, from what I've heard, you certainly had firsthand knowledge about—"

"Shut up."

Lois gasped, but otherwise remained silent. Emma squeezed her eyes shut. Firsthand knowledge? Is that what people thought, that Casey had given in to her relentless pursuit? What a laugh.

Then a worse theory occurred to Emma and she curled her arms around her stomach. Oh no. Surely no one had heard her outrageous claims of being pregnant. Her father wouldn't have told a soul, and Casey's family wasn't the type to gossip. Yet Lois had inferred something…

"You need to grow up, Lois, and learn some manners."

"*I* need to learn manners?" Her outrage was clear. "I'm not the one who slept with every guy in Buckhorn."

Casey snorted. "As I recall, not that many guys were asking."

"Casey!"

"See ya around, Lois."

The sound of Lois's angry, retreating footfalls couldn't be missed. Emma sighed, aware of Casey's approach but unsure what she should say to him. Already she'd caused him problems, but he didn't want to hear her apologies, he'd been plain about that.

She felt steadier now, but still swamped in confusion. Her father didn't drink—never had—and she knew in her heart he never would. What had Lois meant by her comment?

Emma expected Casey to seat himself. Instead, he crouched down beside her. "Em?"

Startled, Emma stared at him.

With concern darkening his brown eyes, he said, "Hey. You okay?"

Casey came from a long line of caregivers. As a doctor, his father tended everyone from infants to the elderly. Being the town sheriff, Morgan set out to protect the innocent, and Jordan was the perfect vet with a voice that soothed and a manner that reassured. Even Gabe, the resident handyman, made a point of lending a helping hand to anyone who needed it.

She understood Casey's nature, but did he think she was made of fluff? "Why wouldn't I be?"

"Lois is a bitch."

Emma couldn't help but chuckle at that. "No, she's just hung up on you. She saw your arm around me and misunderstood."

"She understood." He put his rough palm on her knee with his long fingers curling around her. She hadn't realized the back of her knee could be so sensitive until Casey's fingertips brushed there. "I'm sorry she said what she did."

Trying to ignore his touch, Emma put her hand over his. "It's not the first time, Casey. If you go around alienating your friends over me, you're going to find yourself pretty lonely."

He ignored her warning to ask, "She's called you names before?" As he spoke, he clasped both her knees and Emma had the flashing thought of him pushing her legs open and settling between them. The image had an instantaneous effect on her body: her breath hitched, her belly tingled, her flesh heated. She didn't have the time or concentration for this.

In a rush, she shoved to her feet and stepped away. "Of course she did. Most of the boys from here—men now, I suppose—wanted to get me in bed and most of the girls hated me because of it."

Very slowly, Casey came to his feet. "She's jealous."

How ridiculous. "Hardly. Everyone always knew that I wanted you, but that you always turned me down."

Casey looked pained. "I'm sorry, Em."

"What did she mean when she said you had firsthand knowledge about me?"

He hesitated.

"Casey?"

With a shrug in his tone, he said, "For a while, people thought you ran off because of me." His eyes narrowed. "No one knew about that night, how your father brought you to me. No one knew that I asked you to stay—but you left anyway."

Startled, Emma could have sworn she heard resentment in his tone. But that didn't make any sense. "I'm glad that's all it is."

Sounding almost lethal, Casey repeated, "You're glad?"

He couldn't understand. "I didn't want you insulted, but I don't care what she says about me—I never have."

Casey watched her with brooding intensity. "I don't believe that."

The day had been too tumultuous for her to hold on to her temper. "And I don't care if you don't believe it. I made my choices and I've lived with them."

"Em…"

"I slept around. So what?" Bitterness that had simmered for years suddenly boiled over. "Just because I'm female it's a huge sin to enjoy sex, to enjoy being touched? How many females have you slept with, Casey?"

His jaw tightened.

"Ah. Should I take that blank expression to mean there are too many to count? What about Lois's reference to last weekend? Did you sleep with her then?"

"No."

She found that hard to believe and let him know it with a look. "But because you're male, that's just fine, right? Better than fine. What makes you a stud makes me a whore."

"Stop it, Em."

The furious rasp of his voice didn't register. "No one's ever talked about all the guys who bed hop, the guys who came to me. But a woman…"

"Stop it."

Emma went slack-jawed at his raised voice. Never in her life had she heard that particular tone from Casey. With her, he'd been cajoling, teasing, concerned, sometimes firmly insistent. Always gentle. But never outraged.

Of course, she'd known him only as a boy. Now he was a man.

She blinked at him, a little awed by the level of his anger. It showed in every taut, bunched line of his muscled body. His jaw was clenched, his hands curled into fists. Oh boy.

Emma pulled herself together. She hadn't intended to ever have this discussion with Casey, but since it had begun, she wished she'd chosen a better place than a hospital waiting room.

More in control of herself, and her voice lower now, Emma sighed. "Casey, I'm not ashamed of my past. At least, not that part of it." There were other things, things her family had done, things she'd covered up, the way she'd always pressured him, that still made her hot with regret. But not her sexuality. "I was young and healthy and I enjoyed sex. I still enjoy sex."

A low savage sound escaped him, similar to a snarl. He locked his hands behind his head and paced away.

His reaction stunned her. It almost looked as if he was restraining himself—and had a devil of a time doing so. "If you can't deal with that then you should head on home now. I'll find a ride back to the motel."

Casey turned and stalked to the waiting-room door. For one heart-stopping moment, Emma assumed he was going to storm out in a rage. He was leaving her and her heart hurt so badly she nearly doubled over with the crushing pain. She knew Casey would never love her, but she'd already started hoping that they could be friends.

Instead, he belatedly snapped the door shut to afford them some privacy. When he turned to face her, he still looked livid but he, too, had lowered his voice.

"I don't give a royal fuck how many boys you slept with, Emma."

Despite herself, his wording made her mouth fall open.

Very slowly, with intimidating deliberation, Casey stalked her. "But I do care that you were too young to be making those decisions."

Her chin lifted. "You're telling me you waited?"

"Apparently longer than you did." He pointed a finger at her. "And before you say it, before you assume that being in an all-male household gave me encouragement to screw any female who offered, you should know that I got a lot of lectures on responsibility. Dad, Morgan, Jordan—hell, even Gabe—they all endlessly harped on about ramifications. What might be meaningless sex to me could mean a whole lot more to a girl, especially if she got pregnant, or her folks found out. So, no, I didn't indiscriminately indulge in opportunities."

"And it bothers you that I didn't show that same restraint?" She kept her chin high, but the idea that he'd start judging her now hurt.

"What bothers me is that you did a hell of a lot of stuff because you were always lost and alone." His expression hardened, his jaw drew tight. "And I didn't do enough to help you."

"No—"

He gave her a warning look that made her swallow her automatic denial. "It's my turn, Emma, so you just be quiet and listen."

Emma snapped her mouth shut and began backing up

as he kept advancing. Never had he looked so big, so imposing. So irritated with her.

She bumped into the wall and was annoyed with herself for retreating. She wasn't afraid of Casey. Out of all the things she'd ever felt for him, not once had fear ever been an issue.

Casey crowded into her, caging her in with his body. When she started to sidle away, he gripped her shoulders and held her firm. They stared at each other in silence until Emma gave up and held still.

"I care that you've been lying to me from the start."

"But..."

"I care that I let you get away."

Her eyes widened. *Let her get away?* Far as she knew, Casey hadn't wanted her to stay. Oh, he'd offered her help because Casey was the type of man who could do nothing else. But he'd made it clear many times that she didn't factor into his future. Well, this *was* his future, and just because she'd materialized didn't mean...

His hands kneaded her shoulders absently, while his gaze burned. "And you can bet your sweet ass I care that *I've* never had you." He leaned closer and his voice dropped to a guttural whisper. "I care about that a lot."

Her heart thundered, and her pulse went wild. Unable to maintain eye contact with him so close, Emma looked away. But Casey wasn't allowing that. He put a fist under her chin and brought her face back around, forcing her to meet his burning gaze. His eyes had narrowed with intent, starting a trembling deep inside her. "You quote double standards to me, but you wanna know what's really unfair?"

"No."

He pressed into her until she felt his hard flat abdomen against her belly. Oh God. Her whole body came alive, quivering with primal awareness.

"It's unfair for a gorgeous young woman to keep throwing herself at a guy until he can't sleep nights for wanting her too much. And then she runs off and no other woman will do because he has a taste for her—a goddamned hunger— yet, damn it, she's gone."

"Casey…" She gave the breathless complaint automatically. She couldn't allow herself to believe him. Always, he'd rejected her, wanting no more than friendship. Time apart couldn't have changed that.

His fingers tunneled into her hair, holding her head still. He lowered his forehead to hers and his eyes closed, his voice going rough and deep. "It's unfair because now that you're here again, all grown up and sexier than ever, you no longer want me."

She felt his warm breath on her lips, felt the heat of his frustration, his urgency, which sparked her own. Her body was melting into his, her nerve endings tingling and alive. Not want him? She was dying for him.

"I'm sorry, sweetheart," he murmured against her mouth, "but I don't intend to let you get away with it."

He said that so simply, sort of slipping it in there on her, it took a second for his statement to sink in. When his meaning dawned on her, Emma became alert with a start, only to have any thoughts of rejecting him quelled beneath a ravaging kiss. He didn't ease into the kiss. No, he took her mouth with ruthless domination.

Emma loved it.

All objections scattered, as insubstantial as a hot summer

breeze. Aware of her surrender, Casey groaned low in his throat and tilted his head, fitting his mouth to hers more securely. He continued to hold her immobile, pressing her to the wall. She felt the muscled hardness, the vitality of his body against her breasts, her belly and thighs. She tried to squirm, to get closer, but his grip didn't allow it.

The kiss was an onslaught, never broken, always going deeper, taking and giving, and Emma forgot they were in a hospital with people milling around outside the room.

Casey didn't forget. Slowly, reluctantly, he pulled back. His thumbs brushed the corners of her swollen mouth. Emma fought to get her eyes open.

"I love your mouth, Em. So damn sexy." He nipped her bottom lip, licked her upper, took her mouth again. He sank his tongue in, soft and deep.

Emma groaned.

"I used to imagine your mouth on me," he whispered, "and it made me nuts."

Hearing him say it made her imagine it now. *"Yes."* She would love to taste Casey—everywhere. "Yes." She reached for him again.

Casey stepped them both away from the wall and urged her head to his shoulder, then wrapped his arms around her to hold her tight. He took several long, unsteady breaths, which allowed her to do the same. Emma was so shaken that if Casey hadn't supported her, she thought she might have melted into a puddle on the floor.

"I'm going to give you time, Emma."

She flattened her hands against the firm wall of his chest, relishing the feel of him. Time? She didn't need time. At the moment, she didn't want time. Unless it was time enough to explore him, to kiss him everywhere, to feel him deep inside her. Oh God, she *would* melt.

"I'm going to wait so you won't feel rushed."

She couldn't stop shaking. "I won't."

He went still, cursed softly, then turned his face in and kissed her ear. "Shh. Not yet. First you're going to get comfortable with me again. Then we're going to talk, and I want the truth this time, Emma."

Her heart, which had only just begun to calm, kicked into a furious gallop again. "No…"

"And then." His tongue touched her earlobe, licked lightly inside to make her shiver. "*Then* I'm going to lay you down, strip you naked and sate myself on you." He groaned as if being tortured. "I've got nearly a decade of lust to make up for, sweetheart, so it's going to take me a really long time to get my fill. I hope you're up for it."

Emma shuddered. She had no idea what to do, what to say. But in that single moment, she made a decision. She wouldn't leave Buckhorn again without having Casey first.

If that made her feelings for him harder to deal with, so be it. She wasn't a weak woman with silly illusions. She knew from past experience that Casey wouldn't want her as a permanent fixture in his life. She knew she'd never fit into Buckhorn. She never had.

When she'd left, there'd been a lot of things she wanted. Security, respectability, a close family…and Casey Hudson. But of all those things, it was only Casey who had kept her awake at night.

She had the security and respectability that came with a good job, an attitude adjustment, maturity. She had a family; not her own, but the Devaughns were very special to her and she loved them. She'd attained things of value, but she'd also learned that they weren't enough. She hadn't admitted to herself what was still missing in her life until Casey made it clear that he wanted her.

She'd never be close with her own family; seeing her father again had proven that. But she could have this—she could have her memories of Casey. With everything combined, she'd make that be enough for a lifetime.

She looked into his mellow golden eyes, glittering with excitement. His sharp cheekbones were flushed with arousal. For her. Emma whispered, "All right."

The heat in his eyes flared, but was quickly banked. "God, Emma." He took several deep breaths, leaned back and finally managed a smile. "The minutes are going to seem like hours until I can get you alone."

Emma nodded.

"Until then, let's talk about your dad—and what really happened the night he dropped you on my doorstep."

chapter 8

CASEY SAW the shuttered way Emma guarded herself. Well, too bad. Sometimes the truth proved painful but, damn it, he deserved that much.

He couldn't stop touching her, smoothing her warm cheek, relishing the feel of her. He could barely wait until she was naked so he could rub his hands, his face, over her whole body. He wanted to stroke her breasts, her belly. Between her thighs.

The second she'd agreed with him, he'd gotten semihard and he had a feeling he'd be that way until he got her alone. Heat snaked through him, adding to the sexual tension and making his voice gruff. "Come on, Em. You know you can tell me anything."

She closed her eyes tightly. "People don't just fall into old relationships that easily, Case."

"You and I do." Spending the day with her had reaffirmed that much. Emma looked different, and her attitudes were wiser, more confident. But the closeness between them existed as strong as ever. No other woman had ever touched him so easily. "Regardless of what you ever thought, Em, you've always had a special place in my heart."

"Casey." She sounded strained and covered her face with her hands.

He couldn't keep from kissing her again, but he contented himself by pulling her hands away and brushing his mouth over her forehead. "I care about you—I always have. In all the time you were gone, that hasn't changed."

"No? You want to sleep with me now. That's sure not how I remember it."

Something else that was different—her lippy comebacks. They amused him. "I always wanted you and you know it." He leaned down to see her face. "I think you enjoyed tormenting me, sending me home with a boner, knowing I'd be miserable all night long." The fact that he could tease even when he was this aroused said a lot about Emma and how relaxed he was in her company.

She denied his accusation with a quick shake of her head. "You didn't have to be miserable. I would have taken care of you."

Casey's moan turned into a laugh. "You're still tormenting me. Now, enough with the distractions. What happened that night, Emma? Why were you so desperate to get out of Buckhorn?"

"You don't really want to know."

"Of course I do."

"Then you don't really *need* to know. Casey, I don't want to involve you. It wouldn't be fair."

She looked truly set in her decision, and Casey knew she wouldn't tell him a thing. He was contemplating ways to get around her stubbornness, when the waiting-room door opened and Dr. Wagner stuck his head in. "Am I interrupting?"

Casey stepped back from Emma. To keep her from ushering him out of the room, he said, "Not at all. We're anxious to hear how Dell's doing."

Emma made a sound, clearly aghast at his audacity in including himself. Casey pretended not to hear. She wanted to shut him out again, but he wasn't about to budge. She'd agreed to sleep with him, to accept him as a lover. She could damn well accept him as a friend and confidant too. Whatever Dr. Wagner had to tell her, he could share it with them both.

Lois, peeved and hostile, stepped in behind the doctor. The way she watched Emma was so malicious, it should have been illegal.

Casey had never paid that much attention to Lois before now. He'd thought her cute, a little silly. He'd been out with her once or twice, casual dates that didn't amount to much and definitely didn't go beyond a few kisses. But he hadn't known how catty she could be. Poor Emma, to have put up with her and the other women like her.

He had new insight into what Emma's teen years must have been like in Buckhorn, and it was decidedly worse than he'd thought.

"Let's sit down," Dr. Wagner suggested.

Emma went to a chair and Casey stood behind her, his hands on her shoulders, making it clear to the doctor and to Lois that he was there for her.

Many times in the past, he'd stood in front of her, trying to shield her. He knew now that she was stronger than he'd ever suspected. She had to be to have survived with her naturally generous nature still intact. Standing behind her, offering her support in what she chose to face, and respecting her strength to do it, seemed more appropriate.

The doctor pulled up his own chair facing Emma, and Lois sat beside him. Dr. Wagner pasted on his patented reassuring physician's smile. "Ms. Clark, your father is doing much better today. I see improvement not only in his mental capacity in identifying objects, but also in his mind/eye coordination." The doctor turned grave. "But, to be truthful, for a little while there I thought we might lose him."

"Lose him?" Emma stiffened in alarm. "But I thought..."

"You're seeing him now, with much improvement. For three days he had no clear recognition of most things. He knew what he was seeing, but he couldn't find the word in his memory to identify it."

Emma bit her bottom lip. "I came as soon as I was told, but I had to pack up and I didn't arrive in Buckhorn until late last night. I stopped here first. My father was asleep, so I just looked in on him." She twisted her hands together. "The nurse said he'd be okay."

"And she's correct. But I anticipate quite a bit of therapy not only to help him deal with what he's suffered and his diminished capacity—which should be only temporary—but to help rebuild his coordination. We'll get his meds regulated—blood thinner and blood pressure medicine to keep him from having another stroke."

For several minutes, the doctor explained the causes and effects of a stroke, and Emma listened in fretful silence.

"He'll need to be monitored for TIAs—or mini strokes."

Emma nodded. "The nurse said that he also fell?"

Dr. Wagner's eyebrows rose in surprise. "Your mother didn't tell you he fell off the porch steps when she called you? She said she found him unconscious, which is why she called the paramedics. And good thing too, as I've already said."

Lois made a face. "He'd been drinking, so his wife thought he'd just passed out."

Scowling, Dr. Wagner twisted around to face the nurse. "Incorrect, Ms. Banker. Alcohol had been spilled on him, but he had not consumed any noticeable amount."

When he turned back to Emma, his expression gentled and he reached out to pat her hand. "It's my guess that he was carrying a bottle of whisky when he had the stroke. It spilled all over him and, yes, we could smell it. I had thought to question his wife about it, but haven't seen her yet."

Emma stammered, "Mom d-doesn't get out much."

Casey wanted to roll his eyes at her understatement. Her mother was a recluse. She was seldom seen around town, and apparently she hadn't even ventured out to visit her husband.

"I see." The doctor gave her a long look, then referred to his notes. "Well, he did some further damage with his fall. We got the MRI back on his ankle, and luckily it isn't broken, though it is still severely swollen and I'm certain it's causing him some pain. Add to that the bruising on his ribs and shoulder…well, he took a very nasty spill. I'm relieved he didn't break his neck."

Emma nodded. "Me too."

"You say you're from out of town. Will you be able to stay around to attend him, and if not, is your mother capable of the task?"

"I…" She glanced at Casey, who squeezed her shoulder, then back at the doctor. "What kind of care will he need?"

Appearing to be a little uncomfortable, Dr. Wagner explained, "I don't anticipate he'll go home for a while yet. But when he does, he'll need help with everyday tasks until he regains control of lost motor skills. He'll need transportation back and forth to the hospital for therapy. He may even need help feeding himself, dressing…at least for a while. As I said, his improvement so far is quite promising, but we can't make any guarantees."

"I understand." She waited only a moment before giving a firm nod. "I can be here as long as I'm needed."

Casey wondered if she could stay indefinitely. She'd made a life in Chicago…by all accounts, a happy life that suited her. But her roots were in Buckhorn. Whatever had driven her away the first time, he'd be here with her now, offering her support in whatever way she needed. Maybe it'd be enough.

Emma dropped back in her seat, and Casey noted the weariness in her face. She looked beautiful to him, so he hadn't at first noticed. But now that he did, he felt guilty. She'd been given worrisome news, spent several hours on the road yesterday with only a few hours' sleep to recoup, and then faced her father.

And he'd been bulldozing her straight into an affair. He suddenly felt like a bastard. No, he wouldn't change his mind. He couldn't. But he would treat her gently, give her plenty of time.

"I hope I've relieved your mind," Dr. Wagner said.

"You have. I'm sure I can handle things, as long as you tell me everything I need to know."

"Yes, of course. When he's ready to be discharged, we'll give you a list of his prescriptions, along with instructions on his general care. He'll have regular checkups and you can always reach someone here at the hospital or at my office if you have questions. Thanks to his injured ankle and ribs, he'll spend a good deal of time in bed, so you'll also need to rotate his position until he's back on his feet. He's going to be very sore for a while."

Wearing a half smile, Emma admitted, "I'm a massage therapist, so I know about sore muscles."

"A massage therapist?" Lois asked, looking down her nose.

"Excellent," Dr. Wagner said at almost the same time. "It's too bad you don't live here. I could have used your services last week after a day spent fishing." He chuckled as he rubbed the small of his back. "I'm getting too old to sit on the hard bench of a fishing boat for hours on end. I was stiff for two days. But the wife had no sympathy. None at all."

Emma laughed with him. "I'll be glad to help you out while I'm here. Just give me a call. The desk has my number."

Dr. Wagner brightened. "Careful now. I'll hold you to it."

"It'll be my pleasure. A thank-you for all the good care you're giving Dad."

Casey wasn't at all sure he liked the sound of that, and then he caught himself. Dr. Wagner was a grandpa, for crying out loud. A kind old man who'd known his father forever. Yet…Lois had the same damn thought, given her spiteful expression. She smiled, but it was a smile of malicious intent.

Casey wondered how much Emma would let him help. Considering what he'd learned, he knew it wouldn't be easy for her to be home with both her parents. Yet her father's health dictated that she do just that.

He wanted to do what was best for her, and if that meant

helping her with Dell... He and her father were not on great terms—not since the night Dell accused him of getting Emma pregnant—but Emma would have cleared that up with her father by now. Dell would certainly have realized that he wasn't a grandfather, and Casey wasn't a father.

Not that he didn't want to be. Someday. With the right woman.

He looked at Emma again and felt a strange warmth spread through his chest. Emma was such a gentle, affectionate, sensitive woman, she'd make a wonderful mother.

And if she knew your thoughts, Casey told himself, *she'd probably head directly back to Chicago.* Hell, he scared himself, so he could only imagine how Emma would react.

"You'll be hearing from me." Dr. Wagner shook her hand, then clapped Casey on the shoulder. "I'm off to see the rest of my patients."

He went out, yet Lois lingered. She looked Emma up and down with a sullen sneer. "A massage therapist? Is that what they're calling it these days?"

Casey felt like strangling the little witch for her insinuation, yet Emma only smiled. "Far as I know, Lois, that's what they've always called it. You didn't know that? I'm surprised, since the field of massage therapy has become an integral part of health care, and you *are* a nurse, after all."

Stung, Lois pursed her mouth. "It sounds like a shady front to me. I remember you too well. I can just imagine what you do while *massaging* someone."

Emma leaned toward her, taunting, egging her on. "It is scandalous. Why, I light scented candles and play erotic, relaxing music. But I'm good, Lois, so good, that I get a lot of repeat customers." She held up her hands. "I'm told I have magic fingers and that I can work the tension out of any muscle."

Red-faced, Lois said, "It's an excuse to get naked and get...rubbed."

"You make that sound so dirty!" Emma laughed. "Actually, people with real physical ailments come to me. Strained muscles, stress, rehab after an injury..."

Lois sputtered in outrage. "You should encourage people to see real professionals."

"Oh? You mean like the massage therapists employed by the hospital? I noticed their offices downstairs. They're not quite as well equipped as I am, but they're still adequate."

"They're accredited."

"Me too." Emma fashioned a look of haughtiness. "I'm certified with the AMTA and licensed by the city of Chicago. You know, you look so puckered up, you should really try a little massage. All that frowning ages a person and gives her wrinkles."

"I do see a few frown lines, Lois," Casey managed to say with a straight face. It was strange, but seeing Emma so confident, even cocky, turned him on. "Maybe the folks downstairs will give you an employee discount."

Clearly knowing she'd lost that round, Lois stalked out in a snit.

Unwilling to let Emma leave the same way, Casey caught her elbow. She'd put up a good front for Lois, but he could see that she was miffed over his interference with the doctor. "Do you want to visit with your father some more before we head off?"

She considered it, and finally nodded. "Maybe just to smooth things over before I leave."

Casey hated for her to face him alone again, but he already knew he wasn't welcome. "Hey." He touched her chin and resisted the urge to kiss her. "Don't let him get you down, okay? He's bound to be a little grouchy, all things considered."

"It's not that." She started out of the room. "There are some things my father and I will never agree on, that's all. But I don't want to argue with him here, not while he's hurt and sick."

This time Casey waited for her in the hall, but he could hear them speaking. The words were indistinct, but the tone was clear: Emma calmly insistent, Dell complaining, even whining. Casey winced for her. Under the circumstances, being Dell's caretaker wasn't going to be easy.

When she emerged ten minutes later, looking more agitated than ever, he slipped his arm around her waist. They walked down the hallway to the elevator in silence, but once inside, Casey pulled her into a hug. "Ms. Clark, I'm noticing a few frown lines on you, too."

A reluctant smile curled her lips, but her eyes remained dark with worry. "Is that right? Think I should stop for a massage?"

"What I think is that you should talk me through it. Maybe I have magic fingers too."

The smile turned into a grin. "I never doubted it for a second."

"But first, a day on the lake with the sun in your face will work wonders."

To his surprise, Emma sighed. "Oh, that does sound like heaven."

Aware of a slow, heated thrumming in his blood, Casey urged her off the elevator and through the lobby. Already he visualized her in a bikini, her skin warmed by the sun, dewy with the humidity... He had to swallow his groan to keep from alerting her to his intent. He'd have her alone in the boat, on the lake, with no way to escape. Touching her, kissing her, was a priority.

But first he intended to discover all her secrets. Something had happened to her, something bad enough to make her leave her home. Bad enough to make her leave him.

He wasn't letting her off the boat until he knew it all.

chapter 9

B.B.'S HOT BREATH pelted Casey's right ear as he drove. The dog, like Emma, enjoyed having the top down, his face in the wind.

Emma's long hair whipped out behind her and she constantly had to shove it from her face. In something akin to awe, she breathed, "It's so beautiful out here."

Glancing at her, Casey agreed. Now that they'd hit the back roads leading toward the lake, the foliage was thicker, greener, lush. Blue cornflowers mixed with black-eyed Susans all along the roadway. Cows bawled in sprawling pastures, goats chewed on tall weeds grown along crooked fence posts. Blue-black crows as fat as ducks spread their wings and cawed as the car went past.

The narrow roads forced Casey to slow his speed, but he didn't mind. Watching Emma reacquaint herself with her hometown made every second enjoyable. She waved to farmers in coveralls who tipped their straw hats to her and then lazily waved back. She strained to see tobacco huts and tomato stands and moss-covered ponds. She embraced the wind in her face and the sun in her eyes.

She laughed with the sheer joy of it all.

And Casey felt positively frenetic with lust. It burned his stomach and tightened his throat and kept him uncomfortably edgy.

If, as he'd first assumed, he had only lust to deal with, he'd have already pulled over to the side of the road and taken Emma beneath a tree on the sweet grass. She claimed to be willing and there was plenty of privacy here once you got far enough from the road that no cars would notice you. Making love to Emma with the hot sun on his back and the birds overhead would be downright decadent, something straight out of his dreams.

But he was afraid what he felt for her was more than mere lust. He wasn't sure how much more and he wasn't sure how hard it'd be to convince her of it. Emma seemed hell-bent on remembering how he'd once rejected her, instead of giving them both a chance to get reacquainted as adults. Not that he blamed her. Looking at her now, he couldn't understand how he'd ever turned her down.

Emma was as earthy and sexual and appealing as a woman could be. And she was in her element here.

She belonged in Buckhorn. Did she belong with him?

They'd stopped at the motel where Emma had changed into her suit and a zippered terry-cloth cover-up. Snowy-white and sleeveless, it hung to midthigh, showing off the shapely length of her legs. She'd raised the zipper high enough to rest between her breasts. Casey could see the top of her beige, crocheted bathing-suit bra, which made him nuts wanting to know if it was a bikini or a one-piece.

She wore dark sunglasses and brown slip-on sandals, and she had a large cotton satchel stuffed with a colorful beach towel, sunscreen, a bottle of water and her cell phone. She commented that she wanted the hospital to be able to reach her if they needed to.

Before they'd left the motel she'd also taken the time to call Damon on his phone, and discovered that the car was repaired and he was touring the area. Emma had promised him that she'd be back for dinner. Luckily, to Casey's way of thinking, Damon had explained that he had a date, so Emma should take her time visiting.

Emma hadn't seemed at all surprised or concerned with how fast Damon had gotten acquainted. Apparently he had a way with women, given the fond smile Emma wore while rolling her eyes.

Casey had no idea what Damon had planned, and he didn't much care. As long as Damon stayed busy, he couldn't interfere with Casey's pursuit of Emma.

He turned the car down the long driveway to his family's home. The property here was lined with a tidy split-rail fence to contain the few farm animals they kept. Their menagerie often varied, since some of his father's patients paid for medical services with livestock, which they in turn often donated to the needier local families.

At present, they had several horses, an enormous hog, a fat, ornery heifer and two timid lambs. They'd keep the horses, and Honey had grown partial to the lambs. But the hog and heifer had to go. They terrorized Honey every chance they got. Whenever Honey was around, the damn cow dredged up the most threatening look a big-eyed, black-spotted bovine could manage.

Casey adored Honey, and a day didn't go by that he didn't appreciate her and all she gave to them, to his father. Because Sawyer's first marriage had been such a public fiasco, no one had ever expected him to remarry.

Casey had enjoyed being raised in an all-male household, but having Honey around had been even better. Softer. Over the years, she'd planted numerous flowers along the outside of the fence: enormous white peonies, tall irises and abundant daisies. Something was always in bloom, making the area colorful and fragrant.

Holding her hair from her face, Emma glanced around at the familiar stretch of land. "I thought we were going to the lake?"

"We are." He kept his gaze on the road and off the sight of her creamy skin. "But I want to stop at the house first. I need to change and grab the boat keys."

"You live at home?"

"In the apartment over the garage. I lived in Cincy for a while, just because I thought it'd be more convenient. But it didn't take me long to decide I prefer the forty-minute drive to and from work every day." Now, more than ever, Casey was glad he hadn't moved out of the area.

The sprawling log house came into view. Built on a rise and surrounded by mature trees and numerous outbuildings, it looked impressive indeed. In his younger days, Casey had lived there with his father and his uncles. Morgan now had a house farther up the hill, but not more than a ten-minute walk away. Jordan had moved into Georgia's house with her and the kids after they married, and Gabe bought a place in town with Elizabeth.

Morgan's newest official vehicle was in the yard. Because

so many people in Buckhorn lived off the beaten path or in the hills, Morgan drove a rugged four-wheel-drive Bronco. Misty, his wife, had convinced him to trade from black to white last year. Actually, she'd wanted red, but Morgan had refused that. He said the sheriff's emblem painted on the side would clash.

Casey saw Emma take in the crowd in front of the house. With the dark glasses on, he couldn't see her eyes. But he watched the tilt of her head, the lack of a smile on her pretty mouth.

It appeared Morgan and Misty were dropping off the kids, Amber and Garrett. They stood on the steps, Morgan wearing his tan uniform and Misty in a casual dress. Sawyer and Honey were beneath the shade on the porch, drinking tall glasses of iced tea. Shohn was there, too, with Morgan's dog, Godzilla. All in all, they made an intimidating crowd of people.

When they saw Casey pull up and park beneath an oak tree, the kids raced to the car to greet him. The boys were shirtless and in sneakers; Amber wore a T-shirt and cutoffs and was barefoot.

B.B. twitched his ears, alert to the activity but not overly concerned. When he spotted the kids, his tail started thumping in earnest. Casey hadn't known they'd all be there. He waited, worried that Emma would be upset to be dropped into the middle of his overwhelming family.

Instead, she sat back in her seat with a sound of wonder. "It's incredible, but they look almost the same."

Relieved, Casey reached over and smoothed a long lock of hair behind her ear. "Dad has gray at his temples now, but Honey says it makes him look distinguished."

"She's right. He's still so handsome it's almost unfair.

And Shohn looks just like him. But, if anything, Morgan's gotten even bigger."

"Misty calls him a brick wall." Casey looked at his imposing uncle in time to see Morgan pat Misty on the rump. She swatted at him and he laughed.

Shaking his head, Casey said, "I swear, they still act like newlyweds."

"Yeah, and it's wonderful." Emma sighed. The kids had almost reached them. They were making a clatter, laughing and calling out. "You can see which kids are his. That shiny black hair, and just look at those blue eyes."

Emma opened her door, not waiting for Casey. B.B. jumped out beside her and whined in excitement, practically pleading to be released so he could play with Godzilla. The kids skidded to a halt in front of Emma and then stared.

Shohn squinted up at her. His dark hair was mussed and he had dirt on his knees. "Does your dog bite?"

"Only on bones." She grinned as she said it. "But not leg bones. Just steak bones."

Garrett held out a hand and B.B. licked it. "Can we play with him?"

The dog whined again with the most pitifully pleading expression, amusing the kids.

Because they had plenty of land for running, Casey unhooked the dog's leash. "You guys go easy on him, okay? He doesn't know you yet."

Amber stroked his muzzle and giggled when his tail started furiously pounding the ground. "We'll watch him for ya, okay?"

Casey left it up to Emma.

"Honey won't mind having him loose?"

"'Course not." Luckily, Honey loved animals as much as they all did. Except for big cows and snarling hogs.

"All right." Emma scratched B.B.'s ear, then patted his side and released him by saying, "Go play."

B.B. bounded forward, leaping this way and that in his exuberance at seeing another dog. Godzilla went berserk with his own joy, which prompted the kids to do the same. Amber and Garrett ran off after the dogs, but Shohn hung back, still squinting. "You Casey's girlfriend?"

Casey started to reply, but Emma beat him to it. "I'm a friend and I'm a girl, so I guess you can call me a girlfriend."

"He's got a lot of girlfriends."

Emma's mouth curled. "I never doubted it for a second."

Shohn laughed, but in the next second Casey threw him over his shoulder and held him upside down. "Brat. Quit trying to scare her off or I'll have to hang you by your toes."

Casey pretended to drop him and Shohn roared with laughter. When Casey finally set him back on his feet, Shohn moved a safe distance away, posed to run, and gave a cocky smile. "If she turns you down, Case, I'll take her. She's real pretty."

Fighting a laugh, Casey feigned an attack and, like a flash, Shohn ran off to join the other kids. Casey looked at Emma and saw she wore an ear-to-ear grin, which prompted his own. So she liked kids, did she? A good thing, since there were quite a few in the family. "You're not going to turn me down, are you, sweetheart?"

Rather than answer, she said, "Gee, he reminds me of someone else I know. Now, who could it be?"

Every moment Casey spent with her canceled out the time they'd been apart. He pulled her into his side. "I was shy."

"Ha!"

"Shohn's only ten, but I swear he's girl crazy already. The little rat flirts with every female, regardless of her age. Makes Honey nuts. Dad just shakes his head." He gave Emma a squeeze. "And of course, my grandmother says he reminds her of Gabe."

Emma laughed. "Where is your grandmother?"

"She and Gabe's father, Brett, live in Florida, but they get up this way every couple of months to visit."

Because Casey was lingering in the yard, giving Emma a chance to brace herself for his family, Sawyer left the porch and headed toward them. It seemed he'd been seeing patients, given that he wore dark slacks and an open-necked button-down shirt with the sleeves rolled up. He smiled at Emma without recognition. "Hello."

He held out his hand and Emma took it. "Hello, Dr. Hudson. It's been a long time."

Cocking one eyebrow, Sawyer looked to Casey for an introduction. Casey stared at his father hard, trying to prepare him. "Dad, you remember Emma Clark."

The other eyebrow lifted to join the first. Sawyer still held her hand and now he enclosed it in both of his. If he'd been surprised, he quickly covered it up. "Emma, of course I remember you. It has been a long time. How've you been?"

"Just great." B.B. charged up next to her, with Godzilla in hot pursuit. "Casey said it was okay to let him run."

Sawyer admired the dog for a moment, then nodded. "He's fine, and obviously he doesn't mind the children."

"B.B. loves kids. He's very careful with them."

"He's a beautiful animal." Sawyer released Emma and gestured to the porch. "We were just taking a break. Would you like something to drink?"

She glanced at Casey. "We were going out on the boat..."

"There's time. I need to change anyway."

She pushed her sunglasses to the top of her head and nodded. "Then yes, thank you. I'd love to visit for a few minutes."

Casey was amazed at her. He'd expected her to be uncomfortable, maybe embarrassed. Instead, she waved to Honey, strolled right up to the porch and began greeting everyone with a new confidence that was both surprising and appealing. Any awkwardness she'd felt as a youth was long gone.

Sawyer shot Casey a look filled with questions.

"She's in town to see her father."

"The hell you say? After all this time? It's been...what? Over eight years."

"Dell's had a stroke."

"I heard." In a small town, news traveled fast. "He'll be okay?"

"Doc Wagner seemed to think so." They were still in the yard, out of earshot from the others. Casey rubbed the back of his neck, struggling with how much he wanted to say. But he'd always been able to talk to his dad and now more than ever he wanted to share his thoughts. "About when she left..."

Sawyer clasped Casey's shoulder. "I didn't think we'd ever see her again. I worried about that girl for a long time." He searched Casey's face. "I know you did too."

There was no denying that. Though he'd tried to hide it, his father knew him too well to be fooled. "You know..." He glanced up at Sawyer. "We all assumed the same things back then, with how Dell dropped her off here, and her bruised face, the way she was crying."

"But?"

"But seeing her with him today, I realized we assumed too much."

Sawyer gazed toward the porch where the women and Morgan gathered. "How's that?"

"I took her to the hospital today to visit him."

Again, Sawyer lifted his dark eyebrows. "When did she get to town?"

"Last night."

"And you're already chauffeuring her around?"

"It's not like that. We're…"

Sawyer waited.

"Hell, I don't know." He could just faintly hear Emma speaking on the porch, her tone friendly and natural. He watched her, saw the easy way she held herself, how she greeted Morgan and Misty. He shook his head. "I had a time of it, convincing her to let me hang around. She's different now, but how I feel about her is the same."

"How do you feel about her?"

Casey scowled. "I'm not sure, all right? I just… Seeing her again made me realize how much I'd missed her." He was starting to feel sixteen again, waiting for his father to give him another lecture on the importance of rubbers.

"Nothing wrong with that."

Casey shifted uncomfortably. "Her car broke down on the way into town last night. Gabe fixed it for her this morning, but she needed to visit her dad early so she could catch Dr. Wagner. I drove her, then waited around. And damn, listening to her with her father, well, things aren't as they always seemed."

"Honey is waving at us. Maybe you better catch me up later." They started toward the porch, but halfway there Sawyer asked, "Do you know what you're doing, Case?"

"Yeah." He frowned. "At least I think I do."

"Will Emma be moving back home?"

He shook his head. "She says not. She has her own business in Chicago, and some very close friends there."

"So she's only here for a spell?"

Not if he could help it. "I don't know."

"But you want her to stay?" Sawyer didn't wait for an answer. "Maybe we can help. As for her father, I'd planned to pay her folks a visit anyway, to see if there was any way I could help."

"I'll go with you when you do."

Morgan eyed them both when they finally started up the wooden porch steps. Because he'd spent some time hunting for Emma after she'd run away, Casey had no doubt he was bursting with questions. But Morgan would never deliberately make a woman uncomfortable.

Emma had already been seated in a rattan rocker across from Honey. She'd slipped her feet out of her sandals and had her toes curled against the sun-bleached boards of the porch.

Morgan said, "Why don't you take my boat. It hasn't been out in a while."

"All right." He peered at Emma, trying to read her expression. "Maybe I can talk Emma into skiing."

Emma held up her hands. "Oh no. I need to get used to the boat first before I try anything out of the boat."

Misty crossed her arms over the railing. "I finally learned how to ski, but I look pathetic when I do."

Morgan bit her ear. "You look sexy."

Rolling her eyes, Misty said, "Morgan is starting to drool, so I guess we better get going."

"A date with my wife," Morgan rumbled. "That doesn't happen very often."

Hands clasped together, forehead puckered, Emma came out of her seat. "Before you go, could I talk to you just a minute? I mean, all of you?"

Everyone stared. Casey held his breath.

Making a face, Emma said, "I'm sorry to hold you up, but since you're all here, I figured it'd be a good time to apologize." She sneaked a quick look at Casey. "And don't tell me it's not necessary, because it is to me."

"Damn it, Em…" He took a step up the porch stairs toward her.

Morgan laced his arms around Misty and pulled her back into his chest. "Well now, I suppose we've got a few minutes to spare."

Misty snorted. "And the curiosity is probably killing him."

"Casey's right." Honey leaned forward in her chair. "You don't owe us anything at all. But if you want to talk…"

With his hand on the back of Honey's chair, Sawyer said, "I'm curious too. Where'd you go the night you ran off?"

Casey glowered at his family. He thought about just flinging Emma over his shoulder, as he'd done to Shohn, and carrying her off. But that'd probably shoot any chance he had of getting on her good side. He could tell this was important to her, so he locked his jaw and waited.

Emma turned to Morgan first. "My father told me that you looked for me after I took off. I'm sorry that I put you to that trouble by not explaining better when I left, and I'm especially sorry that any of you worried about me. Kids do dumb things, and that night it didn't occur to me that any of you might worry."

Because no one had ever worried about her before? Casey didn't like that probability, but he knew it was likely true.

She turned to Sawyer next. "I never dreamed that you'd actually look for me."

"We just wanted to know for certain that you were okay."

Honey agreed with her husband. "You were awfully young to go off on your own."

"I know. And I appreciate your concern." Her cheeks dimpled with her smile. "It's why I came here that night, because I knew you'd be nice and that you'd understand. I'm sorry I took advantage of you."

"Enough apologies," Misty said. "Morgan likes to fret—it's why he's a sheriff—and Sawyer's no better. They're both mother hens. Obviously you and Casey have made up now, so all's well that ends well."

Casey took that as his cue to move to her side. Without confirming or denying Misty's statement, Emma said, "Thank you."

But Morgan wasn't ready to let it go. "So where'd you disappear to?"

Misty gave him a frown, which he ignored.

"Chicago. I met some very nice people who helped me figure out what I wanted to do. I finished up school and started my own business. Things have been great."

Bemused, Casey could only stare at her. If he hadn't heard the full story—or rather, a less condensed version—he would have believed her life to be a bed of roses. Damn, she was good at covering up. He'd have to remember that.

"What kind of business do you have?" Honey asked.

"Massage therapy. I have my own small studio."

"Ohmigod," Misty enthused. "I know women in town who drive weekly into Florence for a massage. They'll be all over you if they find out."

"Not that Misty needs to leave home for that sort of thing," Morgan stated, while rubbing her shoulders. Misty just smiled.

"Are you going to be in town long?" Honey asked.

"I'm not sure yet."

Casey caught her hand and laced his fingers with hers. He didn't want to hear about her leaving when she'd only just come home. "We have to get going."

"I thought you wanted to change."

"I will, but I figured we'd swing into the apartment on our way down to the lake." The house overlooked the lake, and from the back, it wasn't too far to walk to reach the shore. Casey's apartment above the garage was on the way, so he decided to just drag Emma along with him. The quicker he got her alone, the better.

"All right." Emma finished off her glass of tea. After slipping her sandals back on, she thanked Honey again.

"Will you be back in time for lunch?" Honey wanted to know.

If things worked out as he hoped, they'd spend the rest of the day together. "We'll grab something on the lake, but thanks." Casey hugged the women, said farewell to the men, and led Emma back to the car so she could get her satchel. They went around the side of the house to the garage apartment. Before Emma could call B.B., he fell into step beside her, along with all the kids. The dog almost looked to be laughing, he'd had such a good time.

"Where ya going?" Garrett asked.

Ruffling his hair, Emma said, "Casey is taking me boating."

Shohn perked up. "How about tubin' us, Case?"

Emma looked at Casey in question. She remembered tubing, Casey was sure. At one time or another, just about everyone on the lake had been bounced around on a fat black inner tube, tied with a ski rope and pulled behind the boat. It proved a bruising ride, one guaranteed to get water up your nose and make your body ache. Kids loved it, but most adults had more sense.

Likely Emma's questioning look meant it was up to him whether or not to include the kids.

He voted *not*. Casey wanted to grab Emma and run like hell. Instead, he told Shohn, "How about we save that for another day? Emma hasn't been home in a long time and I want to let her enjoy the ride, not scare her to death with your daredevil antics."

The boys looked downcast, making Casey feel guilty. Then Amber, the oldest of the bunch at a not-quite-mature eleven, elbowed them both. "You can go tubing anytime, dummy. Case has a date."

Shohn slanted a leering look at Casey and grinned like a possum, but Garrett shrugged. "So?"

"So he wants to kiss her. Don't ya, Case?" Shohn made smooching noises while pretending to hold a swooning female.

Emma surprised him yet again by snatching Shohn up close and kissing his cheek and neck until he screamed uncle. Everyone was laughing, Garrett pointing at Shohn, and B.B. jumping around in glee. Amber looked up at

Casey, her dark-blue eyes twinkling with enjoyment. He hugged his niece, unable to stop smiling. Damn, having Emma around was nice. Without even trying, she fit in—into Buckhorn, into his family. Into his heart.

Emma sat down on the bottom step leading up to the rooms over the garage. Casey smoothed his hand over her head. "I'll go change and be right back."

Panting, Shohn sprawled backward across her lap like a sacrifice, his arms spread out, his head almost touching the ground. "Take your time, brother. Take your time."

Emma laughed too hard to answer Casey, but Amber followed him up the steps and through the front door. She helped herself to a drink of water, then flounced onto his sofa while Casey went into the bedroom to change into his trunks.

"I like her," Amber announced, saying it loud so Casey would be sure to hear.

"Me too," Casey called out to her.

"You gonna keep this one?"

Inside his room, Casey chuckled. He remained endlessly amazed at how different his nieces were from the boys. The girls got together and planned, while the boys got together and scuffled. Occasionally the differences were less noticeable, like on holidays when they were all wild little monkeys, but overall the girls were more mature. "She has some say-so in that, you know."

"Daddy doesn't give Mom much say-so. He just picks her up and totes her wherever he wants her to go."

That picture brought about a laugh. Morgan did seem fond of hauling Misty around. 'Course, he'd seen his father toting Honey a time or two as well—whenever she'd fallen asleep on the couch, and several times when his dad had that certain look, which prompted Casey to give them immediate privacy. In Gabe's case, it was as often as not Elizabeth who was dragging Gabe off to bed. Jordan, however, was more subtle. He and Georgia connected with scorching looks that no one could misunderstand.

Casey finished changing into cutoff jeans, an unbuttoned, short-sleeve shirt and ratty sneakers. He snagged a beach towel and rejoined Amber. "Your mom lets Morgan get away with that because she likes it."

Amber sighed theatrically. "I know. Daddy says Mom has him wrapped around her little finger."

"Your mom and you both." Casey held his hand out for her and said, "Let's go before she runs off with Shohn instead."

"Yeah right." Amber slipped her small hand into his. "She's probably already in love with you. All the women act stupid around you."

Casey's heart jumped at that "L" word, but he said only, "You think Emma acts stupid?"

"No, silly. That's why I think you should keep her."

When they went back down the steps, they found Emma doing tricks with B.B. She threw a stick and he caught it in midair, then brought it back to her. She told him to roll over, to speak, to shake hands. The boys were suitably impressed with his every feat.

Without even thinking about it, Casey looped his arms around Emma from behind and kissed her ear. The kids all stared wide-eyed. "If you think her dog is neat, you should see her car."

That refocused the boys' attention.

"Is it as cool as your car?"

"What color is it?"

Teasing, Emma said, "It's better than his car."

Casey raised an eyebrow, but agreed. "Definitely. We both have Mustangs, but Emma's is a cherry-red classic. You know what that means?"

Garrett nodded. "It's old."

"But in great condition."

Frowning, Garrett said, "I'd rather have a new one."

"That's only because you haven't seen it yet," Emma assured him.

Casey gave her a squeeze. "How about we bring the car by here tomorrow and you rats can look it over?"

"Will you stay for dinner?" Amber asked, and even to Casey, who knew her private agenda, Amber looked like innocence personified.

Shohn aimed a thumb at his chest. "You could go out in the boat with us so I can show you how good I ski."

Emma stiffened with alarm, though why the idea of spending time with his family bothered her, he had no clue. She liked the kids, he could tell that much. And she'd been totally at ease even while apologizing and explaining to Morgan, Misty, Honey and his dad.

He let her push out of his hold and move a few steps away.

She turned to face him, saying, "I might already have plans…" But the words trailed off as she got a look at his naked chest. When a breeze blew by, parting the shirt a little more, Emma's mouth fell open, her eyes flared.

Satisfaction built within him.

Well now, that was nice. He was comfortable in his own skin, so casual around the lake he hadn't really thought about her seeing him when he yanked on the shirt. But Emma seemed to appreciate it. Once he got her on the boat, he'd lose the shirt and encourage her to lose the cover-up. He'd get her in the cove and hold her close, skin to skin...

Like perfect little strategists, the kids started begging Emma to return for dinner. Casey decided he would take them tubing—and soon. They deserved it.

He reached out and tugged on a lock of Emma's hair, then mimicked the kids. "Please?"

She swallowed, closed her mouth, and raised her eyes to his. "I'll try." Her smile was staged. "But I'll probably have to bring Damon along."

Casey groaned, grabbed his heart as if he'd been shot, and stumbled into Amber, who laughed while trying to hold him up.

"Who," she demanded around her smile, "is this Damon person?"

Casey straightened. He hugged Amber, then kissed her little turned-up nose. "He's no one important, sweetheart. Just Emma's friend. And if he comes to dinner with us, why then you can all show him how to catch tadpoles and crawdads on the shore, okay?"

Amber's small face brightened in understanding, and she gave Casey a conspiratorial wink. "Okay, Casey. That sounds like fun." She encompassed the boys in a look, and added, "It'll probably take him a long time to get the hang of it, but we'll be patient—even if it takes hours."

chapter 10

EMMA TRAILED her fingers in the cold water. She loved the sights, sounds and smells of being on the lake, but it all faded away with Casey so near. It wasn't easy keeping her gaze off him. In fact, it proved impossible.

But Lord have mercy, he looked good. He now wore only low-riding cutoffs and he was perched on the driver's seat at the back of the boat, steering one-handed while the wind blew his dark-blond hair and the sun reflected off his smooth, tanned shoulders and the firm expanse of his broad back. He had one muscular, hairy leg braced on the deck of the boat, the other in the seat. She let her eyes follow the line of his spine all the way to the waistband of those shorts...

She jerked her gaze away. Staring at Casey's muscled backside would not help her get it together. The air was hot, but it didn't compare to what she felt on the inside. Casey had matured in ways she hadn't counted on. His body had always been lean and strong, but now he had filled out and his strength was obvious in the flex of muscles in his upper arms, across his chest and shoulders. He wasn't a hulk like Morgan, just nicely defined and very macho.

He was hairier than she remembered too. Not too much, but there was a sexy sprinkling of dark-brown hair on his chest that faded to a thin line toward his navel, then a silkier line still down his belly—and behind his fly.

Emma breathed too deeply, imagined too much, but she wanted to touch him, kiss him.

When they'd first gotten in the boat, B.B. had demanded all her attention. He'd tottered back and forth, looking out one side of the boat then the other, constantly whining. He didn't like the way the boat moved and kept him unsteady. But within ten minutes, he'd settled down and now he watched out the back, his body braced against the casing for the inboard motor. His tongue hung out the side of his mouth and his furry face held an expression of excitement.

Emma had been smiling over that when Casey casually pulled off his shirt and stowed it in the side of the boat. While she ogled him, he suggested she remove her cover-up. She'd declined, and had been trying not to stare at him, without much success, ever since.

The lake was crowded with boats everywhere, more so than she remembered it being in the past. At first Casey had driven at breakneck speed, cutting across the wakes of other boats, bouncing over choppy waves, causing the water to spray into the boat and making her laugh. He'd gradually slowed and moved closer to the shoreline so that now they glided through the water, watchful of skiers and swimmers and noisy Jet Skis.

A flashy cabin cruiser filled with sun worshipers zipped up alongside them. Lounged around the boat, three men and three women waved, prompting Casey to return the greeting.

Emma saw his friendly smile, the way his raised arm showed a tuft of dark hair beneath, how his biceps bulged. She also saw how the women coveted Casey with open admiration, while the men leered at her. She didn't know if anyone recognized her, and she didn't stare back long enough to recognize anyone herself, but before the day was over, his friends would be talking. She hated that, but had no idea how to avoid it. Whether it was fair or not, she *did* have a reputation, and yet Casey was determined to be seen with her.

Her thoughts scattered as he steered the boat into a deep cove at the far end of the long lake, away from the congestion. He didn't bother to speak over the roar of the motor, but every so often she felt the intensity of his gaze settle on her. Little by little he slowed until the motor only purred and the ride was easy and smooth, just gliding through the water.

By the time they were out of sight from prying eyes, she couldn't hold back any longer and moved to the seat behind him.

Casey twisted his head toward her. He wore dark reflective sunglasses, but she could tell by the set of his mouth, the slight flare of his nostrils, that his mind had centered on the very same thoughts.

Without saying a word, Emma knelt on the seat and settled both palms on his bare shoulders, smoothing her hands down to his shoulder blades, then to his sides in a deep, sensual massage. Hot. Taut. Silky-smooth flesh over hard muscle.

Casey went still except for the expanding of his chest and back with each deep breath he took. She loved touching him, stroking him. "Emma..." he said, half in pleasure, half in warning. "Damn, you are good."

She leaned forward and pressed her open mouth to the

spot where his shoulder melded into his neck. She breathed his heated scent while rubbing deeply at muscles, relaxing him and exciting him at the same time. "You're the most beautiful man I've ever seen."

He shuddered and reached back for her hand, then drew it forward to his mouth to kiss her knuckles. He held her that way, with one arm draped around his neck, her breasts flattened on his back. She put her cheek on his shoulder and hugged him. Strangely enough, she felt both content and turbulent.

"I want to show you something, okay?"

So overwhelmed with sensation, Emma could barely speak. She nodded.

He slowed the boat even more to drift into dark green, shallow water riddled with sunken tree limbs and covered with moss. This finger of the cove was narrow, barely big enough for a boat to turn around. Emma worried for the boat's prop, but figured Casey knew what he was doing.

That thought was confirmed when she spotted a skinny weathered dock with uneven boards at the very tip of the cove. It had old tires nailed to the side to protect the boat, with grommets for a tie-up. Casey brought the boat up alongside it, turned off the engine and secured it with the ease of long practice.

Enormous elms grew along all sides of the shoreline, with branches reaching far out across the water to form a canopy over the cove. She could hear the croak of frogs, the splash of carp, the chirp of katydids. The air smelled thick with all the greenery.

Casey brought her around next to him. Every line of his body was drawn tight. "You like it?"

"It's incredible."

"I bought it. There're two acres, and the little cabin up the hill." He didn't look away from her as he explained that. "More like a shack, really. But it's secluded and peaceful."

Emma slipped off her sunglasses to peer into the surrounding woods. Sure enough, halfway up the hill a small house was just barely visible through the thick trees and scrubby shrubs. Like the dock, it was constructed of weathered wooden planks and consisted mostly of a sloping screened-in front porch. A skinny dirt path led down to the dock.

She gazed up at the tall trees, blocking all but a few rays of sunshine, then she listened to the quiet. Her tone low in near reverence, she whispered, "It's almost magical."

B.B. whined, then leaped nimbly from the boat to the dock. He started sniffing, working his way to the shore.

Still staring at her, Casey asked, "Will he be okay?"

Emma nodded. "He won't take off. He just wants to explore the area."

"If he goes too far, he'll find a few cows on the adjoining farm. But that's it. For all intents and purposes, we're alone here."

He touched the zipper of her cover-up, right between her breasts, with one finger. His dark glasses still in place, his voice a low murmur, he said, "Let's lose this now, okay?"

Trembling from the inside out, Emma nodded. "All right." Uncertainty made her feel clumsy. She wasn't shy, really, but it had been a long time since she'd experienced the freedom of the lake. Everyone everywhere wore little more than a suit, some skimpier than others. In compari-

son, hers was modest, concealing as much as a regular bra
and panties might.

But that wasn't the point. She knew Casey would touch
her, knew he wanted to have sex with her, and the very idea
of it had her near to moaning. She kept her attention on
Casey's chest, instead of his face, and dragged the zipper all
the way down. She stood in front of him, while he sat in the
driver's seat, his face level with her breasts, his knees open
around her legs.

With an absorption that shook her, Casey set his sunglasses
aside, reached out and caught the top of the terry cloth and
tugged it slowly down her arms. Amber eyes took in the sight
of her body as he dropped the cover-up on the seat behind her.

Leaves rustled overhead. Water lapped at the shore. A
bird chirped. Neither of them spoke.

Casey wrapped his hands around the backs of her thighs,
making Emma quiver. He stroked her, sliding his palms
slowly and deliberately up over her hips to her waist where
his thumbs dipped in near her navel, back and forth across
her belly. He watched the movement of his fingers, then
leaned forward and pressed an openmouthed kiss to the rise
of one breast, another in her cleavage, lower, on her ribs.

Shaking under the sensual onslaught, Emma braced her
hands against his shoulders. "Casey…"

"It seemed like you were gone forever, but now that
you're back, it's like you never left." He licked her navel,
took a gentle love bite of her belly. In a gravelly voice, he
rasped, "This has been a long time coming."

Closing her eyes, Emma tunneled her fingers through his
thick, warm hair. She stroked his nape, then pulled him
closer. "Yes."

His hands moved back down her body to her bottom. He kneaded her, groaned, closed his mouth around her nipple through the bathing-suit bra. She felt the press of his hot tongue.

"Casey."

In the next instant, he stood and Emma found herself flush against him, his mouth on hers, his tongue sinking deep. He pressed his rigid erection into her belly, his breathing labored, his hands trembling as he touched her everywhere with a gentleness that bordered on awe.

He lifted his mouth and looked at her. The heat in his eyes stole her breath, then he kissed her again, easy, slow. Against her mouth, he said, "Emma, honey, as gorgeous as you are in that suit, all I can think about now is getting you out of it."

Emma looked around the area, which was deserted but still out in the open. "It…it's been a long time since I made out in a cove…"

"Don't." Casey's hands tightened on her and he squeezed his eyes shut. Three deep breaths later, he got control of himself. Despite his obvious turmoil, he cradled her close and spoke quietly near her ear. "I'm talking about making love, not making out. And I thought we'd go up to the cabin. It's clean, and no one ever comes here." He opened his mouth on her neck, pressed his tongue to her wildly thrumming pulse. He groaned again. "I need a long time, Emma. Hours. Days." Her heart thundered, and she heard him barely whisper, "A lifetime."

Her knees nearly buckled. But men often said things they didn't mean when they were aroused. She had to remember that so she didn't set herself up for disappointment.

Flattening her hands on Casey's chest, she levered him back, smiled and said with absolute certainty, "Yes."

B.B. FOLLOWED THEM up the hill and into the enclosed front porch. The dark screening kept bugs out and shaded the room, but let in the fresh air. With the small house buried in the dense woods, it was cool and smelled a little earthy.

The dog did a quick reconnaissance of the area, sniffing everything, pushing his nose into every corner. He decided it bored him, and went back out through the screen door into the yard. They watched him as he wandered down to the dock, found a heated spot beneath a ray of sun. He turned around, circled and dropped.

Emma smiled. "He's so lazy," she said, her voice sounding thick.

Suffering the most raging case of lust he'd ever known, Casey seated himself on the side of the twin-size bed. The white cotton sheets were rumpled and the pillows still bore the imprint of his head from his last retreat three days ago. Then, he'd been considering his life, his future, what he wanted to do. There'd been many decisions to make.

Now all other concerns were pushed aside in his need to have Emma. Again, he clasped her hips and looked at her adorable belly, the way her bra lifted her breasts, how the waistband of the bottoms stretched across her hipbones. The bikini was nearly the same color as her skin, but nowhere near as soft.

"I put the bed in here when I bought the place. It's great for napping, and I like to come here and think."

As bold as ever, Emma straddled his lap, then settled

onto him, groin to groin, belly to belly, breasts to chest. Her eyes were heavy, her face flushed, her lips parted. She touched his jaw with her fingertips while staring at his mouth. "What do you think about, Casey?"

You, he started to say, but caught himself. Damn, she looked ready. But he wanted to go slow, to make it last. He pushed his hands into her bottoms, cuddled her firm cheeks and rested his face against her breasts. "Work. Life. Hell, I dunno." He'd often thought about her, wondering where she was and what she was doing. "I just like kicking back here, getting away from everyone."

Emma nuzzled against his ear. "Do you bring women here for sex?"

He jerked back, offended and annoyed. "Only you, Emma."

Her big brown eyes darkened, and turned velvet with emotion.

Without even trying, she twisted him inside out. "Kiss me, Em."

She did, and damn, she knew how to kiss. Her enthusiasm singed him and left him so primed it was a wonder he didn't slide her beneath him right now.

Patience, he reminded himself. He wanted more than one quick fuck. He wanted… Hell, he didn't know everything he wanted. But he wanted more. Of her. Of this.

Her bra ties slid free easily enough, yet the closeness of their bodies kept it in place. Casey clasped her shoulders and held her away from him. The cups dropped away from her breasts and Emma, while smiling at him, removed the top completely.

Beautiful. Casey held her steady as he leaned forward and

closed his mouth around her left nipple. Her body flexed the tiniest bit in reaction and she made a sound between a groan and a purr.

He locked his arms around the small of her back to keep her from retreating as he feasted upon her. He took his time, loving the taste and texture of her, the small sounds she made. When her nipple was tightly beaded, he switched to her other breast.

At first, the gentle rocking of her body didn't register. When it did, Casey had to look at her. With her head tipped back, her lips parted, her fingers caught in his hair, she epitomized female abandon.

Using his teeth with devastating effect, he further taunted her nipple, until she whispered, "Casey, *please...*"

He shuddered in reaction. "I love hearing you say my name." He couldn't wait any longer. Lifting her to her feet, he quickly finished stripping her. She didn't say a word when he hooked his fingers in the waistband of her bottoms and skimmed them down her legs. She stepped out of the material, he set them aside, and they both went silent.

So often in his dreams, he'd imagined having Emma just like this.

She stood there with her belly pulled tight, her nipples wet from his mouth. His to take. Casey drew a heated breath—and knew he was falling hard all over again.

It should have bothered him. Emma had walked out on him once; she kept secrets from him still. She'd only been back in town for a day and had definite plans for taking off again. But, at the moment, none of that mattered.

Keeping his eyes on the neat triangle of pubic hair between her legs, he unsnapped his shorts and shoved them down, removing his boxers at the same time. He kicked them aside on the dusty porch floor. He knew Emma was staring at his erection. He locked his knees and let her look her fill, but it wasn't easy when his every muscle strained against the need to hold her again.

In a breathless whisper, she said, "I hope I'm not dreaming."

That made him smile and relieved some of his tension. "Come here, and I'll make sure you're awake." The words were barely out of his mouth and Emma was there, her small hands sliding up and over his chest to twine around his neck, her belly pressing into his groin, her mouth turned up for his. She showed no reserve, no hesitation. And the kiss she gave him left him shaking.

Hoping to slow her down, he lowered them both to the bed and moved to her side. The urge to climb on top of her and sink deep into her body was already strong. With her encouraging murmurs and touches, holding back was hell. But he'd been waiting for over eight years so what did a few more minutes matter?

And he had been waiting, he knew that now. The dissatisfaction he'd felt with every female since Emma now made sense. They'd been lacking simply because they weren't Emma. She was special in ways he hadn't realized.

Propping himself up on his elbow, Casey stared down at her.

She shifted, trying to bring him back to her, flesh to flesh. "Casey?"

"Shh." Fingers spread wide, he settled his hand on her belly and felt her muscles contract. "I love just looking at you, Emma."

Her velvety brown eyes, so hungry, so hot, held his as she

caught his wrist and urged his hand lower, between her parted thighs. She started at the first touch of his fingers there, moaning softly, her breath hitching.

Watching her face, Casey gently opened her with his fingertips, stroked over her swollen vulva, her clitoris. She was wet, hot. His own heartbeat roared in his ears.

As he teased, her back arched off the mattress, making her breasts an offering. He dipped down to gently suck on her nipples at the same time he sank his middle finger deep. Her reaction was startling—and damn exciting. Inner muscles clenched tight around his finger, her body shivered, her legs stiffened.

"Casey." So much pleading in one small word. Hell yes, he loved hearing his name, especially the way she said it now, with all the same need he felt.

A rosy flush covered her body, warming her skin and intensifying her luscious scent. Casey took his time suckling her, fingering her, enjoying her. Perversely, the more frantic Emma became, the more she moaned and writhed and pleaded, the more determined he was to take his time, to leisurely make her crazy with lust. And to prove to her that she couldn't feel this with any man other than him.

She was so easy to read, not because her hands clenched fitfully in his hair and her broken moans were so explicit. Not because her hips rocked against his hand, faster, harder. But because he knew this one particular woman better than any other. It seemed he always had. And he knew he always would.

He felt her begin to tremble, felt the stillness that signaled the onset of her release, and he surged up from her breasts to take her mouth in a voracious, claiming kiss.

Goddammit, she was his. She'd always been his. She...

The clench of her nails on his shoulders shattered his thoughts and warned of her release. Heart ready to explode, he rode out the climax with her, kissing her face, murmuring to her, maintaining the steady press and stroke of his rough fingertips between her thighs until she finally pulled her mouth away to gulp frantically for air. She took her pleasure as naturally as a woman should—relishing it, giving in to it.

"Oh God," she groaned as she slumped back into the mattress, still breathing too hard, still shivering. Her eyes were slumberous, heated. Damp with tears.

He wanted more.

He needed it all.

Casey came to his knees to look over her temporarily sated body—temporary, because no way in hell was he done with her. He touched her everywhere, parting her legs wider, stroking her with both hands, catching her already sensitive nipples. He luxuriated in the feel of her warm, soft flesh in places that he'd once considered forbidden to him.

"You care about me, Emma. It's still there—whatever it is between us."

Her eyes were closed, her face turned slightly away. She nodded, sniffed, and more tears seeped out around her thick lashes.

Frowning, Casey trailed his fingers down her body, over her belly, through her pubic hair and between her lips. She was creamy wet now, swollen, throbbing. He watched her eyes open…and thrust three fingers into her hard.

She cried out softly, twisting on the sheets.

"Admit it, Em. Say it." He waited, but she stared at him with that lost expression that had the ability to rip him apart. His teeth clenched. "Tell me it's still there. *Tell me you care about me.*"

She swallowed hard and offered up a small, shaky smile. Looking more vulnerable than any woman ever should, she whispered, "Always, Casey." Her voice broke, and she laid one palm over his heart. "Always."

A tidal wave of feelings took his breath. He couldn't wait a second more. He snagged the condom from his shorts pocket and rolled it on in record time. Emma waited until he started to settle over her, then she rose up and pushed him to his back. Eyes still glistening with tears, that small secret smile still in place, she stared into his eyes. "It's my turn."

Casey groaned. That husky purr of hers would be the death of him. His muscles cramped when she wrapped both hands around his erection and stroked, slow, easy. Again and again.

He was still trying to get himself under control when she lifted herself over him, positioned him against her tender sex, and sank down so languidly he nearly lost it there and then.

"Emma..." His awareness of her was so heightened, he felt everything, every tiny movement and touch. Like the press of her smooth legs around his hips, and her buttocks on his thighs. The way her hands contracted on his chest and how her body squeezed him with each retreat, then softened around him as she sank down again.

Her breasts swayed, drawing his hands, then his mouth. Much as he enjoyed seeing her astride him, she was too far away. Craving the touch of her body to his, Casey sat up and pulled her closer so he could reach all of her, her slim back, the luscious flare of her hips and the firm resilience of her ass cheeks. He kissed her, keeping her mouth under his even as he felt his testicles tightening with his climax.

As she wrapped her legs completely around him, Emma never missed a beat, rising and falling, rising again. She didn't let him hold back, didn't give him a chance to regain control. When he came, she took his harsh groans into her mouth and gave back her own sweet sounds of release. Their bodies strained, clung, and then shuddered roughly. Her arms wrapped around his neck, Emma leaned into him.

Casey felt her heartbeat rioting against his jaw and he pressed a kiss to her breast. Emma's fingers stroked idly through his hair, petting him, hugging him tight every couple of seconds. The contentment lasted for long minutes. He felt at peace, whole in a way that had eluded him until now.

But with the edge taken off his hunger, Casey knew he had to tend to other things. He mentally braced himself, then carefully stretched out on the bed with Emma resting over his chest.

He was still inside her when he kissed her temple and said, "Now we talk."

"Mmm." She toyed with his chest hair, and Casey could hear the sleepiness in her voice, reminding him once again that she was short on rest, heavy on worries. "About what?"

Staring at the warped boards in the ceiling, Casey tightened his arms around her back so she couldn't run from him. "About you." He kept his tone calm, firm. "About what happened that night you came to my house."

She stiffened in alarm, but he couldn't relent. This was too important. She tried to struggle away from him but he stroked her, hoping to soothe her, to offer reassurance.

"Casey…"

He held her close to his heart. "I want to talk about your mother."

"No."

"Yes."

She lifted her face so he could see her disgruntled frown. Casey smoothed her tangled hair back and studied her taut expression. He touched the corner of her mouth with his thumb, and said, "She's a drunk, isn't she, Emma?"

DAMON SMILED at the picture Ceily made in her sundress and sandals. Given the understated outfit, she should have looked innocent. Instead, she looked hot. Tantalizing. Like a wet dream.

He knew women well enough to know she'd spent extra time preparing for him. It showed in the carefully applied makeup, the subtle sexiness of her clothes.

She'd spent the last hour showing him around Buckhorn, not that there was that much to see other than the beautiful scenery. They'd had ice cream, and watching Ceily lick a cone was a special form of foreplay he wasn't likely to forget anytime soon. Damon was sure it had been deliberate. And it had worked.

He'd barely been able to take his gaze off her as they'd waved to a hundred of her "close friends" and browsed the one and only gift shop.

After showing him all the landmarks, she'd driven her small compact to the outskirts of town, parked near a pasture and gotten out. Carrying a small cooler of drinks and with a plaid blanket over his arm, Damon followed her. He had to be careful of cowpatties, a unique concern that.

He wasn't quite sure where Ceily was leading him, but he gladly followed. Walking behind her, taking in the sway of her lush hips, certainly wasn't a hardship.

The humid breeze ruffled her hair and played with her skirt when she twisted to look at him over her shoulder. "There's a beautiful creek right down here."

The entire area looked splendid—the perfect place to build some small vacation cabins or retirement homes. "Is this your property?"

"No, it belongs to my grandpa."

He wondered if her grandpa would be willing to sell. "You've lived here your whole life?"

"Yep." She stopped in front of a crystal-clear creek filled with churning water. The sound alone could mesmerize, but with the wildflowers here and there, birds circling and Ceily close by, it was outright magnificent.

Damon spread the blanket and watched her settle onto it. Ceily wasn't an introverted or uncertain woman. She had a teasing, confident presence that aroused him.

He dropped next to her and slanted her a teasing look. "If I get too hot, do you intend to throw me into the creek?"

Utilizing considerable thought, she plucked a long blade of grass. "I thought we might both cool off when the sun sets."

Damon arched an eyebrow. "Skinny-dipping?"

Her mouth curled while she positioned the blade of grass between her thumbs. "I bet you're a virgin, huh?"

"Was it my uncommon restraint that led you to that conclusion?"

Laughing, she said, "I mean a virgin to skinny-dipping. Somehow I can't see you frolicking outdoors in the buff."

Damon rested back on one elbow. "I'm always up for new experiences, especially when they're initiated by a beautiful woman."

He jumped when she raised both hands to her mouth,

the blade of grass somehow caught between, and gave an earsplitting whistle. When she looked at him for approval, he asked, "Is that how country girls whistle?"

Pushing her hair behind her ear, Ceily nodded. She didn't quite look at him when she idly tossed out, "Wanna see how country girls kiss?"

Feeling a curl of heat, Damon murmured, "That's a dumb question for such a smart girl."

She laughed and came down over his chest, knocking him flat. "I like you, Damon."

"Is that so?" He smiled, enjoying her silly banter. "Show me."

"All right." Her eyebrows lowered. "But I should warn you first that I don't sleep with a guy on the first date."

"Pity." Did she expect him to start complaining? He held his grin back with an effort, ready to disappoint her. He liked Ceily, and he appreciated her honesty. He held her hair away from her face and brushed his lips over her chin, her throat.

"You're not mad?"

"That you've been teasing me? No. I happen to be enjoying your efforts."

"Unbelievable."

Feeling smug, he grinned at her, knowing he had just surprised her. "So how many dates will it take me?"

She stared deep into his eyes, lowered her mouth to his and groaned. "Let's play it by ear."

The second her mouth touched his, Damon was lost. Damn, she was sweet, and yet she was also brazen. A delicious combination.

Slowly the kiss ended. Ceily licked her lips, sighed and

rested her head on his chest. "Want me to teach you how to whistle like that?"

Damon was in the most powerful throes of lust he'd felt in years, and she wanted to teach him how to whistle. He laughed, liking the novelty of it, liking her more by the moment. "That's exactly what I was thinking about. Whistling. And with a blade of grass, no less."

She poked him in the ribs. "Liar."

He tightened his arms around her so she couldn't prod him again. "At the risk of sounding trite, what's a smart girl like you doing in Buckhorn?" Damon could easily picture her in the city, charming one and all.

She pushed up to see his face. "This is home. Where else would I be?"

The way she said it, he felt foolish for asking. Though he'd come with a distinct sense of contempt for the town that had ostracized Emma, Buckhorn had managed to charm him as well. The relaxed air, the openness, the sense of being where you belonged, fed something in his soul. The idea of settling here teased at him. "Your grandfather own a lot of land?"

Her sigh held a wealth of melancholy. "He does, but soon he'll have to sell a major portion of it, including this spot, which is one reason I brought you here. I don't know how much longer I'll get to enjoy it."

"Is he selling to developers?"

"He doesn't want to. But he needs the money, so…" She shrugged.

A variety of emotions clamored for attention. Damon hated that Ceily would lose something important to her, but at the same time his mind already churned with the possibilities. It would be an insult to the land to clutter it with shopping centers or parking lots, but a few cozy cabins spaced out along the creek…well, it'd be lovely. And lucrative.

He couldn't think about purchasing the land without thinking about Ceily as well. She was in her mid-thirties, single, which prompted another question. "Okay, so why isn't a warm, sexy woman like you married?"

Her cheeks dimpled with a smile. "I suppose I have high standards, and all the best men were taken."

"And those standards are…?"

"Mmm. Let's see." Somehow, her hand on his chest just happened to be over his left nipple. If she stroked him one more time, he was going to have to jump into the icy creek on his own volition. "He'd need to be caring, like Sawyer Hudson."

A dark cloud intruded on his contentment. "Case Hudson's father?"

"Yep. Sawyer is a local doctor and everyone in these parts loves him. He's almost perfect, but I'd want someone to be bold and vigilant too, like his brother, Morgan. He's the sheriff."

Damon saw a definite pattern beginning. "For crying out—"

"And gentle like his brother Jordan, handy like Gabe…"

"Enough." Damon rolled her beneath him. In a growl, he said, "I think you're teasing me again."

She laughed up at him, proving him right. "Maybe. But I've always been a *little* in love with each of them." Her gaze moved over his mouth and she added gently, "No one else ever quite measures up."

Damon's eyebrows lifted. "By God, that sounds like a challenge."

She looped her arms around his neck. "Does it?"

Damon had the feeling she knew exactly what she was doing. Never in his life had he felt the need to compete for a woman, and he wasn't about to start the barbaric ritual now. Despite those assurances to himself, he tangled his hand in her hair, tipped her mouth up to his and said, "I don't want to hear you say their names again."

"But—"

He kissed her, not just a kiss, but full-body contact, heartbeat to heartbeat, and long minutes later when he felt her thigh slide up along the outside of his, he lifted his head. Her lips were wet, her eyes smoky.

Satisfied, Damon pried himself away from her and stood. "Now," he said, while trying to subtly readjust himself, "about that dip in the creek…"

chapter 11

EMMA GAVE UP TRYING to get away from Casey. Oh, if she flat out told him to release her, he would. But then he'd wonder at her overreaction, especially in light of what they'd just shared. She didn't want to give away more than necessary.

She settled back against him—a most comfortable place to be—and made her tone as unaffected as possible. Despite her wariness in discussing her problems with him, she felt mellow and sated and emotionally full.

She kissed his chest and asked, "Why do you want to know?"

"I want to know everything about you. When we were younger I was so busy trying to resist you, I never thought to ask some important questions." He patted her behind. "It took all my willpower and concentration to say no."

She smiled.

Casey relaxed his hold to stroke her back. "I always assumed that your dad mistreated you. Did you know that?"

A logical assumption, she supposed, but mostly untrue. "No, my dad never physically hurt me."

"Okay, not physically." He'd caught her small clarification and asked for one of his own. "But he did hurt you, didn't he, by not putting you first, as all parents should?"

Perhaps, Emma was thinking, she should tell him some of it. It would help to show the broad contrasts in their lives and make him understand why she couldn't stay in Buckhorn. It wouldn't be easy for him to understand because Casey had always known love, always had security. Could he even comprehend what her life had been like?

But she'd taken too long to answer him. He turned to his side so that Emma faced him. With a tenderness that felt *almost* like love, he tipped up her chin and kissed her nose. "Trust me, Em."

"I do. I was just trying to figure out how to say it, where to begin."

"Your mother is a drunk?"

"For as far back as I can remember. All our holidays and special occasions were tainted because she'd drink too much, and once she started, she'd keep drinking for days, and then need more days to recover." Somehow, telling Casey about her darkest secrets wasn't as bad as she'd anticipated. He held her, warm and strong, and it made it so much easier. "She got to where she didn't need a reason to drink. She'd just decide to and the times between episodes narrowed until she was drinking almost as often as not." Emma took comfort in the steady thumping of his heart and admitted, "She's not a nice drunk."

Casey's eyes were steady on her face, not giving her a chance to retreat emotionally or hold anything back. "She got violent?"

"Sometimes." That was so awful to admit, Emma immediately tried to explain. "Her judgment was off when she drank. She'd take everything wrong, no matter what you said or what you did. And she'd get furious."

Casey muttered a low curse and gathered her closer.

"It's all right." Emma gave him one truth that she'd learned long ago. "Being hit wasn't the worst part of it."

"No?" He drew a shuddering breath, and his voice sounded raw. "What was the worst part?"

She shrugged. "Being afraid. Not knowing when it would happen, not knowing what to expect or when. I hated walking on eggshells, always being so uncertain."

She'd never talked about her mother with anyone, and now she found there were things about her mother's illness that she wanted to say. "You know what? It was strange, but I got to where I could figure out when she'd drink just from the anticipation in her voice. Or her tone. Something about her mannerisms. I could even talk to her on the phone and I'd hear it and...I didn't want to go home."

Breathing too hard, Casey kissed her temple, her ear. She felt his grim resolve to hear it all, so she continued.

"It might have been a week or a month. It might have been only a few days. But I knew if she started to drink, she'd get drunk." Emma sighed and turned onto her back to stare up at the roof. "Those were the nights I'd stay out."

"So she couldn't touch you?"

"That, and because she's so...ugly when she's drunk. Mean and nasty and hateful. She made me feel ugly, too."

"Oh, Em." He squeezed her tight.

"By the morning, she'd be in a near stupor and much easier to deal with. When she'd finally sober up, she'd be sorry. Really, really sorry. And she'd be sick for days."

"Jesus." He gave a long, disgusted sigh.

She shrugged as if it didn't really matter—when really it mattered too much. It always had. "Dad tried to run interference—he really did. But he's always worked two jobs and he…" Emma squeezed her eyes shut. "He loves her. He'd tell her not to drink, threaten to leave her. And once he even refused to buy her any alcohol. But…that didn't stop her either." Emma hated remembering that night. It still had the power to make her stomach pitch in fear.

She shrugged, shaking off the sensations of old. "Dad loves her too much to ever really enforce any consequences."

"Hey." Casey's big hand opened on the side of her face. "You deserve love too, you know."

"I know." God, her voice sounded far too small. She hated that, hated her pathetic childish weakness when it came to this one topic. She'd grown strong through the years, but it seemed she'd never outgrown her childhood hurt. "That's why being with the Devaughns was so great. They do love me. Damon and I are close. I had a…a normal life with them and it was wonderful."

Only they weren't her real family, just good people. They'd felt sorry for her at first, but that pity had turned to love. She knew it, felt it whenever she was around them. And she loved them in return.

"That's why Damon came with you?"

"He worries," she admitted. "I told him I'd be fine, but he didn't want me to be alone. He hadn't counted on you though." She turned her head toward him and had to smile. He was rumpled from their lovemaking, a little sweaty, his eyes still smoldering. And, for the moment, all hers.

"Damon knew about you, of course. I told him how I'd come to your house that night and he naturally had questions. I was prepared to see you again, Casey, but neither of us expected you to…"

Casey cupped her breast. "Reclaim you?"

"Casey Hudson, there's no way you can reclaim something you never had and never wanted in the first place."

His long fingers continued to caress her, shaping her breast in his palm, gently, easily, as if he now had the right. And she supposed he did.

"I was young too, Emma. I didn't know what I wanted until it was too late. I thought I had to stick to my grand plans and—"

"And I wasn't part of those plans. How could I be? I understand all that, Casey. And I'm so proud of you."

He wasn't looking at her, but rather at her breast. Now he leaned forward and briefly suckled her nipple, making her close her eyes on a moan. She was still sensitive from their recent lovemaking and just that easily her body softened for him again.

He released her only to blow a warm breath over her damp flesh. "I want a chance with you, Emma." His eyes shifted to hers and the moment their gazes collided, she felt pinned in place. "I want you to give us a chance while you're here."

Oh God, that hurt, to even think of something permanent with Casey. She spoke the words aloud, not just for his benefit, but for her own so she didn't start reaching for things she couldn't have. "I have a life in Chicago."

Casey nodded. "I used to think I wanted a life in Cincinnati. But the more entrenched I've gotten there, the more I've realized that I hate the job with my grandfather, am sick of the damn commute and resent my time away from my home." He stared down at her with a thoughtful frown. "Haven't you ever felt that way?"

"No. There were things about Buckhorn that I missed." She tugged on his chest hair and teased, "You, of course. And the water, the air and the…freedom. But you have tons of friends here, and family who love you. I don't. You can't know what it's like to be the outsider, for your own mother to despise you and for your father to care more about her than anything else, including what she does to you. You can't—"

Casey sat up and swung his legs over the side of the bed. Startled, Emma visually traced the long line of his back down to his buttocks. Her throat felt thick.

He turned back to her as suddenly again, his expression devoid of emotion. "You know about my mother, Emma?"

She nodded. Most everyone in Buckhorn knew that Sawyer wasn't really Casey's father. Casey's mother got caught cheating and Sawyer started divorce proceedings. When she birthed Casey, she planned to adopt him out. Instead, Sawyer had been at the hospital with her because she had no one else, and once he held Casey, he'd immediately claimed him as his own. After some nasty gossip— spread mostly by Casey's mother—she took off. No one had heard from her since. But Sawyer, along with Morgan, Jordan and Gabe, had raised Casey, and there wasn't a soul who knew them who would question that Casey had been well loved.

"I looked her up once." His eyes lit with cynicism. "Bet you didn't know that."

"No." Emma, too, sat up and tugged the sheet over her lap.

"Not one of my better ideas. I don't know what I expected, but she wanted nothing to do with me. She was pretty damn plain about that." He rubbed a hand over his face. "I haven't told anyone else, not even Dad."

"I won't ever say a word." Stupid woman, Emma thought, then added out loud, "She doesn't deserve you, Casey."

His smile now was chagrined. "Like your parents don't deserve you? It's true. You're a beautiful person and pretty damn special. I hope you know that."

Such a lavish compliment made her blush.

"I wasn't looking for pity, though, any more than you were. I only told you because I wanted you to see that we do have some similarities."

Emma laughed. "Right."

"We both love Mustangs."

She gave him that one.

"And we both love the water." Casey bent and kissed her throat. "And sex." He nuzzled her breast. "I'd say that's enough to build on."

"You're the only person I know who'd think so, which just goes to prove how extraordinary you are."

That had him raising his head and frowning. "I'm just me, Emma, prone to making lots of mistakes. Taking the job with my stepgrandfather was one of them, though now I'm not quite sure how the hell to get out of it."

"You don't think he'd understand?"

Casey grunted. "I don't know. He's made me the damn heir apparent, and while I hate the job, I'm rather fond of him. I don't want to disappoint him."

"What is it you want to do?"

"Something here. Something simple. Like you—which is

another similarity—I want to have my own small business rather than help run a gigantic organization."

Prodding him, she said, "Like…?"

He laughed. "I don't know for sure, nosy. But I'm thinking maybe I'd try being an accountant and financial planner. I already have a BBA in accounting and an MBA in accounting and taxation. I could get a CFP certification…" He finally noticed the comical confusion on Emma's face and drew to a halt. "Sorry. A lot of mumbo jumbo, huh?"

She couldn't hold back her grin. "Since the closest I got to a college was driving past in my car, and the idea of crunching numbers makes my brain throb, yeah. But I take it you're already qualified?"

He laughed. "For the most part. And I *do* enjoy crunching numbers, especially if I can help people plan better. You know, a lot of folks around here are selling land and not getting what they should. Some of the older people are retiring without enough to live on." He shook his head. "As I said, I'm still thinking on it. And thinking right now, with you sitting there looking like that, isn't easy."

Emma grinned, and hiked the sheet a little higher. "Better?"

"Hey now, I didn't mean you should…"

Emma swatted at him when he reached for the sheet and they both laughed. "Okay," she said when he retreated again, albeit with a big grin, "so that's one mistake you've made. And not even really a mistake because it sounds to me like you've already got it figured out. You know what you want to do—you're just dragging your heels about doing it. I say go for it. What have you got to lose?"

"A great job? Financial security?"

She snorted. "You'll be an overnight success."

He stared at her intently, then suddenly sounding too serious again, he said, "You know your faith in me is downright scary. Always has been."

Her faith was well deserved, but he didn't look open to hearing that.

He put his hand on her thigh and squeezed. "I'm not perfect, honey, and I don't even want to be. I've made more mistakes than I can count." His hand slid higher, under the sheet and up to the inside of her thigh. "But losing you was the worst of the lot."

He kept saying things like that, confusing her so much.

"The night you left me—you and your mother had been fighting?"

"I didn't leave you." Good God, where did he get these notions? "I left Buckhorn."

Casey just waited.

Her calm now shot to hell, Emma said, "Yes." But then she shook her head, trying to pick and choose her words. "Not really fighting, but she was drunk and Dad couldn't reason with her and things just got out of control..." *Boy, was that an understatement.* "I didn't want to stay for that anymore. I decided it was past time to go."

"If your dad hadn't had the stroke, you wouldn't have come back." He made it a statement rather than a question.

"No." This was the hard part, where she had to be really careful. "I'd talked to them a few times, but nothing had changed. They knew how to reach me, and though Dad called every so often, like on my birthday and holidays, Mom only called four times, and two of those times she was drunk."

Casey lowered them both to lie on the mattress. His hands held her face still for the soft press of his mouth to her forehead, chin and cheeks. "Don't let them continue to influence your life."

"I don't!"

"When you avoid Buckhorn because of them?" Put that way, she had no more denials to offer. "You're here now, and who knows for how long? Your dad may need you for months, maybe longer. He might never fully recover. Is your mother capable of taking care of him, considering she has a drinking problem?"

Surely that wouldn't be the case. She hadn't even had the opportunity to consider such an eventuality. Things were happening too fast...

"Give us a chance, Emma. That's all I'm asking. Quit shutting me out and let's see how it goes." He moved against her and added, "Do you think you can do that?"

From breasts to thighs, his hard, naked body covered her. She could feel his erection against her belly, his warm, fast breath. Pushing all probable consequences aside, she reached for him. "Yes."

THEY'D FALLEN ASLEEP. Exhausted, Emma slept like the dead and woke with Casey propped on an elbow beside her, smiling. B.B. was splayed over their legs.

"He snuck in about a half hour ago."

Emma stretched up to peer at the dog. As if he felt her awareness, he rolled to his back and looked at her upside down. Casey chuckled and reached down to scratch his throat.

"I can see this might turn tricky. Maybe I should get another cot and set it up at the other end of the porch."

"Wouldn't work," Emma informed him. "He'd still crawl up here. He's too used to sleeping with me."

"He got dirt and leaves in the bed, but at least he's dry. And he didn't complain at having me here."

"He likes you." Emma stroked Casey's shoulder. "I like you, too."

"Yeah?" His slow smile warmed her heart. "Well, I'll have to remember this combination, huh?"

"What combination?"

"Great sex and a little rest."

Laughing, Emma stretched and said, "The sex was incredible, and I did need the rest." She peeked at him. "But do you think you can add food in there somewhere?"

"Whatever it takes to keep you happy."

If this was a dream, Emma thought, she didn't want to wake up. Casey was so attentive, constantly touching her, kissing her. Sharing details of her mother's sickness hadn't been nearly as painful as she'd feared, because Casey had shared some of himself in return. And best of all, he had no complaints about her dog. Every other man she'd dated had resented B.B.'s interference—which had made them very dispensable. But not Casey. Rather than scold the dog, he'd made room for him and even given him affectionate pats. But then when had Casey ever been like other guys?

After they got dressed, she finally got a tour of the little run-down cabin. It needed some repairs, no doubt about that, but it was still quaint, boasting a stone fireplace currently blackened from use, a minuscule bathroom—which she made use of—and a tiny kitchenette that even had running water. Other than the bathroom being sectioned off, it was all one open room.

Casey showed her where he'd like to erect a gazebo, where he'd clear an area for a picnic table and perhaps a shelter. The charm of the cabin would definitely be the seclusion and the surrounding nature. Casey promised to bring her there often, and Emma already looked forward to the return.

A few minutes later, after Casey insisted on covering her in sunscreen with excruciating, and exciting, attention to detail, they took the boat out again in search of food. First, Casey pulled in to the boat dock with the intention of getting hot dogs and chips. He changed his mind when, seconds after they'd docked, Lois and Kristin, along with a contingent of friends, converged on him. They'd docked their own boat and had been in the process of restocking their drinks and snacks.

It wasn't unusual to run into people on the lake. As Casey had told Damon, people used their boats almost as much as their cars. But to see the two women together...well, that boggled Emma's mind. Her luck couldn't be that bad. She caught Casey's apologetic shrug, prompting her to ask, "They're friends?"

"Everyone knows everyone else around here, babe, you know that."

"But...they both want you!"

That made him laugh, and shake his head at her. "I told you I work with Kristin, and Lois is—or rather was—a friend."

Apparently, he was still annoyed with Lois for her sniping remarks at the hospital. Emma tried to ignore both women as they sent her baleful looks while moving in on Casey. It wasn't easy. They wore tiny bikinis, gorgeous tans, and they were all too ready to play touchy-feely with Casey.

Because of the men who'd accompanied Lois and Kristin,

Emma was grateful that she'd put her cover-up back on. They were being nice enough about it, only barely looking, but judging by their curious attention, she assumed Lois had already clued them in to her identity.

Casually polite, Casey spoke with the women while gassing up the boat. Two of the men, dressed only in snug trunks, walked around the dock to Emma's side. B.B. gave a low growl of warning, alerting Casey to their approach.

One of the young men knelt down, which brought him closer to eye level with Emma. He grinned at her with what looked to be real pleasure. "Emma, I'd heard you were back. It's good to see you again."

Her dark glasses shielded her eyes and gave her a false sense of privacy. "Thanks. I'm sorry…do I know you?"

Chagrin added color to his already tanned face. "You don't remember me?"

"Should I?"

He ribbed his friend and they both laughed. "Naw, I guess not. It was a long time ago."

His friend added, "And you have lost some hair."

They laughed, and the first man held out his hand. "Gary Wilham."

The name jogged her memory, causing Emma to look closer. True, he had a bit of a receding hairline, but he was still quite handsome. And still built like a linebacker… "I remember now. You played football for the school."

"That'd be me."

"Sorry about that. I'm not real good with faces anymore." She and Gary had had a short-lived…thing. She wouldn't call him a boyfriend, and they hadn't officially dated. But if he expected her to be embarrassed, he'd be disappointed.

He kept the handshake brief and merely polite, surprising her. "So." He gave her the once-over. "You look terrific. How've you been?"

Relaxing, Emma said, "Good. And yourself?"

"Real good. You in town for long?"

"A few weeks maybe." Or months. She just didn't know yet.

"That's great." He glanced at Casey, then back to her with casual interest. "Catching up with old friends?" At her nod, he said, "Perfect. We're all going waterskiing. Want to join us? It'll give you a chance to get reacquainted with everyone."

Emma barely had her mouth open to make her excuses when Casey started the boat's powerful motor, making conversation more difficult. The men backed up. Emma turned and saw that Casey, too, wore his glasses—and a very false smile.

"Sorry, Gary. We've already got plans. Maybe some other time?" And he put the boat in reverse before Gary could offer any alternatives.

A little stunned at their hasty retreat, Emma waved to the men bidding her a fast farewell. Once they were several yards out in the lake, she said, "That was rather abrupt."

"He was about to ask you out. As to that, if he finds out where you're staying, he'll probably call."

Suffering faint disappointment at Casey's attitude, Emma raised an eyebrow. "You mean he'll expect to jump back into…old times."

Though his glasses hid his eyes, there was no mistaking Casey's annoyance. "No, damn it. I meant he and every other guy who looks at you will notice what an attractive woman you are and hope to get closer. Reacquainting himself is just an excuse."

"Oh." Emma felt small for projecting her own thoughts onto him. "Sorry."

"As to that, I'd appreciate it if you'd quit putting words into my mouth, okay?"

To give him his due, she winced theatrically. "Okay, I'll try."

"And while we're on the subject, I'd like us to come to an understanding."

That he was heading back toward Morgan's dock didn't escape her notice. "Two questions. One, is our day at the lake over?"

He stared straight ahead. "You're starting to look a little pink, despite the sunscreen. I think you've had enough sun, but I thought we'd head back to the house to eat. If Honey doesn't have anything ready, then we'll grab a bite at Ceily's."

Just hearing Ceily's name made her stomach clench. She swallowed hard, prayed Honey had dinner going, and nodded. "Question two, what understanding?"

His mouth flattened before he huffed out a long breath. In rapid order, he slowed the boat and reached for her hand, then pulled her up and into his side. Still looking severe, he drew her close for a brief kiss. "I have to get back to work tomorrow, but I'll cut my hours short and be home by five all week. That'll give us most of the evening to be together."

Amazed at the plans he made, at the way he wanted to adjust his routine to suit her, Emma could only stare at him.

"I have no right to ask you this," he went on, "but I was hoping you'd spend all your free time with me—and only me."

"My free time?"

He glanced ahead as another boat going at breakneck speed came around the bend. "Yeah. I realize you'll need to be with your father a lot, and I'm willing to do that with you too, whenever I'm around. But I…damn it, Em, I don't want you going out with other guys." He'd sounded belligerent, but just as quickly went tender with a self-conscious laugh. "I swear, it'd make me nuts."

It would take her time to get used to Casey wanting her. "I'd like that."

"Making me nuts?"

She laughed. "No, spending more time with you. But you're right that I need to see my dad often. It's why I'm here, after all. And since it looks like I'll be here awhile, I might need to drive back home to get more clothes…"

"We'll get it all worked out."

We. She really liked the sound of that. But would Casey still feel the same when he found out the truth of why she'd left? He'd asked her to tell him the whole truth, but through lies of omission, she'd denied him that. He'd also asked her to trust him, yet how could she? She knew Casey, knew what a good person he was. He'd been very understanding so far, but he wouldn't be able to understand everything she'd done.

When she'd only planned to be in town for a week or so, she'd thought she might be able to avoid confronting past transgressions. If she needed to stay a month or more, the chances of being haunted by her past increased.

Yet what else could she do?

She'd start by simply enjoying what time she could have with him. And she'd face demons as they arose, not a second before. If it all fell apart in the end…well, it was no more than she'd ever expected.

Probably no more than she deserved.

In the meantime, she'd take what she could—and wait for it all to come crashing down.

chapter 12

BY THE TIME Casey walked her to the motel-room door, it was past midnight. Exhaustion pulled at him, but he hated for the day to end. It had been a unique pleasure, watching Emma interact with his family. She'd helped Honey with dinner, fallen naturally into the routine of serving the kids, and when Gabe showed up with Elizabeth, she'd spent over an hour discussing car motors with him.

Casey knew everyone was curious about her, but they'd also enjoyed her company. Emma was very easy to be with, in a hundred different ways. Maybe if he brought her around them more often, she'd realize what he already knew—that she fit into his life with ease.

Emma turned at the door to smile at him, and Casey had to kiss her again. And once he kissed her, he wanted so much more. Making love to her this afternoon had been deeply satisfying…but not nearly enough. He wanted her again, right now. If she hadn't looked so weary, he might have invited himself in.

He consoled himself with the fact that she'd agreed to see

him every day. He had no doubt that at least part of their time together would be spent in bed.

After a full day in the sun and water, and after the rambunctious attention from all the kids, B.B. was tired as well. While Casey feasted on Emma's sweet mouth, the dog collapsed in a heap at their feet.

Though he told himself merely to kiss her good-night, Casey couldn't resist taking a little more. He flattened his hands on the door at either side of her head, angled his hips in, and relished the feel of her soft, accommodating body flush against his. Emma clung to his neck, taking his tongue, giving him her own. They both groaned at about the same time.

"You're hard again," she whispered against his mouth with what sounded like awe.

"And you're so damn soft," he growled, rubbing his nose against her cheek, her throat, her chin.

She stared into his eyes, slowly licked her lips, then offered, "If you'd like to—"

The door opened behind her.

With a yelp, Emma, who'd been leaning on the door with Casey's full weight against her, lost her balance and fell inward. Because his hands had been flat on the door, Casey couldn't stop himself from falling in too. He tried to brace himself, but his feet got tangled over the dog.

Damon said, "What the hell!" just before the three of them landed hard on the floor in a welter of arms and legs. Damon cursed again, Emma gave an *umph* as she got squashed, and Casey quickly tried to lever himself off her. But B.B. had been jerked awake with a start and found it all great fun. He jumped on Casey's back and knocked him flat against Emma again.

Everyone froze.

Into the silence, Damon, who was on the bottom of the heap, murmured dryly, "Well. My first ménage à trois, but somehow I never figured I'd be on the bottom."

Emma started snickering, while it was Casey's turn to curse.

"I'm being quite crushed," Damon added. "So, Emma, doll, if you wouldn't mind…?"

"I'm trying," she claimed around her giggles. She realized her legs were open to Casey, cradling him. "But Casey—"

Flustered, Casey again felt B.B.'s paws on his back, then a wet tongue—the dog's—drag over the back of his neck. "No, B.B., *down*."

The dog retreated, but stayed close, bouncing here and there, ready to leap in again if anyone looked willing. Casey shoved himself into a sitting position then assisted Emma off of Damon.

Damon, the idiot, just lay there, his hairy legs sprawled out, wearing no more than his underwear. "I'm flattened."

Casey wouldn't mind flattening him. But Emma laughed and poked him in the abdomen. "Get up, you big faker. You're not hurt."

He did, but he groaned and groused in the process.

Casey eyed him. "Do you live in your damn drawers?"

"I was ready for bed, I'll have you know, because unlike the two of you, I returned at a respectable hour."

"Yeah?" Emma grinned. "And when was that?"

"About twenty minutes ago," he admitted with a smile. "And I expected to find you in bed."

"I just bet you did," Casey grumbled.

"But," Damon said, dragging out the word, "you stayed out rather late. So I was listening for you and worrying, as any self-respecting, pseudo-big brother would. When I heard the muted noise at the door, but no one came in, I got curious—and found myself sexually compromised."

Emma apparently thought the guy was hilarious, given how she laughed. That earned her a tender smile from Damon, leaving Casey to feel like a damn outsider. He didn't like it, not at all. But he supposed he'd have to work on tolerating Damon, given Emma seemed so fond of him.

And he had called himself a big brother to her.

It dawned on them all at once that they were seated on the floor. Almost as one they stood, both men assisting Emma.

"Your nose is pink." Damon flicked her cheek with a finger. "Too much time frolicking in the sun?"

"We were on the lake a good part of the day. And it was wonderful. I can't wait to show it to you."

"I look forward to it. I've already explored a bit of the countryside—and you're right, doll, it's spectacular."

Emma brushed herself off, then allowed Casey to draw her into his side. Around Damon, more than anyone else, he felt the constant need to display possessiveness.

"So who gave you the tour, Devaughn?"

Damon went very still while clapping his gaze on Emma. He replied to Casey, but it was Emma who held all his attention. "A friend of yours, actually. Ceily Brown."

Emma gave a tiny jerk. "You were with Ceily?"

He rubbed the back of his neck. "Yes. I met her while having lunch. I thought she was a waitress and didn't realize she was the owner of the place until we'd already been flirting back and forth a bit and things were…in progress."

Startled, Casey asked, "Ceily was flirting with *you?*"

"So?"

Uncomfortable with the idea, Casey shrugged. "So she doesn't…that is, she normally…"

"I know." Damon grinned. "She's discriminating. She told me so."

Emma suddenly turned to Casey. "Well, I suppose we should call it a night." She attempted to usher him—inconspicuously—toward the door.

Casey refused to budge. "What's wrong?"

"Nothing." Her smile didn't touch her eyes. "It's just that it's way past my bedtime and it has been a busy day. I'm ready to drop."

B.B. agreed with that and headed for the bed. Casey decided he'd pressed her enough for one day. He'd made enormous headway already. "All right." He went to the door, but brought Emma with him.

Damon didn't move, he just crossed his arms and watched them. In his underwear. Casey really didn't like him much at all.

"I'll see you tomorrow when I get home. Will you have your cell phone on you so I can find you?"

"Yes. I should be done visiting the hospital by then, but I'll need to think about a run back home."

Damon asked, "We're leaving already?"

Casey scowled at him, but Emma said over her shoulder, "I'll explain in a minute." Then to Casey, she said a firm, "Good night."

He smiled. Then he laughed. His timid little Emma was long gone, and in her place was a woman more exciting than he'd ever known. "Good night, sweetheart." He bent and kissed her, but kept it quick and light with Damon looking on. "Sweet dreams."

EMMA SHUT THE DOOR behind Casey. She apparently heard Damon approaching, because she pretended to faint, falling back against him. "Oh Lord, what a day," she said.

Damon caught her under her arms and laughed. "Made your knees weak, did he?" Seeing her so happy made him happy too. From the second he'd gotten a good look at her, he could see she positively glowed, and not just from too much sunshine. Casey had a startling effect on her, and that told him all he needed to know.

Groaning, Emma straightened, but went to the bed to flop down. "It's too incredible." She stared at Damon in what he could only call wonder. "He wants to see me."

Damon pretended to gasp as he followed her over to the bed. "No! He wants to see a gorgeous, sexy woman? How strange. What do you suppose is wrong with that man?"

Fighting a smile, Emma smacked at him. "It's more complicated than that, and well you know it. And he doesn't just want to see me a little. For as long as I'm here, he asked that we be exclusive."

"He's a possessive ape. I picked up on that right off."

"He is *not* an ape."

Damon noted she didn't challenge the possessive part.

"And Damon, we might be here a lot longer than we'd first planned. Or at least, I'll be. That's what I meant about making a run home. I'll probably need more clothes. But there's no reason for you to stay."

Damon could think of several reasons to hang around, and first and foremost was his astounding reaction to a certain small-business proprietor. Then there was the stretch of land Ceily's grandfather was supposedly going to sell. And his own dissatisfaction with his life…

Emma spent several minutes explaining her father's condition to him, and Damon, as usual, did his best to be a good listener. He had such wonderful, caring parents himself, he couldn't imagine the emptiness she had to feel, knowing hers cared so little for her. Yet, she still suffered with her own sense of responsibility toward them. It was another mark of Emma's generous spirit, and one of the reasons she was so easy to love.

"What are you going to do?"

Propping her elbows on her knees, Emma buried her face in her hands. "I don't know," she wailed with only slightly exaggerated frustration. "I want to be with him. God, to be truthful, I still have feelings for him."

He'd assumed that much all along, of course, which was one reason he'd insisted on accompanying her on this trip. Emma didn't love easily, but when she spoke of Casey, the love she felt for him was more than apparent. "And how does he feel?"

She shook her head and straightened. "At first, it was almost like he thought he'd been slighted...because he hadn't gotten to...uh..."

"Make love to you?" Yeah, Damon could see that. Hudson might consider her the one that got away. He'd been controlling things, keeping Emma at arm's length—right where he wanted her, not too close but within reach. Then suddenly she wasn't around at all and he'd likely floundered with mixed feelings. Far as Damon was concerned, it served him right.

But the way Emma avoided his gaze when she nodded, Damon wondered if the sex issue had already been seen to. It would explain her glow and the heat he'd witnessed in

Hudson's eyes. He almost grinned. "I take it once isn't enough?"

She punched him in the arm. "You know me too well."

"I was talking about him, actually but, yeah, I know you too well. And there's no reason to blush. If you're happy I'm happy."

Absently, she began to stroke B.B., and the big dog gleefully dozed off. Emma was good with her hands and she loved touching. If you sat by her, you could expect to get as many pets as the dog. She made a perfect massage therapist—and she'd make an even better lover.

"I know getting involved with him, even temporarily, is beyond stupid." She winced. "When I leave, it's going to make it so much harder. But I just can't resist grabbing this opportunity."

Watching her closely, Damon asked, "So who says it has to be temporary?"

She blinked at him, laughed a little nervously. "Because it's just sex."

"Did *he* say as much?"

With an uncertain look, she shook her head. "No."

Damon squeezed her knee. "Then I think you need to stop making assumptions and give the guy a chance. If he just wanted sex, seems to me his little co-worker Kristin was more than willing."

She thought about that, then nodded. "True."

"And you definitely need to shake off that dark cloud. You're in Buckhorn two days and already you're reverting to that silly girl I first met."

"I wasn't silly."

He grunted. "You had no clue who or what you were. You

kept trying to fade into the background, to disappear completely, which was very silly because a woman like you is always noticed."

Her eyebrow lifted this time. "A woman like me?"

"Smart, sexy, warm and sincere. Men have built-in homing devices for women like you. You can't be in the vicinity without males perking up—and I don't just mean their attention." He bobbed his eyebrows so she wouldn't misunderstand. "You're around, and men know it."

That had her laughing. "You are so absurd sometimes."

"No more absurd than you. Forget the past, doll. Forget the girl you used to be and the boy you always thought he was. Just take it day by day and see what happens. If Casey Hudson possesses even half the sterling qualities you always attributed to him, I'll be shocked if he doesn't fall madly in love with you." In fact, Damon thought the poor guy was already halfway there. He looked at Emma as if he wanted to eat her up, and he didn't even try to hide it.

"Now—" Damon stood to stare down at her "—it's time to hit the sack. I'm seeing Ceily again tomorrow."

"You are?"

"Indeed. She's a charming little minx, I'll say that for her."

"If you say that *to* her, she's liable to clobber you."

Damon grinned. "I can handle her, don't worry. But she suggested I be ready early, and I'm beginning to realize that, around here, that means crawling out of bed before the sun comes up."

Emma gave him a long look, no doubt wondering how involved he planned to get with Ceily. He could understand her surprise. Hell, he was still reeling himself. Of all the women in Buckhorn, she was probably the last woman he should be spending extra time with, all things considered.

But as usual, Emma didn't pry except to ask, "So you're going to be staying too?"

He sauntered toward his own room, but when he reached the doorway, he looked back at her with a smile. "The infamous Casey Hudson sees me as competition, despite my assurances to the contrary, and I'm finding that amuses me a lot. So, yes, doll, I'm staying. In fact, wild horses couldn't drag me away." Damon couldn't wait to see how the town's golden boy worked this one out.

In the meantime, he'd be working on buying some land—and seducing Miss Ceily. Things looked promising.

And here he'd feared Buckhorn, Kentucky, might be boring. It was anything but.

MORGAN STOOD at the grill, turning burgers, rolling wieners and brats, and seasoning pork ribs. As the official cook for the day, he'd opted for a wide variety to please all the family who'd turned out for the impromptu get-together. All around him, the kids were playing and the animals were running about. Up on the porch, he could hear the wives chatting and laughing. Life was good.

He glanced over to where Casey and Emma sat beneath a tall elm tree, practically glued together. It was just like old times, except that two of Gabe's fair-haired daughters were with them, watching as Emma taught them how to weave clover buds together for ankle bracelets. The girls loved them, and when Casey made a larger one and placed it on Emma's head like a tiara, they giggled.

Sawyer walked up to him. It was his day off so he wore

jeans and a tan T-shirt. "Out of the ten days she's been in town, this is the fifth time Case has had her over for dinner."

Morgan raised an eyebrow. "I knew they were getting tight. But that's sounding pretty serious considering he doesn't usually bring his dates around that often."

"Hell, the days he hasn't brought her here, he's spent with her somewhere else. Everyone in town and on the lake has noticed, which I think might have been his intent. I've never seen him chase a woman like this."

Shrugging, Morgan said, "Usually they're chasing him." He expertly flipped a burger, then stepped back as flames shot upward from the grease. "Misty told me that the gossip among the young ladies is getting kinda nasty. With Emma around, they're all out of the running, and apparently they're not too happy about that."

"What kind of gossip?"

"Oh, that Case feels sorry for her. That he's using her. That she's using him." He shrugged. "Typical catty stuff. Misty was fit to be tied when she got home."

Sawyer smiled. "I take it she straightened them out?"

"That she did. But stop grinning, cuz your wife was right there with her and just as adamant about stopping rumors."

"You're on fire," Sawyer told him, then waited while Morgan retrieved a slightly charred hot dog and moved it to another part of the grill. "You know Honey dotes on him. If Emma makes him happy, then she's all for it."

"She does appear to keep him smiling."

"True. And if she's around, he's by her. Or watching her. Or watching that no one else is watching her. It's bound to cause talk."

Grinning, Morgan said, "Reminds me a bit of me back in my day."

"Reminds me a bit of any guy in love."

Nodding thoughtfully, Morgan said, "Yep. That's about it, I suppose."

Jordan strolled up with three frosty colas, one already opened and half gone, the other two for his brothers. Gabe followed along behind him. "What has you two over here gossiping like old women?"

Shoeless and in a sleeveless shirt, Gabe leaned against a tree. "We could see your frowns from the porch."

Accepting his drink and taking a healthy swig, Morgan nodded toward Casey. "Think he's in love with her?"

Gabe snorted. "That's what has you all puckered up? Well, let me set you straight—yes. He loves her."

Jordan used his wrist to wipe the sweat from his forehead. "Hear, hear."

Sawyer said, "Hmm."

"You like her, don't you?" Gabe glanced over toward Emma in time to see his youngest daughter climb into her lap and give her a hug. "Because I like her fine. She's a pretty little thing. And she's damn good with cars. Almost as good as me." He shook his head. "Gotta admire that."

"She's damn good at neck rubs too."

Gabe squinted his eyes. "Do tell."

Grinning, Sawyer said, "Morgan helped Howard dig out a tree stump. And by 'helped,' I mean he did it himself. He seems to forget he's an old man now."

"I'm in my prime, damn it." Then Morgan raised his nose. "Just ask Misty."

"Yeah, well, prime or not, he pulled more than a few muscles showing off. Emma happened to be here when he started complaining and within minutes she had him blissfully relaxed and half-asleep."

Gabe stared over toward Emma. "Wonder if I could get her to show me how to do that."

"She showed Misty."

"And Honey." The two brothers grinned at each other.

"Needing help with Elizabeth, are you?" Jordan taunted Gabe.

"Naw, but the woman is insatiable. I figured if I could get her to sleep a little more…"

After everyone stopped chuckling, Gabe said, "You're fretting for nothing. Because if I know women—and you know I do—Emma is as much stung as Casey is. It's almost embarrassing, the way she looks at him."

Jordan elbowed him. "Like anything could embarrass you."

"Hey, I'm an old married man, completely oblivious to lecherous looks." He grinned sinfully as he said it.

"We all like her," Morgan pointed out. "But isn't she here only temporarily?"

Sawyer nodded. "That's what concerns me the most. Yet she's the only female Casey has brought around the family this much."

"That oughta tell ya something, I suppose."

Morgan rolled his eyes at Gabe. "Yeah, it tells us that he loves his adoring uncles and values our approval."

"She has mine."

"Mine too."

Sawyer shifted, running a hand through his hair and sighing. "She left here because she didn't like it, or because she had some mighty big personal problems. Whichever, I'd hate to see Case hurt."

"He's smart. He knows what he's doing." Jordan clapped Sawyer on the shoulder. "Of course, a man's finer senses tend to warp a little when he's getting his heart drop-kicked by love."

Morgan nodded. "It's cruel the way a woman can lay you low."

Gabe said, "As long as she's laying me...." The others lifted their drinks in a salute.

Just then, Misty yelled from the porch, "You got the meat ready for me?"

Morgan smiled while the others quickly turned their backs to snicker. "Always, sweetheart, always." Then under his breath to his brothers, "She can't get enough."

Jordan raised his eyebrows. "Yeah, well, your wieners are on fire."

Morgan hurried to move things around on the grill. Gabe glanced up, saw that Elizabeth had joined Misty in setting out side dishes, and yelled, "You ladies getting... *hungry?*"

She smiled back with a look guaranteed to knock the wind out of him. "Ravenous."

Gabe clutched his heart. "Oh God, I asked for that, didn't I?"

Sawyer called to Honey, "Be right there, sweetie." And he blew her a kiss.

Jordan said, "I like Emma's friend, Damon."

"He loosened right up, didn't he? When I first met him, he was such a starched shirt. Nice enough fellow, but so...precise." Gabe said that as though it were a dirty word.

"Put my teeth on edge. Never thought he'd be the type to hang around here this long."

"He's still starched, but it's just his way." Sawyer nudged his brothers as he saw Damon come around the corner of the house, led by Amber and looking far from starched at the moment. Judging by his bare wet feet and wind-tossed hair, Amber had taken him along the bank hunting crawfish and minnows again—a pastime Damon apparently enjoyed, much to everyone's surprise.

Amber had insisted on his first such adventure, but since then he'd gone along willingly and they'd fallen into a routine of sorts. Whenever Damon came to the house with Emma, Ceily usually accompanied them, and they'd go to the shore with Amber and any of the other kids who were in attendance that day.

Sawyer also noted that Damon had his pant legs rolled up, his shirt mostly unbuttoned, and Ceily tucked close at his side. "Ceily sure likes him."

"Likes him?" Gabe grunted. "She's totally besotted, always sashaying around in front of him, batting her eyelashes and whispering in his ear. And he enjoys it—you can tell that much."

"Good for her." Morgan pointed a metal spatula at Gabe. "'Bout time she found someone."

"Hey, I got no problem with her being happy," Gabe groused. "It's just that I always figured it'd be someone local. I hope like hell he doesn't break her heart, or worse, talk her into moving away."

"Moving away would be worse than a broken heart?"

Jordan scowled at Morgan, then asked Gabe, "Why would she move away?"

"I understand he's a well-respected architect back in Chicago." Sawyer shrugged. "Can't see him giving that up."

The men all looked up as a scuffle started between Garrett and Shohn, who were a little too close in age at nine and ten not to compete at every turn. Adam, only slightly more subdued at thirteen, stood to the side shaking his head until Honey raced into the yard and said quite loudly, "That's enough!"

The boys broke apart, grumbled a little and, with Honey prodding them along, headed to the porch.

Morgan shoved a platter of hamburgers at Jordan. "Here, carry this. We better feed the savages before they turn on each other."

Laughing, Jordan took the food. "I can remember Mom saying the same thing back in the old days."

Gabe snickered. "Yeah, but usually she was saying it about Morgan."

"Last time I talked to her, she said she'd be coming to town soon. Seems Casey spoke with her yesterday when she called. He mentioned Emma a few dozen times, and now she's more than a little curious."

Sawyer laughed at Jordan. "Nosy is a better description." The brothers all agreed with fond smiles. "I expect she'll be here before too long."

Their mother lived in Florida with Gabe's father, Brett. After losing her first husband and divorcing her second, she'd found true love. It made them all glad to see her so happy, and since she got to Kentucky at least six times a year, they didn't mind that Brett had talked her into retiring in Florida.

Later, after the food had been devoured and everyone, except the kids, was feeling a little more lethargic, Sawyer seated himself near Emma. She and Casey were on the porch swing, their hands entwined, talking quietly.

"So, Emma, I hear you've been busy."

Her brown eyes warmed with a gentle smile. "Dr. Wagner has scheduled several massages, and so has Ms. Potter. They're both very nice."

"I hear the wives have been in line as well."

She laughed. "Morgan too. But I enjoy it."

Sawyer nodded, having noticed that she was indeed a "toucher." If Emma was near someone, she touched—rubbing a shoulder, hugging the kids, stroking the animals. She was very sweet, very open and friendly, and Sawyer liked her, yet still he worried. "How's your dad doing? Any word on when he might get to come home?"

"They tell me it's still too early to know for sure." Her expression grew troubled. "He had shown so much improvement at first, but this past week there's been no real progress. If anything, he seems more sluggish. They're adjusting his medicine, trying different therapy, but...I just don't know."

Casey kissed her knuckles. "I went with her last night, and she saw him again this morning. He's still talking, not real clear though."

Emma looked away. "He was crying this morning."

Damn. Sawyer glanced at his son and shared his look of concern. But he was a doctor, not just a father, not just a friend, so he put on his best professional face and tried to reassure her. "That's not uncommon with stroke victims. I'm sure the doctor explained it to you?"

She nodded. "Emotional lability, he called it. He said depression is common. I just wish there was some way I could help."

"Hey." Casey put his arm around her. "You're helping a

lot. You're here with him. You've rearranged your life. I'd say that's plenty."

"I'd say so too," Sawyer agreed.

She didn't look convinced. "He's lost so much weight."

That wasn't uncommon either. Sawyer asked, "They still have him strictly on IVs?"

"Yes. They're not sure yet how well he can swallow. I forget what they called it…"

"Dysphagia." Sawyer knew one side of Dell's mouth was weak, so they likely had to be careful of the increased risk of choking. "Emma, it hasn't been that long. Try not to worry too much, okay? He's talking, and he recognizes you. That's pretty miraculous and a good indicator right there." He patted her hand, but he didn't promise her that everything would be all right, because he really didn't know.

A loud beeping broke the quiet, which had Morgan and Damon both reaching for their cell phones, then coming up with frowns because it wasn't theirs. Honey pointed to Emma's purse. "I think it's yours, Emma."

She came off the swing in a rush and fairly dived off the porch to reach the bag she'd left at the picnic table in the yard. Casey stood to watch her, Sawyer beside him. It was the first call that she'd gotten to Sawyer's knowledge and, naturally, it alarmed everyone.

After Emma said a tentative "Hello" into the phone, her lips parted and she slowly sank onto the bench seat at the wooden table.

Casey bounded off the porch steps in one leap and was at her side before she could say, a bit shakily, "I see." He stood behind her and put his hands on her shoulders. Damon sat down beside her. Everyone waited, alert.

Avoiding all the curious gazes, Emma said, "I'm so sorry, Mrs. Reider. Yes, of course, I'll be right there." She closed her eyes. "Yes, I understand."

Mrs. Reider? Sawyer thought. He'd presumed it was the hospital, that her father had taken a turn for the worse. But instead...

Emma pushed the disconnect button on her small phone, tucked it back into her purse and stood. "I'm sorry to rush off, but I need to go." At the word *go,* B.B. hurried to her side.

"I'll take you," Casey said.

She looked horrified by that idea. "No—"

"I'll take you." He wasn't about to be dissuaded, and Sawyer understood why.

Emma looked to Damon, received his nod, and finally agreed. "All right. I suppose you might as well."

He might as well? What the hell did that mean? Sawyer wondered. And why did she look as if the rug had just been pulled out from under her?

Reaching for his shoes and socks, Damon said, "I'm coming too."

"But..." With everyone watching the poor girl, she gave up. "Fine. But I do need to hurry."

Honey worried her bottom lip. "Your father is okay?"

"Yes—that is, he hasn't had a change." She patted the dog, but her smile was a bit self-conscious. "That wasn't the hospital."

Ceily sidled up next to Damon and asked, "Then what's wrong?"

Emma hesitated a long moment before admitting, "It's my mother. She's at the motel where Damon and I are staying. She wants to see me."

Damon looked far too grim, leading everyone else to wonder why a visit from her mother mattered so much. "You ride with Casey," he told her. "I'll drive your car."

Since that was how they'd arrived, she merely nodded.

"Emma?" At Sawyer's query, she turned. For a young woman who'd been smiling moments before, she now looked far too world-weary. It didn't make sense, and filled Sawyer with compassion. "Let us know if there's any way we can help." And he thought to add, "With anything."

She stared at him a long minute before nodding. "Thank you. Dinner was wonderful. Everything was wonderful. I… Thank you."

And then Casey led her away. Sawyer watched until she and B.B. had gotten into his son's car before turning to his wife. Honey hugged his waist. "I'm worried about him, Sawyer."

Sawyer knew exactly how she felt, but he repeated his brothers' reassurances, saying, "He knows what he's doing."

Honey nodded. "I know. But does he know what *she's* doing?"

chapter 13

THE PAST WEEK and a half had been wonderful, but now it was over. All the secrets, all the pretending. She didn't know how or why her mother had sought her out, but she knew their reunion was bound to be difficult—just as her relationship with her mother had always been.

"I don't want you to come up with me."

Casey didn't bother to glance at her. "Why?" His hands were tight on the steering wheel, his expression dark.

What could she tell him? That she didn't want everything to end with such an unpleasant scene? "She's my mother and I'll deal with her."

"You think I would interfere?"

"No, but…" She drew a breath and gave him part of the truth. "It embarrasses me."

Casey pulled the Mustang into the gravel lot. He put it in Park, started to say something to Emma, but then stalled as his gaze lit on something. "I'd say it's too late to worry about that."

Emma followed his line of vision and saw her mother. She

was half slumped at one of the picnic tables, holding her head with one hand, a lit cigarette with the other.

Emma's heart got caught in her throat. Regardless of anything else, of the past and the hurt feelings and the dread, she was seeing her mother again for the first time in years. And she was choking on her hurt.

Her mother's brown hair, like Emma's only shorter, was caught back in a blunt ponytail. She wore dark jeans, a short-sleeved white blouse and sandals. Seeing her like that, she could have been anyone's mother. She could have been a regular mother.

She could have been a mother who cared.

Emma knew better though. Ignoring Casey, she opened her door and stepped out. Her mother noticed her then and stood. She swayed, unsteady on her feet, and had to prop herself with one hand on the tabletop.

Of course, she was drunk, just as Emma had expected.

"Where the hell have you been, young lady?"

The slurred words were flung at Emma without regard for the quietness of the lot or the spectators close at hand. Somewhere in the back of her awareness, Emma knew Damon and Ceily had arrived. She knew Casey was close behind her, leading the dog. She knew Mrs. Reider and a few guests watched from the motel-lobby door.

It's not me, Emma told herself. *What she does, who she is, doesn't project on me.* She knew it, had lived with that truism all these years past, but still her shame bit so deep she could barely see as she made her way to the picnic table.

Her voice sounded wooden as she said, "Mother."

"Don't you call me that," her mother sneered, and Emma saw that familiar ugliness in her brown eyes, in the dark shadows beneath, in the pasty sheen of her skin and the spittle at the side of her mouth.

"All right." Sick dread churned in her belly. She knew her mother would humiliate them both. What she didn't know was how to deal with it. As a child, she'd begged, hidden, run away. But she wasn't a child any longer, and her mother was now her responsibility.

"A daughter would have come to see me by now. You know I'm all alone. You know I needed you. But no. You're too good for that, aren't you?"

"You have my number," Emma reasoned. "You could have—" No. Emma stopped herself. She knew from long experience that there was no reasoning with her mother in this condition. It would be a waste of breath to even try, and would only prolong the uncomfortable confrontation. "Why don't I take you home?"

"Oh no, missy. I don't damn well wanna go home now." She took an unsteady step forward. "I want you to take me to the store, and then we're goin' to the hospital to see Dell."

Emma's heart nearly stopped. Take her mother to the hospital? Not while she was drunk. "I won't buy you alcohol." She didn't bother to reply to her other request.

Her mother looked stunned at that direct refusal. Her eyes widened, her mouth moved. Finally, she yelled, "You just get me there and I'll buy it myself. I'm worried about your father and sick at heart and God knows my only daughter doesn't give a damn." As she spoke, she tottered around the table toward Emma. Ashes fell from the cigarette, which was now little more than a butt.

Just as she'd done so many times in the past, Emma

braced herself, emotionally, physically. Even so, she had a hard time staying upright when her mother's free hand knotted in the front of her shirt and she stumbled into her. "You'll take me," she hissed, her breath tainted with the sickly sweet scent of booze and the thickness of smoke, "or I'll tell everyone what you did."

A layer of ice fell over Emma's heart. It was now or never, and she simply couldn't take it anymore. "What *you* did, you mean."

The shock at her defiance only lasted a moment. "No one will believe that." Her mother laughed, and tugged harder on Emma's shirt. "You, with your damn reputation. You don't have any friends around here. Even that nosy sheriff was always checking up on you. He'll believe whatever I tell him. And you'll go to jail—"

"I'll take my chances."

Enraged, her mother drew back to strike Emma, but her hand was still in the air when Casey pulled Emma back and into his side. Her mother's swing, which would have left a bruise, given the force she'd put behind it, missed the mark by over a foot and threw her off balance. She turned a half circle and landed hard on her hands and knees in the rough gravel. Her cigarette fell to the side, still smoldering.

Emma had automatically reached out to break her fall, but she pulled back. She could feel Casey breathing hard beside her, knew he was disgusted and shocked at the scene—a scene he'd probably never witnessed in his entire life, but that was all too familiar to Emma.

B.B. went berserk, barking and snarling, and Emma, feeling numb, caught his collar to restrain him. She whispered to the dog, soothing him while staring down at the woman who'd birthed her. She waited to see what else she'd do. Her mother could be so unpredictable at times like this.

But she stayed there, her head drooping forward while she gathered herself. Eight years had apparently taken a toll on her too. When she twisted around to look up at Casey, it was with confusion and anger. "Who the hell are you?"

Thinking to protect Casey, Emma said, "He's the sheriff's nephew."

"And," Casey added, his own anger barely under control, "I heard everything you just said."

Slumping back on her behind, slack-jawed, her mother stared from Casey to Emma and back again. Slowly, her lips curled and she pointed at Emma. "Did she tell you what she did? Do you know?" She hunted for her cigarette, picking it up and using it to light another that she fetched from her pocket. She took a long draw, looking at Casey through a stream of smoke. "She tried to burn down the diner."

Emma closed her eyes on a wave of stark pain. She'd held a faint, ridiculous hope that her mother wouldn't take it that far, that she'd only been blustering. That somehow she'd care just a little about her only child.

Barely aware of Casey taking her hand, Emma sorted through her hurt, pushing aside what she could to deal with the situation at hand. Mrs. Reider didn't deserve this scene. She ran a respectable business in a dry county. Having a drunken argument in her lot would probably go down as one of the worst things imaginable.

Slowly, Ceily came up to Emma's other side. She wasn't looking at Mrs. Clark, but at Emma. "You're the one who called and reported the fire that night, aren't you?"

It was so damn difficult, but Emma forced herself to face

Ceily. When she spoke, she was pleased that she sounded strong, despite her suffocating guilt. "Yes. I'm sorry. It's all very complicated and I didn't mean for any of it to happen…"

"Your mother started it?"

Amazed that Ceily had come to that conclusion without further explanation, it took Emma a few moments to finally nod.

"That's a lie!"

Ceily ignored her mother's loud denials, speaking only to Emma. "Why? I barely knew your folks."

It would help, Emma thought, if she had a good solid reason to give, some explanation that would make sense. She didn't have one. "You weren't a target, Ceily. The diner is just the first place she came to where she thought she might find either a drink or money to go get a drink."

Ceily shook her head. "But I don't serve alcohol, and I cash out every night before closing up."

"I know. And if she'd been thinking straight, she might have realized it too. But alcoholism…it's a sickness and when you want to drink, nothing else matters…"

Her mother began protesting again, her every word scraping along Emma's nerves until she wanted to cover her ears, run away again. But she no longer had that luxury. She had to deal with this. "She broke in, and things went from bad to worse… I didn't know what to do."

Damon stepped up and looped his arms around Ceily so that she leaned into his chest. It dawned on Emma that Ceily didn't look accusatory as much as curious. Of course, her reaction would have been vastly different eight years ago, the night it had all happened. The shock, the anger and hurt had likely been blunted by time.

"How did you find her?" Ominous overtones clouded Casey's softly asked question.

Emma winced. Because the fire and Emma's visit to his house had happened on the same night, Casey had a right to his suspicions. "Earlier that day, I'd convinced my father that we had to stand together, to get her help. It was the worst argument we'd ever had. She was furious, and...I couldn't take it. So I went out. But I always cut through town coming home." Here Emma gave an apologetic shrug to Casey. "Your uncle had warned me that he'd run me into juvenile if he caught me out so late again."

"He worried about you," Casey told her with a frown.

"I know." Emma smiled, though she felt very sad that only a stranger had worried, and only because it had been his job. "I came home behind the businesses, as usual, because that way I was less likely to be seen from the street. I found my mom coming out of the back of the diner, and I realized what she was doing. Then I smelled the smoke."

"She'd already started the fire?"

"Not on purpose. It was her cigarette, but..." Wanting to finish it, Emma rushed through the rest of her words. "The fire was small at first and I tried to put it out. But she kept fighting me, wanting us to leave before we got caught."

"Dear God," Casey muttered, and he glared at her mother, who gave him a mutinous look back.

Emma spoke to Ceily. "I knew I couldn't do that. I told her she needed help and that I thought you might let her just pay for the damages if she agreed to go to the hospital for treatment. But she didn't believe me and when I finally got the call through, she..."

"She threatened to blame you?" Casey asked.

Emma turned to him. "Yes. She said she'd tell everyone that I did it. I was...scared. I wasn't sure who might believe her."

"No one would have."

"You might not have blamed me, but—"

"I wouldn't have either," Ceily said.

Damon leaned around to look at Ceily, slowly smiled at her, then gave her a tight squeeze.

Emma couldn't believe they were being so nice. In so many ways, it might have been easier for her if they'd hated her and what she'd done. "I'm doubly sorry then, because I was a coward. The fire was already out of control. I made the call anonymously, went home with my mother and...things got out of control."

"That's how you got beat up that night, isn't it?"

He sounded furious and pained and...hurt? Because she'd been hurt? She glanced at him, but didn't reply because she didn't want to involve him further. "I made plans to leave."

"You came to me."

She shook her head at Casey. He couldn't seem to get beyond that, and she was beginning to think he put far too much emphasis on that one small fact. "With the intent of only staying one night."

"If I'd known that, you never would have gotten away."

"I had to leave. If I'd stayed until morning when everyone started talking about the fire, well, someone would have figured it out. Then I wouldn't have had the option to go."

He scowled, crossing his arms over his chest and appearing very displeased with her assessment. "How the hell did you get out of town so fast anyway?"

Knowing he wouldn't like the answer, Emma winced

again. "I hitchhiked once I got on the main road. Neither Morgan nor his deputy saw me, of course, because they were still busy with the fire. With a lift from two different drivers, I got as far as Cincinnati, then caught a bus the rest of the way into Chicago."

Ceily stared at her in horror. "Dear God. You could have been—"

Damon interrupted Ceily. "But she wasn't. Instead, she found my family and she's now a part of us." He reached out and touched Emma's chin. "And she's suffered a lot over this."

"Damon, don't make excuses for me, please. I should have told the truth long ago. I should never have lied in the first place."

Damon, still holding Ceily at his side, addressed both her and Casey. "It took her a few years to get her life in order. After that, she thought about coming home and confessing all—she honestly did. But her father would beg her not to, and with so much time already passed..."

Emma laced her hands together. "I couldn't bear the thought of my mother going to jail."

Her mother shoved to her feet, outraged by the mere suggestion. "No one is taking me anywhere! I didn't do anything. It was you."

Casey shared a look with Ceily, then received her nod. "No, you won't be going to jail. It was an accident, not arson. And even with the breaking and entering, well, it's been eight years. I'm sure the limitations on that have run out."

Emma was agog, her mother smug.

"But...won't the insurance company want their money back? I know there was a lot of internal damage."

Her mother grabbed Emma's arm in a viselike grip. "Shut your mouth, girl."

Casey stepped forward, but Emma stopped him with one look. She had avoided dealing with her mother for too long. When she'd been a child, she'd had an excuse. But as an adult... It was past time she took responsibility for what she'd done, and forced her mother to do the same. "You're going to get help."

"I don't need any help."

For the very first time in over a decade, Emma felt nothing. Not hurt, not need, not even compassion. "It's possible that legal charges might not apply anymore. But there are other things to consider now. Daddy's stroke is serious. If and when he's able to leave the hospital, I'm taking him with me."

"Whaddya mean, 'with you'? He's my husband!"

"And he's my father. He needs someone who can take care of him, not the other way around. He'll need therapy and supervision and encouragement. You're not capable of any of that, so until you get help, get sober, and stay that way, you're on your own."

The fingers on her arm grew slack, then fell away. "You can't do that." Her whisper was rough with shock.

"Of course I can." Emma swept her arm around the lot. "Thanks to this visit, there are more than enough people who now know that you're incapable of taking care of yourself, much less someone in need of medical attention."

Damon, Ceily and Casey, along with Mrs. Reider and a half-dozen motel guests made up an audience. Two cars had stopped on the road, having also noticed the spectacle unfolding in the motel lot. In a town as quiet as Buckhorn, it didn't take too much to get the gossip going. She wouldn't be surprised to see the whole thing written up as front-page news in the Buckhorn press tomorrow morning. In the past, that would have devastated her, leaving her curled up with shame. Now, she just wanted things resolved.

"Emma?" Ceily smiled at her. "There was never an insurance claim made. I didn't want my premium to go up, and I'd been planning to renovate anyway, after Granddad turned the place over to me completely. So I used the money I'd saved and fixed it up with a lot of help from Gabe and volunteers from the town."

Nodding, Emma said, "I'll reimburse you."

"No, you won't." She turned to Mrs. Clark, who stared blankly down at her feet. "But your mother can pay me one fourth of the money I spent, since there were some things I wouldn't have replaced if it hadn't been for the smoke and fire damage."

"I don't have that kind of money," her mother whispered, looking very lost and confused by it all.

Ceily shrugged. "So get a job. I'll let you make installments."

Her mother's look of horror was almost comical.

"They have a drug abuse and alcohol treatment facility at the hospital," Casey offered, speaking to Emma, not her mother. "We can take her there now." He looked as though he wanted to rid himself of her as fast as possible.

Sadly, Emma now felt the same. Years ago, she'd have done anything to help forge a normal relationship with her mother. She'd begged her, during her sober moments, to get professional assistance. But whenever she was sober, her mother always thought she had control over her drinking. She'd agree to quit, and mean it. But her resolve never lasted and Emma had long since grown tired of her mother's refusal to admit to her sickness.

However, what Emma had said was true—this time she would take her father away if her mother didn't get help. "Mother? What do you say? And before you agree or disagree, you should know I'm either taking you to the rehab facility, or leaving you here. Those are your options. If you stay, I have no doubt Mrs. Reider will give the sheriff a call, and you may well end up with court-ordered rehab anyway."

Her mother stared at her, looking much like a lost child. She was breathing hard, fighting tears, but Emma also knew an excess of emotion came with alcoholism, so she stiffened her spine and waited. Finally her mother nodded, surprising Emma, giving her hope.

"Listen, doll," Damon said quietly, "she's nothing to you now."

Emma knew that wasn't true. A parent was a parent, good or bad, and she would make the best of this. She turned to Damon and offered him a slight smile. "She's my mother." Then she added with a sigh, "And she got us kicked out of here. Mrs. Reider wants us gone as soon as possible."

Damon groaned. Her mother looked away. Mrs. Reider hovered in the doorway, appearing impatient—and curious since she couldn't hear what was being said.

Ceily and Casey spoke at the same time. "You can stay with me." Then they both blinked, and Casey added, "Ceily, honey, you're more than welcome to Damon. By all means, take him. But Emma and B.B. are coming with me."

Ceily hugged onto Damon's arm. "Works for me."

Emma looked at Damon, who grinned and shrugged.

"Sounds like it's all planned out, doll. That is, if you're okay with it."

Casey waited with a sort of tense anticipation they could all feel. But Emma had few choices, and she wanted to be with him. So she nodded. "Thank you."

EMMA WAS SO QUIET Casey couldn't help but worry. Getting her mother to the rehab center had taken far longer, and been more complicated, than he'd anticipated. But throughout it all, Emma had kept her shoulders squared, her emotions in check, and her determination at the fore. She was amazing.

After her mother had willingly signed herself in, Emma made plans to bring some of her things to her. She'd be at the facility for an undetermined length of time, but she'd start dependency counseling right away. Because leaving meant she'd likely lose her husband, she looked resigned to staying. She'd also asked, in a small, fretful voice, if Emma would visit her.

Emma had agreed, but there'd been no embrace between mother and daughter. For her part, Emma appeared motivated by pity for the woman who'd never been a real mother to her. She'd also been so distant, not touching Casey, hardly even looking at him. Casey didn't push her. She needed some private time to come to grips with everything, but under the circumstances that was tough to find. Mrs. Reider's was the only motel in Buckhorn, and any other lodging would put her too far away from her father. Though he wished this were easier on her, Casey was glad she'd be with him, even if it wasn't by choice.

It hadn't taken them long to pack her and Damon's

things. While Emma stood by without saying a word, Casey had called ahead to his father to fill him in on the situation. Emma's silence hurt him, because he knew she was hurting. Dealing with her troubles was hard enough, but broadcasting those troubles to the whole town would be nearly impossible to take. Casey feared he'd just lost a lot of headway in convincing her to stay in Buckhorn.

Damon and Ceily were there when Casey pulled down the long driveway. Damon had used the excuse of bringing Emma's car to her, but Casey suspected he also wanted to see her settled. Thankfully, the kids were out of sight, but Sawyer and Morgan, Misty and Honey all waited for them. When Casey stopped the car at the side of the house, his relatives moseyed inside to give them some privacy.

Casey turned off the engine. "You okay?"

It took her a moment, then she said, "It's strange, but mostly what I feel is relief that it's all out in the open. At least now I can deal with it."

Casey nodded. He could understand that. "It'll be okay."

Her laugh sounded a little watery, too close to tears, before she rubbed her face and drew herself together. "Looks like I'll be spending even more time visiting hospitals, huh?"

Jaw locked, Casey reached for her hand. "You owe her nothing." Far as he could tell, all her mother had ever given her was grief.

"I owe this town. I owe Ceily."

"You didn't cause the damage."

"No, but I kept quiet about it. That's a crime in itself."

"You were a kid, damn it."

She raised a hand. "No, Casey. Don't coddle me by making excuses. I'm fine really. Just… exhausted."

Christ, she'd been seventeen years old, burdened with more than most adults could handle. He had no intention of letting her wallow in guilt, but he let it go for now. "We'll go to bed early," he promised her.

That had her laughing again. "*We* will, huh? Does it bother you that your whole family will know I'm with you?"

Casey gave her a long look before stepping out of the car. B.B. jumped out with him and followed him as he circled the hood. Emma had already opened her own door before they could reach her. With Casey and Emma both carrying bags, they started toward the garage apartment. B.B., now very familiar with the Hudson household, followed along.

Finally Casey couldn't keep his mouth shut, and he said, "It's been a long day for me too, Emma. Don't piss me off."

She abruptly stopped, but since he and the dog didn't, she hurried to catch up. "What are you talking about?"

He'd kept his turbulent emotions tamped down all day— not an easy feat when he damn well loved her and it killed him to see her hurt. Now it felt as if he was imploding, his anger shot up so fast. Dropping her luggage, he whirled on her and gripped her shoulders. "I damn well want everyone to know you're with me, Emma. The whole town, preferably."

Eyes huge, she asked, "There's going to be so much talk. You have to know that Lois and Kristin and probably a dozen of their friends are saying awful things—"

Casey gave her a tiny shake. "I remember being behind the garage with you eight years ago. You were tempting me, driving me nuts, and you even accused me of being a virgin, then had the nerve to act surprised when I didn't deny it."

Her eyes softened. "Any other guy would have, especially since it wasn't true."

"I told you then that I didn't give a damn what people thought. So, why should I care now, especially when the alternative is not having you nearby? I'm not going to suffer a single moment of discomfort over it."

Some of the tension eased out of her and she gave him a genuine smile.

He pulled her into his chest. "Hell, Emma. I'm so proud of you. Don't you know that?"

"Proud?"

"God, yes." He held her back a little. "Look at you, at everything you've dealt with, all that you've accomplished. I don't know another person who could have handled that scene at Mrs. Reider's with so much grace and dignity."

"It was all I could do not to cry."

"Even if you had, so what? You sure had reason enough. But you didn't. You didn't cave in either. You've taken every rotten thing that's been thrown at you and somehow…" His own eyes grew damp, making him curse, making his voice hoarse. "Somehow you've stayed one of the most beautiful people I've ever known."

Breathing a little shakily, Emma moved back into his embrace. They stood there like that a long time, until Emma finally whispered, "Thank you."

Laughing with exasperation at the way she was forever thanking him for one thing or another, Casey locked his arms around her and hugged her right off her feet. "Baby, it wouldn't matter to me if your mother had burned down three buildings. She's not you." He nuzzled her ear. "I'm just glad that you're home."

Once he said it, Casey was afraid she'd again deny that Buckhorn was her home, so he kissed her, making any rebuttals impossible. It wasn't a lusty kiss, though he was more than ready for one of those too. Instead, he tried to kiss her with all the love he felt. It had been a day of emotional upheavals. She wasn't ready to have him start an overflow of declarations. Soon, he'd let her know how he felt. For now, touching her, holding her, having her close, would be enough.

"Come on," he said against her mouth. "We'll get you settled so you can get some rest."

Emma didn't argue, but when they turned around, they saw that B.B. had run off. They located him quickly enough, on the porch with Sawyer and Shohn. Both Hudson males wore wide, satisfied smiles.

Sawyer yelled out, "He was scratching at the door. Seems he wants to come in."

Emma started to apologize, but Casey cut her off. "He can visit with you for a while if he wants."

Shohn gave a whoop. "Can he sleep with me tonight? I'll take good care of him."

Casey said, "Dad?"

"Sure." Sawyer put one hand on Shohn's shoulder. "Fine by me if Emma doesn't mind."

Emma laughed. "He likes to hog the middle of the bed."

"That's okay." Shohn hung on the dog like a long-lost friend.

"He's liable to want to find me before the night is through," Emma warned.

Sawyer rubbed the dog's ears. "If he does, I'll walk him over to you. But you never know, so we might as well let him try it."

Since Casey wanted Emma to himself without the dog in the middle of them, he wrapped up the discussion and hurried Emma on her way. Once they were in the garage apartment, Emma dropped her luggage. "I can unpack tomorrow."

Casey glanced up at her. She'd gone straight through to the bedroom and stood next to his bed, her arms at her sides, her expression watchful. "All right." He smiled. "Are you hungry?"

She shook her head, then licked her lips. "I'd just like to take a quick shower."

Visions of her naked, wet, teased through his mind. "Yeah." He cleared his throat. "Let me get you a towel."

Ten minutes later, he was stretched out on the bed with his back propped against the headboard. He'd removed his shoes and socks and unbuttoned his shirt, but he was still uncomfortably hot. And uncomfortably aroused.

Yet, he knew sex wasn't what she needed right now.

He tried turning on the television, but he couldn't block the sounds of running water in the bathroom. He felt tortured. Even after the sexual excesses of the past week where they'd spent several hours a day at the cabin making love, the need he felt for her hadn't diminished. Hell, if anything, he wanted her more now than ever.

When the water stopped, that only heightened his awareness. But when Emma stepped out with her hair pinned atop her head and her sweet body wrapped only in a towel, he nearly groaned. She was home. She was with him. She was his.

In the face of so much progress in their relationship, he would be patient.

"Don't get up," she told him as she strolled toward the bed and seated herself on the side of the mattress, near his hip.

Casey stared at her, unsure what she wanted at that particular moment, unwilling to do anything that might make her ill at ease with him.

"Your apartment is fabulous." She stared at his abdomen as she spoke. "I knew Jordan used to live here, but I didn't know it was so nice."

Casey nodded absently while noticing the water droplets that clung to her shoulders. The apartment was open and spacious, located directly over the three-car garage. The kitchen, breakfast nook and living room all flowed into each other, with only the bedroom and bath private. "It suits me."

She rested one slim hand on his naked abdomen. "Will your folks expect to see us tonight?"

Casey almost choked on his indrawn breath. She had to have noticed his erection, given that his cock strained against his jeans, leaving a long ridge beneath the material. But the little tease said nothing. "No. That is, they'll understand if we wait till morning."

"They don't object to me being here?"

His dad had probably already figured out that Emma was special to him. As to that, everyone might know, since he hadn't exactly tried to keep it secret. "No, they're glad to have you here."

Using just her fingertips, she traced the line of hair from his navel down to the waistband of his jeans, making him shudder. "Did you lock the front door?"

With Shohn used to visiting whenever he chose, and all his young cousins forever underfoot, he'd taken care of that first thing. "Yeah."

"Good." She unsnapped his jeans and slipped her soft, cool hand inside.

Casey groaned. "Emma…"

Without a single reply, she freed his erection from the restriction of his jeans. Casey shifted, then groaned again when she leaned forward and brushed her cheek against him. He put one hand on her head, racked with mixed sensations. Lust was prominent because he could feel her breath on the head of his cock. But he also felt tenderness, because this was Emma, and with every second came the realization that she was his other half, the one woman meant for him.

She made a small hungry sound, and licked him from the base of his shaft to the very tip.

His hand clenched in her hair, his control fast evaporating. "Babe, wait."

Lifting her head, her dark eyes soft and heavy, Emma said, "Mmm?"

Could a woman possibly be more appealing than Emma was at that moment? He'd never get used to the way she looked at him with so much love in her eyes.

Love? God, he hoped so.

Casey closed his eyes and struggled for a deep enough breath so he could be coherent. "Let me get out of these jeans, okay?"

"All right." She agreed readily enough, stood—and then dropped the towel.

Casey lost it.

"Ah, damn, Em." Catching her about the waist, he tumbled her down into the bed and moved over her. The touch of her naked breasts on his chest, her belly on his abdomen, had him in a frenzy of need.

"Your jeans."

"In a second." Hell, if he shucked his jeans off now, he'd be inside her in the next second. He took her mouth, long and leisurely and deep until they were both panting, then slowly worked his way down her body. Kissing wasn't enough, and he indulged in a few gentle yet hungry love bites that had her gasping and squirming under him. She smelled of his soap, and strangely enough even that enticed him. He suckled her nipples until they were tight and straining, put small kisses on her ribs, dipped his tongue in her navel…

"*Casey.* "

Where seconds before he'd been desperate to sink into her, to feel the clasp of her body tight around his shaft, now he wanted her to be desperate. Kneeling between her thighs, he growled, "I want to taste you."

Offering a soft moan for reply, Emma braced herself, legs stiffening, hands knotted in the sheets. Smiling, Casey bent and nuzzled through the springy curls, breathed in her rich scent, and after carefully opening her with his thumbs, covered her with his mouth.

They both groaned, Emma with a sinuous twisting of her body, Casey with the need to take more and more. He moved her legs to brace her feet against his shoulders, cupped her hips in his hands, and held her still for the thrust of his tongue, the careful nipping of his teeth. He found her small, swollen clitoris and drew it gently into his mouth for the softest suckling, the demanding rasp of his tongue.

Within minutes she was ready to come, but like him, she wanted more. "Casey, wait."

Her breathless plea barely reached him with the taste and scent of her pushing him over the edge. He felt her silky thigh on his jaw, felt her heels pressing into his shoulders…

Her fingers tangled in his hair. "Casey, *wait*. I want you inside me. Please."

Breathing hard, he looked up the length of her body. Their eyes met, his glittering, hers dark and vague.

He took one last, lingering taste of her, then lunged to his feet. After hurriedly stripping off his jeans, he found a condom in the bedside drawer and rolled it on. All the while, he watched her, appreciating the sight she made sprawled in his bed, how right she looked there.

Emma came up to her elbows, but fell flat to the mattress again when he moved over her, hooked her thighs in his arms to spread her legs wide, and slid smoothly inside her body. He felt her tightening with that first stroke and pushed her legs higher so that he was deep, so damn deep. She couldn't choose the rhythm, couldn't alter the depth of his thrusts or change the angle. He was in control.

He heard her broken cry on the second stroke, and shuddered at the sharp bite of her nails on his shoulders as she tried to urge him even closer. On the third stroke, harder, deeper, he relished the start of her release. "That's it, Em. Come for me, sweetheart. Come for me."

Her body arched beautifully, her breasts shivered with the strength of her orgasm, her expression was arrested, her breath low and guttural.

Teeth clenched, muscles straining as he held himself deep, Casey joined her, and as they both went boneless, he found the strength to murmur, "You're mine, Emma. Now...and always."

To his relief, she didn't deny it.

But then Emma was already sound asleep.

chapter 14

DAMON HAD BECOME as much a regular fixture around the Hudson household as Emma. For two weeks now, he and Ceily had been almost inseparable, which meant when Damon stopped in to visit, Ceily was there too. And more often than not, their visits seemed to be at dinnertime.

It was the first time Emma could remember seeing Damon so taken with a woman. That he should be taken with Ceily was nothing short of supreme irony. But she was happy for him, and for Ceily.

Honey and Misty had grown up with an austere father, which meant their dinners had always been rather subdued events. Now they both relished the boisterous, busy meals spent with friends and family. Since they lived so close, with Morgan and Misty just up the hill, and were best friends as well as sisters, they were often together. They claimed to enjoy the extra *rational* female company in Ceily and Emma, which Emma took to mean a woman not mooning over the brothers or Casey.

Certainly, Ceily was too straightforward to moon, but

Emma? She merely hid her mooning. Truth was, she couldn't go five minutes without thinking about Casey—and smiling in absolute happiness. He occupied her every waking moment. The past month spent with him had been, well, the stuff of dreams... because she loved Casey with all her heart.

The more time she spent with him, the more she accepted that she'd actually fallen in love with him as a teenager, and never really stopped. Neither time nor distance apart had lessened the emotion one bit.

But being with him, making love to him every night, waking with him every morning, had strengthened that love until she couldn't imagine how she'd survive when she had to leave him.

Yet she knew that eventually she'd have to do just that.

While Casey was at work, Emma visited her parents at the hospital. Her father was now much improved, and her mother was, if not pleasant, at least sober. Dell had been thrilled to find out his wife had willingly gone into rehab for help. As far as Emma was concerned, that, more than anything, had helped revive his spirit. Her mother was allowed to visit him, and they'd talk for hours. Most of their conversations centered around her mother's complaints, but in his commiseration, Dell's speech had gotten much better, as had his motor control.

Her mother was determined to be there for him. It wasn't easy, and she had a lot of difficult times, but she was trying. Losing her daughter hadn't done the trick, but the possibility of losing her husband was too much.

They were both healing and, for once, Emma thought she might be able to be part of her own family. It would never be the ideal—it would never be the Hudson household—but it was an improvement.

She'd spoken with them about the future, and because they both relied on her now, they were willing to adjust.

Casey had gotten home a half hour ago and, after greeting Emma with a kiss, went straight to the apartment for a shower. With Damon and Ceily visiting again, he knew they'd have dinner with the family, rather than slipping off to the cabin with sandwiches, as they often preferred.

He'd just stepped back into the kitchen, hair still damp, casual clothes now in place of his suit, when Honey announced the fried chicken was ready. Morgan stood to call in the kids, but Casey said, "I wanted to tell you all something first."

Into that breaking silence, Emma's phone rang. She jumped, considered ignoring it, but Casey gave her a crooked smile. "Go ahead. This'll wait."

A little embarrassed, she made her apologies and answered the wireless phone while stepping out of the kitchen for privacy. With so many people in for dinner, the buzz of conversation still reached her.

Her first reaction to hearing Dr. Wagner's voice was alarm. Because she visited the hospital each day to be apprised of improvements, he had never found it necessary to call her. But at his jovial greeting, she relaxed...until he announced that he'd be sending her father home in the morning.

It was the signal of the end, her last remaining excuse for lingering in Buckhorn. She'd already contacted a Chicago hospital about her father's physical therapy once he left the hospital. It was located close to her home and could provide everything he needed. She'd also made plans with a rehab facility for her mother.

Unaware of her melancholy, Dr. Wagner continued. "You

can take a copy of his chart with you, but I've already faxed one to the hospital you specified. Take a day or two to get him settled, then set up routine appointments."

"Thank you, I will." Emma squeezed her eyes shut, but couldn't resist asking, "You're sure he's ready to come home?"

"He's shown marked improvement over the last week. Yes, I'd say he's ready—and anxious. Everyone tires of the hospital in a very short time. And being home with his family is a good therapy in its own way, too."

The quiet drone of conversation in the kitchen had died and Emma wondered if everyone had paused to listen to her. "Thanks, Dr. Wagner. Is there a specific time I should be there in the morning?"

They made arrangements, and while Emma made mental note of all things pertinent, her heart ached. She didn't want to go, didn't want to leave Casey. Didn't want to leave her home.

But how impossible would it be for her to tend her parents here where everyone now knew of her mother's transgressions—and her own. She had to be reasonable, not emotional. She had a thriving business, which had been neglected for almost a month. She had a life, friends, family in Chicago. All she had in Buckhorn was a reputation, and some bad history.

With an invisible vise on her heart, and a lump in her throat, she reentered the kitchen and managed to dredge up a smile. Everyone looked up from the dinner table. "My dad is getting out of the hospital tomorrow."

The expressions varied from surprise, concern, to expectation. Casey merely looked detached, and that confused her.

Emma folded her hands together over her waist. "I'm taking him, and my mother, of course, home to Chicago with me."

Sawyer tossed down his napkin. Unlike his son, he looked far from indifferent. "You're what?"

Honey's eyes were wide. "Oh, but…" She glanced at everyone else, as if seeking help.

Morgan rubbed his forehead and muttered something under his breath. Misty fretted.

But Damon, damn him, looked at Casey with one eyebrow raised. "Well?"

Casey, sighing with long-suffering forbearance, left his seat to stand beside her. "I suppose I'll be going to Chicago too."

"What?" Sawyer pushed back his chair.

Morgan snorted. "Since when?"

"You can't be serious," Honey and Misty said in unison.

Emma gaped at him. "You're not moving to Chicago!"

"Why not?" Casey shrugged, disregarding her shock. "I'd already decided that I wanted to switch jobs—which is what I was about to announce when you got your call."

Everyone started to protest at once, but Casey didn't let it stop him. He held up a hand, silencing one and all. "No, just hear me out. I enjoyed what I was doing up to a point, but now it just isn't enough." He winked at Emma. "Having Emma around helped me to realize what I really want to do."

All eyes turned to Emma, making her gulp.

"Just what is that?" Sawyer finally asked.

"Financial planning. I had thought to open something up here, but…" He shrugged again. "Looks like it'll have to be in Chicago."

Emma's mouth fell open.

Ceily pushed back her chair and joined those who were already standing, which was just about everyone. "I'm going to Chicago too."

Damon dropped his fork and leaned back in his seat. "What the hell for?"

She blinked down at him. "Why, to be with you."

"But I'm staying here."

Emma and Ceily said at the same time, "You are?"

He scowled. "Yes, I am. I like it here." He cleared his throat and, though Emma had rarely seen him this way, he looked uncertain. "I spoke to Jesse about buying his land. We're working out a deal."

Ceily's eyes narrowed. "You spoke to *my* grandfather without telling me?" And then, with her eyes popping wide, added, "He agreed to sell to *you?*"

Damon joined the ranks of those standing. "Well, how else could we keep the land around and not have some city slicker throw a damn water park up?"

"You," Ceily pointed out, "are a city slicker."

"Not anymore," he told her with satisfaction. "I was thinking along the lines of some nice tidy little rental cabins that would blend with the woods. Maybe ten or twelve of them. They'd be unobtrusive but lucrative."

Everyone seemed to be holding their breath. Ceily crossed her arms over her chest. "If you stay here, I'm going to fall in love with you."

Very slowly, Damon smiled. "Yeah?"

She gave a brisk nod. "And when I do, I'll damn well expect you to marry me."

His look so intimate, Emma blushed, Damon pulled Ceily close and kissed her. "It's a deal."

Casey threw up his arms. "Well, since that's settled… Emma, how soon do we need to leave?"

Emma rubbed her ear, utterly befuddled. "Casey…" She

looked around at his family, but none of them appeared willing to help. "You can't leave here."

"Why not?"

Logic remained just out of reach. She shook her head. "This is your home."

"It's your home too. But what the hell? We can make a home anywhere, right?"

Sawyer covered his mouth and, Emma suspected, a smile. She groped behind her for a chair. Honey rushed to scoot one beneath her before she dropped. Morgan gave her an encouraging nod.

They were all nuts. When she finally found her voice, it emerged as a squeak. "Uh, *we?*"

Eyes intent on her face, his sensual mouth tipping in a slight smile, Casey nodded. "Me and you."

"But…it's not just me." He had to understand that. "It's my mother and father and…"

"And me," Damon said. He grinned. "I'm like a brother figure, don't you know."

Casey laughed. "And I'm not just me. Hell, Emma, this lunatic crowd—" he indicated the rapt faces of his family members "—is only a small part of the group."

Morgan scowled at him. "I changed your diapers, boy, so don't give me any lip."

Sawyer choked on a laugh. "Are you hinting that you want some privacy, Case?"

He rolled his shoulders, trying to look indifferent—and failing. "Not particularly. I just want Emma to admit that she loves me."

Her mouth fell open again. At this rate, she'd end up with a broken jaw.

Misty leaned over to put her arm around Emma. "Put him out of his misery, hon. Men hate to suffer, this bunch more than most."

Putting her head in her hands, Emma laughed, or maybe she was crying, or a little of both.

Honey wrung her hands. "I really would hate to see Casey move away. But more than that, I'd hate to see him brokenhearted."

They were all nuts. "Well, of course I love him."

Casey beamed at her. "Way to drag out the suspense, Em. Naturally, I love you too. So, where do you want to live?"

There was a time, Emma thought while she fought her smile, when this situation would have totally disconcerted her. She'd have felt out of place, conspicuous. But now she reveled in the open love exchanged between Casey and his family. She wanted to be with all of them. She wanted to have kids who would join the others in the yard, running and playing, happy and carefree and secure in a way she'd never been able to be. They were a good family to be around—a better family to be a part of.

Tears filled her eyes and clogged her throat, making her voice thick. "I'd like to stay here."

Until Sawyer and Morgan both slumped in relief, Emma hadn't known they were so tense waiting for her answer. But to her surprise, Casey didn't seem any more relieved with staying than he had seemed worried about leaving. He walked over to her and took her hand. "Now we could use some privacy. Feel like a boat ride?"

"Yes."

"But you haven't eaten!"

Casey kissed Honey on the top of the head. "Mind if we take it with us?"

Sawyer had already turned and begun packing food into a basket. "'Course she doesn't." He grinned at his son. "Leave B.B. here since he's still playing with the kids. I'll make sure he gets fed. And while you're gone, Honey and Misty can start planning the wedding."

Casey raised an eyebrow at Emma, and Emma laughed. They were overwhelming, wonderfully so. "Thank you."

Rolling his eyes, Casey said, "You say thanks more than anyone I know."

A mere half hour later, Emma found herself in the small cabin Casey owned, naked, beneath him, and thoroughly loved. Casey continued to nibble on her lips, her ear, her chin. The day was so warm, their flesh had melded together. Casey was still inside her.

"You will marry me, won't you, Em?"

She scoffed. "Like you ever had a doubt."

Raising himself up, Casey stared at her with such a serious expression she got worried. "Doubts? You've filled me with more doubts than any man should ever have to suffer. You left here, when I never thought you would, leaving me to doubt if I'd ever see you again. You came back more wonderful than I thought possible, making me doubt I'd even still have a chance."

"Casey." How could he have been so silly? She'd been his for as long as she could remember.

"Damn, Emma, I love you so much it's scary."

"I love you too. I always have."

"You did a very good job of hiding it." He kissed her, sweet and gentle, then deeper until he had to tear himself away. He cupped her face, rubbed her temples with his thumbs. "I am so proud of you, Emma, but, God, it's unsettling to know you built this happy life somewhere else, and damned if you didn't constantly talk about running back to it. I kept wondering how long I could keep you here, if it'd be long enough to get you to fall in love with me again." He gave her another hard kiss and pressed his forehead to hers. "Believe me, Em, I've had doubts."

Emma squeezed him tight.

"Are you sure you're okay with staying here in Buckhorn?"

She grinned. More doubts? "Yes. I love it here. I'd just convinced myself it didn't matter because I thought I couldn't stay." Then she felt compelled to ask, "Aren't you happy to be staying here?"

"I'm happy to be with you. That's what matters most."

"But," she said, insisting on the truth, "you'd rather be here, wouldn't you?"

"Yes, I'd rather be here."

"It won't be easy, you know. Kristin and Lois have spread a lot of gossip…"

Casey grinned. "Everyone already assumes they're just jealous—and understandably."

"Because I have you?"

He laughed, squeezed her, shook his head. "No, goose. Because you're so remarkable, beautiful inside and out."

Emma lowered her gaze to his tanned shoulders. "There's my mother and father to deal with."

"And your possessive dog and dumb-ass Damon and—"

She slugged him. "Hey!"

Laughing, Casey rolled so she was atop him. "Just teasing. I like your dog just fine."

She gave him a fierce scowl. "And Damon?"

Casey pretended to consider that, until Emma tweaked his chest hair. "Okay, okay! He's a good guy. I like him, now that I've gotten used to him."

"Really?"

"He loves you, and he's in love with Ceily, so he's okay in my book." His teasing over, Casey pressed her cheek to his heart and held her there. "No family is ever perfect, Emma. We'll make do with your folks, and you'll work at putting up with mine, and we'll have each other. Everything else will work itself out."

epilogue

Two Months Later

CASEY PUSHED the recently repaired cabin door open and was nearly knocked off his feet by B.B.'s greeting. With his keen ears, the dog heard Casey's approach before his car had rounded the last bend. By the time he reached the porch, B.B. was always waiting.

"Hey, boy. Where's my better half?"

B.B. woofed, accepted a few more vigorous rubs, then ran outside to chase a squirrel. He seemed to enjoy the isolated surroundings as much as Emma.

Casey listened to the sound of running water and knew Emma was in the tiny shower. Since marrying her a week ago, he'd been about as happy as a man could get.

At her insistence, they'd moved into the remote cabin after renovating it a bit. Spotlessly clean, with walls, windows and roof repaired, it made cozy temporary quarters until Damon finished directing the builders on their modest house on the lake.

To Sawyer and Honey's delight, they'd been convinced

to move nearby, only a few acres away from the main house on the land the family owned. With Misty up the hill and Emma down, Honey claimed she had the perfect female company close by.

Casey tossed his suit coat aside, pulled his tie free and loosened his collar as he heard the shower shut off, replaced with the sounds of Emma humming. Seconds later she emerged from the bathroom in a long pink T-shirt, her hair wrapped in a towel. The second she saw him, her beautiful dark eyes lit up and she came to him for a kiss.

"I didn't hear you come in," she said, going on tiptoe to hug him.

It was the type of greeting he'd never tire of. Casey took her mouth in a long, deep kiss before slipping his hands beneath the bottom of the shirt and cuddling her bottom. "Mmm..." he said. But before he carried her off, they needed to talk. "How'd it go today?"

"Actually, it was great." She stepped away to the refrigerator and poured two glasses of iced tea. In silent agreement they wandered out to the screened porch and sat in the new pair of rattan rockers bought for just that purpose. B.B. took a leap off the dock—something he'd begun doing only days after they'd moved in, then waded up on the shore, shook himself off and plopped down in the sun to dry.

"The nurse is terrific and Dad really likes her. She's firm but friendly. Even Mom is grateful to her for the help. I think she still worries about Dad, even though he's doing better."

With Sawyer's help, they'd located a home health-care aide to take over Dell's physical therapy and keep him on a healthy diet by supplying both breakfast and dinner. Her presence freed up Emma's time, a necessity since she'd opened a massage therapy salon in Buckhorn, and found herself booked solid almost every day.

Emma's mother had stayed sober since that eventful day in Mrs. Reider's parking lot, much to Emma's relief. They were both trying to get along, though Casey doubted they'd ever be close. But now they were civil, and little by little they were building a tenuous relationship. It was a start.

Casey looked at her profile then set his tea aside. "Come here," he told her, catching her hand and pulling her into his lap. "You were too far away."

She smiled up at him. "Quit stalling. Tell me how things went with your grandfather."

He winced, but ended it with a grin. "We negotiated. I agreed to stay on as a consultant for the new hires in my department, and he agreed he wouldn't ask more than four days a month from me."

"Sounds doable. And like it might appease him. I know you didn't want any hurt feelings."

"He was so set on making me his heir."

Emma curled into him. "And you tried."

There was no refuting that. But he wasn't cut out for the corporate life, not when his roots were so entrenched in Buckhorn. "I think he's refocusing on Shohn." Casey laughed. "And if I know my little brother, he'll be running the business by the time he's twenty."

"I don't doubt he could if he set his mind to it."

Shohn had been the best man at their small wedding, and he'd also danced at the reception with every female in attendance. For a ten-year-old, he was an outrageous flirt and bursting with confidence. The women doted on him, calling him cute and audacious and adorable—a chip off the old block. Shohn just grinned throughout it all.

"You'll set your business up soon?"

"Yes." Since leaving Chicago, her life had been constant turmoil. Between the issues with her parents, relocating her home and work, the wedding, she'd barely had time to relax. More than anything, Casey wanted things to settle down into a calm routine. "I'll finish up two more weeks with Granddad so my replacement can make a smooth transition. My new office ought to be ready by then and all the advertisements will have been distributed. By the time the house is built we should be all set."

Resting her head on his shoulder, Emma said, "You don't need to make promises to me, Casey. The new house, the new jobs…they're a nice start, and I'm happy about them. But I'll always be happy, no matter what, as long as I have you."

Casey turned her face up to his so he could see her beautiful dark eyes. They were filled with love, all for him. Though Emma thought his life had always been blessed, he knew he'd just been passing time without her.

His grin started slow, but spread. "You know, sweetheart, though it's usually your line, I have to say thank you."

Tilting her head, she laughed. "What are you thanking me for?"

"You came back home to me, Em. You gave me a second chance to have the only woman I want. You gave me back *me*, because without you I was only half-alive."

Her eyes were enormous, sexy, shining with love. "Casey."

"I love you so damn much. Just as you are, just as you've always been, and however you'll be in the future. You're mine. Now and forever."

CAUGHT IN THE ACT

chapter 1

RAIN DRUBBED THE WINDOW sluggishly, but Mick Dawson could still see out, still see all the different people milling around with colorful umbrellas and hats. He was so intent on watching for her he listened to the conversation with only half an ear. But then, half an ear was the most required when his friends got started on that particular topic.

"See that gorgeous blonde?" Josh Marshall said, deliberately baiting as usual. "The one who just came in? She's wearing a push-up bra."

"Is that right?" Zack Grange kept his tone dry. "How can you tell?"

"I know women." Josh's reply held an overdose of world-weary cynicism. "And I especially know women's breasts." He added, "At your age, I'd think you would, too."

"Yeah, and at your age," Zack retorted, "I'd have thought you'd outgrown your adolescent obsessions."

The three of them sat in the corner booth at Marco's, a casual Italian restaurant they'd first discovered five years ago. It was central to where they each worked, in the downtown area.

They came often, more so every year, it seemed, until now they met almost daily for lunch and often for dinner, too. None of them was married. Josh remained a confirmed bachelor, Zack was now a widower and Mick...well, Mick hadn't met the right woman. His criteria were strict, but to his mind, marriage was forever. He'd seen the worst quite often, marriages made in hell and sustained with sarcasm and cheating and drink. He'd also witnessed that elusive best, unions overflowing with love and trust and support. No way would he settle for less than what he knew could and should be.

Because of their different jobs—each of them stressful—and their lack of romantic ties, meeting at Marco's was about as close to a domestic routine as the three men ever saw.

The restaurant served as a place for celebration—a promotion, a new house, whatever came up that seemed celebration worthy. They also commiserated with each other there, as when Zack's young wife had died and he'd wanted to retreat from life, not seeing anyone, not doing anything except coddling his little girl. Or after Mick had gotten shot in the leg and missed several weeks of work, making him edgy.

Mick's life was all darkness and threats and caution. Ugly. Except here at Marco's, and with the people he trusted—his two friends, his family.

No one else. At least, not yet.

No woman had ever snagged his attention long enough to build a trust, certainly never for anything serious. Until now.

Now he was intrigued.

"Mick, tell this fool that breasts don't lift to the sun like a flower." Josh laughed at his own jest. "If they're damn near touching her chin, she's wearing a push-up bra."

Mick glanced at Zack and grinned. "Josh is an idiot where women are concerned—including his insane fascination with breasts, which, I agree, he should have outgrown years ago."

Josh shook his head in a pitying way. "Men do not outgrow their fascination with breasts. You two are just weird."

"A real woman," Mick told him, "would chew you up and spit you out."

"A real woman?" Zack asked, feigning confusion. "You mean someone with an IQ higher than ten? Why would Josh date anyone smarter than he is?"

Josh said, "Ha-ha. You're just jealous." He grinned and added, "Besides, the ladies have better things to do with their mouths when they're around me. Chewing is definitely out."

All three men laughed. "So," Josh said, "if you two abnormal specimens aren't turned on by a woman's breasts—which should be soft and natural, not shoved heavenward—then what does do it for you?"

Mick groaned. "Didn't we have this discussion back in high school?"

"Yeah, but it's still interesting."

"Bellies," Zack blurted.

Josh raised a brow. "Excuse me?"

For the moment, Mick felt content to just listen.

"I love a woman's belly." Zack leaned back, smiling to himself. "Not all muscled up the way some women want to do these days. Just a nice soft smooth woman's belly." He nodded, confirming his own conclusions. "Very sexy."

Josh considered that, then nodded, too. "Okay, I'll give you that one. Bellies are hot. But not belly button rings."

"No," Zack agreed. "A good belly doesn't need decoration."

"What about you, Mick?" Josh prodded. "Long legs? Great ass? What?"

Mick took another bite of his BLT, almost by rote, not because he was hungry. He considered his reaction when he'd seen *her* for the first time. What had he noticed? What had caught his eye and kept him so interested, to the point he almost felt obsessed?

He glanced out the dim window again. It was a miserable, dank July day, breezy, with fat purple clouds hanging low in the sky.

She should be coming along any minute now.

He'd first noticed her at his old neighborhood. He'd been there to rent out the upstairs apartment of the building he still owned, the same building he'd once lived in as a child. There were a lot of...*unpleasant* memories for him there, along with a few special ones. He kept the building as a reminder to himself that his life had changed, *he* had changed, but he was still a product of his upbringing.

Evidently, she rented from the building next door, because she had come down the walkway to the street and headed toward the post office, letters in her hand. It worried Mick, because no one traipsed around unprotected in that area. To call it rough would be a gross understatement.

But there she'd been, strolling along without a care. He hadn't hesitated to follow her, making certain she remained safe, enjoying the back view of her as she strutted along, her stride long and sure and almost cocky.

The sun was blistering hot that day, shining down on her blue-black, shoulder-length hair, hair so silky it appeared fluid when she moved. Soft, light blue eyes looked beyond everything and everyone, including Mick, as if a great distraction held her. He'd been nearly spellbound by her tall, willowy body with its incredibly long, slim legs and broad, fragile shoulders. Strangely enough, even when she came back out of the post office and went past him, again oblivious to her surroundings, he hadn't noticed her breasts. All his attention had been on her face, with its strong jaw, straight nose, pale eyes.

Mick wondered for an instant what Josh would think of his oversight.

Because he wanted to meet her, wanted to get to know her and have sex with her until he passed out from sheer exhaustion, he wasn't about to discuss her with Josh or Zack. So he merely shrugged. "It's a combination of things, and it's different with every woman."

Before either Josh or Zack could respond to that obscure reply, Mick saw her. Blindly, he laid his sandwich aside and twisted in the booth to better see out the window. Regardless of the drizzling rain, the gray sky, he'd expected her. A little rain wouldn't chase her inside. No, not this lady. She jogged every day around the same time, the same place. Or at least she had for two weeks now. It felt like fate, seeing her first in an area where he owned property, and then here again, where he routinely visited.

Zack, being a reasonable sort, hadn't complained much when Mick had made him move so he'd have the window seat. Josh, though, was unreasonable, always. Outrageous bordering on obnoxious. He'd demanded, all with laughter and taunting grins, for Mick to admit who he was watching for. Mick had refused, but now it didn't matter.

The second he shifted his attention, going on alert, Josh noticed.

"Aha! There you go, Zack. I think we'll get to see this mystery lady any second now."

Mick told him, rather succinctly, what he could do with his speculations. But that didn't deter Josh; if anything, it made him more curious.

Both Josh and Zack twisted around, and they, too, watched through the window. The streets were crowded during the lunch hour. Open umbrellas jumped with the breeze as people milled up and down the sidewalk.

And there she was, weaving in and out of human traffic as she jogged, her head uncovered, her clothes better suited to a bright spring day than drizzling rain. Funny thing was, she went right past them, inky-black ponytail bouncing, rainwater dripping off her nose and darkening her sweatshirt, and still Josh and Zack looked, searching the crowds.

They hadn't realized she was the one.

Mick's body knew that she was. Just seeing her now, bedraggled and wet and distracted, he wanted her. His muscles felt tight, his blood hot, his flesh prickly. Damn, if just watching her jog did this to him, how would it feel to kiss her, touch her, to slide deep inside her and hear her moan out a climax?

He felt the stirrings of an erection and muttered a curse. Insanity, he decided, but it couldn't be helped.

To hide his reaction, he grinned and leaned into the corner of the booth. Now that she'd gone by, he could face Zack and Josh and still keep an eye on her for about half a mile on the long, straight street. He glanced, and saw there was almost no jiggle to her firm little butt in the skintight biker shorts. His large hands would cover that bottom completely, and he'd hold her still, keep her steady for his thrusts….

Josh interrupted his very interesting imagery. "So? What are we looking for?"

"Nothing now." Mick deliberately sipped his coffee, knowing he had to get control of himself. And he had to get her; maybe after he'd made love to her for no less than ten days, he'd be able to get her out of his system.

A comical look on his face, Josh stretched past Zack, nearly knocking his plate off the table, and pressed his nose to the window. He looked and looked and finally said, "Damn it, there's nothing, no one, out there worth staring at!"

Mick and Zack shared a look. Zack shrugged. "If you're only looking for breasts, that could be. Maybe Mick was looking for something else."

Josh frowned at Zack. "No way. You know he's straight. We've both seen him with women."

Mick spewed his coffee. Zack burst out laughing, and several women in the restaurant looked their way. They kept looking, smiling, flirting, and Mick shook his head. "You're drawing attention to yourself again, Josh."

"Me? I'm not the one laughing like an idiot."

"You don't need to laugh," Zack told him, "to be an idiot." Then slowly, as if speaking to a half-wit, he said, "I meant Mick was maybe looking at a woman who wasn't top-heavy. Just because it's your ultimate definition of what makes a woman, that doesn't mean the rest of us agree."

Josh studied Mick. "That right?"

"That you have strange ideas about women?" He took another sip of coffee and shrugged. "Yeah."

"I meant," Josh said, exasperated, "is she… lacking in the upper works?"

"As far as I can tell," Mick told him, a little annoyed and not sure why, "she's not lacking anywhere."

That only perplexed Josh more.

Mick again peeked out the window, and to his surprise, he saw her turn at the corner, cross the street and start back toward him. There was no more jiggle from her front than there'd been from her back. When she was just opposite the restaurant, she slowed and finally stopped. She rested her hands on her knees while she breathed deeply, heedless of the light rain and his avid attention.

When she straightened again, she stretched her arms high. Her shirt rose, showing a very sweet belly that Zack no doubt would have adored. Captivated, Mick continued to stare at her while a slow heat stirred deep inside him. She walked into the jewelry store located directly across from the restaurant, and Mick made up his mind.

Pushing aside his plate, he stood. So many times over the past few weeks he'd considered following her, initiating a conversation, introducing himself. He didn't want to rush her, but he'd dreamed about her twice, so he knew his fascination wasn't about to go away. Now seemed like as good a time as any to make his move. "I'll be back."

Josh and Zack stared at him, blank faced. Mick was aware of a thread of urgency vibrating through his blood. It had been like that from the second he first saw her, and every moment after when he watched her. He couldn't put his finger on it, couldn't tell anyone outright what it was about her that appealed to him, what pushed him over the edge. He only knew he wanted her. *Bad.*

As he dodged cars and puddles in the roadway, and muddy, slick spots along the curb, he wondered—for about the hundredth time—if she'd been in the area awhile, or if she'd only recently moved in when he first saw her. He'd been buried in work for the past two months, putting in seventeen-hour days, so it was possible she'd been close by for longer than two weeks.

He could get another assignment any day, so he had to take advantage of the opportunity now.

He hoped like hell she was single. Since first seeing her, he'd studied her closely. There weren't any rings on her fingers, but then he knew women who didn't wear them, especially while jogging. Not once in the two weeks of his awareness had he seen her with anyone, definitely not a man, but that, too, could be a fluke.

Mick turned up the collar on his windbreaker and darted across the sidewalk, trying to keep as dry as possible. He didn't have to look behind him to know both Josh and Zack would be craning their necks, their noses pressed to the window, spying on him. It was totally unlike him to chase a woman.

It was totally unlike him to be interested enough to bother chasing.

Thunder boomed, echoing over the street and rattling windows just as he stepped through the jewelry store's ornate front door. Air-conditioning hit him, chilling his damp skin. He brushed his hair back from his forehead and looked around. Glass cases were everywhere, some large, some smaller to showcase a certain piece, and there, in the far corner, she stood. Dressed in her running wear she looked very out of place, conspicuous and unique in the upscale, glitzy store. She also looked sexy as the original sin with her skin dewy from the drizzle and sweat, her cheeks flushed from exertion, her hair as much out of the ponytail as in, wet and sleek.

Damn, he thought, annoyed with himself. She wasn't that pretty, was in fact kind of plain. She wore no makeup, but her lashes and brows were as dark as her hair. Her nails were short, clean. She had a nice body, strong and sleek, fine boned, but not overly curved, not typically sexy.

Not the type of body to make him sweat at the sight of her.

She didn't give out signals or flirt or even pay much attention to men, not that he'd noticed.

His eyes widened. God, maybe she didn't even like men. That'd be a kicker, one he wouldn't, couldn't accept. Not when the mere sight of her turned him on. He didn't just want her; he felt as if he had to have her, just as he had to sleep or eat. It was the damnedest feeling, and he wasn't happy with it or himself.

She didn't appear interested in any particular item as she moseyed from case to case, peering inside, then shaking her head and moving on. For the moment, Mick was content to watch her. He slipped his hands into his jeans pockets, then quickly pulled them out again when he realized that negligent pose might expose the weapon in the waistband holster at his back. Being off duty, he didn't need the gun, but he always carried it.

In this day and age, his cover wouldn't have been believable without it. Drug dealers, prostitutes, gamblers…they all expected you to be armed, and if you weren't, you were considered an idiot, or worse.

Usually, even when conditions didn't call for a weapon, he managed to smuggle in the Smith & Wesson 9 mm in an ankle holster. There were times, though, when he had to go without, leaving him feeling naked, and those were the times when he got most tense, when the adrenaline rush was all but blinding. He always wanted a woman afterward, a way to release all that pent-up energy.

He wanted a woman now.

He wanted her.

Moving closer, watching her, he was amazed that she didn't feel his attention, so acute that it had him half-hard again with expectation. It had always been his experience that blatant staring was felt like a stroke of ice. But then, she was a civilian, and he'd already noted the first day he saw her how heedless she could be of her surroundings. It amazed him sometimes that people could survive with so little caution.

The door chimed behind Mick and more people entered. Two men, dressed much like Mick in jeans and T-shirts, wearing sneakers, one in a ball cap. They appeared to be in their mid-thirties, clean, middle-class. As a cop, Mick automatically took in everyone and everything. He'd already noted the two salesladies, the older couple looking at cocktail rings for an anniversary. He picked up on actions and quiet dialogue and expressions.

Caution was as basic to him as breathing. And because he wasn't a civilian, wasn't oblivious, he immediately detected the sudden charge in the air despite the nonthreatening scene and apparently ordinary people. It had come in like the wind with the men, and Mick didn't like it worth a damn. He had a keen sixth sense, and he trusted it more than he trusted appearances.

The woman looked up, around, made brief eye contact with the two men who'd entered, then again with Mick. Their gazes locked and held for an instant, an instant that made his gut clench with awareness. She gave him a small smile, a simple, friendly smile that nonetheless heightened his tension, before she turned away again.

Senses on alert, Mick followed her, not too close, in no way obvious, but keeping her within reach. Because the shop was small and crowded with displays, the air thick and humid from the rain outside, he could detect her scent. It was earthy and rich, warm woman, damp skin and clean female sweat. His heart punched hard, a little fast; his sex thickened. He'd been too long without a woman, too long without any sexual relief. Sometimes being a contrary bastard was a real pain.

Her wet running shoes squeaked on the ceramic tile floor as she browsed, appearing to study the shop, not just the wares but the structure, the setup. Mick frowned as he watched her, further intrigued and a little distracted. Out of the corner of his eye he saw one of the men reach into his jacket pocket, and a silent alarm screamed inside Mick's head.

He jerked around, but not quickly enough.

"Everyone stay still and calm." The guy waved a SIG Sauer .45 around the room with menacing intent. "No one panic or do anything stupid," he said with a sneer, "and I won't have to kill anyone."

Damn, damn, damn. Mick took a quick, inconspicuous glance around. The elderly woman, clinging to her husband, looked ready to faint, while the salespeople stood motionless, frozen in horror. His movements so slight that no one paid him any mind, Mick edged closer to the woman he'd followed. She stared at the gunman, her blue eyes darker now with fascination, but he saw no real fear.

"We'll do our business," the guy in the ball cap said, "and then leave and no one will be hurt."

Mick didn't buy it for a second; the words sounded far too rehearsed, far from sincere. And there was an anticipatory expression on the man's face.

Things never worked out the easy way—not life, not love, sure as hell not an armed robbery.

The second man hitched his gun at the saleswoman. "You, come open the register and make it quick."

She balked, more out of surprise than rebellion. Mick had a similar sensation. They were surrounded by diamonds and gold of unbelievable value, yet this idiot wanted what little cash might be in the register? The robber had to realize that most sales would be handled with credit cards or checks; his demand didn't make sense.

Mick's hands twitched. He wanted to grab his gun; he wanted to be in control. Right now, control meant keeping everyone alive. It meant keeping *her* alive.

Without warning, the man who'd issued the order shouted, "*Now*, goddamn it!" and everyone jumped, the saleslady screeching and stumbling over her own feet as she rushed to obey.

A predictable panic reaction, Mick thought, to the threat of sudden violence, not something a robber intent on keeping things calm would have instigated. Mick's suspicions rose.

The older woman quietly wept, one saleslady turned

white, the other shook so badly she had a hard time working the register. Before she could get it open, distant sirens broke the quiet, making both men curse hotly. Mick tensed, waiting for another outburst, for them to turn and run, for them to retaliate by shooting the saleslady. He'd learned early on that criminals did the most absurd and unaccountable things, often causing death without reason. He prepared himself for any reaction.

But what they did took him totally by surprise.

They didn't yell, didn't run. They focused their blame on the young woman next to Mick.

"*Bitch,*" the guy in the ball cap snarled. "You set off an alarm."

Startled, she blinked, looked around, backed up two paces. "No," she breathed. It was the first time Mick had heard her voice, which quaked with fear, bewilderment. "I don't even know where—"

The man took aim at her and, without thinking, Mick blocked his path. Both gunmen froze at his audacity. He felt the woman's small hands against his back, clutching at his jacket. He felt her face press into his shoulder, was aware of her accelerated breathing, her trembling. She was deathly afraid, and anger surged in his blood.

His voice as low and calm as he could make it, Mick said, "She's a customer. She doesn't know where the alarm is."

He was ignored.

"Everybody get down!" As the guy in the ball cap yelled his order, a car screeched up in front of the shop, motor idling. The customers all dropped to the floor, panicked, including the woman at Mick's back. He felt her jerky movements, could hear her panting in terror.

Mick moved more slowly, his mind churning as he tried to buy himself some time. If he could get his gun... His elbow touched the woman's wrist, he was so close to her. She, like the others, had stretched out flat, covering her head with her arms, shaking. Mick kept himself balanced on his elbows, ready to move, watching without appearing to watch.

The sudden shattering of glass—again and again as each case was destroyed—caused the older woman to wail, the saleslady to whimper. The woman next to Mick never made a sound. He wanted to look at her, to somehow reassure her, but he didn't dare take his attention off those weapons. The two men grabbed a few large items of jewelry, but it was as if they destroyed the store just for the sake of destruction.

It was by far the most pathetic, disorganized and unproductive robbery Mick had ever witnessed—and that made him more suspicious than anything else might have. By rights, they should have known where the most valuable items would be, and should have concentrated their sticky fingers there. Instead, they seemed to take whatever was at hand without thought to its worth. No one robbed a jewelry store without casing it first, without knowing what would be found inside and where.

The two men finally headed for the door. The tension tightened, grew painful, static crowding the air until it seemed impossible to breathe—and the bastard in the ball cap turned to fire.

Mick moved so fast, he barely had the thought of moving before he was over her, his arms covering her head, his muscular body completely blanketing her delicate one. Though she was tall for a woman, about five-nine, she was small boned and felt fragile to his six-three frame. He was plenty big enough, and more than determined enough, to be her protection.

She gasped at the feel of him on top of her and immediately stiffened, forcing her head up, twisting. "No! What are you doing?"

He jammed her head back down, then cursed when her cheek hit the hard tile floor. Knowing what she likely thought and wishing he could spare her, Mick said into her ear, "Be still."

She wiggled more furiously, trying to free herself, confused and frightened, unsure of his intent. "He's going to—" Mick began to explain, and then it was unnecessary.

The crack sounded loud and startling; the sudden pain in his right shoulder was a lick of pure fire. For only a moment, his arms tightened around her and he ground his teeth together. "Oh God," she whispered, trying to turn toward him.

Mick grunted, but didn't move. No, he wasn't about to move. For whatever reason, they wanted her dead, but they'd have to get through him first.

He felt the blood spreading on his back, sticky and warm; he was aware of the woman squirming beneath him, gasping, crying. But it wasn't until he heard the door open that he rolled and drew his gun at the same time. He blocked the awful pain, any distractions, and got off a clean shot through the glass door, clipping the man who'd tried to shoot her. The hollow-point bullet hit him high in the left thigh before he could get into the car. The leg crumpled beneath him and he went down in an awkward heap, howling in pain, grabbing for the open car door in desperation.

The car lurched away, spewing gravel and squealing tires, tossing the man back. The side of his head cracked solidly against the curb. He lay there unconscious, sprawled out like a wounded starfish.

Surging to his feet, Mick ran out the door. He spotted the car, drew careful aim and fired again. The back window exploded, but the car didn't slow. It careened around the corner on two wheels and disappeared.

Already the streets had filled with onlookers, people too damn stupid to stay inside and away from gunfire. Mick's arm rapidly went hot, cold and then numb; his fingers throbbed. His hand shook as he tried to hang on to his gun, to steady himself.

Josh and Zack appeared, having witnessed the tail end of the robbery from the restaurant. Josh, smooth as silk, slipped the gun from Mick's hand and dropped it into his trouser pocket. They'd arrived just seconds before the police cars. More people from all over the street converged, whispering, curious. Josh caught Mick's upper arm and supported him. "Jesus, man. You're shot."

Zack came to his other side and yelled, "Someone call the paramedics. He needs an ambulance." That made Mick laugh, since Zack was an EMT. Zack shook his head wryly and pulled out his radio, putting in the call himself.

"Here, sit down," he said, and led Mick to the rain-wet curb.

"I don't want to sit in a damn puddle," Mick grumbled. "I'm fine." Fine enough that he wanted to find the woman. He looked around, and when he didn't immediately see her, terror started to take hold. He located the elderly couple leaning against the brick building. The old woman clung to her husband and cried, while he peered around in dismay and impotent anger. Mick saw the two salespeople, huddled together, dry eyed but white as snow, apparently in shock. Cops swarmed everywhere, separating the witnesses so they couldn't share stories. Two police cars took off to give chase, while another radioed in the call. An officer headed Mick's way.

Where the hell is she?

When the cop reached him, frowning, his hand resting on his holster, Mick said quietly, "I'm Mick Dawson, Vice." He started to reach inside his jacket for his badge, but his arm wouldn't cooperate and he cursed.

Josh said, "I'll get it." He retrieved the badge and flipped it toward the officer, who nodded and yelled for someone to get a blanket.

Frustrated, Mick could do no more than stand there, getting weaker by the second, while Zack gave instructions into his radio and Josh more or less held him upright.

Zack told the officer, "The ambulance is on its way. I'm an EMT. I'll see to him until it gets here."

The officer, frowning in worry, handed Zack the blanket and then set off to clear the street.

Mick started to pull free, desperate to find the woman and make certain she was okay, but just then she stepped around the elderly couple. Her face, her beautiful face, was creased with worry, with disbelief. From a slight distance, they stared at each other, and there was no distraction in her gaze now, no oblivion. The horror of what had just happened darkened her eyes to midnight.

A bruise discolored her cheekbone from when he'd pushed her head down. His stomach cramped with that realization. She trembled all over, and Mick shook off Zack to go to her, needing to hold her, to apologize, though he didn't even know her name, had no idea who she was or why the robbers had wanted to kill her.

Zack, who'd been looking at the wound in his shoulder, drew him back. "Damn it, Mick, you're ready to drop."

Mick started to deny that, but then his legs gave out, and if it hadn't been for Josh and Zack supporting him, he'd have been sitting in the middle of the sidewalk instead of on the curb with a folded blanket beneath him. His vision swam, closed in.

"You're losing a lot of blood," Zack said in his calm, professional voice, but Mick heard the concern, the anger, as his friend began first aid.

"Don't let her get away." Mick meant to say it loud and clear, an order that couldn't be ignored. But the words emerged as a faint whisper, and that infuriated him. He'd finally met her—sort of—and he sounded weak, looked weak.

At the moment, he was weak. Too weak.

But she'd felt so good beneath him for that brief, charged moment, adding to his adrenaline rush, further arousing him though they'd been in the middle of a very dangerous situation. It was so absurd, but even as he'd braced for that bullet, he'd been aware of her under him, her ass cuddling his groin, her head fitting neatly under his chin.

He forced his head up and said again, trying for more than a whisper this time, "Don't let her get away."

He knew Josh heard him because he leaned closer. "Who?"

"In…the running clothes. Black hair." That was the very best description he could muster under the circumstances.

Josh looked up, eyes narrowed as he scanned the crowd and then settled on someone. He said, "You've got it, buddy. Now you just rest. I'll take care of it." He got to his feet and stalked forward purposefully, saying in a tone that brooked no argument, "Miss? I need to see you, please."

And Mick blacked out.

chapter 2

"WHERE IS SHE?" The sound of his own voice, foggy and dark and thin, appalled him. Mick tried to clear his throat, but it was impossible.

"Shh," he heard Zack say. "Take it easy."

Mick struggled to open his eyes, then wished he hadn't. What the hell had they done to him? His shoulder didn't hurt, at least not at the moment, but he felt as if his brain might explode, and every muscle he possessed was sluggish, refusing to cooperate with his brain's commands.

More cautiously this time, he cracked his eyes open and found Zack on guard at his bedside. Where was Josh? Where was *she*?

"The woman?" he asked again, and he sounded like a dying frog.

Zack lifted a glass of water with a straw to Mick's mouth. He wanted to tell Zack to jam the straw in his ear, but he couldn't. He gave in to his thirst and took several quick sips. He started to move his arm, and fire burned down his side. *Now* his shoulder hurt. He ground his teeth, hissing for breath.

"The anesthesia is wearing off," Zack explained. "You'll be groggy a little longer, but overall you're fine. They left the bullet in—that's two for you now, right? Taking it out would only have caused more damage. You lost too much blood already."

Mick was still registering what Zack had said when his friend leaned forward and growled, not two inches from his nose, "You scared the hell out of me! Don't you know if you get shot you should stay down? Swinging your arm around that way just encouraged it to bleed more."

Mick grunted, as much from the pounding in his head as in reply. "Where the hell is she?"

Exasperated, Zack sighed. He didn't need to ask *She who?* "Josh has been keeping a close eye on her, since right before you passed out and bashed your damn head on the ground. Yeah, that's why your head feels like it's splitting. I'm surprised you don't have a concussion, as hard as you hit. If you didn't have to be so damn macho, if you'd just tell someone when you were ready to faint—"

"I did *not* faint." Mick's voice, his words, were gaining strength, and he grumbled, "I passed out from blood loss."

"Yeah, well, they look about the same when you drop right in the middle of a crowd."

It hurt, but Mick narrowed his eyes and said, "Zack? Come closer."

Zack, filled with new concern, leaned down close.

"Where the hell is she!"

Zack jerked back and grimaced. "All right, all right, you don't have to bust my eardrum. You said, all ominous cloak and dagger, 'Don't let her get away.' Neither Josh nor I knew if that meant she should be arrested, or if she was the lady you'd been watching for."

Mick jerked—and the sudden movement squeezed the breath right out of his lungs. Damn, he'd forgotten how badly a bullet hurt. Through clenched teeth, he snarled, "You didn't…?"

"Turn her over to the cops? Nope. They questioned her, of course, but Josh followed them to the station and then picked her up afterward. She's fine, just shook up and babbling about you being a hero—no surprise there, I suppose. She claims you took that bullet for her, and she wants to see you, overflowing with gratitude and all that, but, of course, since we didn't know what the hell was going on…"

"I'm going to kill you."

Zack grinned. "We collected her for you, but she's none too happy right now. Josh is more or less, er, detaining her. No, don't look like that. You know he wouldn't hurt her. But he's taxing himself; it's been over four hours, after all."

Four hours! Mick wanted to groan again, thinking of her waiting that long, Josh coercing her into hanging around….

"No," Zack said, correctly reading his mind, "she didn't want to leave, she wanted to see you. And she's not happy when she doesn't get what she wants. She's actually—" Zack coughed. "She's a very determined lady."

Zack looked at Mick's IV and added, "Evidently, she wants you."

That was a revelation, one he could easily live with. His head pounded, but Mick held back all wimpy sounds of distress and said, "Get her for me."

"Don't be an idiot! You're hardly in any shape to start getting acquainted." Zack stood, towering over the bed. "I assumed once you came to, you'd explain what the hell's going on, we could then explain it to her, and then we'd let the lady go home so you could get some rest."

"Do *not* let her leave here alone." Mick had awakened with a feeling of panic, again seeing that gun aimed at her—just her, no one else, and for no apparent reason. Until he figured things out, he wanted her watched. He wanted her protected.

It pissed him off royally that he had to ask others to do that for him.

"Mick, we can't just refuse to let her leave."

Giving Zack a sour look, Mick said, *"Get her."*

"Damn, you're insistent when you're injured."

"And I've heard more 'damns' from you in the last five minutes than I have since your daughter was born."

Zack shrugged. "Well, Dani isn't here to listen and emulate. Besides, it's not every day I see a friend shot."

"You say I need to recoup, Zack?"

"That's right."

"So how is it going to help my recuperation when I get out of this bed and kick your sorry ass?"

Zack hesitated before giving in with a laugh. "I can't fight you now, because you're already down and I feel sorry for you. If I let you get up and attempt to hit me, you'd probably start bleeding all over the place again and rip your stitches, and I'd have to let you win." He held up both hands. "Stay put. I'll find out how soon you'll be moved to your room and when Delilah can join you."

Pain ripped through his shoulder as Mick did a double take. "Delilah?"

Zack stared. "Don't tell me you didn't even know her name."

"So?" Learning her name hadn't been his top priority. Touching her had, and he'd accomplished that while also protecting her. A nice start, except for the fact that someone wanted her dead, and had shot him trying to accomplish the deed. But he'd figure that one out eventually. In the meantime, he had no intention of letting anyone hurt her.

"So you took a bullet for a complete stranger?"

Very quietly, Mick asked, "Wouldn't you have done the same?"

And because Zack already had once, long ago, he turned and walked out.

The second Zack pushed aside the curtain and left, a nurse stepped in, ready to check Mick's vitals and reassure him. She lingered, and Mick couldn't help but smile at her, despite his discomfort and his current frazzled frame of mind. She was about five years older than he, putting her in her early thirties. She was attractive even in sensible white shoes and a smock. She smoothed his hair, her fingers gentle, while she explained that he'd be there overnight, but would likely leave in the morning, and that they'd put him in his own room very soon.

Still being polite, Mick was careful not to encourage her. He wanted to meet Delilah, wanted to talk to her, hear her voice when she wasn't frightened, see her smile again. She was the only woman he wanted at the moment, and he was relieved when the orderly showed up and announced it was time to take Mick to his room.

Any minute now he'd meet her, really meet her. And he promised himself that not long after that he'd kiss her…and more. He didn't know how he'd manage that, all things considered, but he would. He had to taste her, had to stake a claim in the best way known to man.

He discounted his wound. It wouldn't slow him down; he wouldn't let it slow him down.

He needed her.

"I'M CAPABLE OF WALKING on my own."

Josh, the man "escorting" her to Mick's room, gave a disgruntled sigh and removed his hand from her arm. He'd been pushy and demanding, a total stranger insisting she follow his orders. She'd done so, once she realized he was a friend of the man who'd protected her.

But she didn't like him, and she definitely didn't like the distrustful way he loomed over her. He pretended gentlemanly qualities, but she knew he held on to her so she couldn't get away. She'd already told him a dozen times that she had no intention of leaving.

Not that Josh paid any mind to what she had to say.

He had "slick" written all over him, from the way he held himself to the way he noticed every single female in the vicinity. She understood his type. Josh was one of those men who felt superior to women, but covered that nasty sentiment with charisma and a glib tongue. No doubt, given his good looks and outrageous confidence, women regularly encouraged him.

Del just wanted to get by him so she could meet the other man, the one who'd risked his life for her.

Josh slanted her one of his insulting, speculative looks. "I hope you don't go in there and give him any grief."

When she didn't answer him, he added, "He did save your sorry, ungrateful little butt, after all."

She could hardly ignore that! Del whirled and stuck a finger into his hard chest. "I know. I was *there*," she snapped.

Her control, her poise and any claim to ladylike behavior were long gone. Today had been the most bizarre and eventful day of her life. "You're the one who doesn't seem to understand that I need to see him, that I should have been there with him all along, to thank him—"

He glared at her, rubbed at his chest and walked away. Del had to hurry to catch up to him. A few seconds later they turned a corner, and Josh pushed a door open. "Here we go," he said. And then under his breath, but not much under, she heard him mutter, "Thank God."

Through the open doorway, Del could see the occupied hospital bed, and she drew up short. Heavy emotion dropped on her, making her feel sluggish in the brain— which was a first. Her breath caught. Her stomach flipped. Her heart fluttered.

He lay almost flat, his long, tall body stretching from one end of the narrow bed to the other. She remembered his height when he'd covered her, protecting her and all but dwarfing her despite her own height. She remembered the power of him, too, the vibrating tension and leashed strength.

His beautiful, dark brown hair now looked disheveled, spikey from the earlier rain and his injuries and... Her bottom lip quivered with her loss of composure.

He was the most beautiful man she'd ever seen, though she hadn't really seen him until he threw himself on top of her and saved her life. At first she'd thought he was with the robbers, and she'd known so much fear she'd actually tasted it.

Instead, he'd taken a bullet meant for her.

Her heart stuttered to a near stop. What kind of man did that? He didn't know her, owed her nothing. She'd barely noticed him in the store before that.

But when he'd chased the bad guys just like a disreputable Dirty Harry clone, she'd looked him over and hadn't been able to stop looking. He'd been all hard, flexing muscle, animal grace and speed.

Now he was flat on his back in a hospital bed. She sighed brokenly, choking on her emotions.

He turned his head at the sound she made, and those deep brown, all-consuming eyes warmed. A slight, heart-stopping smile curved one side of his mouth, and he looked sexy and compelling. In a deep, dark voice hoarse with pain, he whispered, "Hi."

Just like that her heart melted and sank into her toes. There was so much inflection, so much feeling, in that one simple hello. Vaguely, she heard Josh saying, "Delilah, meet Mick Dawson. Mick, Miss Delilah Piper."

Del paid no attention to Josh, her every thought and sense focused on the large dark man in the bed. In the bed because of *her*. No one had ever done anything even remotely like that for her. Her life in the past few years had been, by choice, a solitary one. Even before then, though, her relationships had been superficial and short-lived— nothing to inspire such protective instincts.

The reality of what he'd done, what he'd risked for her, threw Del off balance emotionally, just as the sight of him stirred her physically.

Without another thought, she moved straight to the bed. Mick looked at her, still smiling, but now with his eyes a bit wider, more alert, a little surprised. She sat near his hip and stroked his face. She *needed* to touch him, to feel the warmth of his skin, the lean hardness of his jaw…. Unable to help herself, she kissed him.

Against his lips, she said with heartfelt sincerity, "Thank you."

He started to say something, but she kissed him again. It felt...magically right; she could have gone on kissing him forever. His mouth was firm, dry. Five o'clock shadow covered his jaw, rasping against her fingertips, thrilling her with the masculinity of it. Heat, scented by his body, lifted off him in waves, encompassing her and soothing her. He tasted good, felt good, smelled good.

A little breathless, bewildered by it all, Del said, "I'm so sorry. It should be me in that bed."

"No!" His good arm came up, his hand, incredibly large and rough, clasped her shoulder, and he levered her away. For a man in a sickbed, he had surprising strength and was far too quick.

And he looked angry. And protective.

Excitement skittered down her spine, while tenderness welled in her chest.

The door opened again and Zack, the man who was a little nicer than Josh, started in. He jerked to a halt when he saw them both on the bed, nose-to-nose. Startled, Zack began to backpeddle, only to change his mind once more when he spotted Josh standing in the corner, smirking.

"Uh, Mick?" Zack sounded ridiculously cheerful and vastly amused. "I see you're feeling...better."

Josh chuckled. "I imagine he feels just fine right about now, since she's in here."

Slowly, not wanting to upset Mick, Del stood and cast a quick glare at both men. In her fascination with Mick, she'd all but forgotten them and how they'd bulldozed her, refusing her every request, evading her questions.

"I'd have been with you sooner, but they wouldn't let me," she said to Mick, feeling piqued all over again. "I didn't know what was going on or why—"

"Only family could see him before he got to his room," Zack said, some of his cheerfulness dwindling.

Del had heard the same lame explanation at least ten times, yet Zack had pretty much stayed with Mick, except for when he'd taken a turn guarding her so Josh could look in on him. They were friends, not family, or so they'd told her, so their excuses held no weight. They'd insisted she come to the hospital, insisted she wait around, and then they'd refused to let her do anything useful—like see Mick and thank Mick and...

She brushed her stringy bangs out of her face, still annoyed, still frustrated. "You could have taken my suggestion and told them I was his wife. Then they'd have let me in."

Josh choked; Zack raised one eyebrow and looked at Mick. Mick grinned, then reached out for her hand with his good arm, which meant stretching across the bed. When she took his hand, he said, "I'm sorry you were worried." And in a quieter tone, "Are you all right?"

Dismissing the other two men, she again sat on the bed. She wanted to kiss him some more, but his friends were standing there, not only ogling them, but bristling like over-protective bulldogs. Besides, after her run through the rain, and the burglary, she probably wasn't all that appealing.

"I'm fine."

Mick touched her bruised cheek with gentle fingertips. His eyes were nearly black with concern. "Damn, I'm sorry about that."

His tone made her heart beat faster, made her skin flush

and her insides warm. They'd only just met, but she felt as if she'd known him forever.

Catching his wrist, she turned his hand and kissed his palm. Again he looked surprised, and if she didn't miss her guess, aroused. His eyes were hot, his cheekbones slashed with color. He stared at her mouth.

Was it possible he felt the same incredible chemistry?

Del had to clear her throat to say, "You saved me. I'm sorry I freaked. I thought…well, at first I thought you were with them and you intended to…"

"I know." He continued to stare at her mouth, which made her belly quiver, her nerves jump. "I'm sorry I scared you."

The irony didn't escape her. Here he was, in bed, wounded, and he kept apologizing to her. She'd never met a man like him. "You kept me alive," she stressed, which discounted any side effects, such as a small bruise, as unimportant. "I'm the one who's sorry. Well, not sorry that I'm alive, but sorry that you got hurt in the process."

"It's just a flesh wound."

Zack coughed and Josh snorted.

She looked at his two friends, then peered at Mick suspiciously. Was it worse than she thought? But the nurse had told her he'd be okay.

Her ire resurfaced and she said to Mick, "I wanted to come in and see you, but they wouldn't let me. Waiting was awful. When we found out how long it would be, I planned to go home and shower and change, and try to make myself presentable, so when you came to I wouldn't be such a sight, but he—" she directed a stiff finger at Josh "—wouldn't be at all reasonable about any of it."

"Don't blame Josh," Mick said, smiling just a bit. "I asked him to keep you around."

"You did?"

"I was afraid you'd disappear and I wouldn't get to see you again."

His words were so sweet, she forgot about her sweat and ruined clothes and stringy hair. "I wouldn't have done that, I swear! I would have come right back."

Again she leaned down and kissed him, but this time he was ready for her and actually kissed her back. His tongue stroked past her lips for just a heartbeat, then retreated. Her breath caught and she sighed. *Oh wow.*

With a numb mind and tingling lips, she heard him rumble in a low voice, "I want to see you, Delilah."

She lowered her voice to a mere whisper. "I want to see you, too. I just wish I'd had time to clean up. I'm all sweaty and I have mud on my feet and my clothes are limp and wrinkled. I smell like a wet dog."

His hot gaze moved from her eyes to her mouth and back again, his expression devouring. "You smell like a woman."

She almost slid right off the side of the bed. Much more of that and she'd be sweating again, that or she'd self-combust.

He was just so darn sexy! The dark beard shadow covering the lower part of his face made him look dangerous. After witnessing him in action that afternoon, she knew he *was* dangerous. His brows were thick, his lashes sinfully long, his high-bridged nose narrow and straight, his mouth delicious. And those dark eyes… This man had singled her out and risked his life to save her. It was beyond comprehension.

It was the most exciting thing that had ever happened to her.

Only a thin hospital gown and a sheet concealed his entire gorgeous, hard body from her. She looked him over, saw the width of his chest, the length of his legs. His feet tented the sheet, and as her attention slid back up his body, she noticed something else was beginning to tent, as well.

She returned her gaze to his, saw the burning intensity there, and froze. He wasn't embarrassed and made no attempt to conceal his growing erection.

Using his left hand, Mick lifted her fingers and caressed them gently. His eyes were direct, unapologetic, and when she glanced at the other two men, it was to see them looking out the window, at the ceiling, anywhere but at the bed.

She was unimpressed with their show of discretion after everything they'd already put her through. It didn't matter that they'd directed their attention elsewhere; they were still in the room, their presence noticeable. They'd more or less forced her to stay, at Mick's request, but it was obvious they still didn't want her alone with him.

If they'd really been polite, if they'd trusted her at all, they'd have left the room. But no, they weren't ready to budge an inch. She supposed they didn't know her well enough to trust her and, after all, he'd just been shot, but still…

Mick looked vital and strong and all-male, and his effect on her was beyond description. She'd long since decided men weren't worth the effort, but oh, she hadn't met this man yet.

"Are you sure you're going to be okay?" She gripped his hand hard, trying to accustom herself to the unfamiliar feelings of tenderness and worry and explosive desire. It had been forever since she'd felt so much awareness for a man. Well, actually, she'd never felt it—not like this. Which was the main reason she seldom dated anymore. Men didn't appreciate her emotional distance.

She felt far from emotionally distant now. "The nurse said you'd be fine, but…"

"Yeah." His voice was rich with promise. "I should be out of here soon."

"Tomorrow," Zack said, still keeping his eyes averted, "as long as you agree to take it easy. They'll send you home with antibiotics and painkillers, but knowing you—"

A noise in the hall alerted them to more visitors. Mick released his hold on Del and bunched the blankets over his lap to hide his partial erection just seconds before a man and woman pushed through the door. They entered in a rush, heading straight for Mick.

Not being much of a people person, Del faded aside, inching into the corner opposite Zack and Josh. Mick frowned in displeasure at her retreat, and Josh said, "No worries. I've got it covered." When he moved to stand between Del and the door, Del realized he meant that he'd continue to keep her around.

As if she'd leave now!

Del's attention snagged on the pretty blond woman now hovering over the bed, kissing the top of Mick's head, his high cheekbone, his chin. "Thank God you're all right!"

The woman's lips were all over Mick, and Del didn't like it at all. But she knew she had no right to complain.

"I made Dane drive like a demon to get us here."

"Angel," Mick protested, all the while grinning widely so that Del knew he didn't really mind her attention at all, "you didn't need to rush. I'm fine."

Del wondered if Angel was her name or an endearment.

The woman pressed her cheek to Mick's. "But you were shot!"

Zack laughed. "I told you on the phone he'd be all right."

"I had to see for myself."

Josh crossed his arms over his chest and smiled. It was apparent to Del that they all knew each other, that these were more of Mick's friends. These people Josh trusted; she could see that.

Feeling like an outsider, or worse, an interloper, Del frowned.

"According to the doctor," Josh said, addressing Angel, "he'll need some baby-sitting."

Zack nodded. "Luckily the bullet hit at a tangential entry. It was expended enough that the force didn't carry it into the chest cavity, which could have injured his lung, or in a through-and-through injury that could have caused more damage to his arm."

"Yeah," Mick mumbled, tongue in cheek, "I'm real lucky."

Del's heart ached for him. This was the most she'd heard, and it hadn't been revealed for her benefit. Rather, the information was for the new arrivals, especially the woman with the lips.

The female who was trusted.

It all sounded so horrendous, worse than Del had imagined. If the shooter had stepped just a little bit closer, if his aim had been a little higher… She closed her eyes, fighting back a wave of renewed fear and impossible guilt. Mick could so easily have been killed.

Her eyes snapped opened when she heard Angel say, "You'll come home with me, of course."

Del had no real rights to jealousy or possessiveness, but

she felt them just the same. Who was this beautiful woman who felt free to kiss and touch Mick?

And then the thought intruded: was he married?

Del's stomach knotted. She tried to see Mick's hand, but couldn't with both people crowded near his bed.

The man with Angel said, "The kids would love a chance to fetch and carry for you. They adore you, you know that."

With incredible relief, Del realized that if they had kids, they must be a couple. Which meant Mick was safe from any romantic entanglement with Angel.

Del was just beginning to relax again, feeling on safer ground, when yet another couple pushed through the door. This woman was lovely, too, but the man with her held her close to his side, leaving no doubt that they were together. He was large and dark and so intense he looked like Satan himself. Del stared, but no one else seemed alarmed.

Mick even rolled his eyes. "Angel, did you drag Alec and Celia down here, too?"

Angel touched his face. "They were visiting when we got the news. Of course they insisted on coming."

The room was all but bursting with large men. Josh and Zack were big enough, but their physical presence was nothing compared to Dane's and Alec's, both of whom were in their prime and exuding power.

And Mick, even flat on his back and wounded, was a masculine presence impossible to ignore. He had an edge of iron control, of leadership, that couldn't be quelled by an injury. All in all, the men made an impressive group. Del expected the walls to start dripping testosterone any moment.

She watched them all, memorizing names and studying faces as they shared familiar greetings. The women were all-smiles, and even Dane looked somewhat jovial. Alec, however, looked capable of any number of nefarious deeds.

Just as Del thought it, she saw his piercing gaze sweep over Mick from head to toe, and he grinned a surprisingly beautiful grin, making his black eyes glitter and causing Del to do an awed double take.

"I knew you wouldn't go much longer," Alec drawled, and even his deep voice sounded scary to Del, "without getting yourself shot again. It's a nasty habit."

"I'll try real hard to keep that in mind," Mick said.

"Zack tells me you got shot on purpose this time." Alec crossed his massive arms. "At least I try to avoid it when possible, and when Celia isn't around."

Celia, slim and elegant, leaned over Mick's bed and kissed his forehead. To Del's way of thinking, there was far too much kissing going on, and far too many visitors. At this rate, she'd never get him alone.

But that concern was secondary to another. Judging by what Alec had said, this wasn't the first time Mick had been shot. Del looked at Josh and Zack, to judge their reactions to that news. Their expressions were impassive, leading her to believe they already knew Mick had been shot before this.

"Don't let Alec tease you, sweetie," Celia said. "He's glad I got him shot. Otherwise we'd never have ended up together."

Alec looked very dubious at her statement, whereas Del was completely floored. What in the world did these men do that they took turns catching bullets?

Celia continued, saying, "If you stay with Angel, then we can visit you."

Del knew that any second now Mick would agree to

Angel's offer, and then she'd lose her chance. She took a
deep breath, unglued her feet and tongue, and declared,
"I'm taking him home with me."

The room fell silent, and as one, all eyes shifted her way.
The women and two men stared, as if seeing her for the
first time.

Mick smiled.

Under so much scrutiny, Del squirmed. Thanks to the
rain and her long jog and the events at the jewelry store, she
looked like something out of a circus sideshow. But determination filled her. She wasn't a coward and she wouldn't
start acting like one now.

Moving out of the corner, she edged in around Angel,
who kept kissing Mick's forehead. Del got as close to him as
she could, then stated again, "I'll take care of him." She
made her voice strong, resolute.

Angel blinked, looked at the other people, then back at
Del. "You will?"

"Yes. After all," Del explained, "it's my fault he's hurt."

Everyone's gaze shifted from her to Mick. Expressions
varied from male amusement, astonishment and fascination, to female speculation.

Del wanted to wince, to close her ears so she wouldn't
have to hear what Mick might reply to her appalling assumption. They were strangers in every sense of the word,
but he'd claimed to want to see her again. What better opportunity would there be than for her to take him home?
She'd never played nurse to anyone before, but how hard
could it be?

She stood by his bed, refusing to budge, blocking Angel
and her lips, in particular, and waited in agony.

Expectation hung in the air, along with a good dose of confusion.

Mick grinned, managed a one-shoulder shrug and addressed all six people at once. "There you go. Looks like it's all taken care of."

"WHAT DO YOU KNOW ABOUT her?"

Josh looked down at Angel and shrugged. They stood in the hallway outside Mick's door, which was as far as Angel would go. "Not a damn thing," he said, "except that Mick is in a bad way."

Angel pressed a hand to her chest, looking as if she'd taken the bullet herself. "The wound?"

Josh knew how close she was to Mick—practically a surrogate mom even though only nine years separated them. Mick's real mother, from what he understood, had been plagued by too many personal weaknesses. She'd died long ago, and Angel and Dane's family had become Mick's. "I'm sorry, I meant that he's been acting…infatuated."

Relieved, Angel bent a chastising look on him. "Mick is a grown man, a very levelheaded man. He doesn't get infatuated."

Josh knew that, which only made it more baffling. Beautiful women flirted with Mick and he hardly noticed. But this one… Josh shook his head. "Call it what you want, but today he chased her down, took a bullet for her without even knowing her name. And according to Zack, the first thing he asked about, even before he got his eyes open, was Delilah."

A slow smile spread over Angel's face. "This is wonderful!"

"Did you hear me?" Beyond respecting her a great deal, Josh knew Angel was one of the chew-'em-up-and-spit-'em-out women Mick had mentioned during their lunch, so he carefully measured his words. "Today, just a few minutes ago, is the first time he officially met her. Before that, he just watched her jog every day." Josh thought about Mick's preoccupation with Delilah and added, "She's not even all that eye-catching."

Angel smacked him on the shoulder. Not hard, but it still stung.

He refused to rub it.

"Looks are nothing, and you should know it by now. Besides, I think she's cute."

Dane, carrying two colas, strolled up behind her. He handed one to his wife and asked, "Who's cute?"

"Mick's woman."

Grinning, Dane said, "That little dynamo in there telling him she won't leave now that he's awake, not even to go home and get a change of clothes? And if she does leave, she absolutely will not take a bodyguard with her?" Dane laughed as he sipped his drink. "Both Alec and I offered, at Mick's insistence. Alec even promised her we wouldn't leave him alone, that one of us would be sure to stay with him until she returned. But she's not convinced. If anything, that seemed to have the opposite effect on her."

"I wonder why."

"Because she likes being difficult," Josh pointed out, disgruntled.

Dane grinned. "Actually, I believe she's jealous of Angel."

Angel frowned. "Of me? But Mick and I are like…"

"You don't have to convince me," Dane told her. "But then I know you both well. She doesn't."

"Why would she need a bodyguard?" Angel asked,

changing the subject. Dane spent a few minutes explaining about the bizarre aspects of the robbery, and Mick's concerns.

"For whatever reason, I don't think Mick has told her that he's a cop," Dane said. "He tried telling her she could be in danger, but she's blowing the whole thing off as nothing more than a fluke, or a coincidence. I get the feeling he'll have his hands full with that one."

Josh glared toward the closed door. "After spending several hours with her today, I can tell you that she's about the most contrary woman I've ever met. All she did was bitch at me."

Dane raised both brows. "Let me guess, you tried treating her as you do most women, flirting, teasing—"

"Condescending," Angel added.

"I was charming!"

"—and," Dane continued, "she was too smart to fall for it."

"She wants to do things her own way," Josh grumbled, still amazed that she'd taken exception to his manner, "and damn the consequences. She's far too...independent and stubborn for my tastes."

Barely stifling a chuckle, Dane clapped him on the shoulder. "It's good for you, teach you a little humility around the ladies."

Josh wasn't interested in learning humility, thank you very much. He and the ladies got along just fine. Delilah Piper— well, she was just an aberration, a woman who couldn't be swayed with sound male logic, smiles or compliments. In fact, she'd been rude enough to scoff at his compliments, as if she'd known they were false, which, of course, she hadn't because he was damn good at flattery when he chose to be.

Josh felt renewed pique; no woman had ever scoffed at him before. "Do you want me to go drag her out of there?"

Dane's expression filled with anticipation. "Oh yeah, I'd love to see you try."

True, Josh thought. Knowing her—and, after spending hours closed up with her in the waiting room, he did indeed feel that he knew her—she'd probably kick him someplace dirty. His groin ached just thinking about it. She'd threatened to do him in once today already, when he wouldn't agree to label her Mick's wife, just so she could sneak in and see him sooner. Obstinate woman.

And besides, brute force wasn't something he'd ever used on a female. He'd only been mouthing off because he'd used up his other tricks on her without success. "I'll see if I can dredge up some diplomacy," he told Angel and Dane, and sauntered into the room with all the enthusiasm of a man headed to the gallows.

One look at Delilah and he was again filled with confusion. What was it about her that had Mick going gaga? The woman was... *lanky*. That's the only word he could think of that described her. Her arms and legs were long, her body slim, her breasts small. She appeared delicate when he knew she was anything but.

He had, however, noticed that she had a very nice tush, not that it made up for the rest of it.

And now she watched him, on alert, as if he had no right to be in the room seeing one of his best friends. His gaze met Alec's and Alec shrugged. Celia stared wide-eyed.

None of them were used to Mick being thwarted. Most times, he told people what needed to be done and they did it. Mick had an air about him that demanded obedience. Women especially went out of their way to make him happy. Not that Mick took advantage of his appeal to women. Just the opposite, he seemed unaware of how they gravitated to him and he was the most discriminating male Josh had ever known. Beautiful women came on to him, but more often than not, Mick showed no interest at all.

Until now.

According to Angel, Mick had been that way since he was sixteen. Always a take-charge guy, always irresistible, but at the moment he looked ready to pull his hair out.

With flagging patience, Mick said, "I want you to be comfortable, Delilah. Go home and take the shower you mentioned earlier. Change your clothes if you want, get something to eat."

"I'm not hungry and I'm used to the clothes now." Her every word exuded stubbornness, though an edge of desperation could be heard, too.

Alec and Celia stood at the foot of the bed. Celia shook her head and Alec narrowed his eyes in contemplation.

Mick looked tired and frustrated and pained as he said, "I don't need you to baby-sit me, Delilah."

Josh decided enough was enough. Mick wasn't in top fighting form or the conversation never would have gone on for so long. He hated seeing his friend this way, wounded and weak.

Josh had handled plenty of women in his day. This one was no different—at least not in the most important ways.

"Of course you need a damn baby-sitter." Josh leaned against the wall, ready to take on Delilah and win. "Good God, Mick, you were dumb enough to get shot in the first place, then dumb enough to pass out. I can understand why she doesn't trust you now to do as the doctors and nurses tell you. You'd probably yank out your IV, wouldn't you? Or get up and parade around the room until you keeled over again. If she doesn't stay right here like a good little mother hen to make sure you behave yourself, you might even—"

Predictably enough, Miss Delilah exploded. She went stiff as a spike, sputtered, then practically shouted, "Don't you talk to him like that, Josh!"

Celia jumped a good foot at Del's explosive outburst. Alec coughed to cover a laugh. Zack, always laid-back and calm, watched the drama unfold with interest. But then Zack knew Josh and likely suspected his motives.

"Well," Josh reasoned, extravagant for the sake of their audience, "why would you refuse to go home and change out of your rumpled clothes unless you didn't trust him to act intelligently?"

Delilah fried him with a look before bending down to Mick. She said very sweetly, "I'll be right back."

When she stalked around the bed, both Celia and Alec scurried to get out of her way. Josh didn't know if it was the scent of mud and sweat that motivated them, or the intent look on her face.

As she passed Josh, she snagged his shirtfront and dragged him out after her. Biting back a victorious laugh, Josh looked over his shoulder in time to see Mick chuckling. Josh sent him a salute.

Once in the hallway, Delilah rounded on him. She opened her mouth to speak, but he beat her to it. "You need to shower. I can see sweat stains under your arms, and I can smell you."

Her face flaming with color, she kept her gaze glued on Josh, then turned her head the tiniest bit and sniffed. She wrinkled her nose and frowned.

Josh almost laughed. Truth was, Delilah smelled kinda nice, like shampoo and lotion and woman, not that he'd ever tell her that. Calmly now, because he didn't want to offend her, he said, "Mick needs you here. I know that. Hell, you're all he's talked about since he came to."

"Really?" She looked skeptical, and hopeful.

"Yep." Seeing her uncertainty, Josh softened. Most of her aggression had been on Mick's behalf, so he couldn't really hold it against her. "He'll be uneasy if he thinks he's imposing. You don't know him like I do. He's not used to relying on anyone. Do you really want to start a relationship that way?"

She stared down at her muddy sneakers and mumbled, "No."

Such a small voice for Delilah! And he noticed she didn't deny the relationship part. Good. At least that meant she was as interested as Mick. Josh would hate to think his friend was the only one smitten.

"He also doesn't want you to be alone. He doesn't worry about women often, so you could show a little gratitude and go easy on him."

Seconds ticked by before she finally admitted, "I didn't— don't—know those men." She looked at him, her eyes troubled. "And I don't want a total stranger waiting around on me while I shower and change. I don't like to impose on others, either."

Josh wanted to curse, to end this awful day by heading home and phoning a reasonable woman, a doting woman who'd give him the comfort of her body and her feminine concern. He did not want to spend more time with this particular woman, who treated him as an asexual nuisance.

But he knew what he needed to do. He drew in a breath

and made the ultimate sacrifice. "All right. Then let me take you home. You can do what needs to be done, then I'll bring you back. You can stay until visiting hours are over. I know he'd appreciate that."

As if he hadn't made the grand offer, she said, "Maybe Zack could drive me home?"

If it wasn't for Mick... Josh drew a deep breath and reached for control. "Zack can't. He has a four-year-old daughter and he needs to get home to her."

"Oh." Delilah eyed him, apparently liking his plan as little as he did. "I suppose Dane or Alec would be okay...."

He should have said fine, should have let Mick deal with her. Instead, he heard himself say, "Dane and Alec just drove two hours to get here, and I'm sure they'd like to spend their time visiting Mick, not chauffeuring your stubborn butt around town."

Stiffening, she said, "I could take a bus...."

"And Mick would still worry. Someone shot at you today, lady." From what Josh understood, someone had singled her out as a victim. It didn't make sense, and he understood Mick's concern. "You witnessed a burglary and it doesn't matter that you told the police you didn't recognize anyone, that you have no idea what's going on, it's still strange."

She didn't relent, and he said, his patience at an end, "Hell, I promise not to speak to you, all right? I won't even look at you if it'll make you happy."

Using both hands, she covered her face. Her normally proud, straight shoulders hunched and she turned partially away.

Thinking she was about to cry, Josh froze. Damn, but he couldn't deal with weeping women. There was nothing he hated more, nothing that made him feel more helpless. His stomach tightened, cramped. Delilah acted tough and talked tough, but she was still female, delicately built, and she'd been through an ordeal.

But she didn't so much as sniffle. "I don't mean to be nasty," she said from behind her fingers. Her voice was miserable but strong, and devoid of tears. "It's just..." She hesitated for a long minute, then dropped her hands and sighed. "I feel so responsible."

Josh's hostility and impatience melted away. She'd been involved in a robbery, shot at, stuck in the hospital all day in wet, grubby clothes with total strangers. If he'd known her longer, he'd have offered her a hug. But he'd just met her—and so had Mick. Josh was still worried. It wasn't like Mick to fall so hard so fast. He'd never even seen Mick trip. On rare occasions, Mick dated, and then moved on.

Josh couldn't think of a single female, other than family, who Mick would have invited to stay at the hospital with him. Not only would he have found it an intrusion, he was far too private to want anyone around him when he wasn't up to full speed.

In his line of work, Mick naturally had to be careful, and that caution had carried over into other aspects of his life. Or perhaps it had always been there, left over from a less-than-wonderful childhood. But whatever the reason, Josh could tell that for this woman, Mick was throwing caution to the wind.

Settling for a friendly arm around her shoulders, Josh steered her back toward the hospital room. "The last thing Mick would want is for you to feel bad. About anything. As to responsibility, it sure as hell isn't *your* fault those idiots showed up and started shooting. Okay?"

"Thanks." She nodded, and even managed a small smile for him. Josh was struck by that smile, and for the first time, he had an inkling of what Mick felt.

They walked through the door, and she seemed to forget all about Josh the second her gaze landed on Mick. Nonplussed, he watched her hurry back to Mick's bedside. "Josh is going to drive me home, but I'll be right back."

Mick's surprise at the quick turnaround was plain to see as he looked from Josh to Delilah and back again. Josh winked. Oh yeah, he'd have fun ribbing them later with this one. He'd gotten her to do what the rest of them couldn't. He hadn't lost his touch, after all.

"Don't worry, Mick," Josh said, feeling in good humor for the first time since the shooting, "I'll keep a real close eye on her."

That earned him a frown from both Delilah and Mick. Delilah apparently didn't think she needed to be watched, and Mick obviously didn't want any male looking at her too closely. Jealousy, Josh decided, and was glad he'd never suffered such a miserable emotion.

"You really don't have to rush," Mick told Delilah after dragging his attention away from Josh. But it was plain to Josh that Mick wanted her back where he could be the one keeping an eye on her, protecting her, not any other man, not even a friend he trusted. He was also in pain and doing his best to hide it. Damn stubborn fool.

Delilah glanced around the room. "Will your visitors stay all night?"

"No," Mick said, making the decision before anyone else could answer.

Alec coughed again. Celia rushed to assure her. "We'll be

at a nearby hotel for the night, but we'll stay here until you get back. How's that?"

As if it was up to her, Delilah nodded. "That'd be perfect. Thank you." Then she bent to kiss Mick again. "I'm going to give my cell phone number to the nurse, just in case." She turned to Josh. "Are you ready?"

"I'll be right there."

She looked suspicious at his delay, but didn't question him on it. She turned and moseyed out.

The door had barely closed before Angel and Dane came back in. Angel propped her hands on her hips and said, "Now that she's not within hearing distance, tell me the truth. Does your shoulder hurt?"

With a crooked grin, Mick admitted, "Hell, yes." Then he turned to Zack. "If you could see about some pain medicine…?"

"The doctor ordered it for when you woke up, but you were too bullheaded to take it."

"It would've made me sleepy."

Josh shook his head. "And God forbid he miss a single second of Delilah Piper's visit."

Zack, always something of a peacemaker as well as an EMT, laughed. "I'll go get your nurse and she can take care of you."

Josh walked over to the bed, where both Dane and Alec now hovered. Josh knew they were dying for some answers. Together the two men ran a private investigations firm, and they could sniff out trouble without even trying.

"The other men got away. The police are still looking, but they haven't turned up anyone."

Mick's curse was especially foul. "What about the one I shot? Did they find out anything from him?"

"The idiot had ID on him. He's Rudy Glasgow, and he's still unconscious." Josh knew that despite Mick's injuries, he'd want to know it all. Still, he hesitated before saying, "It doesn't look good."

Mick dropped back onto the pillow with an aggrieved sigh. "I know my shot to his leg didn't put him under. Was it the head wound from when he fell?"

"Yeah. You two mirror each other—both shot, both with conked heads. Only his was worse. He rattled something in his skull and the docs don't know when he'll come to, which means they don't know when he'll be able to answer questions, if ever. You were lucky that you landed more on Zack than the concrete when you fell."

Not amused, Mick cursed again.

"I also turned your gun over to the officer first on the scene. He insisted, of course, and with you passed out cold…" Josh shrugged.

"That's standard procedure," Mick assured him, not worried. "I'll be issued a new one."

Josh nodded. "I notified your sergeant and he's getting in touch with Internal Affairs."

"Which means I'll have to see the damn psychiatrist, too." He groaned.

"Just procedure?" Josh asked, though he already knew any shooting required a follow-up visit with the shrink, just to keep the officers healthy in mind and body.

"Yeah." Mick looked weary beyond belief. "When she leaves here tonight—"

Dane held up a hand. "We won't let anything happen to her. I promise."

And Josh assumed that meant one or both of them would

be tailing her the rest of the night, even after she finished her hospital visit. Delilah wouldn't like it if she knew. But then, Dane and Alec were damn good, so she wouldn't find out unless they wanted her to know.

Alec looked thoughtful, and with his intense, dark features, the look was almost menacing. It had taken Josh some time to get used to him. "So you think the robbery was a sham? Just an excuse to shoot her?"

"They aimed for her head," Mick rumbled in disgust, describing how he'd covered her, and the shooter's angle. He gave details he hadn't given when Delilah was in the room. "They didn't threaten anyone else. Hell, they didn't even look at anyone else."

"But why her?" Dane asked.

"I haven't got a clue. Far as I can figure, she was just a customer, like the other two in the shop."

Though Mick said it, he didn't look quite convinced. Josh didn't like any of it, especially since his friend seemed determined to be in the middle of it all. "I'd better get out there or she'll leave without me."

"She doesn't have a car here, does she?" Mick asked, concerned over the possibility.

"No, but believe me, that wouldn't stop her. Prepare yourself, Mick, because she's about the most obstinate, bullheaded woman I've ever run across." He squeezed Mick's left shoulder. "Take it easy while we're gone."

"You won't let her out of your sight?"

"Just when she showers." He grinned at Mick's warning growl. It amused the hell out of him how possessive his friend had gotten, and how quickly. "Quit worrying. I'll bring her back safe and sound."

chapter 3

MICK WATCHED JOSH GO, and though he trusted Josh im-
plicitly, he cursed the injury that kept him confined to bed.
"She could have been killed today."

Angel sat beside him on the narrow mattress. "Is that why
you agreed to go home with her? So you can protect her?"

He nodded, but he saw that both Alec and Dane knew his
reasons were more varied than that. And more territorial,
more sexual. Protecting wasn't the only activity he had in
mind. He'd never burned for a woman before, but now he
felt like an inferno ready to combust.

Why the hell would someone want her dead?

Mick remembered the way she'd been looking the place
over, the way she'd initially smiled at the men—a smile he'd
considered merely polite, stranger to stranger.

Zack came back in, the nurse trailing him. She gave Mick
a dose of morphine through his IV, and seconds later the
discomfort receded and lethargy settled in.

Mick relished the relief from the searing pain, even while
he fought to stay awake and sharp enough to think.

"Relax," Dane ordered him.

"I have to figure out what's going on." A vague sense of impending doom, of limited time plagued him.

Dane shook his head. "No. You're in no shape to start snooping around. Let it go for now. The bastard who shot you isn't going anywhere, and he won't stay out forever. When he comes to, you can question him. Or better yet, let someone else do it."

"No." Even with the morphine clouding his mind, Mick knew he wasn't about to pass up the opportunity to get some answers. "I need to call my sergeant, to tell him I want to stay advised. And I need to talk to the head nurse. I need to—"

Angel pressed her fingers over his mouth. "You need to sleep. I have a feeling when Delilah gets back, you'll be determined to stay awake and alert."

Alec cocked a brow while cuddling Celia to his side. "He wouldn't want to miss a minute of that, as Josh said."

Mick relaxed, thinking of Delilah's emotional strength, her boldness, how she'd kissed him, her taste, her heat. They were right—he didn't want to miss that. In the next instant, he fell asleep.

MICK WOKE TO THE SOUND of quiet tapping. The room was dim, with only one light glowing in the corner. The curtains were all closed, but he could tell it was night. He'd probably slept another four hours or so, and it enraged him. There was a lot to consider, a lot to do, not the least of which would be getting to know Delilah.

The tapping continued, light and quick. He bit back a groan as he turned his head on the soft pillow and zeroed in on the source. There, sprawled in the room's only chair, a laptop resting across her thighs, was Delilah.

God, she was lovely.

A nurse had evidently brought her a pillow and blanket in an effort to help make her comfortable. The padded lounge chair could have served as a bed in a pinch. Delilah had the back reclined, the pillow behind her shoulders, the blanket thrown over the arm of the chair.

Her rich dark hair, freshly washed, swung loose and silky around her shoulders. The light from the laptop cast a soft blue halo around her. Her eyes looked mysterious, purposeful, as she typed away. Mick watched her, aware of the acceleration in his pulse, the expanding sexual tension.

She'd changed into a pair of baggy jeans and a miniscule, snowy-white, cropped T-shirt. Her sandals were off, tucked beneath the chair, her bare feet propped on the edge of the counter in front of the window. Two flowering plants now sat there, no doubt from Angel and Celia.

Delilah's slim legs seemed to go on forever, and Mick, still only half-awake, pictured them around his hips, hugging him tight while he rode her, long and slow and so damn deep. He visually followed the trail of those incredibly long legs, and when he came to her hips he imagined them lifted by his hands, her legs sprawled wide while he tasted her, licked her and made her scream out a climax.

A groan broke free from him and Delilah jumped, nearly dumping her laptop. "Mick!"

Heat throbbed just below his skin. He was so aroused he hurt, but he'd done nothing more than look at her and give his imagination free rein. What would it be like to actually have her?

He swallowed and said with a drawling, raw deliberation, "I don't suppose you'd like to give me another kiss?"

Slowly, her gaze glued to his, she set the laptop on the floor and stood. "I didn't mean to be so brazen earlier. I just…it amazed me that anyone would do what you did."

"So you kissed me?"

Arching one dark brow, she half laughed. "I wanted to devour you, actually."

The shadows in the room did interesting things to her body. "Do you always say exactly what you think?"

She shrugged. "I guess so. I know I shouldn't, but I'm out of practice when it comes to this sort of thing."

"You can say whatever you want to me, okay?"

She nodded. "You saved my life, and you got hurt in the bargain. I saw you and I just…wanted to kiss you."

That didn't sound right to Mick. "So it was about gratitude?"

"Yes…no. I'm not sure." She made a helpless gesture, then shifted her feet and tucked her silky hair behind her ear. "The thing is, touching you seems…right."

He understood that. Touching her seemed right, too. Hell, devouring her seemed right. He'd have gladly gotten started right that minute, but she stood there, waiting, uncertain, very different now that they were alone. She wasn't as defensive, and there was no reason for her to be protective.

No woman had ever been protective of him. Except Angel, but that was back when he'd been a boy. With Delilah it felt different.

"Everyone else has left?"

"Yes. Angel and Celia gave me the number of the hotel where they're staying so you could call if you needed them.

The man, Alec, said you had his cell number if you wanted to make sure he was on duty. Whatever that means."

Mick nodded, understanding perfectly. Alec would wait and watch for Delilah to leave. He'd protect her until Mick could take over. There wasn't a more capable or harder man than Alec Sharpe. Knowing he'd keep his eye on Delilah gave Mick a new measure of relief.

When he didn't speak, she gestured at the flowers and said, "The women bought these in the gift shop."

"That's just like them."

She fidgeted. "They're…friends of yours?"

"More like family. As close as family can be without all the baggage."

"Oh." A mix of emotions crossed her features—confusion and relief. "Josh and Zack said they'd be in touch in the morning."

"I figured as much." She stood there before him, barefoot and fidgety, and Mick used the opportunity to look at her. The loose jeans hung low on her slim hips, showing a strip of pale belly between the waistband and the hem of her shirt. He saw the barest hint of her navel, enough to fire his blood, to make his mouth go dry.

He glanced at her breasts and found himself smiling. She was indeed small, but still so damn sexy he ached all the way down to his toes. As he stared, her nipples tightened, pushing him over the edge.

He needed her closer. Because she looked uncertain, he asked, "You didn't like kissing me?"

"I did!" she blurted, then bit her bottom lip. She twined her fingers together and shifted her bare feet again. "I just didn't want you to think that, you know, just because you were nice enough to save me that you had to…"

"Had to what?" Inside, he grinned, knowing what she thought, but in the mood to tease her.

"You know. Be sexual with me." His gaze shot to her face and she rushed to add, "I wasn't sure if you felt the same way I did. I mean, you're incredible. Gorgeous and sexy and hard and…what woman wouldn't want you? But I'm just me. I didn't know if you wanted to—"

Just that quickly, his humor fled. "I want to."

"You do?"

He was hard, and there wasn't a damn thing he could do about it. "Come here, Delilah."

As if reassured, she strode to the bed and sat beside him, this time to his left. "You want me to kiss you again?"

Unwilling to rush her or scare her off, he didn't move. He wanted her to be as free as she'd first been, taking what she wanted from him, when she wanted it. Was there a better male fantasy than having a bold woman who knew her own mind and went after what she needed?

Holding himself still, Mick said softly, "I'd love for you to kiss me again."

"You don't need anything first?" She searched his face, looking him over, he assumed, for signs of discomfort. "A drink? More pain medicine?"

I need you. "No."

Tentatively, she laid a hand on his chest. "You're so warm," she whispered, her fingers lightly caressing, edging under the loose neckline of the hospital gown. "I watched you sleep for a while and it made me nuts." She glanced at him, meeting his gaze. "You even look good when you sleep. I had to get out my laptop to keep busy, just so I wouldn't end up touching you. I didn't want to wake you."

Mick had no response to that, other than a rush of heat. The thought of her watching him and wanting him fed his awareness of her, making it more acute.

She touched his throat, then slid her slender fingers over his uninjured shoulder. "I think," she whispered, watching the progress of her hand, "that you're about the sexiest man I've ever seen."

If they'd been anywhere other than a hospital room, he'd have pulled her under him. He shifted, felt the pain deep in his shoulder and cursed.

She quickly pulled away, then poured him a drink of water and lifted the straw to his mouth. "Shh. This will help."

Getting her under him would help, but he didn't say so. He drank deeply, hoping the icy water would cool his urgency, return a measure of his control. It was insane to want a woman this way.

After setting the paper cup aside, Delilah again rested her hand on his chest. Her gaze locked with his. "Your heart is racing."

"I'm horny," he explained, because anything more eloquent was beyond him while she continued to touch him.

Her light blue eyes twinkled and her lush lips curled into a satisfied feminine smile. "No sex for you, at least not until you're healed."

That "not until" stipulation—which pretty much guaranteed he'd eventually have her—about stopped his heart. Without another word she leaned down and touched her mouth to his. She was gone before Mick could respond.

Her blue eyes were warmer, softer, and he rumbled, "Again."

She looked at his mouth, bent, stroked his bottom lip with her hot little tongue. "Do you like that?" she breathed.

He groaned.

Still so close he tasted her breath, she asked, "You're not married or anything, are you?"

"No."

"At first, I was afraid Angel or Celia—"

"No." Using his left hand, he touched her hair. Warmth, softness. "I love your hair." He tangled his fingers in the silky mass and brought her mouth back flush with his.

"Thank you," she murmured, and obligingly gave him the longer kiss he wanted.

Dull pain pushed at Mick, but he blocked it from his mind. It was nothing compared to the feel of her. "Open your mouth."

She did, then accepted the slow, deliberate thrust of his tongue. He stroked deep, taking her mouth, exploring all the textures and heat, and the taste that was uniquely Delilah.

They both groaned.

Delilah pulled back. She touched his jaw and asked, "Did I hurt you?"

He had to stop this or he'd lose it completely. "Of course not."

"I'm not married or anything, either."

Mick, still on the verge of a meltdown, managed to lift a brow at that candid disclosure, and she shrugged. "I just thought you should know," she said, her words coming in soft, uneven pants, "being as we're...well, doing this."

"This?" She stayed close and the scent of her, lighter now and touched with lotion and powder, filled him. He wanted to wrap himself in it, wanted to hold her close to his body until their scents mingled.

"The whole sex thing." She drew a breath, but kept her gaze steady, unwavering. "I assume that's where we're headed. I mean, I'll have you all to myself in my apartment and I want you. I assume you want me, too."

He could hardly believe what she'd just said. No woman had ever come right out and so boldly stated her intentions to have an affair with him. Women sometimes chased him, but they were subtle, never so up front with their motives. They teased, flirted, advanced and retreated.

They didn't advance and advance.

"What is it you do?" she asked, unconcerned with his bemused astonishment—maybe even unaware that she'd astonished him. "I've never known anyone who carried a gun and shot people."

He should have been prepared for that, because he knew she'd ask. But he was still stuck on that affair statement, attempting to get his head back together—a near impossible feat because all he could think about now was starting that damn affair. The sooner the better.

"Mick?"

He wanted to tell her the truth, but he knew nothing about her except that she evidently had an enemy, someone who wanted her dead, someone who would have succeeded if that bullet hadn't been sidetracked by his shoulder. He also knew she was eccentric, a woman heedless of her surroundings, honest to a fault, brazen and stubborn one minute, shy and uncertain the next. And he knew she wanted him, not as much as he wanted her, but enough.

His innate caution warned him against going too fast.

Thinking of Dane and Alec, he lied. "I'm a private investigator."

Her eyes widened with unrestrained excitement. "Seriously?"

She looked so comically surprised, he grinned. "Yeah." Starting things off with a lie wasn't the best course of action, but he had few choices until he found out what was going on. If all went as planned, he'd be able to tell her the truth soon enough. She'd understand his reasoning and forgive his deception. He'd see to it.

"Wow." She settled on the side of his bed, her hip against his, her hand still resting on his chest. "I could use you for research."

Mick did a double take, momentarily getting his mind off the idea of pulling her down on the narrow bed beside him. "Research for what?"

She shrugged in the direction of the laptop. "I'm a writer. I'm always looking for easy ways to research. From the horse's mouth is always the easiest."

A writer? Now, somehow that fit. The creative types were always a bit different, as far as he knew. "What do you write?"

"Mysteries." She waggled her eyebrows. "Fun stuff. Whodunits with a few laughs and some racy romance thrown in."

It was Mick's turn to say, "Wow." Then he added, "Have you ever been published?"

"Well, yeah." She seemed to consider that a stupid question.

She'd said it so casually, as if it were nothing. He'd never met a novelist before, and now he planned to sleep with one. "How many books have you done?"

"I've had four published so far, with two more in the

works." She nodded toward her laptop. "I'm working under a deadline right now."

"How old are you?" Mick didn't think she looked old enough to have one book published, much less four. He'd always pictured writers as more seasoned, scholarly types.

His question made her grin. "Twenty-five, almost twenty-six. I sold my first book when I was twenty-three."

Mick eyed her anew. A mystery writer. He had to shake his head at the novelty of it. And here he'd claimed to be a PI. A match made in heaven. "I'll be damned," he said, still dealing with his amazement. "Maybe I could read one sometime?"

"Sure. I'll show them to you when we get to my apartment. By the way, I drove myself here so I could take us both home tomorrow. Your friend Josh was pretty ticked off about it. He was going to tattle, and you should have seen his face when we found you asleep. He looked so frustrated, I thought his head would explode. Of course, for that one, it might be an improvement."

Mick closed his eyes. Some maniac had tried to kill her, and here she'd been on the road alone again, vulnerable. He could just imagine Josh's frustration. "Delilah."

"Del."

"Excuse me?" He opened his eyes again and stared at her. Hard.

"If we're going to be friends, you may as well call me what everyone else does."

"And everyone else calls you...*Del?*" It sounded like a man's name to Mick.

She shrugged. "It's what I've always gone by. Only my father called me Delilah, usually if he was angry, and he died a few years ago. Now I only use my full name when I write."

Mick wondered how her father had died, if she had any other family left.

He shook off his distraction. He'd have time to ask her about her family later. Keeping his tone stern, he said, "Josh was right to be angry. Someone tried to shoot you today. You shouldn't be alone, not until I—" He pulled back on that, quickly saying instead, "Until the police can figure out what's going on."

She flapped her hand at him, waving away his concerns, then let it settle on his abdomen. He nearly shot off the bed. Every muscle in his body clenched and his cock throbbed. He'd never been in such a bad way before.

If she moved her fingers just a few inches lower, she could make him feel so much better. He closed his eyes against the image of her soft hand holding him, stroking him. Too fast, he was moving way too fast.

"I don't think," she murmured, watching her hand on his body, "that they were really shooting at me. Why would they?" She looked up at him, her hand thankfully still. "I mean, they aimed at me, but I think it was just a random thought. They were criminals and they got thwarted because the police showed up, and they were mad, so they wanted to shoot someone."

Nearly choking on an odd combination of explosive desire, frustration and protectiveness, Mick asked, "And you think they chose you, a woman who didn't have a thing to do with anything, a woman just visiting the store? They didn't look rattled or frenzied. They looked like they meant to shoot you—you specifically—before they took off."

Her fingers spread wide and her brow furrowed. "I don't know. I didn't notice anything like that."

Her baby finger was a quarter inch from the head of his penis. His body strained, fighting against his control. He *needed* to lift his hips, to thrust into her hand.

"You," he rasped, "are the person they accused of setting off an alarm, when you hadn't moved and weren't anywhere near anything that could have triggered an alarm."

That made him think of something else, and he forced himself to concentrate on things other than her touch. "How did the cops know? Did anyone tell you?"

She stared blankly at his bandaged shoulder, deep in thought. "The officer who questioned me said someone on the street noticed the guns when he was walking by, and he used his cell phone to call them."

"Honey, listen to me." Mick put his left hand on her bare waist, between the bottom of her shirt and the top of her jeans. Her skin was smooth and warm, her muscles taut. "Did you recognize either of them? Was there anything at all familiar about them?"

"No, of course not." She looked at her hand on his abdomen, then at his erection. He read her thoughts as if she'd spoken them aloud. Instinctively, he tightened, which brought forth a moan of pain from both physical discomfort and sharp anticipation.

"You're in a bad way," she said in a hushed, husky tone filled with understanding and her own measure of need.

He wanted to howl. He wanted to ask her to go ahead and stroke him, hard and fast, that she use her mouth…

"Delilah…"

"Del," she whispered, and started to glide her hand lower.

Using his left hand, Mick caught her wrist. His hold was tight, too tight, but he felt stretched so taut he was ready to snap. "I'm in worse than a bad way," he rasped. "I'm on the very edge, and if you touch me I won't be able to control myself."

She tilted her head, staring at him as if she didn't quite grasp his meaning.

"I'll come," he said bluntly, then watched for her reaction.

She stayed still, but probably only because he held her slender wrist in an iron grip, refusing to let her move.

"This is difficult for me," he explained, watching her, needing her to understand. He felt more tension than he had at fifteen, when he'd seen his first fully naked female, there for the taking. He'd lost control then; he was ready to lose control now. He ground his teeth and insisted, "I'm not usually like this."

Her eyes, warm and heavy-lidded, looked him over. "You're hurt, in bed. This is a strange situation."

"It has nothing to do with any of that and everything to do with you. I want you bad, and have since the first time I saw you."

He could tell that admission pleased her. "Today?" she asked,

Gently, he lifted her hand away from his body so he could carry on a coherent conversation. He brought her hand to his chest and kept it there. "I saw you two weeks ago, near a building I own. You were heading to the post office."

Her frown reappeared. "I never noticed you," she said. Then, chagrined, she added, "I was probably plotting, and I don't pay much attention then. My mind tends to wander."

He thought about how she'd been examining the jewelry store, studying it, prowling from one corner to the other. "Plotting...what?"

"My book, of course."

She said it as if it should have been obvious to him.

"So," she asked, "you saw me a few weeks ago?"

"And many times since then. I eat at Marco's a lot, and you—"

"Jog by there a lot." Her smile was very sweet. "Whenever I have a deadline, I need to get outside at least once a day to clear my head so I can really think and plot. So I jog. But I've never noticed you before."

"I've watched you almost every day. Today when I saw you actually stop and go into the jewelry store, I decided it was time to introduce myself."

Her countenance darkened. "Instead you saved my life."

They stared at each other. The air was charged, until a nurse started backing in, dragging a cart with her.

Delilah moved so fast, Mick was stunned. She snagged the pillow from her chair and dropped it over his lap. To the nurse she said, "Time to check him again?"

The nurse looked over her shoulder and smiled. "I'll only be a minute." Then she turned to Mick. "For an injured man, you're about the healthiest thing I've ever seen."

Mick was in no mood for small talk. "Is that right?" he asked, while watching Delilah.

"Yep. Great lungs, great reflexes. The epitome of health. I wish everyone would take such good care of their bodies."

Delilah made a choking sound at that observation. "I'll, uh, just get out of your way." She tapped a few buttons on her laptop, closed it and set it on the window ledge. She picked up a large tote from the floor and swung the strap over her shoulder, saying to Mick, "I'm going to run down to the coffee shop and grab a bite to eat. Do you want anything? You slept through dinner."

The nurse said, "We can still get him a tray."

Delilah leaned close and whispered, "It was nasty-looking stuff. I'd pass if I was you."

The nurse heard and grinned. "The coffee shop has pretty good sandwiches and chips and desserts. You're not on a restricted diet, so if something sounds good…"

Delilah started out. "I'll surprise you."

"Delilah—"

"Del," she said, then added, "Don't worry. I'll be right back. We'll pretend we're having a picnic."

And before he could warn her to be cautious, she was gone. Mick sank back against the pillows, the ache in his shoulder receding to no more than a dull, annoying throb. The nurse offered him more pain medication, but he passed. He needed all his wits about him to deal with Delilah Piper. Otherwise, he thought, grinning shamelessly, she'd probably take sexual advantage of him in his weakened physical shape.

He could hardly wait.

The nurse finished her poking and prodding, changed his bandage, and then, at his request, handed him the phone.

He called Josh. A woman answered—no surprise there— and Mick heard her grumbling, heard the squeaking of bedsprings, before Josh came on the line.

"You're either feeling much better or much worse if you're making a call."

"Much better," Mick told him, and he knew it was only a partial lie. "Can you bring me a change of clothes tomorrow? The nurse said I should be ready to get out of here by eleven."

"Sure thing, but it'll have to be early. I'm on duty starting at eight."

As a fireman, Josh worked varying hours, usually four days on, four days off. On his off days—today being one—he spent a lot of time with women.

Zack, an EMT stationed right next door to the fire department, was just the opposite. He spent all his spare time with his daughter and only rarely made time for women, and then only when his hormones refused to let him put it off any longer.

"If it's inconvenient, I can ask Zack."

"It's no problem. I'd planned to check up on you anyway, just to make sure your little woman hadn't done you in."

"You don't like her?" Mick asked, not really caring, but curious all the same. Personally, he found everything about Delilah unique and enticing, even her damned stubbornness, which had earlier about driven him nuts.

"She's...different."

True enough, Mick thought.

"And she took exception to me right off the bat."

Mick grinned. That was probably a first for Josh.

"She's not like other women, and she'll take some getting used to. But it appears she's as nuts about you as you are about her, and I suppose that's all that really matters." There was a muffled sound as someone snatched the receiver away from Josh and he apparently wrestled it back. Mick heard him growl, "Just hang on. I'll only be a minute."

Chuckling, Mick said, "I won't keep you."

"S'no problem. She'll wait. So, what's it to be? Jeans? And I guess some type of button shirt?"

"That'd be easiest. I'm sure you can find your way around my house."

A feminine whisper, insistent and imploring, sounded in the background. Mick grinned again. "G'night, Josh."

"Hey, before you go, you should know that Alec is hanging around, waiting to take care of things for you."

Mick appreciated the subtle way Josh explained that with his lady friend listening. "Thanks. I'll ring him next."

He disconnected his call with Josh and punched in Alec's number. He imagined Delilah would return any minute, and he wanted to make sure things were set first.

"Sharpe."

"It's me, Alec. Where are you?"

"Hanging out in the parking lot."

"Damn, I hate to do that to you."

He could hear the smile in Alec's tone when he said, "Celia's with me. It's no problem."

That made Mick smile, too. He could just imagine the two of them necking like teenagers. Alec was still a bad ass of the first order, but with Celia, he was a pussycat. "Why don't you head out and I'll call you when she decides to leave?"

The door opened and Delilah came through, her arms laden with paper bags and disposable cups of steaming liquid. Mick eyed her cautiously, not sure how much she'd heard.

She set everything down and turned to him with a smile. "Is that Josh?"

"No, it's, uh, Alec." He could hear Alec laughing in his ear. He knew they all appreciated the unique effect Delilah had on him.

"Alec?" That surprised her, he could tell, but not for long.

"Well, tell him to go home and go to bed. I'm not leaving tonight, so I don't need a bodyguard."

Mick scowled. "Delilah…"

"Del." She sat on the side of the bed and took the phone from his hand, then said into the receiver, "I'm going to stay the night. But thanks for thinking of me, anyway."

And then she hung up.

chapter 4

AT TEN O'CLOCK, the doctor gave Mick the okay to leave, together with a long list of instructions. Del listened intently and felt confident that she could take care of everything that needed to be done.

Angel and Celia, along with their husbands, had come and gone already. They'd been there since early morning, but because Delilah now realized that they were in fact Mick's family, she enjoyed the attention they lavished on him. He treated both women with an avuncular ease, not with the heated awareness he'd shown her.

Unfortunately, Josh had shown up, too, at the crack of dawn. She'd been asleep when he'd arrived, and was forced to awaken to his scowling face. He'd seemed suspicious of her overnight stay, as if he thought she might have molested Mick in his sleep. Stupid man.

Though Josh was uncommonly handsome, and could be witty when he chose to be, she wasn't at all certain she liked him. Whenever he looked at her, his demeanor plainly said he found her lacking. He distrusted her interest in Mick, and showed confusion at Mick's interest in her.

Nevertheless, she did appreciate his friendship with Mick. Willingly, he'd brought Mick clothes to wear home, then insisted she leave the room while he helped Mick dress. She would have stubbornly refused—*she* wanted to help him dress!—except Mick had wanted her to leave, too.

Delilah had already washed her face and brushed her hair and teeth while his family visited. They'd shown up just as Josh was leaving, and she couldn't help but feel a twinge of poignant sadness, seeing how loved he was. He had a good family, loyal friends, and she envied him that.

Hoping to make a better impression on them today than she had yesterday, she'd applied a little makeup and exchanged her slept-in T-shirt for a dark-rose tank top. Though the hospital was cool, out the window she could already see heat rising off the blacktop in the parking lot.

Now that they were alone again, Mick paced around the room, waiting for an orderly to bring a wheelchair. To Del's discerning eye, he looked ruggedly handsome with his morning whiskers and tired eyes. He also looked a little shaky. She wanted to coddle him, but she'd already figured out that he wasn't a man used to relying on others.

"Does your family live close?"

He glanced up at her, clearly distracted. With his arm in a sling and his eyes narrowed, he looked like a wounded pirate. "A coupla hours away. They'll be back over the weekend, I'm sure." His dark gaze sharpened. "Will that be a problem?"

"To have them visit? Of course not. For as long as you stay with me, I want you to be completely comfortable. It'll be your home, too."

He looked undecided, as if there was more he wanted to say, then he just shook his head. "We need to come to a few understandings."

"Oh?" Seeing Mick flat on his back in bed was one thing. Him standing straight and tall—all six feet three inches of him, moving around the room with flexing muscle and barely leashed impatience—was another. He was an intimidating sight. An arousing sight.

"I want a few promises from you." He stalked toward her, as if ready to pounce, and she felt her heart tripping.

She was a tall woman, meeting many men eye-to-eye. Not so with Mick. He looked down at her, his dark eyes drawing her in, and without thought Del went on tiptoe and touched her mouth to his.

He froze for a beat, then slanted his head to better fit their mouths together, and caught her with his good arm at the same time. He carefully gathered her close, his large hand sliding up her back to her nape and holding her immobile.

Del was acutely aware of his arm in the sling between their bodies. Her breast brushed against the stiff cotton restraint and she shuddered, trying to keep space between them so she wouldn't inadvertently hurt him.

"Relax," he whispered, and then his hand left her neck to coast down her spine, down and down until he was squeezing her bottom, cuddling, drawing her up and in until her pelvis nudged his groin. He made a rough sound of pleasure.

Del pulled her mouth away and rested her forehead on his chest. "This is incredible," she groaned.

"I know." He kissed her temple and asked, "How many bedrooms do you have?"

Her nerve endings jumped with excitement. "I have two, but I was thinking we'd—"

The orderly pushed into the room with the wheelchair and gave them a cheery greeting.

Del felt heat flood her face, more so when Mick gave her a scorching look of understanding. He started to pick up the small bag of items he had to take home, but Del rushed to beat him to it.

"You just sit," she said, trying to regain some composure, "and I'll get this." Mick kept her so flustered, she could barely think, and she almost left her laptop behind. Without preamble, the orderly plopped nearly everything into Mick's lap and started out the door. Del hustled after them.

"It's stupid to ride in a wheelchair when I'm perfectly capable of walking."

"And smooching," the orderly said in agreement, even more cheerful now that he knew what he'd interrupted. "But it's hospital policy."

Mick stayed silent until they got into the car and were on their way. He seemed inordinately alert, watching everything and everyone, and he soon had Del on edge.

"Do all PIs act like you?"

Mick didn't bother to glance her way when he said, "Yeah."

"Are you going to do this the whole time you're with me?"

Again, he said, "Yeah." But then he turned to face her. "You were shot at, Delilah. I wish I could blow it off as bad luck on your part—being in the wrong place at the wrong time—but I can't. Not yet. Not until the police have a chance to talk to the guy I shot, and that can't happen until he comes to."

She bit her lip. "Do you think he'll die?"

"I doubt it." He turned to look back out the window, hiding his expression from her, but she heard the contempt in his tone when he added, "But don't feel bad if he does."

"I wouldn't. I mean, I don't. He could have killed someone."

"That's about it."

Given his surly tone, she decided a change of topic was in order. They stopped at a light and she looked Mick over. His hair was thick and shiny and a little too long. The whiskers on his face, combined with the tiredness of his eyes, made her heart swell. Today he wore the softest, most well-worn jeans she'd ever seen on a man. They hugged his thick thighs and his heavy groin and his lean hips and tight buttocks.

Her pulse leaped at the thought of that gorgeous body beneath the clothes. Tonight, she'd get to see all of him. She'd make sure of it. She was so wrapped up in those thoughts, she almost missed the light turning green.

She eased the car forward, while her thoughts stayed attuned to Mick.

The shirt Josh had brought him was snowy-white cotton, buttoned down the front, and looked just as soft as the jeans. The thick bandage on his shoulder could be seen beneath, as could the heavy muscles of his chest, his biceps. "The doctor says you can shower," she told him with a croak in her voice. "But he doesn't want you to soak."

"Right now, a shower will feel like heaven."

"Will you need anything in particular? I could run by your place after I drop you off and pick you up anything you need."

"Josh grabbed me a change of socks and boxers. Angel's

taking care of the rest later today. For now, whatever soap and shampoo you have will work." He glanced at her, smiling just a bit. "Do you use scented stuff?"

"No."

His eyes went almost black. "Good. I love the way you smell. I'm glad it's you and not from a bottle."

Del tightened her hands on the wheel. Boy, much more of that and she wouldn't make it home. Luckily, he stayed silent for the rest of the ride, and Del didn't bother trying to draw him out again. Her heart couldn't take his idea of casual conversation.

She pulled up to the garage in front of her building. She had to pay extra to park her car there, but she knew if she left it on the street, it'd likely get stripped. She said as much to Mick as she turned off the ignition.

"Yeah, I know. I told you I own that building next door, right?"

Del rushed around to his door to help him—and got a disgruntled frown for her efforts. He was suddenly in an oddly defensive mood, and she didn't understand him.

"You told me. I wasn't sure if you meant the building to the left or the right."

He grunted. The building to the left was a shambles. His building was nicely maintained. "Alec used to rent from me, before he married Celia. The agency where he works is located between here and where he lives now."

Del cocked a brow. "If he doesn't live *here* now, why did he follow us?"

Mick jerked around. Wary, he asked, "What are you talking about?"

She rolled her eyes. "Your friend is pretty hard to miss,

looking like Satan and all. I saw him a few cars behind us. I suppose this is more of your protection?"

Tilting his head back, Mick stared at the heavens. "Something like that." When he looked at her, she could almost feel his resolve. "I don't have a gun right now. The cops confiscated it as evidence."

Del gasped. "They're not going to accuse you of anything, are they?"

"No, it's routine to take any weapon used in a shooting. I'll get another one before the day is out, but until then, I wanted someone armed to keep an eye on things."

Fascinating. He spoke about guns with the same disregard that she gave to groceries. "This is all really extreme, you know."

"It's all really necessary, as far as I'm concerned." Then he added, "Trust me, honey. This is what I do, and I'm not willing to take any chances with you."

That sounded nice, as if he might be starting to like her. But maybe, Del thought, all private detectives were as cautious as Mick. She had no comparisons to go by; she'd never known a PI before.

Shrugging, she decided not to fight what she couldn't change, and hefted out her laptop. She put the leather strap of the carrying case over her shoulder along with her tote, and then reached inside for his bag.

Mick caught her shoulder with his left hand. "Something we need to clear up."

Del peeked up at him. He looked too serious, almost grim. Getting to know this man, with all the twists and turns of his personality, would be exhilarating. "Yes?"

He relieved her of his bag, then her laptop, holding both

casually in his left hand as if they weighed no more than a feather pillow. "I'm not an invalid."

Her temper sparked. "No, of course not. But you are wounded and you're not supposed to strain yourself."

Without warning, he leaned down and gave her a loud, smacking kiss. His expression was amused and chagrined and determined. "It doesn't strain me, I promise."

"But you can only use the one arm."

Slow and wicked, his grin spread. "I can do a lot," he whispered in a rough drawl, "with one arm."

Her stomach curled at the way he said that and what she knew he inferred. She cleared her throat. "I see."

"Good. Now lead the way."

She didn't want to. She wanted to insist that he let her help him. He'd done enough already, more than enough. Too much. The man had a bullet in him, thanks to her.

She turned and marched toward the front stairs. The entry door was old and heavy, and she hurried to open it, anxious to get Mick settled inside.

Together they climbed the steep stairs to the upper landing, where she used her key on both of the locks for her apartment door, one of them a dead bolt. Being a runner, she made the climb with ease, breathing as normally as ever when she reached the top. She half expected Mick, with his injuries and his load, to huff at least a bit, but he didn't.

He did, however, keep a vigilant watch. "I'm relieved to see the landlord keeps the place secure. Not all the buildings in this area are safe."

Del looked at him over her shoulder as she reached inside and flipped a wall switch. She didn't tell him that she'd had the dead bolt installed recently. The front door opened directly into her living room, and one switch turned on both end-table lamps. She said only, "I'm not an idiot. I wouldn't endanger myself."

She tossed her tote onto the oversize leather sofa to her right and reached for her laptop. Mick, who'd been looking around, taking in her modest apartment, held it out of reach, lifting it over his head as if he didn't have a bullet in his other arm, as if the pain wasn't plain on his face. His strength amazed her.

"Where do you want it?"

Sighing, Del pointed to her desk in the corner, where a half wall separated her kitchen area from the rest of the room. Her desk was the only modern, truly functional piece of furniture she had. A computer occupied the center of the tiered piece, with a fax machine, a printer and a copier close at hand. There were file folders and papers stacked everywhere, notes, magazines, interviews she hadn't yet put into the file cabinet behind the desk. Reference books littered the floor.

Mick lifted a brow and boldly glanced at her papers as he set the laptop down.

His curiosity would have to be appeased another time, Del decided. She took his arm and steered him toward the narrow hallway on the opposite side of the room. "The bathroom is this way. You can shower while I change the sheets. Are you hungry?"

He'd never admit it, she knew, but he looked ready to drop, pain tightening his mouth and darkening his eyes. Twice she'd seen him rub at his temples when he didn't know she was looking. The doctor had told her that he was as likely to have headaches from his fall as pain from his wound. Del had a hunch the two were combining against him.

"After you finish," she said gently, but with as much authority as she could summon, "you'll need to take your medicine."

Mick stopped in the bathroom doorway and caught her chin with his hand. His gaze burned, touching on her mouth, her throat, her breasts. "After I finish," he said, his fingertips tenderly caressing her skin, "I intend to see about you."

Her knees almost went weak. "Me?" It was a dumb question; she knew exactly what he meant.

Nodding slowly, he said, "All that teasing you've been doing, all that talk about starting an affair, and your bold touching. I'm beyond ready."

She really did need to learn a little discretion, she thought, now wishing she hadn't told him all her intentions. But she was used to going after what she wanted, and he'd been irresistible, a man unlike any she'd ever known. Everything about him turned her on, from the protectiveness she'd never received before, to his strength and intensity, to his rough velvet voice and drool-worthy bod. The man was sexy emotionally and physically, and she wanted him.

She caught his wrist and kissed his palm. "Mick, you need to rest. There'll be plenty of time for…"

He carried her hand to the thick erection testing the worn material of his jeans. Her heart dropped to her stomach, then shot into her throat.

"You think," he whispered roughly, his eyes closing at the feel of her hand on him, "that I can rest with that? The answer is no."

Her palm tingled and of their own accord her fingers began to curl around him. He lifted her hand away, leaned down and kissed her. "I just need fifteen minutes to shower and shave."

Carrying his bag into the room with him, he turned and closed the door, leaving Del standing there with her lips parted and her eyes glazed and her muscles quivering. She sucked in a breath and let her head drop forward to the door, bracing herself there until she stopped trembling.

His effect on her was startling, almost too much to bear. She'd given up on men as too much trouble, with not enough payoff. But with a mere look, Mick could make her hot, and when he touched her, or she touched him, the need was overwhelming.

She heard the shower start and realized she hadn't reminded him to be careful. She leaned close and said loudly, "Don't soak your shoulder! The doctor said that was a no-no."

Just as loudly, he retorted, "I was there, Delilah, remember?" And then she heard the rustling of the shower curtain and knew he was naked, knew he was wet....

She turned and hurried away.

When he'd answered her, he'd sounded distinctly irritable. Well, hell. Heaven knew, he was likely to be doubly so when he found out she had no intention of making love with him today. It would be too much for him, and there was a good chance he'd injure his shoulder anew.

No, she couldn't let him do that.

She also couldn't let him go unsatisfied. She closed her eyes, feeling wicked and sinful and anxious. There was only one thing to do. Granted, *she* was likely to end up the frustrated one, but that was a small price to pay to a man who'd played her hero, a man who'd saved her life. And she had no doubt he'd make it up to her later. She may not have known him long, but she knew that much about him already. The man wanted her—more than any man ever had.

It was a heady feeling. She liked it.

She especially liked him.

MICK FOUND HER in the kitchen, staring into her refrigerator as if pondering what to fix. A glass of iced tea sat on the counter.

He shook his head, not yet announcing himself. Foolish woman. How could she possibly think he'd want food when she stood there looking more than edible? Oh yeah, he wanted to eat her up. And he would, slowly and with great relish. "Delilah."

She whirled around, first appearing guilty, then abashed when she saw his naked chest. He'd done no more than pull on snug cotton boxers; he had no need of the sling right now, though he kept his right arm slightly elevated to relieve his shoulder of pressure. The bandages there were made to withstand showers and would dry soon.

Any clothes he would have put on would just be coming off again, so he hadn't bothered with them, either. By look and deed she'd made her willingness, her own desire, clear. It didn't matter that he hardly knew her, not when everything about her felt so right.

He braced his feet apart and let her look her fill.

Her eyes widened and then traveled the length of him. Twice. She touched her throat. "If I looked as good as you, I'd have skipped the boxers."

Though he appreciated the sentiment, Mick was too far gone with lust to manage a grin. "Want me to take them off?"

She shook her head and said, "Yes. But not yet. If you were naked now, I'd forget you're hurt and do something I'd regret."

"Like what?" She continued to stand there, her gaze returning again and again to his straining hard-on, which the snug cotton boxers did nothing to hide.

"Like throwing you down on the floor and having my way with you."

He did grin this time. "The bed is right around the corner. Why don't we go there now?"

Just that easily, he saw her resolve form, harden. He may have only known her a day, but he already knew that look.

"You need to take your medicine. Good as you look, I can see that you hurt."

The pain in his shoulder and head were nothing, certainly not enough to make him want to wait another day to have her. "I'll take a pill after I've sated myself with you."

Her gaze locked on his. "Oh boy, you don't pull any punches, do you?"

"From what I remember last night in the hospital, neither do you." And to encourage her, he added, "But I like it when you speak your mind."

She nodded. "Okay, yes, I want you to sate yourself with me. I want to sate myself with you, too." Her expression was one of worry, regret. "But I figure that'd probably take me hours, maybe even days, so we should maybe put it off until you're not likely to die on me."

Damn, her brazen words mixed with the sweetness of her expression and the obvious worry she felt for him was an aphrodisiac that fired his blood. She was a mix of contradictions, always unique, sometimes pushy and too stubborn. Mick took two long steps toward her, ignored the continual throbbing in his shoulder and head, and gathered her close.

He wasn't prepared for her stiffened arms, which carefully pushed him back again. Shakily, she said, "We have to make a deal."

The need stalled, replaced by innate suspicion. What possible deal could she need to make at this moment? Thoughts flew through his head as he remembered numerous deals offered to him by prostitutes, drug dealers, gamblers, people from his youth and the people he now came into contact with every day of his life.

He also thought about the robbery, about her uncommon interest in the jewelry store, her interest in him, her willingness to bring a near stranger into her home and have sex with him.

By nature, he was overly cautious. From his upbringing, and then working undercover, he'd become suspicious of almost everyone and everything.

Because of his background, he often doubted the sincerity of women in general.

Dropping his hands so he wouldn't accidentally hurt her with his anger, Mick growled, "What kind of deal?"

She blinked, confused by his temper. Carefully, her words no more than a whisper of sound, she explained, "I can't stand seeing you in pain. I want you to take your medicine first, then we'll go to bed."

Mick made sure no reaction showed on his face, but once again she'd managed to take him off guard. Her deal was for him, not for her. "The medicine makes me too groggy."

"Not for fifteen minutes or more. I've watched you after you take it. It doesn't kick in right away, and you only go to sleep when you let yourself."

Still not touching her, he said, "What I have in mind will take more than fifteen minutes."

She inhaled sharply at his words, then touched him, her hand opening on his chest, her fingers splayed, sifting through his body hair. The reflexive clench of his muscles brought a sharp ache to his temples, his shoulder.

"You're welcome to stay here until you're completely re-covered," she said, still stroking him with what seemed like acute awe, probably attempting to soothe him, when in fact each glide of her delicate fingers over his muscles wound him that much tighter. "There'll be plenty of time for both of us to indulge ourselves."

He didn't answer right away, trying to figure her out in the middle of an intense arousal that kept rational thought just out of reach.

"Please," she added, both hands now sliding up to his shoulders. One edged the bandage that came over his shoulder from the back. "I won't be able to enjoy myself for fear of hurting you."

He didn't want that. He fully intended for her to experience more than mere enjoyment. He wanted her ripe with pleasure, numb with it. He wanted to give her the kind of explosive release she'd have only with him.

Yet, she was right. In his present condition, it wasn't likely to happen. With her insistence, she was probably helping him to save face.

Mick brought her close and said against her hair, "I'm sorry. I'm not used to wanting a woman quite this much." He wasn't used to wanting to *trust* a woman, either. But he wanted to trust Delilah. He wanted to involve himself with every aspect of her life. He needed to tie her to him in some way.

Nodding, she said, "I know the feeling. You blow my socks off."

He tilted her back so he could see her face. Her honesty humbled him, and pleased him.

"We haven't discussed it," he said, thinking now was as good a time as any, "but I want you to know the nurse was right, I come with a clean bill of health—in all ways. Not only have I always been discriminating, but I'm very cautious, too."

That brought a beautiful smile to her face. "Same here. I can't claim to have been a recluse, but I haven't met many men that I wanted to get involved with. Not like this, not enough to let them interrupt my life. And men take exception to that. They don't like to be neatly compartmentalized."

"Is that right?"

She nodded. "You may not have noticed, but I get really wrapped up in my work, and most of the time I'm not even aware of men around me. At least, not for long."

Mick grinned. "I noticed. At first I wondered if maybe you were a lesbian."

Her mouth opened, then closed. She frowned at him, her pale blue eyes burning bright. "I'm not."

His grin widened. "I noticed that, too."

Still scowling, she said, "Not that there's anything wrong with—"

"Of course not. But I have to tell you how glad I am that you're interested in men."

"I'm interested in *you*."

He appreciated her clarification. "Which means I'm one lucky bastard."

She snorted. "If you were so lucky, you wouldn't have gotten shot." She turned and grabbed up the pills. "Take these."

He downed them in one gulp, washing the bitter taste away with sweetened tea.

"Are you hungry? You really didn't eat that much yesterday, and you hardly touched your breakfast."

He'd been too caught up in his thoughts, in mentally organizing all the things that had to be done that day, to concern himself with breakfast. And the truth was, he felt hollow down to his toes. He could probably eat two meals, but not yet. "No. I just want you. And now that I've swallowed the damn pills, time's wasting."

Her eyes warmed, the vivid blue darkening. She took his hand and turned to lead him down the hall. Without looking at him, she said, "Let me see if I can help you to sleep soundly for a few hours."

It took a great deal of resolve not to turn her against the wall and enter her right there, standing up, without the benefit of a soft mattress. At twenty-six, he'd known lust, but he'd never known anything like this, an all-encompassing need to devour a particular woman.

Her bedroom was small, holding a bed that would barely accommodate his size. The beige spread was tossed half off the bottom of the mattress, pooling on the floor and showing matching beige sheets. Across from it sat a triple dresser with a mirror, the top cluttered with papers and candles and receipts.

A wooden rocker sat in front of one window. The other window held an air conditioner, softly humming on low, keeping the room pleasantly cool. Over the bed a ceiling fan slowly whirled, barely stirring the air but making the room comfortable.

The building didn't have central air, of course. None of the buildings on her street did. Some of them didn't have heat, either. Thankfully, Delilah's apartment building was kept up, just as Mick kept up his building next door. And she wasn't on the first floor, so she could open her windows without fear of intruders.

Her bedroom wasn't what you'd call neat, not with laundry piled on the chair and shoes tossed haphazardly over her closet floor, but it was orderly. He had the distinct impression Delilah could walk into this room and find anything she needed without effort.

She went straight to the bed and propped up the pillows. "Sit here."

Bemused, Mick allowed her to take control. She always seemed less reserved when she was the aggressor, as if taking control gave her more confidence. He wanted her without inhibitions, so he gladly let her lead.

He settled himself, easing his injured shoulder back against the headboard. Delilah stood in front of him and unsnapped her jeans. The sound of her zipper sliding down nearly stopped his heart. Transfixed, he watched her disrobing in front of him. There was no false modesty, no timidity, but no real brazenness, either. She revealed her body with a no-nonsense acceptance that touched his heart; she wouldn't flaunt, but neither would she cower. Mick tightened his fists in the bottom sheet and held himself still.

He'd been half-afraid he was rushing her, moving too fast. But judging by her willingness now, she was finally as ready as him.

But then, he'd been ready from the first moment he saw her.

chapter 5

DELILAH'S JEANS DROPPED, and she smiled at him as she stepped away from them, using one foot to nudge them aside. "I'm not as perfect as you," she stated, again with that simple acceptance of her own perceptions, "but somehow I have a feeling that won't bother you."

Oh, he was plenty bothered, on the point of going insane. Her comments weren't geared toward gaining compliments, but he could only give her the truth. "You're the sexiest woman I've ever seen."

Her mouth twitched and then she laughed. "Yeah, right. With small boobs and a straight waist and gangly limbs?"

He wanted to correct her, to point out everything he found enticing, yet when she caught the hem of her tank top and tugged it over her head, he went mute. His heart struck his rib cage, his breath caught.

The bra she wore had no shoulder straps, and the cups only half covered her. When she flipped her hair back, he could have sworn he saw the edge of a mauve nipple.

He swallowed hard. "This is insane. Come here."

"In a minute. Don't you want me naked?" she teased.

"God, yes." He shifted his legs. He was uncomfortable, drawn tight, ready to come from just the sight of her. "I want to touch you, too." *And taste you and bury myself deep.*

Reaching behind her back, she unhooked her bra and let it drop. Her breasts were round and firm, with small, tightly puckered nipples now darkened with desire.

She left her miniscule panties on and walked toward him, her gait long and sure and purposeful. Without reserve, she climbed into the bed and straddled his lap. Mick groaned as her rounded bottom nestled on his thighs and her breasts came even with his face. He reached for her.

"Shh," she said, catching his right arm and holding it still. "Let me. You just sit back and relax."

Blood rushed through his head. He gritted his teeth and nodded. He didn't tell her that relaxing was out of the question.

"Tell me what you want." As she spoke, she looked at him and touched him, and his vision narrowed to only her.

"I want to taste you."

Her eyes smoldered, encouraging him even as her hands attempted to ease him. It was a wasted effort. Each soft stroke of her hands—over his chest, his uninjured shoulder, his waist, his throat—inflamed him.

He saw the pulse fluttering in her throat when she asked huskily, "Where?"

"Everywhere, but for now, I want your nipples."

Her thighs tightened around his, giving her away. She wasn't nearly as detached or in control as she pretended. He didn't quite understand her forceful determination, but he knew at least part of it was inspired by reciprocal lust.

She drew a shaky breath and slowly, so slowly the anticipation damn near killed him, she leaned forward.

Mick struggled to stay calm. He couldn't stop himself from bending his knees, forcing her farther forward, couldn't stop the flexing of his cock against her tantalizing ass. But he made certain to gently kiss the rounded softness of her breasts, to nuzzle against her until she moaned. He teased her, licking close to her nipple but not quite letting his tongue touch it.

She twisted, attempting to hurry him, but Mick held himself in check. She needed to catch up to him—if that was possible.

With a rough, impatient sound, she finally murmured, "Mick, please…"

He placed a wet, soft kiss directly over her nipple, briefly drawing her into the heat of his mouth with a gentle suction, and then releasing her. It wasn't easy, considering he wanted to feast on her.

She moved against him, one small jerk on his thighs before she stopped herself. Panting, she said, "I like that."

"I thought you would." He did it again, then again and again until she gasped for breath, until her hands settled in his hair and her nipples were tight wet peaks. Likely with more force than she realized, she brought his mouth to her breast, saying without words that she now needed more.

And he suckled her, strong and deep and long.

The combined sensations rocked him: the taste and feel of her on his tongue as his mouth tugged at her, the heat of her sex pressing insistently against his abdomen, her scent and softness and her unique determination.

The physical bombardment on his senses was enough,

leaving him confused and wild with need. But the emotional storm also overwhelmed him. He wanted to consume her savagely, brand her as his own, hear her cries and feel the bite of her nails. And he wanted to hold her gently to his heart, to let her feel protected and know that he'd take care of her. Basic, elemental instincts rolled through him in a way he'd never felt before.

As he continued to tongue and suck, her back arched and she released a ragged moan. Then she moved against his thighs, a riding motion that rubbed the damp silk of her panties along the length of his shaft.

He replaced his mouth with his fingers and said harshly, "Kiss me, Delilah."

She did, stealing his breath as her tongue licked in to tease his. As wild and out of control as he felt, she was more so.

"Let's get these panties off you," he murmured, knowing he couldn't last much longer.

She pulled away, trembling, gasping for breath. Her head dropped forward. After a moment, she dipped down and kissed his throat, her mouth open and hot and wet. Mick wanted to protest, but he loved the feel of her mouth on him.

The pills had muddled his mind some and it took more effort than he could dredge up to stop her as she sank lower, biting at his chest, hotly licking his own nipples, tasting and teasing him.

His arm hurt like a son of a bitch and his head continued to throb dully, but raging lust and crushing need overrode it all. Using his good arm, he tangled his fingers in her silky hair, letting it slide over his chest and then his abdomen as she moved lower and lower down the length of his body.

When her tongue dipped into his navel, he nearly shouted with the pleasure of it. "God, Delilah," he managed to rasp, "baby, you have to stop."

She ignored him. Her hand crept up his tensed thigh, higher and higher until she cuddled his testicles for a brief, heart-stopping moment before grasping his erection and slowly stroking.

He stiffened, all sensation, hot and thick, rushing into his groin. Her mouth, still gentle but hungry, kissed him through the cotton boxers, and the pleasure-pain was so excruciating it blocked everything else.

He cursed, feeling himself sinking, out of control. He had to stop her, but he didn't want to. He wanted her to—

As if she'd read his mind, she eased the boxers down.

"No," Mick protested with a long groan, knowing he sounded less than convincing. The damn pills had melted away his determination, made him forget all his plans. He could only focus on Delilah, on what she did, how she touched him.

"I've been thinking about this all day," she breathed.

He opened his eyes, needing to watch. The look on her face mirrored his own emotions of fire, need, possession. She watched her hand driving him to distraction, her grip firm, her thumb curling over the end of his erection with each long stroke, pushing him closer and closer....

Mick felt a surge of release and desperately fought it off, but she saw the drop of fluid at the head of his penis and leaned forward.

He shuddered, cursed, held his breath—then shouted in

reaction when her mouth closed over him, not tentatively, as he'd expected, but sliding wetly down the length of him, taking all of him in, sucking.

Maybe if he hadn't taken the damn pills, maybe if it had been any woman other than her, he could have controlled himself.

But from the moment he'd seen her he'd wanted her, and he couldn't hold back, couldn't stop himself from coming. His fingers knotted in her hair and he held her head to him, not that it was necessary because she didn't pull away. She drew him deeper and made a low sound of pleasure that he felt in his soul. He tightened, surged, and experienced the strongest release of his entire life. He growled with the force of it, his body taut, arching, his mind going blank.

His only realization in that turbulent moment of rioting sensation was that no other man would ever touch her; she was his, and he intended to keep her.

MICK DIDN'T SLEEP LONG this time, probably no more than an hour, but he awoke half-frozen. The air conditioner, on the highest setting, hummed loudly, and the ceiling fan whirled overhead. He felt his hair blowing, felt his skin prickle with goose bumps.

He'd passed out just as she'd left him, half propped against the headboard, his legs now limp, his shoulder cushioned by a soft pillow. At least she'd pulled the spread up to his waist, he thought, a bit disgruntled.

He felt like an idiot as he looked around and realized the room was empty. He cursed. Then cursed again when he pushed the spread away and became racked with chills. It was like sleeping on the wing of an airplane, for crying out loud!

He swung his legs to the floor, stood—and nearly fell. Weakness had invaded every muscle. The pain pills had no effect on his aches, not after that mind-grinding orgasm, where every muscle in his body, clear down to the soles of his feet, had knotted in pulsating pleasure. She'd wrung him out—no doubt that had been her intent.

He grunted, unable to believe what she'd done, and unwilling to accept that after she'd done it, he'd had the gall to fall asleep.

If the room hadn't felt like a meat locker, he'd probably have been hot with embarrassment.

He glanced down at his boxers, still around his thighs, and shook his head. It was too much, far too much.

He straightened his underwear, whipped the spread off the bed and around his shoulders to ward off the cold, then went to the window to turn the unit down. The air conditioner sputtered and died with a sigh.

Forcing himself forward on shaky limbs, Mick left the bedroom. The apartment was quiet, other than the rattling of pans in the kitchen area. On his way down the hall, he decided to take the offense. Delilah knew he'd wanted to make love to her, but she'd taken the choice away from him. *How* she'd taken it away had been beyond incredible, but still, she needed to know that he wouldn't be so easily manipulated. Not ever again.

He was appalled that he'd proved so easy this time. But then, maybe that's why she'd given him the pills, to weaken his resolve. He'd be sure to ask her that.

When he reached the arched kitchen doorway, she had her back to him, stirring a pan of something on the stove. Whatever she was cooking smelled good, as did the coffee in the coffeemaker. She'd pulled her tank top back on, but not her jeans, and the sight of her bottom in the silky panties did a lot to obliterate his other concerns.

Before he got distracted, he asked, "Did you talk me into the pain pills so you could keep us from having sex?"

She yelped, dropped her stirring spoon and jerked around to face him. Their gazes locked.

The sight of her face made his mind go blank, his heart trip. *She'd been crying.*

"Delilah?" he asked around a sudden lump of emotion. Damn, that bothered him. He didn't get lumps of emotion. In his job, he saw the worst life had to offer and he handled it dispassionately, with a distance that could be applauded. Always, from the time he'd been a young boy, he'd kept his emotions in check.

But God, she looked like hell with her eyes swollen and wet, her cheeks blotchy, her nose red. Seeing her made his heart thump.

She bit her bottom lip and turned to the stove again. He heard her sniff. "Yes."

Mick shook his head. He wanted to hold her, to comfort her. Yet she'd turned her back on him. "Yes what?"

"Yes, I gave you the pills so you wouldn't complain when I…eased you. It was the only thing I could think of. I didn't want you to strain yourself, and the doctor said it was too soon for you to have sex."

Talking with Delilah was like wading through syrup. He kept getting stuck, but damn, it was sweet. He cleared his throat, forcing the emotion away so he could think and react clearly. He slowly approached her and stood at her back, close enough to breathe in her sexy scent and see the enormous pot of spaghetti sauce she stirred. "You spoke with the doctor about us having sex?" Her initiative amazed him—and aroused him.

"Yes. Right after I bought the condoms."

Mick paused. *Bought the condoms?* Before he could ask, she said, "I snuck them into the bedroom, in the nightstand drawer, just in case you didn't go to sleep after you came."

She spoke as bluntly as any man, but then, she'd done that from the first, speaking her mind with candor. Unlike other women he knew, she didn't measure her words. She was so female she made him crazy, yet she didn't always act female. Damn if that didn't arouse him, too.

Hell, everything she did aroused him. Just moments before he'd thought himself fully satisfied, but now... "The hospital sells rubbers?"

She glanced at him over her shoulder, and he watched one fat tear track down her cheek. "Yeah, of course they do. It's a hospital, and they understand about unnecessary risks."

She'd managed to distract him, after all.

Mick shook his head and wrapped one arm around her waist. Resting his chin on top of her head, he asked, "Why are you crying, sweetheart? Did I hurt you?"

"Of course not." She leaned into him, then pushed back with a frown. "You're shivering." Twisting, she put her hand to his forehead in a maternal gesture of concern. "Are you sick?"

"Just cold." He turned her back around and laced his hands over her middle. Her bottom pressed into his groin. "The room was like ice."

She nodded. "I figured you'd like it cold. Most men get warmer than women, right?"

He had no idea, but he doubted any man would relish the igloo accommodations she'd provided him. She'd obviously had some sexual experience, and she was comfortable with her body, with her sexuality. But she was far from knowledgeable about the opposite sex. Mick shook his head at the added contradictions. "Why are you crying?"

She shrugged and leaned back against him. "I'm just a little sad. I'm sorry you have to see me like this. I'm a terrible crier. Very ugly. The news just took me by surprise."

"What news?" He rubbed his chin against her hair, spread his hand over her belly. He loved the feel of her, her softness, her sleekness. She was so feminine, but not in a frail way.

"A guy I know died. I just read it in the paper."

Mick stiffened, caught between conflicting reactions. He wanted to comfort her from any upset, and he wanted to jealously demand information about the guy who'd made her cry. He must have been important to her to bring on the tears.

It shouldn't have mattered. They'd only just officially met, and hadn't officially consummated their relationship yet. But it did matter. A lot.

"Who was he?" Mick asked, keeping her pressed into him by his hand on her belly.

After a long, shuddering sigh, she put the spoon down and turned into his arms. Her face nuzzled into his chest and she whispered, "Just a guy who helped me with research." He felt her wet cheek on his pec muscle and groaned.

"I'm sorta known for my research methods, you know," she continued. "They've become part of my publicity." She leaned back to stare up at him earnestly, and in case he hadn't understood, she clarified. "For my books, I mean."

"How is research a publicity stunt?"

She lifted one shoulder. "People are amazed by the strangest things. But whenever I write about something in a book, I try to experience it first so that I get it right. When I can't experience it, I try to talk to someone who has."

"So what type of research did this guy help you with?" Mick hoped like hell it wasn't a love scene. He could handle anything but that.

Turning away, she reached for a napkin and mopped her eyes. Mick heard another loud sniff. "He was a small-time criminal. I had a scene in my book where a guy stole a car. I couldn't really steal a car—" she glanced at him and added "—not without getting arrested, I'm sure."

"Better not to try it," he agreed, smiling.

"That's what I figured. So I hired this guy, and he took me through all the ins and outs of car theft. For a criminal he was a really nice guy."

Mick glanced at the coffeepot. "Mind if I have a cup?"

"Oh, of course." But she didn't let him get it himself. "Sit down and I'll pour it for you."

Since his knees were still shaking, Mick sat. More than most things, he hated being weak, and for now there was nothing he could do about it. He pulled out a chair at the black, wrought-iron parlor table and gratefully dropped into it.

"Cream or sugar?"

"Black, please."

She set the steaming mug in front of him. His first sip made his body hair stand on end, and he nearly spat it back out. His throat raw, he rasped, "Damn, that's strong."

Delilah didn't take his comment as a complaint. She smiled, looking adorable in her skimpy top and panties, her nose bright red. "I figured you being a man and all, you'd want it strong."

It was a wonder new hair hadn't sprouted on his body. He coughed, and because he didn't want to hurt her feelings, he said, "I think I'll take the cream and sugar, after all."

She happily got them for him, then went back to the stove to check her sauce. To Mick, it looked like there was enough to feed an army. Hopefully, she didn't expect him to eat it all—because he was a man.

Making sure she didn't notice all the sugar he dumped into his coffee, he asked, "So where did a nice woman like you meet a car thief?"

"In prison."

The mouthful of coffee—still too bitter to enjoy—got spewed across the table. He continued to choke as Delilah grabbed up a dish towel and patted his back.

"Mick! Are you all right?"

He wheezed, trying to regain his breath enough to speak. With his eyes squeezed shut, he finally demanded, "What the hell were you doing in prison?"

Tilting her head, she smiled. Given her swollen eyes and the tear tracks on her cheeks, it didn't have the usual effect on his libido. "More research." She chuckled. "You didn't think I meant I'd been serving time, did you?"

Actually, he had, but he wasn't dumb enough to say so. Relief warred with confusion. "Of course not. But can you explain all this research for me?"

She pulled out her own chair at the table. "Okay, but

don't let me forget the spaghetti sauce. Your friends are coming over for dinner and I want to impress them."

"Josh and Zack?"

She snorted. "I meant your other friends, the ones you said were like family."

"Dane and Angel are staying for dinner?" He didn't like putting her out, especially since she was so upset.

"I invited them. Angel called and said she had your things, and wanted to know when it'd be a good time to drop them off. I know she's still worried about you, and she doesn't exactly trust me, so I thought this would be a way to make her feel better."

Cautiously, Mick asked, "What makes you think Angel doesn't trust you?"

Del made a face. "I'm not dumb."

Mick let that go. He'd have to talk to Angel first to see what had been said. He knew Angel would never insult Delilah, but she was protective. "Why do you want to impress them?"

"They're like your family. I like you, so of course I want them to like me."

Mick almost told her it didn't matter what anyone else thought, that he intended to make her a part of his life. But he'd never gotten so deeply involved with a woman, and to do so now, at Mach speed, was just plain foolish. He liked her, all her quirks and unique qualities. He liked her different way of viewing things and her outspokenness mixed with occasional glimpses of uncertainty. And God knew, the sexual chemistry between them was explosive.

But most of her background was still a mystery to him. So he forced himself to be cautious, to go slow. He tucked a tendril of her silky hair behind her ear and asked, "Are you sure you're up to a dinner party?"

"Why wouldn't I be? You're the one who got shot."

"*You* were the target. And you've been crying."

She waved that away, ignoring his first comment and only responding to his second. "I'm overly emotional about the people I care for. There aren't that many. Being a writer keeps me isolated, so I don't get into the social swing of things often. Neddie became a friend as well as a teacher. We had a lot of fun hot-wiring my car."

This time Mick just stared. She gave an impatient sigh and went on. "It's true. We were alike in a lot of ways, reacting to our place in society. Neddie became a misguided criminal, just trying to fit in. I became a writer."

"It's hardly the same thing."

"Of course not. I just meant that we understood each other. Neddie was wrong, and he knew that. But he always said he never hurt anyone who didn't deserve to be hurt. Anything he did, he did among other criminals, including stealing cars. And from what he told me, I believe him."

"Criminals always have excuses, Delilah."

"Well, he was a nice criminal, okay? And very patient. We took my car to a deserted lot and practiced on it for hours. Once I got the hang of it, Neddie timed me."

Mick's left hand, resting on the tabletop, curled into a fist. "You went to a deserted lot with a convict?"

"Can you imagine how the cops might have reacted if they'd seen me hot-wiring a car around here?"

She needed a keeper. *She needed him.* He drew a calming breath, something he found himself doing often around her. "Back up and tell me what you were doing in prison."

"I had a character in a book who had spent a good portion of his life in prison. I couldn't very well write that without knowing what the inside of a prison was really like."

"Ever heard of research books?" he asked dryly.

She laughed. Though he knew her humor was aimed at him, he was glad to see her mood lightening. "I use research books when I have to. But I think it's always better to get first-hand, in-person information whenever I can."

"You said that's part of your promotion?"

"Yep. It didn't start out that way. But then this one reporter got wind of it when my last book hit the *New York Times* bestseller list. She interviewed me and asked me all kinds of questions about my research, and since then the media is real accommodating. They always make a fuss about my way of researching."

His head throbbed. "Media?"

"Yeah. Silly, huh?"

His tongue felt on fire as he sputtered, "You're a celebrity."

Delilah wrinkled her nose and with a note of dismissal said, "To some people, I guess."

"You do this often?"

She shrugged. "Often enough. I was on a talk show once, and not too long ago I got featured on the news."

"The news?"

"About my newest book, and my research for it. It was fun."

In that moment, a thousand questions went through his mind. What the hell was a celebrity doing living in this neighborhood? How much money could she possibly make and what other types of research had she done?

Could any of that have to do with the incident at the jewelry store?

Before he could start on his interrogation, and that's what it would have been because he fully intended to get a lot of answers, she said, "We better get a move on. Everyone will be showing up in about half an hour. I still need to shower and change and make the bed and boil the spaghetti and fix a salad—"

Mick caught her hand as she rose. He tugged her between his legs. "I can help."

This time her laughter had the desired effect. He got hard as a stone. "Mick," she said playfully, and cupped his neck in both hands. "I think I can handle a shower on my own."

Damn, that brought an irresistible image to his mind. Delilah naked and wet, water streaming down her body, over her belly and between her thighs....

He released her hand and curled his arm around her waist, keeping her close when she tried to impatiently edge away. "I meant," he said, his voice now hoarse, "that I can handle spaghetti or a salad."

"No," she said in that unrelenting tone he already recognized. Delilah was used to making all the decisions, and used to holding her ground.

He'd have to work on that flaw.

She leaned down and quickly kissed him. "Not one-armed, you can't, and the doc specifically said you shouldn't use your right arm."

Mick was ready to explain a few things to her, but she added, her voice sweet and cajoling, "Please, Mick. Just let me take care of you, okay?"

He opened his hand on the small of her back, then slipped it down her spine to her bottom. He filled his palm with one firm cheek. "All right," he agreed. "But on one condition."

Her eyes narrowed. "What?"

"Tonight, after everyone is gone…" He let his fingers drift lower, pressing in to touch the heat of her, pleased with her gasp and small moan. "Tonight you'll let me show you exactly what I *can* do with one good arm."

Breathless, she said, "Sex is—"

"I know, not on the agenda." His fingers caressed her. "But I can return your favor of today."

Her lips parted, her eyes glittered and her cheeks looked warm. Several heartbeats went by, then she whispered, "Yes, okay."

Mick felt like a conquering warrior now that she'd given in to him at least a little. He grinned and smacked her butt. "I'm glad you can see reason. Now go get your shower. I'll pull on my jeans and park myself in front of the TV."

"And you won't lift a finger?"

He stood, kissed her forehead and replied, "Not until tonight."

With a comical look on her face, she turned the sauce down to warm and left the room. Mick flexed his aching shoulder, winced and decided to make a fresh pot of coffee while Delilah was otherwise occupied. He could only imagine Dane's expression if he took a gulp of that thick, bitter brew. It would probably prove amusing, but then Mick would have to drink it, too, which would negate all the fun.

So far, her coffee, her air-conditioning and her lack of discretion in dangerous situations were the only things he had trouble with. Those things aside, Delilah Piper was one hell of a woman. With each passing minute, he fell a little harder.

chapter 6

IT TURNED OUT TO BE a hectic evening, and Delilah was glad to see it winding down. Not only had Dane and Angel come to dinner, but Alec and Celia had called, and she'd invited them along. She figured she might as well get the family gathering over with. She was used to people not understanding her, to assumptions that her preoccupation with her stories was sheer daydreaming, motivated by lack of intelligence or attention.

She wasn't used to caring, to going out of her way to be accepted, and she'd felt on edge. Added to that was her urge to write. She had a deadline looming, and her mind kept wandering to her story.

Then Zack had dropped in with his four-year-old daughter, Dani. She was about the cutest thing Delilah had ever seen, and strangely enough, writing took second place to other thoughts. Dani had blue eyes like her father's, but her hair was blond and curly, and she had dimples when she smiled.

It took only a moment for Del to see that the little girl adored Mick. With her father's admonition to be careful of

Mick's injury, she'd rushed to him, climbed into his lap and kissed his cheek as if he were a favorite uncle. Then she'd given him three more kisses to "make him all better." Mick had claimed to feel much improved on the spot, which prompted Dani into giggles.

Something about seeing Mick with a little girl in his arms made Del's heart swell. It was an incongruous sight, Mick so strong and darkly handsome, holding such a delicate, fair child. But it also looked very right, as if Mick were made to be a father.

Del frowned at that. Their relationship, started only a day before, hardly warranted thoughts of parenthood. She shook off the strange aberration and concentrated on being a perfect host.

She wasn't used to entertaining and she definitely wasn't used to so much company. But she didn't resent the intrusion on her writing time. In fact, it was all really nice.

During dinner, Josh phoned, and minutes later another man called for Mick, though he didn't introduce himself and Mick didn't tell her who it was. During his whispered conversation, she saw Alec and Dane share a look.

Her small apartment felt like Grand Central Station. Celia kept watching her closely, as if she was waiting for something, though Delilah had no idea what. Both she and Angel were cautiously nice.

Other than Mick, Del hadn't entertained a man in ages. And she'd never entertained a man's family before now. She had no idea if she was doing things right.

Mick caught her alone in the kitchen getting ready to make more coffee. He wore the sling again, but he still managed to drag her close for a kiss.

"Dinner was great."

He sounded sincere, and she smiled against his mouth. "Thank you." It had been a guessing game, trying to figure out how much sauce and spaghetti to make. After she'd done her best calculation, she'd doubled it for good measure. And that was a good thing, because the men had eaten far more than she'd ever anticipated. "Everyone is so nice. I like them."

"Even Zack?"

"His daughter is wonderful."

Mick laughed at that careful evasion. "You still holding a grudge?"

That sounded infantile, so she shook her head. "No, of course not. I understand why they were so protective of you."

"They were protective of *you*, Delilah."

She didn't agree, but saw no point in arguing. "I suppose for Zack to have such a sweet daughter, he must be a good father."

"He is that." Mick stroked her hair, then added, "Zack likes you. He told me so."

Staring at his chest, Del asked, "What about the others?"

He tipped up her chin. "Angel is cautious because I don't normally get involved with women."

Del wasn't at all certain she understood that. "You're not a virgin."

He choked on a laugh. "No."

"Then what do you mean—"

"I mean I'm real choosy. I already told you that, right?"

"The same is true for me, but maybe for different reasons. I've never had much time for men."

"You're making time for me."

There was no denying that. But Mick was…different. Well worth any effort.

"And," he added, still explaining Angel's reserve, "we've been moving pretty fast."

Delilah chewed over that obvious bit of information. "She's afraid I'll hurt you."

His eyes warmed, and his hand on her cheek was so gentle. "She's afraid you could, and that's a first." He kissed her again. Then once more. "Damn, I have to quit that or they'll wonder what we're doing in here."

She didn't want him to quit. "We're just kissing."

"I want to do a lot more."

So did she. "Tonight, I wouldn't mind—"

His hold tightened. "Tonight," he growled, "it's your turn."

Her heart tripped. She was still aroused from the afternoon. She'd been aroused since the second she saw Mick in that hospital bed.

Knowing he wanted to touch her and…do things to her made her whole body feel tight and too hot and somehow empty. Sighing shakily, she said, "All right."

"An agreeable woman," he teased, and took her mouth with a kiss that curled her toes and made her breasts tingle.

A knock sounded on the wall behind them. Mick lifted his head and turned.

Del groaned, then went on tiptoe to peek over his shoulder. Celia stood there smiling. Alec stood next to her, looking amused.

"I—I was just about to make more coffee," Del stammered.

"Why don't you let Alec do that?" Mick suggested, putting his good arm around her shoulder.

That idea didn't sit right. "But he's a guest."

Alec raised a brow and gave Mick a curious glance. "I don't mind. Coffee is my specialty. Besides, I think my wife is dying to ask you something."

Celia elbowed him, then stepped closer. She looked anxious, her hands clasped together, and she kept glancing from Del to Mick and back again. Finally she blurted, "Are you *the* Delilah Piper? I mean, I saw some books on your shelves and I know it seems crazy, but…"

Mick looked at Del with surprise, and Celia stood there holding her breath. "That's me," Del said.

Mick frowned. "You've heard of her, Celia?"

"Are you kidding? She's fabulous! One of my favorite authors."

That got Del's attention. "Thank you. You've read me?"

Celia rushed closer. "Each and every one. Ohmigosh, that last one had me on the edge of my seat. When the car went off the bridge into that river…" She shivered, as if remembering the scene.

"I did that, you know," Del told her. When Celia stared wide-eyed, Del nodded. "It's true. Of course, I took some lessons first, so I wouldn't drown myself, but then we found this old bridge that no one uses anymore, and the instructor and I took the car right off the side."

Beside her, Mick growled, "What the hell are you talking about?"

And in an awed whisper, Celia said, "Angel didn't believe me that it was you. I mean, that you're the author who really did all those things."

"The coffee will be done in a minute," Alec said, interrupting another angry outburst from Mick. "Why don't we go back in the living room and Celia can grill you like I know she's dying to?"

Del loved talking about her work, and she allowed herself to be tugged into the room. Mick held her hand tight, and as soon as her backside found a couch cushion, he demanded, "What the hell do you mean, you drove your car off a bridge?"

Angel gasped. "Then it's true? It's really you?"

Mick didn't give her a chance to answer. "Delilah, what's going on? What are they talking about?"

"You don't know?" Alec asked, then shared a look with Dane. To Del, all those shared looks felt like a conspiracy. Regardless of her attempts, she was still an outsider in their group.

"Know what?" Mick's gaze narrowed on Del, dark and almost...predatory. A hush fell, everyone watching with expectation.

Del turned in her seat to face Mick, unsure of his sudden change in mood. He sounded angry for some reason, and he looked more than a little disturbed.

Maybe he needed another pain pill, though he kept refusing them. "I explained how I do my research, and about the interviews, Mick."

"You said you visited a prison, not that you drove your car into a river."

She took exception to his tone, especially in front of their guests. She wanted the visit to go well, not be ruined by an argument.

Attempting to sound reasonable in the face of his growing ire, she explained, "I knew what I was doing. I took diving lessons and a class that teaches you how to keep from panicking. I learned all kinds of neat things. You see, under murky river water you sometimes get disoriented because it's so dark." She shivered. "Really nasty, if you want the truth. But if you let out just a little of your breath, the bubbles will rise and show you the way to the surface."

Mick groaned.

"Also, if you stay calm, your heartbeat is slower and you use less oxygen, so you can hold your breath longer. I wasn't very good at that part of it, though. I couldn't hold my breath long at all. Still, it was pretty exciting to—"

"Drive your car," Mick rasped in an ominous voice, "deliberately off a bridge?"

Del frowned. Unlike Angel and Celia, Mick didn't seem at all impressed with her career. Not that she expected or needed him to be impressed. In fact, it was kind of refreshing that he didn't seem in awe.

She was used to a variety of reactions, most of them gushing, some fascinated, even disbelieving. But not angry. That was a reaction she'd never encountered. "It was kind of neat."

"*Neat?*"

That one word held a wealth of scorn and incredulity. Del lost her temper, too. "I may have done a lot of…eccentric things, but it's my life and I can damn well—"

"What other eccentric things?" he demanded. "What else have you done?"

She heard Dane mutter something, and Alec chuckle in return. Those two seemed to find everything amusing, and this time Del had the distinct impression they were laughing at her, or rather her predicament.

Indignant, she gave them each a look of censure, not that it had any visible effect; Dane winked at her, and Alec continued to smile. *Men,* she thought, and decided to ignore their misplaced humor.

Though her heart hurt and embarrassment threatened, Del stood and walked to her bookcase. She pulled out her first book and addressed the women, while deliberately disregarding the men—Mick especially. "For this story I learned skydiving."

"I've always wanted to try that," Dane admitted.

Despite her resolve to ignore him, Del glanced his way. "I learned how to do it without a chute. Another jumper passed me one in midair."

Mick closed his eyes and groaned. He definitely sounded in pain this time.

"For heaven's sake," Del said, thoroughly exasperated. "I *had* a chute! I just pretended I didn't. And there were plenty of other people jumping with me, trained for that sort of thing. Rescue jumpers were there in case something went wrong. Besides, we practiced a lot first in simulated jumps before I actually did it."

Angel piped up and said, "I remember the villain in that book had to steal a chute off another man. That man almost died, but being the male protagonist, he didn't."

"I never kill the male leads." She looked at Mick. "That would ruin the romance aspect of the books."

He groaned again.

Celia, like a true adventurer at heart, asked, "Did you take a chute off someone else?"

Alec immediately hauled her to his side and wrapped his brawny arm around her shoulders. "Don't even think it," he warned, and he looked deadly serious, his expression fierce. Celia just smiled.

"I didn't want to go that far," Del said, a little distracted. It fascinated her the way Celia and Alec interacted. He looked so savage, so menacing, yet Celia wasn't the least threatened by him. Just the opposite; Celia cuddled closer. "I learned how to put a chute on in the air."

Mick bolted to his feet. He looked ready for a full-fledged rage. The only other time she'd seen him like that was the day of the robbery, when he'd rolled to his feet after being shot, and raced out the door. That day his eyes had been nearly black with rage—as they were now. His jaw had been clenched tight, too—as it was now.

She wasn't quite sure what to make of him.

Lifting her chin, Del pulled another book off the shelf. "In this one, I learned how to navigate through an underwater cave."

"That was the creepiest scene," Celia whispered. "There were sharks and poisonous snakes. It gave me nightmares." Then she added, "It was also my favorite book."

Del went to her desk, pulled out a pen and signed both books. She handed one to Celia and one to Angel. "Here, a gift."

Celia clutched the book to her chest. For a long moment she was speechless, then she blurted, "Thank you!"

Angel looked amazed. "You don't have to do this."

Del shrugged. "I get some copies for my own use." She hoped to change the subject so Mick would quit scowling. It didn't work.

Attempting a relationship was hard work. Now she remembered why she'd never much bothered. Of course, that was before Mick, with guys who were easy to dismiss.

She couldn't dismiss Mick.

Angel scooted to the edge of her seat. "Where do you get your ideas?"

She'd been waiting for that question; without fail, it always got asked. She smiled, then for almost half an hour answered questions and explained about her work and laughed and had fun. Mick didn't appreciate hearing about her research techniques, but the women, especially Celia, hung on her every word.

When Del admitted that she had a looming deadline and intended to put in a few hours of writing that night, Alec pushed to his feet. "We need to be heading home. It's getting late and Celia—" he gave his wife a cautious look "—is getting ideas."

Dane also stood, saying in an aside to Del, "Alec is a worrier."

Del looked at the big dark Alec, towering protectively over his petite blond wife. He looked like a marauder, not a worrier. "If you say so."

Angel leaned against Dane and sighed. "We'll let you get to your work."

Del blushed. "I didn't mean to run everyone off."

"Not at all. Dinner was wonderful and the company was even better. But the kids will be getting antsy at their grandmother's."

"You have children?"

"We have two," Angel told her. "Grayson, who's twelve, and Kara just turned ten."

"Our Tucker is nine now," Celia said, "and looks just like his daddy."

Alec's frown lifted into a smile of pride. "The kids would love to meet you, Delilah."

Mick forestalled Del's reply by saying, "I'll tell you all about them tonight."

Del seemed to be the only person who heard his lingering undertone of annoyance.

Angel bent a fond look on Mick. "He does love talking about the kids, so prepare yourself."

"That's because they worship him," Dane added. "It's almost nauseating how they fawn all over him. Especially Kara. The boys aren't quite as bad as she is. But as you probably noticed with Zack's daughter, females love Mick."

Angel elbowed Dane hard, which made him grin and kiss her mouth. Del had already noticed what an affectionate bunch they were, always touching and teasing and kissing.

Mick obviously loved these people, and they loved him, but now, rather than making her feel excluded, the sight of them all together touched her heart and made her yearn for things she'd never considered before. They were wonderful people.

At the moment, though, Mick was busy throwing them all out.

Del watched as Mick herded everyone toward the door. She had the distinct feeling he wanted privacy so he could yell at her. Not that she'd let him. No one had yelled at her since she was a little girl, and she wasn't about to let Mick start now.

Celia surprised her by giving her a hug and telling her she'd cherish the book. Del felt a little silly. It was only a book, but she enjoyed Celia's enthusiasm.

Angel followed suit and hugged Del, too, whispering in her ear, "It's so nice to see Mick confused by a woman." She leaned back and grinned. "Thank you for taking such good care of him."

"My pleasure."

Angel's mouth quirked. "I can see that it is."

Mick stood at the door until everyone had gone. Del didn't wait around for him to start complaining or questioning her. She gathered up the coffee cups and carried them to the kitchen.

He stepped up close behind her. "Delilah."

She could feel the tension emanating off him in waves. It made her tense, too. "Call me Del."

Her hands shook. She refused to turn and face him, choosing instead to rinse out the cups and put them in the dishwasher.

He ignored her order. "Why," he asked in a barely audible growl, "do you do all this crazy stuff?"

"You mean like bringing strange men home to my place? I was just wondering the same thing."

She'd meant to distract him from his grievances, but her ploy didn't work.

"Hell, yes, that's part of it. Don't you have any sense of self-preservation at all?"

She tightened her hands on the edge of the counter. "I learn what I need to know and I don't take unnecessary risks."

He stepped closer, crowding her against the sink. His anger was there, pulsing between them. But there was something else, something more. Her skin prickled with awareness as she felt his erection nestle against her bottom. Her breath caught.

"Tell me why you do it, babe."

She swallowed hard. "The media claims I do it because I like writing about heroes, about guys who can win against all odds, solve twisted mysteries and get the bad guy every time. They psychoanalyze that I'm setting myself up as a heroine."

"Are you?"

"No." It was difficult to think with him so close, and so aroused. "My parents say I've always been too creative and too frenetic. I'm not content to sit idle."

His hot breath touched the side of her throat as he spoke. "I can see that." He nuzzled her, making the fine hairs on her nape tingle, her breasts swell. "You've got more energy than any woman I've ever met. And you don't think about things, you just act."

"You're...you're complaining?" His words sounded disgruntled, but his touch was so gentle, so exciting.

His good arm came around her waist and squeezed her. "The things you've claimed to do are insane, Delilah."

"Look who's talking! A man who deliberately takes a bullet in the back." She forced enough room between them so that she could turn and face him. Her hand trembled from a mix of anger and excitement as she reached up and touched his jaw. "What if that bullet had hit something vital? A lung or your heart or your spine? You could have been killed."

"I'm trained to react."

She snorted at that bit of idiocy. "They don't train you to get shot, do they? I thought PIs did sleuthing, not gunplay."

He looked away from her gaze and focused instead on her mouth. "We do what we have to do."

"And that includes nearly getting killed for a stranger? At least I take every precaution when I do my research."

His eyes, when they met hers again, were so dark, so

intense that Del felt consumed by him. "I couldn't bear the thought of that bullet hurting your soft skin," he whispered. He leaned lower and kissed her, tiny biting kisses from her throat to her ear, to where her neck met her shoulder.

Del shivered, then forced herself back in control. "I can't change who I am, Mick. This is what I do, what I enjoy doing."

He pressed his face into her throat and simply held her. It was a tender, possessive embrace and made her heart rap hard.

"Not since before Angel married Dane have I felt the need to protect someone."

She slipped her fingers through his silky hair, over his neck and the hard joint of his shoulder. "I don't need you to protect me," she assured him softly. Then, touching the bulky bandage on his back, she added, "I don't even want you to try to protect me. Especially not when you get hurt in the bargain."

His head lifted and he stared at her hard. "*Tough*. We've forged a bond, you and I, whether you like it or not." He tangled his hand in her hair and tipped her head back. "You *did* take me in, not just into your home but into your bed. If you didn't mean it, you shouldn't have started it."

"Mean it?" She found it hard to breathe with him watching her so intently, as if he could see her soul. "What… what does that mean?"

"It means you're mine now."

He continued to study her, probably waiting for her to refute his claim, but Del had no intention of doing so. No one had ever wanted to protect her. No one had ever wanted to claim her.

She swallowed. "I was going to clean the kitchen—"

"Leave it," Mick ordered.

"—but I'd rather go to bed with you."

His jaw hardened and his pupils flared. He caught the back of her head and drew her up for his kiss. He tasted so good, and she leaned into him until she heard him groan.

"Mick…" Very gently, she pushed him back. "You should take your medicine."

"Not this time, sweetheart."

"Your shoulder—"

"Will be fine. I promise." He took her hand and started toward the bedroom.

Del admitted to herself that she wanted to let him have his way. Never in her life had she felt so hungry for a man. Never had a man been so hungry for her.

The bedroom door closed behind them and Mick leaned against it. "In the morning," he said, "we're going to talk. Without distractions."

Del had no problem with that plan. "You'll tell me more about the kids and how you and Angel met and about your background?"

There was only a slight hesitation before he nodded. "All right."

"I'm curious about you, Mick."

His gaze moved over her, hot and anxious. "We haven't had much time for talking, but we'll catch up. For now…"

"For now, I want what you want."

He pushed away from the door, his smile slow and lazy. Hot.

"As long as you don't hurt yourself," she qualified.

Mick again caught the back of her neck and lifted her to her tiptoes. Against her mouth he said, "You can help me out by taking your clothes off."

She smiled. "And yours, too?"

"God, yes."

MICK KNEW HE SHOULD HAVE put off the lovemaking in favor of getting a few things straightened out, but he seemed to have little control around her. That in itself was a worry. He was used to an icy indifference in most situations, an iron discipline that never wavered.

Especially where women were concerned.

Too many things didn't add up, and now that he understood the lengths she went to for research—his blood nearly froze every time he thought of it—new questions were beginning to surface about the robbery. He couldn't let lust make him lose sight of the possibilities.

She kicked out of her sandals while unbuttoning her blouse, and his discipline shattered. She didn't undress slowly to tease him. Rather she tore her clothes off as if she felt the same burning urgency as he.

Mick braced his feet apart to keep himself steady while she stripped bare. Her frenzy fired his own.

Tomorrow they would talk. But tonight, he'd make her his in every way.

chapter 7

IN NO TIME, Delilah stood before him wearing only a lacy bra and skimpy panties. He was so hard he hurt. He could feel the hot pulse of blood through his veins, the heavy, rhythmic beating of his heart.

Slowly, savoring the moment, Mick walked to her. With just his fingertips he touched one taut nipple straining against her bra. "Don't move," he whispered, and bent to take her in his mouth.

Her moan was raw and real and satisfying. Mick took his time, suckling her, teasing with the tip of his tongue, the edge of his teeth. He felt the heat rising from her slim body, her restless movements, her heavy hot breath.

"Mick, please." Against his instructions, she tangled her fingers in his hair and tugged. He straightened and began working his own buttons loose.

He held her gaze as he asked, "Are you wet for me right now, Delilah?"

Her pupils dilated, she shook her head. "I don't know."

"Check for me."

Her lips parted. "But..."

"Put your fingers between your legs," he urged, "and tell me what you feel."

Her pulse thrummed wildly in her throat. She swallowed hard, her gaze locked with his, and when her hand moved between her thighs, Mick had to bite back a groan. He locked his knees against the wash of raging lust.

"I...I'm swollen. And hot."

Triumph exploded through him. "And?"

Trembling, she whispered, "And wet."

He cursed low. The damn shirt pulled at his shoulder as he tried to wrest it off. Delilah stepped up to him, her entire body quivering. "Let me."

With gentle hands she eased the shirt from him, then went to her knees to work on his jeans. *Not this time,* he told himself, seeing her on her knees, knowing how ready she was for him.

He let her get his jeans unsnapped and unzipped, then he stepped away. "Stand up, Delilah."

"But—"

"It's your turn tonight, remember?"

Staring at his erection, she licked her lips with blatant insinuation and said, "I know."

Mick laughed, a harsh, hoarse sound. She looked as if she wanted to make a feast of him, and that nearly cost him his control. "You are such a tease." Then, with more command in his tone, he said, "I want you to finish stripping, then sit in the chair."

Startled, she cautiously stood and looked over her shoulder. The chair was piled with clothes, positioned in front of the window. Her bewildered gaze met his. "The chair?"

"That's right." He looked at her breasts, straining against the lace. "Take off your bra. I want to see your nipples."

She glanced again at that straight-backed, hard-seated chair. A shiver ran through her before she reached behind herself to unhook her bra. The position thrust her breasts out more. Mick hardened his resolve, doing his best to remain unaffected by the luscious sight of her. Looking at him, Delilah dropped the bra. Her breasts rose and fell with her accelerated breathing.

"Now the panties," he said, feeling sweat dampen his back and shoulders. His hands shook with the need to touch her, but instead he went to the chair and removed the clothes, dropping them onto the floor. He turned to face Delilah—and she was breathtakingly naked.

As if she was overwhelmed, her head hung slightly forward, her hair shielding her expression. Her long legs were pressed together, her knees locked. Her hands flexed, opening and closing in small, nervous movements.

Mick was caught between wanting to stand there and look at her forever, and needing to be inside her now, this very instant.

Her nipples had flushed a dark rose, puckered tight. The black curls between her thighs looked silky, shielding her secrets.

"Don't be shy with me, Delilah."

Her head lifted, their gazes clashed. "I want to throw you down on the carpet. I want to strip your jeans off you and taste you again." She licked her lips, panting. "I don't understand it, but I'm not shy with you at all. I just want you. A lot."

Mick held out his hand. "Then come here. Let me help you."

She strode to him, her small breasts jiggling, her silky dark hair swaying. He caught her and held her away, but tipped up her chin so that she looked at him. "I want you to sit in that chair and let me pleasure you."

She blinked hard and a slightly worried frown pulled at her brow. "Couldn't we just—"

"No." Mick moved her to the chair and urged her onto the hard seat. He smiled at the way she sat so straight and proper, her spine erect, her knees together and her hands in her lap. But not for long.

Going down on one knee, he sat back on his haunches. "Open your legs as wide as you can, Delilah."

Her shoulders stiffened and color rushed into her face. "What are you going to do?" she asked, both breathless and excited.

"I'm going to kiss you." He glanced at her face, then back to her sex. "Here." Pressing his fingers between her thighs, he cupped her in his warm palm and felt her spontaneous jerk. Though she was tense, her breathing suspended, he could feel her, soft and wet, just as she'd said.

Shifting slightly, he stroked her, his fingertips opening her more, touching her distended clitoris. "Relax for me," he murmured.

Instinctively, she curled forward before catching herself and, with some effort, leaned back in the chair. She took several deep breaths, and her thighs went limp, yielding to him as he pressed her legs wide. "Scoot to the edge of the seat."

Her head tipped back and her eyes closed. He saw her

throat move as she swallowed audibly. "Mick, I feel...
exposed."

"You are exposed," he whispered, watching as she slid
forward in a delectable sprawl. "I wish I had two good arms
right now so I could touch you everywhere."

Her eyes snapped open. "You're not hurting, are you?"

"Shh. I'm fine." He moved between her thighs and leaned
forward to kiss her mouth, taking his time, enjoying her
while he breathed in the spicy scent of her arousal. She
curled her fingers around his upper arms and held on,
making no move to push him away.

He could feel her impatience and drove her as far as he
could, wanting her to remember this night forever. When
she couldn't stop squirming beneath him, he cuddled her
breast in his left hand. He wanted to hold both breasts, but
his right arm and shoulder felt numb with pain.

He teased her nipple, stroking with his thumb and carefully
tugging until her back arched. "Give me your other breast."

Her eyes slowly opened. "What?"

"I want you in my mouth."

Understanding dawned and her look turned equally hot
and gentle. She cupped her breast and raised it high. At the
same time her other hand went to the back of his head and
brought him forward.

At the sight of her offering herself so sweetly, Mick
growled. He kissed her softly at first, plucking with his lips,
lapping with his tongue. She moaned, pressing herself into
him, and he suckled greedily, unable to get enough of her
taste, her incredible scent. Delilah moaned and writhed and
managed to raise herself enough to rub against the fly of his
jeans.

Mick cursed the injury that kept him from taking her in all the ways he wanted.

"Mick!" She cried out, straining against him.

It was too much. He moved back and opened her legs even more. Her pink flesh glistened, wet and ready, and he leaned forward to taste her deeply, his left hand curving around her bottom and holding her still.

Delilah raised her hands and covered her own breasts, crying, moving with his mouth. He loved the taste of her, so hot and sweet. He pressed his tongue into her, slow and deep, then stabbed with quick motions, swirled and licked and teased, and when he knew she was near, when he felt the tremors going through her slender thighs, her belly, he caught her clitoris and drew on her gently.

Her contractions were so strong she nearly escaped him. Fingers biting deep into her soft ass, he held her close and did his best to block the pain of his injury, enhanced by her thrashing.

With one long, last, shuddering moan, she stilled. Her breathing remained ragged, loud, and she seemed boneless in the narrow chair, her long limbs sprawled for him, around him. Her hands dropped to her sides.

Shaken, Mick put his good arm behind her and rested his face on her belly. Though he stayed perfectly still, which eased his physical aches, his mind still reeled and his emotions rioted.

Damn, he thought. This level of connection was more than he'd expected, more than he'd even known existed.

It scared him spitless, because he wasn't a hundred percent sure he could trust in it, in her. He just knew he wanted her now, and he couldn't bear the thought of any other man with her like this.

His arm tightened and he forced himself to say lightly, "You okay, sweetheart?"

"Maybe."

He raised up to smile at her. "The taste of you is enough to make me insane."

Her eyes remained closed, but she smiled. She took several deep breaths to calm her racing heart and said, "Know what I'm thinking?"

He lightly kissed her belly button, then nuzzled the soft skin of her stomach. "Vague, soft, happy thoughts, I hope."

"I'm thinking I want you inside me."

Mick clenched his jaw. He wanted to be inside her, but he didn't see how he could. Much as he hated to admit it, he wasn't invincible. His arm hurt like a son of a bitch, more so with every breath.

Her position in the chair had taken a lot of the physical stress off his arm and shoulder, but her soft moans had caused his muscles to tighten, to flex, and now his pain felt very real.

Delilah sat up. She cupped his face in her hands and said, "Did I tell you I took riding lessons?"

His shoulder screamed a warning, but his erection was more than willing to listen. "On a wild stallion, no doubt?"

Her smile was still softened by her climax. "No. As a little girl, my parents gave me riding lessons. C'mon." She pushed at him gently until he moved back and gave her room to stand. She reached a hand down to him, and with a laugh, Mick came to his feet.

"First," she said, "a pain pill for you. And no arguing. I promise to make it worth your while."

Mick pulled her up short. "You don't have to do this, sweetheart."

"But I want to." Her expression clearly showed her confusion. "I'm not doing you a favor by making love to you. What you just did...it was so wonderful. I had no idea."

Mick wanted to know which part had surprised her, but he kept quiet.

"The only thing is that now I feel empty." She flattened her hands on his chest and stared up at him. "I meant it when I said I want you inside me."

Holding her gaze, he slid his hand down her belly. "My fingers would probably do," he said, and matching actions to words, he pressed two fingers deep inside her.

"Oh, God." Still sensitive from her climax, she dropped her head forward and curled her hands, clutching at him. They both breathed hard. "That's...that's wonderful," she whispered, delighting him with her honesty, her openness.

Her hand moved down his body and curled around his hard-on.

Mick had to fight to keep from coming the second she touched him. He felt primed to the max, and her hand was so soft and feminine. "Delilah," he warned, closing both hands around her shoulders.

"This," she whispered in a sultry voice that coasted over him like rough velvet, "will feel even better."

He had to laugh, though it sounded more like an agonized groan.

She released him, patted his butt and said, "Now quit trying to distract me." Taking his hand again, she led him toward the kitchen, where she kept the pain pills. "I have the feeling you like to control everyone and everything, but I've been on my own too long for that nonsense."

She wasn't looking at him, so it felt safe to smile. She was the most endearing woman he'd ever met.

Her insight was also uncanny. It was true he liked to have control, but more than that was the fact he wanted to take care of her, protect her. He'd never even come close to feeling that with any woman other than Angel, and then it had been a clear-cut feeling. They'd both been going through bad times and had quickly learned to trust each other, to help each other. They were friends and there'd been no confusing possessiveness or lust or this irrational need to make her a part of him, to somehow meld her body and soul with his own.

He loved Angel, just as he loved Dane and their children, and by extension Alec and Celia and Tucker. He'd protect any one of them with his life, but that instinct had never been put to the test. Dane and Alec were more than capable of taking care of their own, so Mick's sense of protectiveness was blunted by their presence.

Not so with Delilah. There was nothing and no one to soften the raw edge of volatile emotions consuming him.

He knew it was too much, too strong and overwhelming. It put him at risk, a risk he'd never faced before because he'd never met a woman who hit him so hard on a gut level.

He had absolutely no idea how to deal with her.

She stopped beside the kitchen counter, unmindful of her nudity, although Mick relished the sight of her under the bright fluorescent lights. While she filled a glass with water, he looked her over. Her shiny dark hair was mussed, half hanging over her brow, framing those incredible, bright blue eyes. Her lips were still slightly reddened from her climax, her cheeks still flushed.

Her nipples still tight.

He sucked in a breath and accepted the pill she handed him, tossing it back and washing it down with the entire glass of cold water. Delilah stepped behind him and peered at his shoulder.

"I think we should change the bandage."

He didn't want her taking care of him, and turned to face her. "It's fine."

She propped her hands on her slim hips and frowned up at him. He'd never had a naked woman remonstrate him before. It put a new slant on things.

"I'm changing your bandage, Mick." When he started to speak, she interrupted, saying, "It's early yet and I have a feeling you won't be falling asleep despite the pain pill."

"God, I hope not." He still smarted over the fact that he'd fallen asleep on her earlier.

"Then that means, being as you're so determined and you refuse to listen to common sense or a doctor's orders, we'll be making love for some time yet. You need to be comfortable and relaxed so that you don't hurt yourself."

He gave her a lazy smile, eyeing the glossy dark curls over her mound and the long length of her legs, now braced apart as if for battle. "Relaxed, huh? You think your lovemaking is so boring I'll be able to just sit back and yawn?"

Her eyes got heavy, her smile wicked. "I think you need to let me handle things. It'll be a novel experience for you. I'll be gentle...but thorough. I promise."

He must be getting used to her, Mick thought, because

her boldness didn't shock him at all, it just fired his lust. He shook his head, but heard himself say, "All right."

Her soft smile broke into a triumphant grin and she turned, giving him a view of her saucy behind as she marched away. Crooking one finger, she called back to him, "Come along, now. I'll see to everything."

He was in so deep he could barely breathe, and strangely enough, he didn't give a damn. Everything would work out, he'd see to it.

Later.

DEL COULDN'T REMEMBER ever having so much fun. Mick was astounding, giving over to her and trusting her. At least as far as his body was concerned. His thoughts were still a secret, but she understood that. Her life wasn't one she openly discussed, either. Not that it had been bad, only that it had been different, and not many people understood her or her choices.

At the moment, she had Mick stretched out on his back, a pillow cushioning his head, his shoulder freshly bandaged. Together they had showered, touching and teasing anew, then taking turns drying each other. While she'd brushed her teeth, he'd commented on her body, complimenting her in the most outrageous ways.

She returned the favor, savoring the sight of him naked at her sink, his razor and aftershave there as if they'd always been a part of her home, as if they, as well as he, belonged with her.

He had an incredible physique, tall and strong and wholly masculine. While he brushed his teeth with amazing dexterity, considering he used his left hand, she watched the play of muscles in his shoulders and biceps. Still damp from the shower, his dark hair clung in curls to his nape and temples. Her blood raced at the beauty of him.

There wasn't a single flaw to his body—except for that obscene bullet wound.

Her heart nearly broke at the sight of it, and without thinking, she'd moved to kiss him above and below his stitches, where dark bruises marred his olive skin.

His groan, one of mingled awareness and physical pleasure, encouraged her. He'd braced his hands on the sink and allowed her to do as she pleased—and she pleased quite a bit.

After that, she'd spent a good fifteen minutes just touching him, caressing his aching muscles and hopefully massaging away some of the pain and stiffness from the injury.

Even with his head dropped forward and his body totally relaxed, Mick still looked so powerful, so strong and capable. It made her stomach jumpy to know he wanted *her,* desired *her.*

Had nearly died for her.

He grew impatient with the subtle touches and teased, "Is it your plan to taunt me all night? Because I'm a hair away from taking control again."

She laughed at him, then squealed as he hurried her to the bed. She had to regain the upper hand so he didn't do more damage to his injury, and it took her several minutes to convince him that she needed to wrap his shoulder again.

He'd finally given in, but only because she let him touch her anywhere he wanted while she saw to that chore. It was apparent that, even though she lacked his physical beauty, Mick felt the same fascination for her body that she felt for his.

Now he reclined in her bed, his eyes dark and hot, watching her as she leaned over to the nightstand and withdrew a condom.

"I hate to sound unsophisticated," she said, "but I've never put a rubber on a guy before. Tell me if I do it wrong."

He didn't reply, merely watched her as she tore the small package open and reached for him. She felt the subtle clenching of his muscles, the heat rising off him in waves. She glanced at his jaw and found it locked hard.

"Like this, right?" she asked, knowing she was pushing him, and enjoying it.

"Good enough," he growled, and his abdomen tensed as she slid the condom over the head of his penis and then midway down its length.

Del surveyed her handiwork. "Not bad," she announced, trying to drag out the anticipation as long as she could. It wasn't easy; already her hands were shaking and a weakness seemed to have invaded her bones. Mick was thick and hot and silky in her hand.

"I've always been really careful," she whispered, trying to regain lost control, "about protection. Not that I'd mind having children someday, but not until I meet the right man."

His body taut and expectant, Mick rasped, "I want kids someday, too."

Del soothed him, stroking his right arm, his chest and shoulders. She met his smoldering gaze and asked, "With the right woman?"

"Yes."

Sliding her leg over his hips, she positioned herself. "Well, this woman is going to make you crazy with pleasure tonight."

His back arched. "I'll get my turn," he told her.

She laughed. "Not until the doctor says you're able." Slowly, so slowly every nerve ending sparked, she lowered herself. He'd barely penetrated at all, just the thick head of his penis inside her, her inner muscles gripping and quivering around him, when she stopped with a gasp. "It's…it's been so long for me," she muttered, trying to explain, her words broken and breathless and fast. Already she felt stretched, uncomfortably tight, yet tantalized. "I'm…I'm not at all sure."

Mick strained beneath her, sweat dampening his forehead, his chest. Delilah knew she couldn't wait any longer or he'd hurt himself. Swallowing back her own discomfort and uncertainty, she braced her hands on his chest, drew a deep breath and pressed down until he was fully, completely inside her.

An explosive curse broke from Mick. She whimpered in response. For long moments, neither of them moved except for a slight trembling of rigid muscles and a spontaneous flexing of sexes as they each struggled to adjust.

Forcing her head up, Delilah looked at Mick through a sweltering haze of sensations. "Are you…all right?"

"No." His left hand lifted, spread wide over her hip. "I need you to move, baby."

Del licked her lips. "It's just that you're…bigger than I thought."

Without his permission, his hips rose, pressing into her, deepening his penetration. "I can't do this," he groaned.

And Delilah's heart tumbled over.

"Mick." Leaning down, she kissed his mouth, his throat, licked at his salty skin. Very gently, subtly, she rocked her hips. His fingers contracted on her flesh, biting hard as he urged her to continue.

She slid up, her wetness making it easy and smooth, then

all the way down again, harder and faster with each turn. Suddenly, despite his injury, Mick gripped her hips in both hands and pumped into her, holding her tight to him, not letting her retreat. He looked feral and explosive and so sexy she felt her own climax begin.

This was what she'd wanted, him filling her, his body a part of hers, wild and real with no reserve between them. She tipped her head back and cried out her pleasure, then heard Mick's answering moan of completion.

A few seconds later his fingers went lax and she lowered herself to nestle against him. He grunted, and she mumbled, "Did I hurt you?"

It took him a little while to answer, but she didn't mind. She felt the bellowing of his chest beneath her ear, felt his sex still deep within her. "Mick?"

Using his left hand, he smoothed her bottom. "I'm feeling no pain. Even my brain is numb."

She didn't want to, but she raised herself to her elbows. "Will it hurt you if I sleep here with you?"

His dark eyes opened. "It'd kill me," he said huskily, "if you didn't."

Tears clung to her lashes. She hurried to blink them away and sat up more. After a deep, calming breath that helped to chase away the excess emotion, she said, "I'm ready for bed. You?"

The way he looked at her told her she hadn't fooled him one bit. He knew she was mired in sentiment, that making love with him had thrown her for a loop. She'd had sex in the past, but this wasn't sex. This was… She wasn't sure what to call it. Sex had been easy to give up, but she couldn't imagine giving up Mick.

More tears clouded her vision, but he didn't seem to mind. In fact, he looked…satisfied.

Del snorted at herself as she swiped at her eyes. He'd come, so of course he was satisfied. "I'll just get rid of the condom and turn on the air conditioner and—"

Mick moved out of her reach. "I can take care of myself, thank you, and I'll set the air conditioner. I'd like to wake up without hypothermia."

"I set it too cold?" She watched him climb from the bed, and was gratified to see he shook just a bit, too.

He stood in front of her and touched her chin. There was a silly smile on his face, in contrast to the male triumph in his dark gaze. "Yeah. You set it too cold," he agreed. "I'm a man, not a polar bear."

Then he went down the hall to the bathroom. Del stood there, bemused, until she heard the water turn off and the toilet flush.

She rushed to straighten the bedclothes and reposition Mick's pillow. She'd sleep on his left side, to keep from injuring his shoulder, she decided.

He walked into her room, as comfortable with his nudity as she was. After setting the air conditioner a tiny bit higher, he got into bed as if sleeping with her were nothing. She wasn't sure if she liked that or not, considering it seemed like a very big something to her. But then he turned off the light and settled back, and when she crawled in next to him, he put his arm around her, drawing her close. The darkness added a new level of intimacy, filling her with contentment.

Her mind peaceful, her body sated, she kissed his chest and asked, "Will you tell me if you get uncomfortable during the night?"

"No." She pushed up to frown at him, but he only laughed and pressed her face back to his chest. "Shh. Go to sleep, Delilah. You've worn me out and I need to recoup so I can get even tomorrow morning."

Feeling smug, she said, "You'll have to wait to even the score. I have to go out in the morning."

His arm tightened. "Where to?"

"Neddie's funeral is tomorrow."

"Neddie?"

Because she'd already told Mick all about him, she sighed. "Neddie Moran, the man who helped me with my research."

A volatile silence followed her statement, then seemed to detonate. Mick turned, pinning her beneath him in one hard, fast movement, his expression furious. "Neddie *Moran* is the criminal who taught you how to steal cars?"

Watching him warily, she said, "Yeah, so?" He'd sounded ready to fall asleep one moment, then outraged the next. "Mick, you're going to hurt your arm."

For some reason, he looked astounded that she would even mention his arm. He jerked around and flipped the light back on. "Forget the morning. We've got to do some talking right now."

"We do?" Del scooted up in the bed and pulled the sheet over her breasts.

"Damn right we do. Do you know how Neddie Moran died?"

"He drowned."

"He didn't just drown. Someone else drowned him." Mick drew a breath. "Sweetheart, he was murdered."

chapter 8

MICK AWOKE TO AN EMPTY bed. Again.

This time, in light of everything he now knew, fear hit him before anything else. He glanced at the bedside clock. Three-thirty. They'd finished their talk almost four hours ago. Where the hell was she in the middle of the night?

He was out of the bed and heading for the door on silent feet before he'd even given himself time to think about it. The reality of her association with known criminals had his skin prickling with unease, his every sense on alert.

She saw no connection between Neddie's recent death and her own very near escape from death.

Mick, however, was positive that the two events were in some way related. She'd associated with Moran, formed a strange friendship even, and now the man was dead. It had been tricky, telling her what he knew of Moran's death without telling her how he knew, or giving away confidential information. The death was still under investigation, but thanks to reporters, it was public knowledge that Neddie had been drowned in the river, so Mick had no problem sharing those details.

Not that they'd swayed her. The most he'd been able to get out of her was a promise that she'd let him escort her to the funeral. Mick planned to avoid even that, using a deception to keep her away, while he had men checking into any possible associations between Neddie and the robbers at the jewelry store. He didn't like himself for it, but he felt it necessary to protect her.

Hours of talking to her had proved that reason and logic wouldn't work. Not with Delilah Piper, and definitely not when she felt an obligation to a friend.

Mick went only a few steps down the hallway before he saw the dim blue light of her computer shining in the otherwise dark apartment. He heard the light tapping of her fingers on the keyboard, and peered around the hallway corner.

Sitting there in front of her computer, her glossy hair mussed, a T-shirt her only clothing, Delilah looked totally absorbed in her writing. Mick leaned against the wall and watched her, aware of a strange twisting in his heart.

Never had he allowed himself to consider hearth and home and a family of his own. He'd become so discriminating with women, so particular, that he'd doubted any woman would have ever appealed to him on that level.

But standing in a dark hallway looking at Delilah, he felt a contentment unlike anything he'd ever known. She was a woman of constant change and contradictions. She made him hot with her careless, comfortable air, and she kept his emotions turbulent with her daring and her stubbornness. And now that he'd laughed and argued and made love with her, he couldn't imagine not having her in his life.

Insane, he insisted to himself. But his pulse continued to riot and his lungs constricted, and only a small part of that reaction was due to lust. Hell, he shouldn't even have felt lust. It hadn't been that long since she'd wrung him out.

But he looked down at himself and, sure enough, he was already semihard. What could you do with a woman who affected you so strongly, except keep her close and make sure she didn't have the chance to affect any other man the same way?

Delilah paused, bit her lip, stared at nothing in particular and then smiled and began typing again. Mick shook his head. She amazed him, amused him, and she turned his libido red-hot.

Not wanting to startle her, he said softly, "Am I interrupting?"

She glanced up, then held one finger in the air, indicating she needed him to wait.

He should have been annoyed. They'd finished making love for the first time and she'd sneaked away to write, and now had the gall to make him wait. He smiled. No woman had ever treated him as she did, and damned if he didn't like it. Probably because her reactions, her responses, were all so real. Delilah didn't have a deceptive bone in her body. She said what she thought, did as she pleased, and that meant she could be trusted—the most appealing factor of all.

Mick sidled closer and stood behind her. He moved her heavy hair off her nape and used his thumbs to stroke her.

Delilah froze, then twisted to face him. "Um...I can't write with you there."

"Why not?"

She frowned, then turned off her monitor. Shadows closed in around them. "It makes me jittery for anyone to look over my shoulder. I don't want you to read anything out of context and think it's lame."

"I wasn't reading," he explained, still holding her neck easily between his hands. "I was considering the possibility of dragging you back to bed."

Delilah faced the computer again, her hands in her lap, her head bent forward. Finally she said, "I'm running behind, Mick. I need to finish up this scene, okay?"

"It's almost morning."

"I know. But the scene is there now, in my head." She twisted again, this time in a rush. "I'm sorry. I know this probably seems odd to you. But writers write…whenever. And I do have a deadline that is quickly closing in." She shrugged. "I've never had anyone live with me, so I've never had to not write when I wanted to. Know what I mean?"

Mick grinned. She meant that she didn't want him to interfere with her writing, but was trying to be tactful. He said only, "How long do you think you'll be?"

Again she shrugged. "I don't know. As long as the words are coming, I want to keep at it. Once this scene's done, I'll have some free time before I need to start the next one."

A thought occurred to Mick: if she stayed up all night writing, perhaps she'd forget about the damn funeral, and he wouldn't have to deceive her. "Okay, sweetheart. You take your time, okay?"

"You don't mind?"

"Of course not. There'll be times when I'll be gone all night working." Even in the dim shadows, he saw her scowl and had to fight from laughing out loud. "I'm sure you'll be understanding, too, won't you?" he teased.

Very grudgingly, she muttered, "I guess."

"Then I'll see you in the morning."

She continued to stare up at him. "Since you're here anyway, will you give me a good-night kiss?"

"My pleasure." Mick made it a kiss to singe her eyebrows—and felt himself burned instead. In that moment, he wondered if he'd ever get enough, if a lifetime of tasting and touching her would ever satisfy him.

He had his doubts.

"Wow," she said when he lifted his mouth. "You think I can work a kiss like that in with a murder scene?"

Mick stared at her blankly and she waved her hand toward the computer. "That's where I'm at in the book. All your talk about Neddie and connections and conspiracies gave me an idea for the murder scene. Do you think my hero would stop in the middle of trying to chase down the escaping madman to kiss the heroine?"

Mick shook his head. "If the heroine was you, I'm sure of it."

He saw the white flash of her teeth, then heard her chuckle. "You're outrageous. Now go on before I totally lose my train of thought and end up with them making love in the middle of the street instead of doing the responsible thing."

Thinking of the "responsible thing," Mick pushed any remnants of guilt from his mind. He'd do whatever was necessary to protect her. "Take as long as you need," he said. "Good night."

As soon as he turned away, he heard the tapping on her keyboard resume. Madmen and making love and responsibility. Somehow they were all tied together with Delilah, and probably with her research pal, Neddie Moran, and the shooter, Rudy Glasgow, and the robbery.

All Mick had to do was find out how.

His mind filled with possibilities, both intimate and protective, so it was no wonder he slept fitfully. He had just awakened again when he felt Delilah slipping into bed beside him. He glanced at the clock and saw that it was only an hour or so until dawn.

Turning toward her, he slid his good arm beneath her head and murmured sleepily, "Did you finish your scene?"

"Yes." She snuggled down, fitting herself to him as if they'd been doing this for most of their lives. That's how it was with Delilah, natural and comfortable and *right*. Her hand settled on his chest, her fingers twining in his body hair, caressing. "I'm sorry I woke you."

"You didn't." Mick pressed his mouth to her crown, drawing in the sweet scent of shampoo and Delilah. "I've been thinking."

"You should have been sleeping."

"I'll sleep with you." He felt her smile against his chest. "What were you doing in the jewelry store, honey?"

Startled, she looked up at him, then with a shrug, nuzzled into his side again. "I was researching."

Their voices were both low, mere whispers over the hum of the air conditioner and the lazily twirling ceiling fan.

"What kind of research?"

Her fingertips sought and found his nipple, toying with him, making him stiffen even while half-asleep. "In this book," she whispered, "the hero has to break into a jewelry store and steal something that the madman is after, before he can get it. So I was trying to see how I'd break into that store if I was a madman."

Mick chuckled. "Neddie couldn't tell you how to do that, huh?"

"He told me a lot of things, gave me a lot of ideas, but not details on a robbery." She pressed her face against Mick in a show of emotion. "I'd contacted him about it, and even left a message, but he hadn't returned my call. I realize now that he probably couldn't."

Shit. If she'd left a message on a machine, then that could be the link that had led them to her. Mick squeezed her closer. No way in hell would he let anyone hurt her. "What exactly did you say on the message?"

"Mick." She rose up on one elbow to look at him. "I do like talking to you in the middle of the night like this, but—"

"Actually, it's morning," he said softly, pushing a curl away from her face.

"That's my point. I really would like to get some sleep."

He chuckled. "No sparing my tender sensibilities, huh?" That made her frown with concern, and he added quickly, "I'm just teasing."

"Are you sure? Because I guess I could stay awake and talk more about this if you really wanted to."

"Actually," he murmured against her mouth, "I was thinking about sports."

She again pushed away, peering at him through the dark with interest. "Are you an athlete?"

Snorting, he said, "Hell, no."

"You don't like sports?"

"I have no idea. I just never played any."

"But all little boys play baseball and football and—"

"I didn't."

She seemed to have forgotten all about sleeping, and her frown was back. "Well, why not?"

He didn't want to talk about his childhood, about his mother's shortcomings. Not now. Preferably not ever. "I was thinking about a sport you taught me."

Despite his best effort, there was an edge to his tone, a deliberately forceful change of subject that she picked up on. She might often be obtuse to her surroundings, but Mick found she was very attuned to him. It unsettled him, and turned him on.

She cupped his jaw in a gesture so tender, his heart ached. "What," she asked, lightly touching the corner of his mouth, "have I taught you?"

"Riding." He rasped the word, forcing it past an emotional lump in his throat, desperate to change his ache to a physical one, one that she could easily appease.

In the next instant, Delilah kissed him—everywhere. The emotional and the physical commingled, a variety of needs that stirred him on every plane.

After she rolled the condom onto him, she mounted him with a smile and leaned down to kiss his mouth. She slid her body onto his with a snug, wet fit, and whispered wickedly, "Giddyap."

DELILAH GROANED as she managed to get one eye open. Her entire body ached in places she hadn't known she had. And her butt was cold.

She forced her head up and saw that Mick had kicked the covers to the bottom of the bed. Her front, curled into his side, was warm enough. But her behind faced the air conditioner and was numb with cold.

When she looked Mick over, gloriously naked, she quickly heated. Until she noticed the alarm clock.

"Noon!"

Beside her, Mick groaned and he, too, opened one eye. "What is it?"

"I overslept!"

"Don't worry about it," he mumbled, and tried to draw her close again.

"But Neddie's funeral! I'll never make it now." She couldn't be sure, but Mick looked very satisfied over the situation. Del frowned. "Did you keep me awake all night on purpose?"

Both eyes opened and he stared at her breasts. "Yeah."

"Mick!"

"I'm not into making love with comatose women, so of course I had to keep you awake."

"Oh." She subsided, but only a little. "That wasn't what I meant."

"All I did," he informed her, reaching out to smooth his hand over her hip, then her belly, "was mention riding." He glanced up, his dark eyes unwavering. "You're the one who did the rest."

Because he was right, and because his hand felt too good on her body even now, she flushed. "I feel terrible," she admitted.

Mick cupped his fingers between her legs, fondling, seeking. His voice morning-rough, he crooned, "I think you feel very nice."

She frowned at him and said, "I'm sore, so forget it."

His smile made him look like a pirate. A dark sexy pirate, set on pillaging. "I'll be understanding," he promised, "and run you a nice hot bath. I'll even get the coffee." Then he added deliberately, "But forgetting about it is impossible."

"Mick." She said his name on a sigh.

His tone, his look, turned serious. "You're about all I can think of these days."

She melted. And she wasn't that sore, she decided. But he'd taken her words to heart and slid out of the bed. He stretched, careful of his wounded shoulder, and she sighed yet again at the sight of him. *Much more of this,* she thought, shaking her head, *and I'll begin sounding like a wounded coyote.*

"Since it's already too late to make the funeral, would you like to come with me today?" He looked expectant—and just a bit too watchful.

"Where are you going?" she asked.

"I need to set up something with a therapist for my shoulder."

"I thought the doctor said to give it two weeks first."

Mick shook his head. "I can't wait that long." He flexed his right arm, winced, and added, "I don't like being less than a hundred percent."

He started out of the room and she scurried after him. He detoured into the bathroom, so she had to pull back. Damn, he shouldn't be pushing himself. But how could she stop him? He far outweighed her and had double the stubbornness she possessed.

She waited in the hallway until she heard the bathwater start. She called through the door, "Mick?"

The door opened and he snagged her, pulling her inside. He looped his left arm around her waist, kissed her pursed mouth and said, "You soak while I get coffee. I'll shower when you're done."

"You're supposed to be resting!" she said, trying for a stern expression.

"Making coffee won't tax my meager strength, I promise." He kissed her nose and swatted her on the behind left-handed. "Now, soak."

"Take your medicine!" she yelled to his back.

She was submerged in the hot water, letting it ease her aches and pains, when Mick came in carrying two mugs of steaming coffee. To her disappointment, he'd pulled on jeans, and she frowned at him. "No fair me being naked and you being dressed."

He handed her a cup of coffee. "It's the only way I can guarantee we'll make it out of here today." He grinned and added, "Otherwise I'm likely to join you in the tub. You're a helluva temptation."

She ignored his outrageous compliment and sipped—and moaned with pure, unadulterated pleasure. "Oh, that's good."

"Just what I wanted to hear. I'll take over all the coffee duties."

"You could just show me how to do it."

"I'm not quite that trusting."

Wondering just how trusting he might be, she splashed him. "So you're saying you don't like my coffee, either?"

"I had a hairless chest before drinking it."

Del tried to feign insult, but she ended up laughing instead. "Okay, so I made it stronger for you. I thought all men wanted their coffee strong and black."

He nodded. "So you know a lot of men with iron stomachs, impervious to the cold, fearless and reckless and invincible?"

"No, but that's how I write them," she teased.

Sounding far too serious, he asked, "Is that the kind of man you were looking for?"

Del considered getting serious, too. She considered telling him he was exactly what she'd been looking for, even though she hadn't realized it until she met him. Instead, she shook her head. "I know the difference between reality and fiction, but I don't have much experience with men's preferences. And for the record, I wasn't looking. I didn't really think there was room in my life for a man, not since I've kinda thrown myself into my writing."

Mick put the toilet lid down and sat. "You really enjoy writing, don't you?"

Her need to write wasn't always a pleasant one. "I suppose it's a love-hate relationship. I feel the craving to write almost all the time. Sometimes it's inconvenient. People think I'm dumb because I plot a lot. They consider it daydreaming, and write me off as being too fanciful. But I doubt I'd feel like me if I wasn't writing."

She hesitated, then tilted her head to look at him. "I hope you can understand. There'll be a lot of times when I'm trying to listen, but my mind will go off track. And I get up a lot at night to write. It seems like as soon as I try to sleep, my brain starts churning and I just can't shut down."

"I'll persevere."

"It doesn't mean I'm not aware of you. It doesn't mean you're not important."

"I understand."

His acceptance was just a tad too quick, making her suspicious. "Do you? Not many guys I've dated have."

He gave her a measuring look, then asked, "Have you dated many?"

"Sure. In my younger days, when I was curious about things."

"Things?"

She grinned. "Sexual things, though the sex was never enough to keep me…engaged for long. I outgrew my curiosity and my fascination with men. These days, writing is more interesting, and more important than any guy—especially when I have a deadline, which I almost always do." She thought about that, and added softly, "Of course, those guys weren't as important as you."

Mick looked down at his coffee cup for a long moment. "Because I protected you?"

"Partly," she agreed. "No one has ever tried to protect me before. You blew me away, putting yourself in line for a bullet."

"What about your folks? Surely they're protective."

"I guess." She idly soaped her arm, thinking about her family. "They're wonderful, and they love me, but with two older, more serious brothers, I'm kind of the odd duck."

Mick didn't say anything to that, just continued to encourage her with his silent attention.

"You can imagine how they all reacted when I told them I wanted to be a writer." She laughed, remembering. "They told me to get serious, and when they saw that I *was* serious, they worried. Especially whenever I did research. Now, though, they're really pretty proud."

"Are you close with them?"

"Oh, sure. And my brothers are great. They're both married and have kids and houses. They still worry on occasion, but meeting you would probably fix that."

Mick went still. "Did you want me to meet them?"

She'd rushed things, she realized, and said, "Not yet."

He frowned. "You said I'm different than the other guys you dated."

"Well…yeah. I never invited any of them to move in with me."

"How am I different?"

She shook her head, lost to rational explanations when it came to her response to him. "I don't know. Everything just feels different with you, sort of sharper edged. Better. I hope that doesn't alarm you. I mean, I won't start pushing for more."

Mick set his coffee aside and stripped off his jeans. "What if I push for more?"

Del felt her mouth fall open as he stepped into the tub behind her, forcing her to move up while the water sloshed inside the tub and over the sides. His hairy legs went around her, and he tugged her back into his chest. Against her ear, he whispered, "Delilah?"

"Then…" She swallowed, trying to get her thoughts collected. "Then I guess we'll just take it one step at a time."

He cupped his hand and poured water over her breasts. "Are you still sore?"

Her heart swelled and her stomach curled in anticipation. She leaned back, closed her eyes and whispered breathlessly, "No."

chapter 9

THEY SETTLED INTO a nice routine. Mick didn't want Delilah in his house, where she might see evidence of him being a cop, so he had Josh and Zack alternately bring him more clothes as he needed them. Now her closet was filled with his things.

A dozen times he thought of telling her the truth, of explaining why he'd started the deception in the first place. But he'd only known her a little over a week, and working undercover made him more cautious than not.

Their relationship grew every day. He'd have a chance to tell her everything eventually.

Meeting with his sergeant had been difficult. Mick had set it up so that Angel and Dane would be visiting when Josh came by. They drove out for pickup pizza, and Mick slipped away to meet with the sergeant. He got a new gun, which he hid away, and an update on the robbery—which wasn't promising, since they hadn't discovered anything new.

He'd eventually have to see the shrink, as policy dictated anytime a shooting occurred. But under the circumstances, the sergeant was willing to give him more time for that.

Though he could have driven himself, Mick claimed soreness to keep Delilah with him when he went to physical therapy. She took her laptop and wrote in the waiting room while he went through a series of increasingly difficult exercises meant to bring him back to full strength. It was slow going, and frustrating, to say the least, but he knew it wouldn't be much longer before he could make love to her as he wanted to, without concern for his injury.

Often he woke at night to an empty bed, and he'd hear her in the other room, tapping away at her keyboard. Rather than go back to sleep, he usually waited for her, and they'd make love when she crawled back in beside him.

Her unusual routine suited him just fine.

There didn't seem to be any dwindling of the devastating chemistry between them, but little by little they were both less alarmed by it, and now they wallowed in the near-violent sensations. Delilah proved inventive and curious, and she had no shyness with his body, taking everything she wanted and giving back as much in return.

Ten days had passed before his sergeant called and told him Rudy Glasgow was finally awake and coherent and ready to talk. But strangely enough, he only wanted to talk to Mick. He'd actually awakened from his coma a few days earlier, but had remained stubbornly silent and still too weak to leave the hospital. There'd been no sign of the other men, but Mick wasn't giving up, and neither was the police department.

His sergeant told him to give Detective Faradon, the lead investigator for the case, a call. Mick peeked in at Delilah, saw she was totally engrossed in her story, and punched in the numbers.

He spoke briefly with Faradon before requesting that the detective use Delilah's number only for emergencies. "Anytime you need to get in touch with me, just call my place and leave a message. I'll check the calls often."

"Running a secret life?" Faradon asked.

Mick ground his teeth together. He didn't want Faradon to know that he was still keeping secrets from Delilah. "I don't want her to overhear anything," he said as an excuse. "It could taint the case if she learned of anything important."

"Just telling you is risky," Faradon agreed. "We're only keeping you informed because you were shot, which makes you damned involved, from where I sit."

"Thanks." Mick rubbed the back of his neck. "I'm glad you understand. So, you got a pen handy?" He recited his home number to Faradon, then they briefly discussed the condition of the man in the hospital before hanging up.

Now all Mick needed was an excuse to get away from Delilah. He didn't want her to know that he'd be talking with Rudy Glasgow, yet he'd made such an issue of going nowhere without her, she was bound to be suspicious if he tried to leave on his own now.

As usual, she sat at her computer working when he finished making lunch and approached her. She was nearing the end of the book, and according to her, that's when she got most involved with the story. She had to tie up loose ends and wrap up the novel with a punch. Mick considered the way her mind worked, conjuring up so many twisted mysteries, and he shook his head. "Hungry?"

Glancing up, she asked, "Who was on the phone?"

Mick stalled, then said, "Just a friend."

"Josh? Zack?"

He hated lying to her, and often he didn't even need to. She hesitated to pry, so if he just shook his head, she'd let it go at that. Sometimes it seemed to him that Delilah went out of her way to give him his privacy, to not push. That bugged him, since it took all his concentration to keep from pushing her. She came to him willingly, accepted him in all ways, but there were still pieces of her that remained hidden. It made him nuts.

Instead of answering her specific question, he asked, "What do you have planned today?"

She accepted the sandwich he handed her and took a healthy bite while shrugging. "Writing. More writing. I hope to finish this weekend. Why? Did you need me to take you somewhere?"

It amused Mick to see how she dug into her sandwich. Sometimes when she wrote she forgot everything else, including food. When her hands began to shake, then she'd remember and grab a bite to eat.

Other times she did nothing but eat while writing. She kept a variety of snacks in her desk drawer—white-chocolate pretzels, caramels, peanuts, chips. She shoveled food away like a linebacker, yet she stayed so slim, even delicate. Her metabolism astounded him.

Settling his hip on the edge of her desk, Mick shook his head. "No, I don't want to interrupt you today. Looks like it's going well."

"It is. I've thought about this scene for ages. It's a fun one to write. Really gruesome."

He laughed at that. "Then you stay home and finish up, but I do need to go out for just a little while."

"Without me?"

"Unheard of, I know, especially with how I've depended on you." He studied her face, seeing the hurt and something more. "You don't really mind, do you?"

She hedged, saying, "Why do you need to go out?"

Going with a sudden inspiration, he touched the end of her nose and smiled. "It's a surprise."

She flopped back in her seat and gave him a mock frown. "Not fair. What kind of surprise?"

"Now if I told you that, it wouldn't be much of a surprise, would it?"

She hesitated, fiddling with the crust on her sandwich. "You don't need to buy me things, you know."

He nodded gravely, playfully matching her mood. "I know."

She didn't look appeased by his response. "You sure you're okay to be on your own?"

"I'm a big boy, Delilah."

"Ha! Don't I know it." Her lecherous grin had him laughing again.

Damn, how he loved her shifting moods, how he loved…

Oh no. He pulled up short on his wayward thoughts, frowning at himself for letting such a deep insinuation intrude. He'd known her all of ten days—if he disregarded the two weeks prior to their formal meeting. He cared about her, more so every hour. No denying that. And he was drawn to her on the most elemental levels.

But it was far too soon to be thinking beyond that. Far, far too soon.

She mistook his frown and sighed. "Okay, I won't play mother hen, but please don't overdo it. It hasn't even been two weeks since you were shot."

Glad of the misunderstanding, he nodded. "Cross my heart."

Mick was ready to leave ten minutes later. He reminded Delilah to keep her door locked and not to let anyone in when he wasn't there. She was still skeptical about any personal threat, but she placated him by agreeing. She had few visitors, other than his friends, but she received mail from her publisher and agent regularly. She promised Mick she would be extra careful, and he finally left.

He was anxious to get some answers, anxious to face the man who'd put a bullet in his back.

The man who'd tried to kill Delilah.

The thought burned Mick, put a fire in his gut and a vibrating tension in his muscles. His sergeant had warned him not to overstep himself, to keep his cool, and Mick had agreed, even knowing it wouldn't be easy. The case was out of his hands, turned over to Homicide, and they could have refused to keep him involved. But they'd agreed to let him in to talk to Rudy Glasgow, in hopes he'd be able to get additional information.

Knowing Delilah would stay in her apartment alone all day made it easier to be away from her. She'd said she intended to write, and Mick believed her. Once she got involved with her stories, not much, including him, could pull her away.

He found her intensity rather endearing.

An around-the-clock watch had been placed on Rudy's room, even while he'd been unconscious. As Mick approached, the present guard came to his feet and set his magazine aside. Glancing down, Mick saw it was a periodical on martial arts. He smiled.

"Dawson, with City Vice." Mick held out his credentials for the guard to verify.

He nodded. "I was told to expect you."

"Has anyone else been in to see him? Has he talked to anyone else?"

The young officer rubbed the back of his neck. "Far as I know, he made a call to his lawyer and told the lead investigator that he'd speak with you. That's it."

"He called a lawyer?"

"Almost first thing after waking up. I heard he was real insistent about it."

Mick supposed that with an attempted-murder charge on Glasgow's head, getting a lawyer would be a huge consideration. "He's doing okay now? They expect a full recovery?"

"Yeah. He's a bit weak and shaky yet, and his leg is still healing, so they're planning to keep him another day or so, but then they'll ship him out." The guard grunted. "If you ask me, he's ready to go now, just dragging it out for the sake of a cushy bed."

Mick didn't doubt the probability of that. He pulled the door open.

The room was similar to the one he'd stayed in, only the shades were tightly drawn to keep it dim, and the TV played loudly. Mick took it all in with a single glance, then lounged against the wall. "You wanted to see me, Glasgow?"

Rudy Glasgow glanced over at him. His face was pale, his eyes shadowed, testimony to his physical state. It didn't move Mick one bit.

Rudy studied Mick for a long minute before grinning and motioning him closer. "I won't bite. Hell, even if I did, I doubt you'd feel it, I'm so damn weak."

Mick refused to respond to that prompt. He went straight to the matter most important to him. "Why'd you try to shoot her, Glasgow?"

He had to shout to be heard over the television, and it annoyed him. Rudy had soft sheets under him, plump pillows behind his head, a mostly eaten meal still on the tray beside his bed. Except for his elevated leg, wrapped in gauze where the bullet had struck, and the guard outside his door, he seemed to be pampered.

It grated that a criminal—an attempted murderer—should be treated so gently.

With a long, lethal look, Rudy said, "That bullet may have crippled me for life."

Mick bared his teeth. "No shit? That's the best news I've had all day."

"Screw you," Rudy suddenly said, lifting himself forward in a surge of anger. He kept his tone low, his voice a growl barely audible over the sound of the TV. His right hand twisted the sheet at his side.

Mick raised a brow, glad to see he'd riled the man. In his experience, information was always more forthcoming when your adversary was upset.

The information he got wasn't quite what he'd been expecting.

Slowly, by tiny degrees, Rudy's hand opened and he rested back on his pillows. He breathed deeply, as if that small fit of temper had taxed him, then a sardonic light entered his tired eyes and he actually chuckled. "But then," he said, "she's already doing that, isn't she?"

"Doing what?"

"Screwing you." He laughed again.

Feigning ignorance, Mick asked, "What the hell are you talking about?"

His laugh was bitter and mean. "That double-crossing bitch you protected. Oh, she covered her ass real good, I'll give her that."

Impatient, Mick barked, "Turn that damn television down. I can barely hear you."

"You heard me just fine, but I'll keep the set on so no one else hears. This conversation is between me and you. What you do with it after that is your own business."

"You planning on telling me something important, is that it?"

"Damn right. You," Rudy rasped, and thrust a finger at Mick, "are making cozy with an accomplice."

"Is that so?" Mick forced himself to speak casually, though a tightness invaded his chest. "And who would it be?"

"The woman you protected!"

"The woman *you* tried to kill?"

"She had it coming!"

Finally, Mick thought, finally he'd get some answers. He summoned a pose of boredom, when inside he seethed with anticipation—and something else, something damn close to dread. He blocked it; *he had to know.* "How do you figure that?"

"Because she was in on the robbery."

Mick laughed, though he didn't feel even an ounce of humor.

Rudy seemed beside himself. "Why the hell else did you think she was there?"

Mick stayed silent, not about to encourage him.

The man smirked. "My lawyer has been in contact with

her, you know. He told me that she's got you moved in and under her spell. She even bragged to him that you wouldn't prosecute her, not while she's keeping you happy in bed."

"You expect me to believe this?" Mick knew Delilah hadn't talked to any lawyers. He'd been with her twenty-four-seven. Protecting her, he thought… No, he wouldn't let doubts intrude because of this scum! Delilah was an open, trusting woman. A gentle woman.

Who drove her car into rivers and learned how to hot-wire cars. A woman who kept company with criminals…

Mick shook his head. He knew every damn call she'd gotten. From her agent, her editor… But then, he'd just taken her word on that, when the strangers had called and she'd excused herself for a private conversation.

"You know she's a damn publicity hound," Rudy continued. "Don't you read at all? This is her biggest stunt yet, though we sure as hell didn't know about her twisted ending until we heard the cops coming. Then we realized she'd tipped them off. There was no other way they could have known we'd be there."

Icy dread climbed Mick's spine, chilling him on the inside, making his voice brisk. "A passerby claims to have seen you through the front window, and he called the police on his cell phone."

Rudy waved that away. "She set the whole thing up, including the guy who placed the call. Think about it—what was she doing there when she didn't buy anything? And why the hell would a real successful writer live in that dump she calls home?"

Mick had often wondered the same thing himself. But what did he know about a writer's salary, successful or otherwise? And for that matter, what did Glasgow know about how Delilah lived?

Feeling edgier by the second, Mick demanded, "Why tell me this?"

"Why?" Again Rudy leaned forward, and this time he shook a fist. "Because I'll be damned if I'll sit here and rot while she goes scot-free!"

"So you think I'll go to the police and have them arrest her? That I'll ask to have her prosecuted?"

"Cut the crap. You don't need to go to the cops because you *are* a cop. I know it, and more importantly, *she* knows it, regardless of your lame act about being a PI."

Mick's heart thudded to a standstill. How did this man know what he'd said to Delilah, unless Delilah had told him? Feeling as if a fist was tightening around his windpipe, he managed to say, "A cop?"

"That's right. You must really think she's stupid, but believe me, she's a clever one. She hadn't counted on you being in the jewelry store that day. She'd told us she just wanted to take part in the robbery, to experience it because of her twisted way of researching things. We'd get the goods and she'd get her insight. She promised to pay us nicely for our trouble.

"But then I guess she decided it'd work out better for her if she got rid of us. If anyone got wise to what really happened, she'd be off the hook. It would have been our word against hers, and she's fast becoming a celebrity, while we all have records. Without any proof to back us, she'd have walked away with a ton of fresh publicity, and we'd all have done time."

"You still don't have any proof—or are you stupid enough

to think I'm going to believe you?" Mick had bluffed with the best of them, and right now he felt as if he'd gambled with his heart.

"Just hear me out."

"Not if you're only going to spout bullshit."

Again, Rudy's hands fisted in the sheets, and his face turned an angry red. "When she realized I knew the truth about how she'd set us up, she saw you as a way out. I bet she came on real strong, didn't she? I can tell by your expression she did." Rudy laughed. "She figures you'll protect her, but I want you to see justice done. That's what cops do, right? They arrest the criminals."

Mick narrowed his eyes. "Or shoot them in the leg."

"Bastard!"

His shout was so loud, the guard stuck his head in the door. "Everything okay in here?"

Mick didn't even look at him. "Get out."

Holding up his hands, the guard said, "Just checking," and backed away, letting the door hiss shut behind him.

Mick took a step forward. His heart hammered, but he kept his expression impassive, blank. "Give me one good reason why I shouldn't take you apart."

"Why the hell would I lie? And think about it—how would I know all this otherwise?"

"Your buddies who got loose?" He stood right next to the bed now, staring down at Rudy, fighting the urge to do him more damage. "We haven't rounded them up yet—but we will."

Rudy groaned, but more out of frustration than pain. "Believe me, they're long gone. Not a speck of loyalty in their veins. No, the only one I've spoken with is my lawyer, and he gave me some gritty details that just about pushed me over the edge."

Mick didn't want to hear any details. "Give me the lawyer's name."

"Not yet." Rudy absently massaged his leg. With deep satisfaction, Mick watched the pain cloud his face. "Not until she gets what she deserves."

"Why would she tell the lawyer anything? It would only incriminate her."

The man shook his head. "He's in love with her. He would never do anything to hurt her, including sharing this information with you. He only told me because he wanted me to understand that she had no intention of getting involved in this mess, that I couldn't count on her to help me out."

"Ah." Mick made a tsking sound of false sympathy. "So you have no one to corroborate this ridiculous tale, huh? Too bad." The sarcasm didn't work as well as he'd hoped; he still felt ready to shout with rage. The *ridiculous* tale was far too close to sounding plausible to suit him.

"I don't need anyone to confirm my story. You already know it's true."

"Not so," he lied. "I don't believe anything repeated by an attempted murderer and bungling thief."

The man looked dumbstruck, then florid with rage. "She really did get to you, didn't she? I understand she wore you out that first night, drugged you, then used her mouth to put you to sleep. But you're a good sport. I mean, you paid her back in kind, right, once you'd gotten a little rest and your friends had all gone home?" Rudy jeered, his voice grating down Mick's spine. "For a wounded man, you were tireless, I'll give you that. But then with her in the saddle, what man wouldn't be?"

A red haze of pain and anger nearly blinded him. "You son of a bitch." Mick grabbed him by his hospital gown and twisted, lifting him a good six inches off the mattress. Disappointment threatened to buckle his knees. He had begun trusting her, caring about her, even lo—

No! None of that mattered now. The only way Rudy could have known the intimate details of Mick's first night with Delilah, especially the playful reference to riding, was if she'd told someone.

And why would she do that unless what Glasgow said was true? He couldn't believe he'd let his lust for her override his professional instincts.

Anguish tore through Mick, obliterating his reason, filling him with bitter regret.

On the heels of those overwhelming sensations was refreshing fury, a reaction he knew how to deal with, an emotion that gave him back his breath—and his strength. He let the rage overtake him.

He released Rudy with a wrenching motion that made the man choke and hold his throat.

Mick backed away, knowing he'd gone over the edge. He wouldn't let her hurt him like this. He wouldn't let her make him forget his duty, his responsibilities.

Goddamn it, he'd been the worst kind of fool, but no more. He didn't verify or deny Rudy's claims, he simply turned on his heel and walked out, but he heard Rudy alternately gasping and laughing behind him.

Hot purpose drove Mick, made his steps long and hard and impatient.

The guard tried to speak to him, but Mick's throat was all but closed, his thoughts, his feelings agitated, even violent. He had to collect himself, get himself under control.

And he had to see the lead investigator on the case. He had evidence to share—and he wouldn't feel sane until he did.

DELILAH HEARD THE KNOCK and left her desk. Mindful of her promise to Mick, she asked, "Who is it?"

"Josh," a voice called back, and, leaving the chain on the door, she cracked it open.

Not only Josh stood there, but Zack, too. They made a mismatched pair, she thought, seeing them both smile at her. Josh with his dark green eyes and blond hair always reminded her of a slick cover model. He had cockiness stamped all over him, and he knew his effect on women. She shook her head. His effect was wasted on her. She had eyes only for Mick, and she liked it that way.

"Can we come in?" Zack asked.

If Josh looked like a model for *Playgirl,* then Zack, with his kind blue eyes and bone-straight, light brown hair, looked like a model for the Sunday ads, maybe for comfy house slippers. He looked warm and cozy, like a man meant for a family.

Josh was excitement. Zack was comfort.

Mick was both those things and more. He was everything. Too quickly, he'd become so important to her.

She held the door open so they could enter. "Mick's not here."

They both drew up short, and Josh, in the rear, almost ran into Zack. "What do you mean, he's not here?"

Delilah shrugged. "He said he had a surprise something or other to do and left at lunchtime, almost four hours ago. He didn't want me to go along."

They shared a look. "You promised to stay in?" Josh guessed.

She shrugged. "I had writing to do, anyway. But this overprotectiveness is getting absurd." She gave them both pointed looks to let them know they were grouped in with the overprotective absurdity. After all, they backed Mick up every time he warned her to be cautious. She wondered how they thought she'd lived this long without them all looking over her shoulder, protecting her every step of the way.

Zack put his arm around her. They were both overly familiar, treating her now as if she and Mick were a longtime couple. They'd come around almost every other day, and had learned to make themselves at home. "Grant the guy the right to worry."

"He doesn't return the favor." She didn't mean to sound complaining, but it sure came out that way.

"Meaning?" Zack asked in a gentle tone.

"Meaning he doesn't want me to ever worry and he looks annoyed if I do."

Josh dropped onto her couch. "'Course he would. He's a guy."

Del warned him with a look. "Your sexist attitude is going to get you into trouble someday." At first Josh's attitude had rubbed her the wrong way, but now she accepted him, even liked him. In small doses.

Zack nodded. "I've told him the same, but this time he's right. Mick can take care of himself."

She laughed at them. They saw everything in black-and-white, especially where men and their roles in life were concerned. Men were supposed to protect, to defend, to cherish. Even Josh, with his variety of girlfriends, treated them all as special. And Zack made his beautiful little girl the center of his life.

That thought brought another, and she asked, "Where's Dani?" She enjoyed visiting with the child. Dani wasn't the average four-year-old. She was too precocious, too aware of her surroundings.

"Gone to the movies with a neighbor and her daughter. She said to give you a hug from her." So saying, Zack pulled Del close and squeezed her, rocking back and forth.

She laughed and pushed herself away. Never in her life had she been touched so much. Her parents, once they'd realized she was different, had given her space—not necessarily space she wanted, but evidently space they needed. They hadn't known how to deal with her, so they'd dealt with her less.

Not so with these guys. The less they understood her, the more determined they were to figure her out. And in the process, they coddled and cuddled her a lot. They made her laugh, made her exasperated, made her feel important, wanted.

She enjoyed it all, the intimate, hot touching she and Mick shared, the friendly touching and camaraderie she got from Mick's friends, and the emotional touching, the acceptance, the welcome. Not a day went by that she didn't hear from one or another of Mick's family or friends.

It had never occurred to her how isolated she'd become. She wrote in a void, emerging only for research and publicity. But then Mick had saved her life, and in the process, changed it irrevocably.

"When do you expect him back?" Josh asked, even as he picked up the TV remote control and started looking for a sports channel.

Zack turned the television off. "Dolt, did you consider that she might be busy?"

Josh glanced at her. "You busy?"

Feeling rather conspicuous now, Del gestured at her desk, littered with small sticky notes and research files. "I was just writing the last chapter."

"Then we can hang out and wait for Mick?"

Zack groaned. "Writing is work to her, you idiot. How can she work if you're here disrupting her?"

Josh looked totally bemused by the idea that he might be a bother to anyone, and Del relented. "Not at all," she said. "I'll enjoy the company. I really don't know how much longer Mick will be, though." She glanced at the wall clock and saw it was nearly five. "I thought he'd be back by now."

Zack glared at Josh, which made Josh raise his brows in a *what?* expression, before asking, "You're sure you don't mind?"

"I've been writing all day. My legs are cramped." Then a thought hit her and she said, "I haven't been out running once since Mick moved in. I miss it."

Again they shared a look, and it was Josh who said, "It's not safe for you to be out traipsing around until they catch those other guys."

"Yeah, right," she scoffed. "Who's to say they'll ever catch them? Am I supposed to stay cooped up forever?" Josh opened his mouth and she rushed to say, "Don't answer that! I know what *you* think already."

He grinned shamelessly. "I was just going to say to wait until Mick is completely healed and I'm sure he'll run with you. In the park. Or someplace else that's safe."

"But not here," Zack added.

"No, not here."

Del sat down on the couch next to Josh. "Why not here?"

Josh frowned, measuring his words. "Being the intense writerly type that you are, you may not have noticed, but this area is pretty hazardous."

"Hazardous how?"

He glanced at Zack for help. Zack sat on her other side. "Unsavory types live around here."

"Really?"

"Well, yeah…you never noticed?"

She chuckled at his disbelief. "Of course I did. I also noticed the variety of people who live here, old and young, black and white and Hispanic, male and female, friendly and hostile. I love the atmosphere, the constant chaos. No matter what time of night I'm up to write, there's something going on outside. People feed my inspiration, and I write better in places like this."

Zack reached over and tweaked a tendril of her hair. "You're a nut, sweetheart."

She swatted at him, laughing.

Josh agreed. "Most women I know want to avoid the criminal element as much as possible. You're the first person I've heard who wants to embrace it."

"I write about the criminal element, remember? Most of my mysteries revolve around a villain. Besides, I go where my villains go. And that makes for some fun travel."

"Yeah?"

"Yup. I love moving."

They were just getting into that discussion when Del's doorbell rang. She glanced at both Zack and Josh, then started to get to her feet.

Josh stopped her with a hand on her arm. "Mick?"

Shaking her head, she said, "Not unless he lost his key."

Zack moved past them both. "I'll get it."

Del smiled at their determination in keeping her safe. She didn't bother telling them that she received a lot of special delivery packages from her editor. No, she just sat back and indulged them in their maleness.

When Zack opened the door, she saw two people there, a man and a woman dressed in suits. The woman gave a faint, stony smile. "Is Ms. Delilah Piper in, please?"

"Who's calling?" Zack asked suspiciously. At the same time, Del stood to better see.

The woman looked past him. "Ms. Piper?"

"That's right." Del started toward the door, but Josh kept pace at her side.

The woman flipped open her bag to display a shiny, very official badge. "I'm Detective Darney, with the city police department. This is Detective Breer. Would you mind coming with us to answer some questions?"

Josh bristled, eyeing the badges as if to verify their authenticity. "What's this about?"

At his tone, the male officer spoke up. "She's wanted downtown for questioning. That's all…for now."

Confused, Del asked, "Questioning about what?"

Both Josh and Zack flanked her, and Del appreciated their solid, comforting presence. She felt off balance and a little frightened.

Detective Breer ignored Josh and faced Del instead. "For possible involvement in the jewelry store robbery," he intoned, his voice so deep Del felt her skin prickle.

"*What?*" She thought she shouted the word, but it came out as only a vague, rusty whisper.

Detective Darney looked sympathetic. "You've been named as an accomplice," she gently explained. "But before any charges are filed, we'd like to talk to you."

Del had no idea what to do; she'd never faced a situation like this! She turned to Josh with a blank stare, hoping for direction. He looked furious and concerned. "Don't worry, sweetheart. We'll be right behind you."

"Mick…"

Zack gave her a squeeze. "We'll get hold of him. I promise."

She nodded, reached for her purse, and then Detective Darney had her arm, leading her out the door.

chapter 10

AT LEAST THEY HADN'T handcuffed her, Del thought with a struggling sense of humor to temper her despair. Her throat felt tight, her chest hurt and her stomach was queasy. She almost faltered as she was led through double glass doors and into a long corridor, but the police station wasn't a place to make a scene.

Detective Darney's heels tapped on the tile floor on one side of her, while Breer's heavy steps echoed as solid thuds on the other. They had her caged in—guarding against her escape? Absurd, almost as absurd as the interrogation room where they stopped.

Detective Breer pulled a chair out for her. "Would you like a cup of coffee?"

Numbness seeping in, Del shook her head. The proffered courtesies, in light of the situation, were almost laughable. She drooped down into the chair.

The plastic-covered seat squeaked beneath her. Her blouse stuck to her back from the heat and her tension, forcing her to lean forward. Sweat gathered between her breasts. The unmarked car she'd ridden in had icy-cold air-conditioning, but this room was hot, stuffy, closing in on her. Suffocating.

Once while doing research, she'd been in a room just like this. She knew the procedure and the protocol, and tried to calm herself with the fact that she knew what to expect, though she'd certainly never thought she'd find herself in the position of being an actual suspect.

Still, she wouldn't panic. It was all a misunderstanding. And thinking that, she said, "If you get hold of Mick Dawson, he could explain to you that I was just a victim."

As if she'd summoned him, Mick strode in. He had another man behind him, and both of them wore frowns, but Mick's was darker, and very grim. Del didn't understand, and she couldn't stop herself from saying in some surprise, "Mick!" and then, as relief washed over her, "Thank God you're here."

His black-eyed glance lacked any emotion as he took a seat at the end of the table—a good distance from where she sat.

Anxiety smothered her. Mouth dry, pulse racing, Del looked down the expanse of the table to Mick. It meant something, that awful distance he'd instigated, but for the life of her, she couldn't imagine what. When he'd left her at the apartment that afternoon, everything had been fine.

He'd even told her he planned to get her a surprise gift.

Thinking this wasn't exactly the surprise she'd hoped for, Del twittered nervously. The silly sound just sort of escaped on its own, a girlish giggle, a forerunner to hysteria, making her edgier. She slapped a hand over her mouth. She didn't understand...any of it.

She swallowed hard and reached for composure. "What's going on?"

The man who'd entered with Mick held out his hand. He was large and beefy, and had salt-and-pepper hair neatly trimmed above his elongated ears. Watery, pale blue eyes were closely spaced to an overlarge nose. His suit fit his square frame loosely, and a wrinkled tie hung crooked around his neck.

He looked like a wonderful character, Del thought, someone she could put into a book. She knew she shouldn't be thinking such inane thoughts at the moment, but all other thoughts cut like tiny razors, and her mind naturally shied away from them.

She couldn't bring herself to accept the man's hand.

He eased back, putting his hand in his pocket. The other held a clipboard. "Ms. Piper, I'm Detective Faradon, lead investigator on the robbery you were involved in." He checked his clipboard, then rattled off the date and time and location.

Del concentrated on finding her breath and centering her thoughts. She had to deal with this—whatever it might be. "Could you please tell me what this is all about?"

Rather than sit, Faradon propped his hip on the edge of the table. Del expected the table to collapse under his weight, but it held.

She skipped another glance at Mick. He was staring at her with such stony concentration that it struck her like a physical blow, forcing her to flinch away.

The other two detectives watched her as well. It was like being on display, or caught in a hangman's noose, and it hurt.

"Ms. Piper, are you acquainted with Rudy Glasgow?"

She shook her head, then stopped abruptly. "Yes, he's the man in the hospital, the man Mick shot."

"So you do know him?"

"I know of him." Her heart beat too hard, too fast. "I've read the accounts since the shooting. His name has been in the papers. He's…he's unconscious."

"Not anymore." The man surveyed her through lowered, bushy brows. His expression turned speculative, calculating. Finally, he said, "He claims to know you."

Forgetting her sweaty blouse, Del dropped back hard in her chair. Her spine offered less support than an overcooked noodle. "He's wrong," she replied flatly.

"He claims," the man continued, glancing at his clipboard, "that you set the whole thing up as a publicity stunt."

Del's gaze shot to Mick and locked with his. Neither of them blinked. Dear God, surely he didn't believe such an idiotic story.

She shook her head. "No."

"That's it?" Mick asked, his voice harsh and loud in the closed room. "No other explanations?"

Del searched his beautiful face, his once gentle face, and her heart crumbled. The flat, compressed line of his mouth, his locked jaw and dark flinty brown eyes showed his distaste.

For her.

Del winced with a very real pain. *He'd already found her guilty in his mind.* She wanted to reach out to him, to touch him, but she couldn't. She didn't think he'd let her.

"Mick?" she whispered.

His expression hardened even more and he looked away. It hurt worse than anything she'd ever felt. She murmured to his averted face, "I can't believe you just did that. I...I really can't."

He gave her another sharp look, but this time she dismissed him.

Looking down at her hands, Del said, "I don't know Rudy Glasgow, and I didn't set up the robbery for a publicity stunt. I don't do that."

"You have been known," Detective Breer pointed out, "for your extravagant research tactics."

"Tactics that have never hurt anyone or broken any laws." She felt hollow, stiff. Wounded. "I was there that day, as I've already said, to see how a robber would set things up, but—"

"Isn't that something of a coincidence," Detective Darney asked, her voice soft in comparison to the men's, "that a robbery would take place while you were doing your research for a robbery?"

"Yes." Del's stomach churned with an awful dread. "It's an incredible coincidence."

"You've spoken with him."

Del jumped at the lash of Mick's accusation. She didn't quite look at him when she asked in a small voice, "Who?"

He rounded the table until he faced her from the other side, giving her no choice but to meet his gaze. "Glasgow. I saw him today." He slashed a hand through the air, impatient, provoked. "He knows *things*."

"What kind of things?"

After glancing at the other people in the room, Mick narrowed his eyes on her. "Things you and I have done. Intimate details that he couldn't have guessed at."

Detective Darney turned away. The men stared at her, their

attention burning hot. Embarrassment hit her first, then a wave of remorse for what Mick had clearly thrown away.

And finally her temper ignited in scalding sensation. It chased away the numbness and burned away the hurt. Her heart raced, her pulse pounded.

Very slowly, she came to her feet. "I haven't spoken to anyone about anything we've done."

"He knew it all, Delilah. He knew *details*."

She stared over his shoulder, her mind racing as the ramifications of that sank in. "Then he…he found out some other way."

"How?"

"It's not my job to figure it out." She turned pointedly to Faradon. Sweat gathered at the base of her spine. She itched from the prickling of fear, mortification, loss and anger.

"All of you," she said, addressing the whole room, "you are looking at the wrong person. I don't know Rudy Glasgow. I haven't spoken with him."

"You've told no one?"

She glanced at Mick, overcome with sadness. His distrust would not be easy to forgive, and he would be impossible to forget. But she had no choice now. "What we've done, Mick…well, it was special to me." She got choked up and despised herself for the weakness. She wasn't used to declaring herself in front of a crowd, especially a hostile crowd. And she didn't delude herself; this crowd was hostile. They'd already condemned her.

She cleared her throat and made a last stab to reach him. "I would never have discussed our personal situation with anyone, much less the man who shot you."

For a long, sizzling moment, Mick stared at her, and she

held herself still, hoping he'd smile, that he'd tell her he believed her. That he'd apologize.

He jerked away, cursing softly. His back to her, Mick ran a rough hand through his hair, and Del found herself stupidly concerned for his injury. She could feel his tension, his anger.

She ignored everyone else in the room. At the moment, the only one who mattered was Mick. What the others thought could be straightened out later. She said steadily, "If you just think about it, you'll know I couldn't have done that. That I wouldn't have done anything like that. You know me."

"Barely," he said, still not facing her.

She wavered on her feet. That he could say such a thing after everything they'd done together, after everything she'd felt for him…

She called herself a fool, even as she begged, "Don't do this."

His gaze cut toward her, accusing. "He said you were counting on our relationship to keep you safe from the law."

Mick's insinuation was clear. He chose to believe a man who'd shot him in the back, rather than her. Del forced herself to straighten. Later, she'd have to decide how to deal with her broken heart.

Right now, she had to figure out what to do to make the detectives believe her. That had to be her top priority.

But how? She looked around at them—and saw pity from the lead investigator, interest from Detective Breer and understanding from Detective Darney. Del hated it all, and accepted that they all considered her guilty.

"Are you arresting me?" She was proud of her steady voice, the strength in her demand.

Faradon tapped his clipboard against the table. "Not just yet. But I don't want you to leave town."

"Fine." Del turned to walk out on wobbly legs, but he stopped her.

"Ms. Piper?"

She froze.

"I may have more questions later. I trust you'll cooperate with me?"

She turned to face him. "The man wanted to kill me—or so everyone keeps telling me. Now that he's come up with this outrageous tale meant to incriminate me personally, I have to believe it was a deliberate act against *me*. Of course I want him convicted and his cohorts found. I'll help you any way I can."

Looking a little bemused by that heartfelt speech, Faradon murmured dryly, "Thank you."

Del pushed the door open and walked out. Her neck hurt, her stomach coiled. Tears burned behind her eyes, and she fought them back.

She wanted to run, as fast as her legs could carry her. Just as she hadn't known such wonderful elation existed until she'd met Mick, she hadn't known anyone had the power to hurt her so badly.

But she held her dignity intact and walked, head held high, back down the long corridor. She was more than a little aware of Detectives Breer and Darney following behind her.

When she reached the front desk, Josh and Zack stood there, impatient and worried. Zack reached for her first, pulling her into a warm, tight embrace that was just what she needed, but not who she needed it from.

"Hey," he said, squeezing her a bit tighter, "are you okay? You're shaking."

Swallowing back a choking sob, she nodded against his chest and allowed herself the luxury of being held by him for one moment more. Then she pushed away.

Josh touched her cheek. "Mick didn't return my page yet."

It took two attempts before the words would come out. "No need to page him. He's here."

Josh and Zack frowned, their expressions mirroring each other. The irony struck her, and she almost laughed. Not only would Mick not help her, but... "He was the one," she said, trying for a note of self-mockery in place of desperation, "who evidently brought the new evidence to the police."

Josh didn't appear convinced. "Honey, are you all right?"

"No, no I'm not." Any second now she was going to throw up. Not because of Rudy or the robbery. She was innocent, and sooner or later they'd all realize it.

No, she was sick at heart, and sick inside, because she loved a man who'd just turned his back on her, and she had no idea how she was going to recover.

A deep breath, then another, didn't really help. "Being that you're Mick's friends, not really mine, and being that he now thinks I'm a... Well, I'm not sure what he thinks." She shook her head, understanding now why he'd kept his thoughts so private—because he'd never trusted her. "All I know is that it's ugly, that everything has changed, and I have no doubt you'll both back him up as you always do. So—" she fashioned a smile out of her stiff lips and tried not to notice the concern in their eyes, the caring "—I guess this is goodbye. It's been swell, guys."

She hurried out front, with both of them rushing behind her. A taxi rounded the corner onto the adjacent street, and she jogged across the parking lot to hail it, just wanting to escape, to be alone—as she'd accustomed herself to being. She had the cab door open when Josh grabbed her arm.

"Delilah, wait."

She looked up at him—and saw Mick standing in the station doorway. "He can explain," she said, tears filling her eyes to the point where everything blurred. "Goodbye."

Josh had no choice but to release her. She didn't look back to see them talking. She knew what Mick would tell them, what he believed, and she couldn't bear to see them turn on her, too. She'd finally gotten comfortable with them, accepted them as a part of her life, a disruptive, unruly, fun part.

And now it was over.

She dropped her head forward and covered her face. *How?* she wondered, wishing she could understand what had happened, how it had all gone so wrong in the blink of an afternoon.

The man Mick had shot was no longer unconscious. And he'd told Mick something, found some way to convince him that she was involved. Mick had said he knew personal things, intimate things. That had to mean details of their lovemaking.

Judging by the way Mick had looked at her, *he* hadn't told a soul, so he'd assumed that she had done the blabbing. To a criminal. To a man who'd tried to kill her and had shot him.

And then the shock of it hit her. She felt chilled to the bone, shivering with realization, revulsion.

The cabby pulled up to her apartment, and Del handed him a twenty, not even thinking about getting change, or how much she'd tipped him. She stumbled to the steps leading to her apartment and stared up at the front door.

There was only one thing for her to do.

She had to leave.

MICK HATED TO ADMIT IT, but he was relieved to see that Josh and Zack had followed Delilah to the station. That meant she hadn't been alone when the detectives took her. He'd regretted sending for her almost immediately, but then he had a lot of regrets, and they all centered around her. He had to stop thinking with his emotions and start using his head instead.

He turned to Josh as he approached, but wasn't prepared for the solid pop in the left arm his friend delivered.

"Ow, goddamn it!" Awkwardly, he rubbed his arm and glared at Josh. "That hurt."

"Good." Josh looked ready to take another swing, this one at Mick's head. "What the hell did you do to her?"

"To Delilah?"

Zack rolled his eyes. "No, to Queen Elizabeth. Of course to Delilah. She came out of here nearly in tears."

"Not *nearly* in tears," Josh accused, his nostrils flared like a charging bull. "She was crying, damn it."

Mick hurt from his hair to his toenails, and not all of it was physical. The idea of Delilah crying only added to his pain, making it more acute when he'd thought he couldn't hurt any worse. Dully, wishing he could undo the past, or somehow change it, he said, "She's not who you think she is."

Zack went very still, then stiffened. "What did you do?"

To see his two best friends rallying to her defense added one more bruise to his already battered conscience. He'd wanted them to accept her, and vice versa. But now it hardly mattered.

In the briefest terms possible, Mick explained the situation. He hated going through it again, hated rehashing all the ways he'd been duped, all the ways she had lied.

When he finished, Josh popped him again.

Mick squared off, unwilling to let Josh's hostility continue. "Will you quit that!"

Pushing himself between them, Zack said, "Josh has a point."

"A point?" Mick stared at him, incredulous. "All he did was hit me!"

"Because you needed to be hit," Zack explained, always the cool one, always the peacemaker. "Jesus, man, you don't know anything about women. I realize you don't date much—"

"Look who's talking."

"—but I figured you'd have picked up some things just from being around Josh, if only by osmosis."

"I know more than I care to," Mick grumbled in return. He knew that he was a lousy judge of character, that he'd allowed his gonads to overrule his good sense. That few people could be trusted, but he was too damn stupid to learn that lesson.

"Not," Josh said, pressing forward again, "by a long shot."

Mick was amazed by Josh's red-eyed, aggressive attitude, which went well beyond defensive friendship for Delilah. *He was acting territorial.* Mick closed the space between them in a heartbeat. "What the hell does she mean to *you?*"

"More than she does to you, obviously!"

Again, Zack wedged into the middle, chest to chest with

Mick, forcefully moving him a few feet away from Josh. "Quit baiting him, Josh. And Mick, he's right. Why the hell didn't you talk to her privately?"

"I'm a cop," he reminded them, with an enormous dose of sarcasm and a chip on his shoulder so large his knees almost gave out. "I'm supposed to bring in the criminals." No sooner did the words leave his mouth than he winced. He sounded just like Rudy.

Josh shook his head and all but shouted, "You're also in love, you ass."

Mick stared at him, and wondered if he could reach him before Zack intervened. Probably not, judging by Zack's watchful attention. Mick settled for saying, "Go screw yourself."

"Oh yeah, that'll fix things." Josh threw up his hands. "Do you have any idea how rare a woman like Delilah is?"

Possessiveness bristled along his nerve endings, despite what had just transpired in the interrogation room. "Not more than a few days ago, you were calling her strange!"

"Strange, unique, rare." Josh shrugged. "But that was ten days ago, before I really knew her."

"You're keeping count!"

"She's damn special."

Zack nodded. "Very special."

"Did either of you hear me?" Mick demanded in a shout, so frazzled and confused he knew his hair should be standing on end. "She's dealing with Rudy. She was in on the whole thing."

Zack leveled him with a pitying look. "I don't believe it."

"Neither do I," Josh added. "If you'd talked to her privately, maybe she could have explained."

"She had a chance to explain in there," Mick roared,

stabbing a finger toward the station, "and all she did was deny any connection to him."

"Maybe because she has no connection, and maybe because you threw her for one hell of a loop." Josh squeezed his eyes shut. "God, she looked so hurt, it's breaking my damn heart, and I'm not the one in love with her."

Zack raised a brow over that, but refrained from saying anything.

"She's crazy about you, Mick. She trusted you." Disgust filled Josh's tone. "And you just tossed her to the wolves."

Mick looked away from the accusation in Josh's eyes. "All I did was have her questioned."

"All you did," Josh said, grabbing him by his shirtfront and shaking him, "is show her that you don't care two cents for her feelings, that you don't trust her and that you'll gladly believe a man capable of murder rather than hear her side of things."

Put that way... Mick shook Josh off and paced across the parking lot. Heat rose from the blacktop in waves, adding to his frustration, making him sweat.

His first sight of Delilah in the interrogation room had showed her to be wilted, stunned. By the time she'd walked out she'd mustered up a bit of stiff-backed pride. But the incredible vibrancy that he'd thought an integral part of her had been gone. He shook his head, wanting to dispel the image of her beautiful blue eyes clouded with distress. "I was...sick when I got done talking to Rudy."

"Sick and stupid," Josh sneered.

Zack grabbed Josh. "Will you knock it off! This isn't helping, and to be frank, I'm beginning to be a bit suspicious of your interest myself."

Josh glared at him, then at Mick's questioning gaze. Finally, he shrugged. "If Mick wasn't interested in her, I'd have been hot on her trail. So what?"

Already on a short fuse, Mick exploded. "You miserable son of a—"

This time Zack had to leap between them, shoving at both men hard to keep them from coming to blows. "You're both causing a scene, damn it!"

Around Zack's body, Josh taunted, "What's it matter to you, buddy? You just threw her away." And then, as if that wasn't enough to curdle Mick's blood, he added, "I think I'll go *console* her."

Another struggle ensued, while Zack did his best to keep the two of them apart. Josh, muttering a sound of disgust, finally gave up and stepped away. "Fine, you still want her? Well then, go after her. But *listen* to her. And don't you dare make her cry again."

Mick, red in the neck and teeth gnashing, subsided as well. He didn't really want to take his rage out on a friend. It took him several moments, but he finally got the words out. "You honestly think there might be another explanation?"

They both nodded at him. Josh said, "I believe in her. She may be good at coming up with elaborate plots for her books, but she'd never hurt someone she cared about."

Mick wondered if, after what he'd just put her through, he could still be counted among those she cared for.

"And no way," Zack added, "would she take a chance on innocent people getting caught in the cross fire just for publicity."

Mick groaned, hearing the ring of truth in their words. Josh walked away from them both and went to stand near a telephone pole. Zack squeezed Mick's uninjured shoulder. "Yep, I'm afraid you might have blown it. Better to get there as quick as you can and start your apologies. If you give her too much time to consider what you've done, she may not be able to forgive you."

Mick stared at his feet. "I can't imagine what explanation there could be. Rudy knew things that no one should have known."

"It would be easy enough for him to guess that you were sleeping together. That doesn't take an Einstein."

"He knew...details. Specific details that went beyond—"

"I understand," Zack rushed to say, before Mick could stumble on. But Mick noticed there was a gleam of curiosity in his eyes, too.

He straightened. "I'll give her a chance to talk to me, one on one. And I hope like hell you're right, that she can clear this all up."

"Ha. I think you better do more than that. You better get down on your knees."

Mick glared at him, but as he walked away, he didn't rule out the possibility of begging. He'd never felt so miserable in his life—not when Angel had been threatened and he knew he couldn't protect her, not even when his mother had died in a stranger's shack, an empty whiskey bottle beside her. No, the thought of losing Delilah was a gnawing ache that kept expanding and sharpening until his guts felt on fire and his chest threatened to explode.

Even if she had been in on the scheme, he didn't want to lose her. He'd find a way to keep her out of jail, keep her straight, even if that meant keeping her in bed, under him, from now on.

Before he reached his car, he was running.

It occurred to him with a blinding flash of insight that if his friends were right, if Delilah was in fact innocent, he'd just left her alone and vulnerable. Anything could happen to her.

He stepped on the gas and made it to her apartment in record time.

JOSH SAW ZACK GLARING at him and he grinned, though his grin felt more sickly than not. "What?"

"Don't use that innocent tone on me. What the hell were you thinking?"

Forcing a chuckle, Josh shook his head. "I just worked him into a lather. He needed to be shook up or he'd have stood around here pondering all the possibilities, and by the time he realized we were right, it would have been too late. I saved him some time and heartache, that's all."

"So everything was an act? You're not hung up on her?"

Josh winked, and lied through his teeth. "Not at all. You know I like to play the field."

"Huh. I know you've never had a woman show complete and utter disinterest in you before."

"True." Delilah had gone from not noticing him, to grudgingly accepting him as Mick's friend, to displaying a fondness that bordered on sisterly. From the start, she'd made her preferences known, and it had been Mick all the way. Josh laughed. "I tell ya, I can live without it ever happening again."

Zack turned to look at the road. "I hope Mick doesn't kill himself getting over there."

"I just thought of something," Josh said, and reached for the cell phone clipped to his belt. "Since we both know

Delilah didn't have any part of sharing that information, someone must have been spying on them."

"But how?" Zack asked. "Mick claims it was very personal in-the-bedroom stuff."

Josh grinned. "Yeah, I wish he'd elaborated on that." Zack laughed, never guessing exactly how big a lie that was. The last thing Josh wanted to hear was the personal sexual details between them. It ate him up.

Delilah, with her contrary ways and openness and brutal honesty, had stolen a piece of his heart. It was the damnedest thing he'd ever experienced, and while he was thrilled all to hell and back for Mick, he couldn't help wishing that he'd found her first.

He shook off his melancholy. Right now, all he wanted was for Mick and Delilah to be happy, and that meant Mick had to get her to forgive him. To that end, Josh wanted to figure out what had gone wrong.

"You think someone could have seen in through the bedroom window somehow?"

"I don't know," Josh admitted, "but I know who could find out."

Awareness lit Zack's eyes. "Alec?"

"You betcha." He punched in a series of numbers and waited until the call was answered. "Alec Sharpe, please. Yeah, it's an emergency."

Only a few seconds passed before Alec took the phone. "Sharpe here."

It would have taken far too long to explain, so Josh merely said, "Hey, Alec, this is Josh. Mick is kind of in trouble and you need to get over to Delilah's apartment."

To Josh's surprise, Alec didn't ask any questions, didn't

ask for details of any kind. He said only, "I'm on my way," and the line went dead.

Zack looked at Josh as he closed the cell phone. "Well?"

Josh shrugged. "He, uh, he doesn't say much, does he? But he's heading over there now." He glanced at his watch. "Figuring he was at the office, I think it'll take him about forty-five minutes."

Zack frowned in thought. "With what I've heard about Alec, I wouldn't be surprised if he made it in thirty."

Then they stared at each other. Josh shifted, looked up at the broiling afternoon sun and then the glare off his car's windshield. He propped his hands on his hips and tilted his head at Zack. "You got anywhere you need to be?"

After glancing at his watch, Zack said, "Not for a few more hours. Dani was going to the pizza parlor after the movie."

They'd been friends so long, they often shared thoughts without words being spoken. "Think we should?" Josh asked.

Neither one answered, then in unison they said, "We should."

chapter 11

MICK SAT OUT FRONT for several minutes, stewing in his own misgivings. He hated to admit how much he hoped, prayed, that Delilah could come up with an alternate explanation. Even now he wanted to hold her, to tuck her close and tell her everything would be all right, that he'd keep her safe and keep scum like Glasgow away from her.

He groaned. It was entirely possible that she'd set up the whole robbery, that he'd gotten shot because of her.

It was even probable, given the facts at hand.

Cowardly bastard, he accused himself, and jerked his car door open. He'd face the outcome, whatever it might be, just as he'd faced everything in his life, good and bad.

He took the concrete steps two at a time. The long flight of stairs leading to the upper level didn't slow him down, either. He bounded up them, anxious to speak to Delilah, to figure things out.

He started to knock, then decided to use the key she'd given him. She might refuse to let him in under the circumstances, so he unlocked the door and stepped quietly inside.

The apartment was silent, causing his instincts to scream. Mick reached to the small of his back and pulled out his gun. He'd armed himself right after seeing Rudy in the hospital. He hadn't worn the gun before that because he hadn't wanted to make Delilah suspicious, and he was only a mediocre shot with his left hand. But he'd felt naked without it.

Every light in her apartment blazed, and things were scattered everywhere—boxes on the floor, cushions pulled loose from the sofa.

Fear for her clawed at him. Mick crept forward, away from the open door, then quickly ducked as the chopping block from the kitchen whooshed past him, barely missing his head. It fell to the floor with a clatter, the wood neatly splitting down the middle. He whirled and aimed.

Thrown off balance by the impetus of the attack, a small body tumbled forward and landed against his chest, warm and familiar. Mick automatically raised his gun to the ceiling while catching her.

He and Delilah stared at each other.

Slowly, Mick lowered his arm to his side, watching her warily. She stepped back and away from him, then covered her mouth, breathing hard. "Ohmigod." Her fingers over her open mouth trembled. She shook her head. "I'm sorry. I didn't know it was you."

All color had leeched from her face. Her eyes appeared huge and distressed. Everything inside Mick melted, all the suspicions and the worry and the anger temporarily replaced by the need to protect her. "Are you all right?"

Seconds ticked by while they stared at each other. She shook her head again. "No."

That was all she said before turning away and heading for

her bedroom. Obviously, no one else was in the apartment, given the way she went about her business.

Mick followed her into her room, and the first thing he saw was the suitcase opened on the bed, partially packed.

His knees locked; his healing shoulder pounded with a renewed ache. "You going somewhere?"

She didn't look at him again, though her face remained pale and he could see her hands trembling. "Yes."

His throat tightened. "Where?"

"I can't tell you in here."

A frown pulled at his brows. "In here in the bedroom?" he asked, perplexed by her odd behavior.

She shifted impatiently. "No, here in my apartment."

"You heard what Faradon told you." He strode toward her, uncertain but determined. He wouldn't let her get away from him. "You're not to leave."

Her scathing glance stopped him in his tracks. "I can't very well stay here. But don't worry. I'm not skipping town. I'll still be around for you to persecute."

"Prosecute," he corrected automatically, then caught himself, realizing she'd said it on purpose. He clenched his teeth, counting to ten. Attempting a softer, more reasonable tone, he said, "I don't want to prosecute or persecute you, babe."

She went to her dresser, picked up an armload of items and dropped them haphazardly into the suitcase. "Get out of my way," she said as she started past him to the hallway. "What are you doing here, anyway? And why are you creeping around with your gun out? Were you going to shoot me?"

She didn't wait for an answer to that outrageous insult, but marched into the hall.

"You know damn good and well I wouldn't shoot you! I wouldn't do anything to—"

"Hurt me?" She stopped abruptly. "It's a little too late to make that claim, isn't it?"

"Delilah…"

In a hurry to finish packing, she rushed off. Was she leaving her apartment rather than throw him out? Did she think he intended to stay with her still?

Actually, he hadn't thought that far ahead, but the idea of leaving her, of not having her next to him at night, her soft body his to touch, her gentle breath warming him, gave him a lost, sick feeling in the pit of his stomach.

He put his gun away, then knotted his hands to keep from reaching for her. She looked…breakable. Fragile.

She stopped in the middle of the floor, as if uncertain what to do next. Her gaze landed on her computer, and she dove toward it with a purpose, quickly pulling cords and disconnecting the monitor.

Mick used that opportunity to clasp her shoulders. Touching her made him feel better. "Delilah, listen to me."

She jerked away so violently, she almost lost her balance. "Don't touch me," she said in alarm, her eyes huge and round and filled with wariness. "Don't you ever touch me again."

They watched each other in silence. Mick was the first to finally speak. "Tell me what's going on."

For a long minute, she stared at her hands. "All right." She took a deep breath, met his gaze defiantly. "I fell in love with you. I trusted you. I knew it was too soon for that, but I couldn't seem to stop it. And you've broken my heart. I really don't think I can ever forgive you."

Her words were damn difficult to take, filling him with

elation—because she loved him—and the heavy weight of sadness, because he didn't know if he could do anything about it. He chose his words carefully, watching her, gauging her reaction. "Because I turned you in?"

Her eyes closed and a tiny, very sad smile appeared. "No, because you'd think that about me at all." She looked at him again. "Here I was, letting myself go crazy for you, and you hadn't really learned anything about me at all."

The need to hold her was a live thing. He barely resisted it. "Can we back up just a bit?" When she didn't answer, he asked, "Why are you in such an all-fire hurry to leave now?"

She gave a broken sigh. "And here I thought you were so smart. Smart and brave and honorable." She reached for his hands and enfolded them in her own. Leaning so close he thought she would kiss him, she whispered near his ear, "I didn't tell anyone anything. I figure you didn't, either. That means my place has to be bugged."

Mick stood there, stupefied, watching her lean back, watching her wait for his reaction. Bugged?

A stillness settled over him, slowing his heartbeat, squeezing his lungs. *Of course her place was bugged.*

But it would have to be worse than that. Just listening wouldn't have given anyone such specific details of their first night together. No, that was something that had to be seen, too.

Almost in slow motion, Mick looked around, heart pounding with acceptance. He caught Delilah by the shoulders. "Come on."

"Where?"

"To my car. I want you out of here."

She dug in her heels, resisting his efforts. "I'm not your

responsibility anymore. I can take care of myself, just like I've always done."

"We can't talk here," he insisted.

And she added with a note of sadness, "We don't need to talk anywhere. We're through."

He hadn't been willing to accept that when he'd thought her an accomplice; no way in hell would he accept it knowing she was innocent and in danger. And he didn't doubt her now, not at all. Maybe he was too anxious to find an alternate explanation, one that didn't incriminate her in any way. But this time he was going by his heart, by his guts, not by his damn pride or his conscience.

He gripped her shoulders tighter, opened his mouth—and heard someone say, "Am I interrupting?"

They both whipped around, and Mick shoved Delilah behind him. Alec lounged in the doorway, one black brow quirked in question, his equally black eyes speculative.

Mick caught Delilah's hand, dragged her resisting behind him, and stepped out into the hallway. Without a word, Alec followed. They moved to a corner and there, where no one could possibly hear, Mick asked, "What the hell are you doing here?"

"Josh called and said you needed my help." He looked at Delilah, his gaze speculative. "What's going on?"

"Damn." Mick quickly explained the possibilities to Alec. Several times Delilah tried to wiggle her hand away from him, but he held tight, and she seemed reluctant to make a scene.

Alec didn't appear the least surprised by any of it, but then he was a specialist when it came to espionage equipment. "Probably a Minicam," he said. He put his large hand on the side of Delilah's neck and bent to look her in the eyes. "You okay?"

She didn't so much as glance at Mick. "I'll survive."

Alec considered that, holding her gaze for a stretch of time, then shook his head. "I think you should go on home with Mick. Let me check things over here and… No?"

She shook her head. "I'm not going home with Mick."

"Yes, you are," Mick told her. "Alec, I just need a sec to talk to her."

Her gaze glued to Alec's, Delilah bared her teeth in what she probably thought looked like a confident smile, but instead showed her tension. "I'm *not* going home with Mick."

Alec raised his brows, waiting for Mick's response. He was saved from that fate when pounding footsteps sounded on the stairs. They all moved at once, Mick again shoving Delilah behind him while drawing his gun, and Alec stationing himself in front of them both.

Josh and Zack skittered to a halt at the sight of them blocking the hallway.

"Uh, we decided you could use some backup," Josh explained.

Mick growled, knowing Josh thought he couldn't apologize to Delilah correctly on his own.

Delilah mistook him, though. From behind Mick she muttered meanly, "Some watchdog you are if you need those two."

Mick turned to frown at her.

Alec sighed.

More footsteps sounded. Dane, gun in hand and arm extended, reached the top of the stairs in a crouch. Everyone blinked at him.

Alec said, "You got my message."

"Yeah." Dane came to his feet and tucked the gun away in a shoulder holster. "What's going on?"

Delilah stepped around Mick, glaring at all five men. "Do you all run around town armed?"

Josh and Zack shook their heads. "Of course not."

Alec, Dane and Mick said at the same time, "Yeah."

She turned away in exasperation. "I need to finish packing."

"Packing?" Josh asked, his tone filled with alarm.

"You're going somewhere?" Zack tried to step in front of her.

Alec caught her by the back of her shirt, then quickly held up both hands when she rounded on him. "Don't slug me, just listen up, okay? You can be pissed off at Mick all you want. Hell, I would be, too."

"Me, too," Josh and Zack said almost in unison, earning Mick's glare.

"But," Alec continued, "you have to think here. Don't go putting yourself in danger just to spite yourself. I don't know where you intended to go, but with everything we've just found out, even you have to realize you need someone who can protect you."

Dane crowded closer. "Just what the hell is going on?"

Mick groaned. "God, I'm getting tired of explaining this."

"Then let me." Delilah drew herself up, and she wore the meanest expression Mick had ever seen. It relieved him, because at least some of the shock, some of the hurt, had been replaced. "Mick went to the hospital to see Rudy Glasgow."

"He's awake?" Dane asked.

"Yeah," Mick said. "Unfortunately, he is."

"While there," Delilah continued, "Rudy convinced him that I was part of his little gang, a criminal to be arrested."

Her tone was so nasty, the men all held perfectly still as if frozen by her censure.

"You see, Rudy knew personal stuff—and no, none of you need details—about what we'd done here in the apartment."

"In the bedroom," Zack supplied, earning a hot glare from Delilah.

"So, of course," she practically sneered, "Mick had to believe the worst about me."

Mick swallowed hard. She'd have them all lynching him before she finished. Already Josh was seething again, and Zack kept giving him reproachful looks. Dane and Alec just seemed resigned. "Delilah—"

"He convinced his connections in the police department to have me picked up for *questioning*."

Everyone looked at everyone else. Dane ventured, "Connections?"

Mick shook his head. "Never mind." Delilah didn't yet know he was a cop, and he had a feeling now wasn't a good time to tell her. He had enough amends to make without confessing his own deception.

"She thinks her apartment is bugged," Alec finished for her, cutting to the chase, "which would explain things."

"Ah." Dane nodded. "That'd make sense, I guess."

"It explains it better than thinking she had a hand in that damned robbery," Josh pointed out unnecessarily.

Zack elbowed him hard.

Defensive, Delilah crossed her arms over her middle and repeated, "I am not going home with Mick. I can take care of myself."

"You know," Alec said, his lowered brows making him look more than a little fierce, "this could have all been a ploy. Why tell Mick you were involved unless someone wanted him to get angry with you, to walk away from you?"

"Which would leave you alone and unprotected," Dane finished for him. He nodded. "Someone wants to get to her, but that's impossible with Mick watching over her. So they instigated this little separation."

Still determined, Delilah said, "I have a deadline."

"Good Lord," Mick muttered, unable to believe she'd be concerned with that now.

"I don't have time to debate with you. I just want to get settled down and finish my work."

"Someone is after you, damn it!"

Even when Mick shouted at her, she didn't meet his gaze. She stared down at her feet and said, "I'll be very careful."

She turned toward the apartment door, and again she got pulled up short. Josh, standing tall and resolute beside her, held her arm. "If you don't want to go home with Mick, come to my place."

Raging jealousy shot through Mick. Growling, he took an aggressive step forward, and both Alec and Dane flattened a hand on his chest, stalling him.

Delilah smiled in regret. "I can't do that, Josh. I'd drive you crazy in an hour."

"Not so."

She shook her head stubbornly. "No, it's out of the question. I wouldn't consider imposing on you."

"Then come home with me," Zack said. "Dani would love to have you there."

"No," she answered gently, looking a little amazed by the offers. "I don't sleep regular hours, and I'd be disruptive and—"

Dane shrugged. "You know you're welcome to our place, or to Alec's."

Alec nodded. "Absolutely."

"But either way, Delilah," Dane continued, "you can't be alone. It isn't safe."

Mouth open, she shook her head. "I don't believe this. You people hardly know me. You can't really want me underfoot. And if there is some type of danger, I could be bringing it to your homes!" She shook her head again, more violently this time, as if making a point. "No, I could never do that."

Dane turned to Mick. "Why don't you go in with Alec and look around? I'd like to speak to Delilah alone a second."

"About what?" Mick asked suspiciously, afraid Dane might bury him further. He was beyond pleased that everyone had jumped to her defense, had rushed to assist her, but he'd have been happier if she'd had no alternative but to give him another chance.

"About life and love and reality."

Josh grinned. "Can I listen in?"

"No." Dane caught Delilah's arm and dragged her toward the steps. "This'll only take a minute."

DELILAH WENT GRUDGINGLY. Truth was, she didn't know what to do. Her only plan had been to get out of the apartment. She felt...dirty. Not just from Mick's impossible and hurtful accusation, but by the sickening possibility that someone had been watching her, someone had seen her making love to Mick. She shuddered with revulsion.

Dane put his arm around her shoulders and stopped at the landing at the bottom of the stairs. It was slightly cooler here, but not much. She felt hot and irritable and irrevocably wounded.

"You asked why any of us would want to take you in."

"I've never known people like you," she admitted, glad for something to think about besides the invasion of her privacy.

"We'd do it for Mick. We love him, and it's obvious you're important to him. He'd go out of his head if he screwed up this badly and something happened to you. I don't want to see him hurt that way. He's been hurt enough in his life."

The thought of Mick suffering because of her made her sadder than ever. Damn it all, she still loved him—and that was sheer stupidity on her part. Nursing her hurt, she said, "Yeah, he cares so much he thinks I'd get him shot."

"Men in love do stupid things. Our brains get all muddled. It's not what we expect, and we don't know how to deal with it."

"He's not in love."

"Wanna bet?"

"He's never said so."

"In words, maybe. But from the start he's been fascinated with you."

She scoffed, and Dane added gently, "Delilah, he took a bullet for you."

She shrugged off that irrefutable fact. When he'd thrown himself on top of her, he hadn't even known her name, so he couldn't have had feelings for her then. And since then…well, since then everything had been too fast. She was confused, so no doubt he was, too. "Mick is a hero," she reasoned. "He'd do that for anyone."

Dane laughed. "I agree, he's pretty damn heroic. But

he's still human, so you have to allow him some human faults. Like bad judgment on occasion, and jumping to conclusions. And acting before he's really thought things out—which is what I think happened today."

"Do you have any idea how badly it hurts for him to think that of me?" Her heart, once full to bursting with love for Mick, now felt cold and hard, a dull ache in her chest.

"Yeah, I do. I made the same mistake with my own wife once."

That got her attention. Delilah stared at him, fascinated.

"It's a long story," Dane said, "and I won't bore you with the details now, but I let her think I was my deceased twin, because I thought she'd had a hand in trying to murder him."

Delilah felt her mouth drop open, her eyes widen. "That sounds more outrageous than the stuff I put in my books."

Dane winced. "I know." Then he smiled. "I fell in love with Angel before I got around to telling her the truth. When it all came out in the open, she hated me. Or at least I thought she did. *She* certainly thought she did. Circumstances not a lot different from what you're dealing with now kept her with me. And it gave us a chance to work things out."

"You think I should go home with Mick so he can make amends?"

"I think you should give your relationship every chance to work out the ugly mistakes. It's not like you two met under normal circumstances. You've been shot at, he's been wounded, someone is obviously after you for some reason—that's enough in itself to make any relationship difficult."

"I guess."

Dane hugged her close. "One more thing. Mick wouldn't risk his life for just anyone. From what he said, he was already mesmerized by you before the shooting. He'd watched you, and thought about you. I understand it happens that way sometimes."

She rubbed her face, so tired and washed-out and confused she could barely order her thoughts enough to keep talking. "I don't know."

"You're feeling muddled, too," Dane pointed out, while gently rubbing her back. "All the more reason you should give things a chance. Go to his place, rest up, talk. I'm not saying to forgive him tonight, but at least let the opportunity exist for him to make it up to you. Give him a chance to explain. Who knows? Maybe he'll say something profound and you'll be able to forgive him."

They heard a noise and looked up the stairs. Mick stood at the top. Had he heard their conversation? His gaze on Del, he said, "We found something."

"We'll be right there." Dane put his arm around her and started her walking. "It's been a rough day. Wouldn't you like to go sit down and let your mind rest for a few minutes?"

Mick waited for them, watching Del closely with his intense, probing gaze. He almost seemed to be holding his breath, he stayed so still.

"Delilah?"

The gentleness, the hope in the way he whispered her name, broke Del's resolve. She nodded. "I'll go with you."

He let out his breath in a rush.

"But this doesn't mean I forgive you."

He nodded. "I haven't forgiven myself. For now I just want to get you settled and know you're safe." Then to Dane he said, "It's an optic fiber Minicam. High-tech stuff, run from the apartment next door."

Dane halted in midstep. "Next door?"

"Led in through the vents on the connecting walls." He glanced at Del, and she could feel his suppressed rage. He held himself in check for her, but he was more furious than she'd ever seen him. "Which included all the rooms except the kitchen and the bathroom."

Thinking of the eyes that had been on her, watching her while she wrote, slept, while she made love with Mick, made her stomach lurch. In the next instant Mick was there, gathering her close despite the trouble between them. "I'll find them, babe, I swear."

Giving herself a brief respite from her pride, Del rested her head on his shoulder. God, it felt good to have him hold her again.

When Dane went ahead into her apartment, Mick led her toward Josh and Zack. He touched her chin, bringing her gaze up to his. "I think it'd be best if you waited in my car. I'll only be a minute."

Josh threw his arm around her shoulder—and Mick promptly removed it. He said under his breath, "You've pushed enough today, Josh."

Josh just grinned, and Del had no idea what they were going on about.

"Have you ever noticed the neighbors next door?" Alec asked Del as he reentered the hall.

She gathered her scattered emotions. Now was no time to fall apart. "I know most everyone else in the building, but I thought that apartment was vacant."

"Does your landlord live here?"

"Afraid not." She wrung her hands, still shaken by having her worst suspicions confirmed. "I can call him if you want to check it out."

Mick shook his head. "We'll need to notify Faradon. He'll get a search warrant."

Del looked from one male face to another. "So what do we do now?"

"We get you settled and safe." Mick's eyes narrowed. "And then I'm going to see Rudy again."

chapter 12

DELILAH WAITED INSIDE Mick's house while he carried in her computer equipment, which she'd insisted on bringing along. Alec had checked the hardware and software for bugs and declared everything clean, so there was no reason for her to miss her deadline.

A severe headache left her somewhat nauseous, but she wasn't sure what to do. She'd never been in Mick's home before. Whenever he'd needed something, she'd offered to bring him home, but he'd always gotten someone else to take care of it.

Now she realized why. He hadn't wanted her inside his personal domain. That would have been too close to suit him. He wanted to keep her as distant as he could while still being intimate with her. And she, like a fool, had given him the perfect opportunity by moving him into her apartment.

"Where would you like me to put it?"

She turned to see Mick standing in the doorway, his arms filled with her monitor and keyboard, watching her. Josh and Zack stood behind him, loaded down with more equipment.

Del glanced around and shrugged. "I guess the bar counter would work as well as anywhere."

Mick didn't move, even though Zack and Josh were making impatient noises behind him. "You can use my desk."

"No, thanks." She walked away. The last thing she wanted was to further invade his privacy.

Almost an hour passed before they had her settled in. Dane had trailed them during the move, watching to make certain they weren't followed. The whole thing seemed very cloak-and-dagger to Del. Despite her profession, she'd never expected to be on the receiving end of a real mystery. Mysteries were figments of her imagination, not reality.

Mick's house, moderate in size, probably forty years old, had a quaint coziness about it. Del stood at the kitchen sink looking out the window. His backyard faced a cul-de-sac, and some distance away she could see a pool filled with playing children, another family grilling out on their patio. It all seemed so...domestic. Hard to believe she was here because someone wanted her dead.

Zack slipped his arms around her and rested his chin on top of her head. "You'll be all right."

She patted his hands where they crisscrossed her waist. One thing she'd realized through all this was that Josh and Zack were now her friends, too. She cherished that fact. "You think so?"

"I know there's no way in hell Mick's going to let anything happen to you."

She laughed at that. "Oh, I dunno. He just might decide I'm a criminal again and hand me over to them."

"Nope, ain't gonna happen. You've thrown him for a loop is all, and believe me, that's not easy to do." He kissed her temple, then asked, "Did I ever tell you how hard it was to make friends with him?"

She shook her head.

"He was so closed off, so damned isolated from everyone and everything. Because the fire department and the life squad are located right next door to each other, Josh and I were friends before we ever met Mick. But we all ate at Marco's and every day we'd see Mick sitting there alone. He'd just eat and leave."

It wasn't a pleasant image, his self-imposed isolation, and Del's heart softened in spite of her efforts to the contrary.

"One day some guys came in drunk and started causing problems." Del heard an odd note of enthusiasm in Zack's tone. "They were loud, disruptive, making a mess and scaring off customers. It was interesting, watching Mick go on alert, seeing how he took it all in and waited to make a move, without even appearing to notice. A waitress asked the men to leave, and one of the guys stood and took an aggressive stance. There were four of them, but Mick never hesitated to jump to her defense.

"He told the guy—nicely—to back off. A punch was thrown, and within seconds, Mick had the guy flattened. The others tried to rush him, three against one, but Mick didn't have any problem handling them." Zack chuckled. "He sure got Josh's respect that day."

"You two didn't help him?"

"He didn't give us a chance," Zack claimed defensively. "At least not with the actual fight. But afterward Josh insisted on buying him a drink—*insist* being the operative word, because Mick was hell-bent on keeping to himself—and the rest is history. It still took us half a year to get him to loosen up, to finally realize we weren't in cahoots with the bad guys. But we've been pretty close ever since."

"You're saying Mick doesn't come by trust easily?"

"You have to get him there kicking and screaming."

She smiled, thinking that a pretty apt picture. "Why?"

"Now that's something you'll have to ask Mick."

"I'm glad you're not telling *all* my secrets, Zack."

Zack gave Del a reassuring squeeze and turned to face Mick with a grin. "Just trying to help out."

Josh stood next to Mick. "Good luck. I just got read the riot act for that very same thing."

"You," Zack said, "had it coming."

Mick actually smiled. "You know, Zack, sometimes it's hard as hell to tell whose side you're on."

"I'm on the side of the right and just." He saluted Mick. "I suppose you're ready for us to make our exit?"

"I wouldn't be that rude."

Josh snorted. "He told me to get the hell out." So saying, Josh went to Del and hugged her right off her feet. "If he gives you any problems, call me."

Over Josh's shoulder, Del saw Mick's expression harden, and she quickly disengaged herself. "I'll be fine."

Josh teased, "But just in case…"

Zack grabbed him by the back of his shirt and dragged him away. "I need to get home for Dani, so we'll see you both later. Mick, if you need anything, just let us know."

Mick didn't answer; he was too busy watching Del.

She shifted uncomfortably, then heard the front door close. *Now what?* she wondered.

Mick came a step closer to her. She felt hemmed in by his imposing silence and the cold sink at her back.

She wasn't sure what she expected, but he only said, "You look exhausted. Why don't you take a warm shower while I hook up all your computer stuff? Or are you hungry? I can fix you something to eat."

She shook her head, very unsure of herself and the situation. "A shower sounds nice. But I…I don't know where it is."

Appearing pained, he closed his eyes, then opened them with a rueful sigh. "I'll show you around."

It was a two-bedroom house with hardwood floors and a small cream-and-black tiled bathroom. He showed her his bedroom, his air watchful, then the guest bedroom across the narrow hallway. Del peeked into both rooms.

His dark gaze pierced her careful reserve. "You can use whichever room you want." Unnamed emotions deepened his voice.

"Where will you sleep?"

"Wherever you want me to."

Well, heck. That put the decision back on her, and she felt too unsteady to force the issue at the moment. She gestured toward the smaller room. "I'll use this one."

With no inflection whatsoever, Mick said, "All right. I'll put your things in there." He led her back into the bathroom. "Towels are in the linen closet right here, and shampoo and stuff is already on the tub ledge."

He started to turn away and she reached for him. The muscles in his forearm tightened when her hand closed around his wrist. "Mick?"

He looked from her hand to her face. "Yeah?"

Del wanted to groan. He was so stiff, so…formal. She had a feeling he was trying not to pressure her, but she wished he would… No, she didn't know what she wanted.

"Is there any chance they know where you live?"

"No. We weren't followed today. Dane made sure of that, and I trust him. And only my closest friends, and the people I work with, have my address."

"But…"

In the briefest of touches, his fingertips grazed her cheek. "I've got a lot of explaining to do, honey. I wanted to wait until I got you here, so you couldn't change your mind about staying with me. But now I think I have to come clean."

Del stiffened. "If you're going to hurt me again, Mick Dawson—"

"No." His fingers tunneled into her hair, stroking her warmly. "I swear, I'll do my best never to hurt you again. But what I have to say will probably make you madder than hell."

She could deal with mad, she supposed. "All right."

"Take your shower, get comfortable, then we'll sit down and lay everything out in the open."

She wasn't at all sure she liked the sound of that, but figured he was right. From here on out, she wanted, demanded, honesty. If he couldn't give her that, they had nothing.

MICK GAVE A SATISFIED NOD. He'd managed to accomplish a lot while she showered. But then, she'd stayed in there forever. Too many times to count he'd wanted to check on her, to make sure she wasn't crying or upset, but he knew getting too close to her while she was naked and wet would be his downfall.

So he clenched his teeth and worked. He had her computer, printer and fax machine all set up in a neat little organized corner. He'd given her his own padded desk chair, and taken one from the dinette set for himself. He'd hung her clothes in the closet, changed the sheets on the guest bed—a bed that had never been used. Canned chicken noodle soup simmered on the stove.

He'd called his sergeant and explained things, and spoken with both Faradon and Dane. Unfortunately, the apartment next to Del's was indeed empty, but they had been able to get some fingerprints. Running them would take some time.

Mick had just finished cutting two sandwiches into halves when Delilah walked in.

Her wet hair was combed straight back from her forehead and she'd pulled on loose shorts and a T-shirt. Barefoot as usual, she padded toward him and pulled out a chair. "I hadn't realized I was hungry, but the soup smells good."

Mick was so tense even his knuckles hurt as he put some soup in a bowl and set it before her. They ate in silence. When she was almost finished, he said, "I'm not a private investigator."

Her head lifted, her eyes wide and cautious. "You're not?"

Because he couldn't stop himself, Mick pushed his bowl aside and took her hand. "At first I lied out of necessity. I can't tell everyone the truth, that's just a fact of my job. Why I continued to let you believe the lie, I'm not sure. I told myself that we didn't know each other well enough. Too many things didn't add up." He met her beautiful blue eyes and admitted, "Actually, I think I was just afraid."

"Of me?"

He looked down at their clasped hands. She was so small boned, so delicate despite her height. She had a willowy appearance, and he wanted nothing more than to protect and cherish her. "It isn't easy to admit, but you scare the hell out of me."

Time stretched taut while she pondered those words. She turned her hand in his and returned his hold. After taking a deep breath, she said, "Okay, so what do you really do?"

"I'm a cop. I work undercover."

She stared at him, silent.

"I'd just finished a bust when I met you, which is a good thing, since I don't have a medical release to get back to work yet, and I hate turning over a case to someone new. It screws up the work that's already been done."

Still holding his hand, Delilah rested her free arm on the table and leaned forward, her animosity and distrust replaced by curiosity. "That's why you were armed?"

"Dane and Alec really are PIs. But yeah, I never go anywhere without my gun. Used to be a gun would make you stick out as a cop, but these days *not* having a gun would be a bigger giveaway. The world has turned into a nasty place."

She chewed her bottom lip. "What you do, is it dangerous?"

"Sometimes." Lying to her was no longer an option. "I mostly deal with prostitutes and drugs and gambling. Because of what I do, I live well away from where I work."

"I noticed."

Of course she had. Delilah was no dummy, he thought with a sense of pride. Even more encouraging was the fact that she hadn't yet pulled away from him. He took hope. "Rudy knew I was a cop. He said you knew and had told him."

He felt her slight emotional withdrawal when she stated, "But now you know that isn't true."

He rubbed his thumb over her knuckles, trying to soothe her. "I assume he heard me on the phone, talking to my sarge while I was at your apartment."

"Where was I?"

"The shower, the bed, involved in writing."

"Oh."

"Delilah...I'm sorry."

"No, I understand."

"Do you? Because I sure as hell don't." Self-disgust rose in his throat. "That first night I spent with you, I should have told you the truth."

"As I remember it, that first night I was too busy seducing you," she said, her tone lighter, more accepting.

"And here I thought I was the seducer."

Her face suddenly paled and she swallowed. "All the while, someone watched us."

"Don't think about that." Mick wanted to pull her into his lap, to hold her close. Instead, he redirected her thoughts. "If one of Rudy's cohorts did hear me, they still wouldn't know I was undercover. The station protects my identity."

Mick could see her researcher's mind at work. She frowned thoughtfully and said, "I think I understand how all this works, although I've never interviewed an undercover officer before."

"Now's your chance," he teased, so relieved that she wasn't angry, he almost felt weak.

"You drive your personal car to the station, but then trade up for an undercover car?"

"Not exactly. No uniforms ever know who's undercover. There's a special place where we switch cars, provided by the city. Once a car gets burnt up—"

"Burnt up?"

"Recognized." She nodded and he continued. "Then we get a new car."

"Something old and disreputable?" she asked, her nose wrinkling at the thought even as her eyes lit up with interest.

He shrugged. "Sometimes. But sometimes we get a fancy car. You never know. It depends on the case."

"You work with a partner?"

"Not exactly, but no one ever works without backup. We all carry pagers and cell phones—another common tool among criminals, thankfully. If something goes wrong, we have special codes we can dial to get help fast."

They talked for over an hour. Delilah surprised him with her understanding. But then maybe it was just her desire to learn about his profession that swayed her. He told her about how wires could be detected with special devices that ran through TVs. If the TV reception got wavy, meaning it had picked up the wire's reception, a perp might know he'd been set up, and things could get hazardous real quick.

Mick told her about his jump-out bag. It held a mask to cover his face when he made arrests, so the perps wouldn't recognize him. And about his vest, which he wore even when it was ninety degrees outside. He described the SIG Sauer guns some punks carried, and the hollow-point bullets used to make a bigger wound.

Everything he told her, no matter how gruesome, only made her curious for more. In so many ways she delighted him, excited him, alternately brought forth his lust and his protectiveness.

When she started yawning, Mick stood to put their bowls in the dishwasher. "I think it's time for you to get some rest. After everything I put you through today, you have to be exhausted."

He turned to see her rubbing her eyes tiredly. "I'm wiped out." But she didn't stand, didn't make a move to go to bed. She just stared at her hands.

Mick closed the dishwasher and stood at her side. "You don't have to be nervous here, Delilah. My house is secure, and Faradon has someone driving by every fifteen minutes. You're safe."

"I know." Still she didn't move.

Mick knelt down beside her. "What can I do?" he asked. He searched her face, and wished like hell he had some answers. "I know I can't make up for not trusting you, but I'll do whatever you need me to."

She stared at his hand on her knee. "You don't owe me. What you did…it's understandable. I just wish you'd talked to me first. Together we might have…"

"I'm a bastard, I know." He worked his jaw, then pointed out, "You haven't yelled at me at all."

Her slender shoulder lifted in a halfhearted shrug. "At first I was too devastated to yell. Then too hurt. Now…well, now I understand."

"I'd feel better if you'd yell."

Her soft mouth curled at his words, which weren't quite facetious. "There's no point to it."

And Mick had to wonder if that meant she considered him a lost cause, not worth the effort of a good yell.

Time, he'd have to give her time. "Come on. I think I'm ready for bed, too."

Looking at him through her inky lashes, she stood. He couldn't decipher her mood, and hated the helplessness he felt.

They went down the hall together, and Mick allowed

himself to hold her for just a moment. He kissed her forehead and stepped away. "If you need anything, or want anything, I'm right next door."

She nodded. "Good night."

Mick stared at that damn closed door for far too long before taking himself off to bed. He doubted he'd get any sleep, and in fact, he wasn't tired at all. His body hummed with tension, with leftover adrenaline.

He left his door ajar so he'd hear her if she called out. Lying there in the darkness, he went over all the possibilities, but couldn't come up with a good reason why Rudy would want her dead.

It had to be linked to Neddie Moran somehow. It was just too much of a coincidence for her to have known Neddie before he was killed, and for Neddie's death to have taken place so close to the attempt on her life.

Mick turned to the bedside table and picked up the phone. Hitting the lighted numbers, he called Faradon.

"It better be important," Faradon grumbled. It sounded to Mick like the man was eating, but then Faradon probably ate a lot. He was as big as a bear.

"Did you find any connection between Neddie Moran and Rudy Glasgow yet?"

"Nope, not a thing so far. But then it could be Neddie knew one of the other guys, and without their names, we're lost. The prints'll probably help. Don't worry, we'll keep digging. We're bound to turn up something soon."

Frustrated, Mick had just replaced the receiver into the cradle and settled back when his door squeaked open.

Delilah's silhouette was outlined by the faint light coming through his windows. "Mick?"

Mick's body thrummed to life as he propped himself up on one elbow. Unless his eyes deceived him, she wore only a T-shirt. He forced the raw hunger from his tone and asked as gently as possible, "You okay, babe?"

She crept closer, hesitated. "I don't want to sleep alone."

Those softly spoken words had a startling effect on his libido, an even bigger effect on his heart. Mick lifted his sheet, inviting her into his bed.

She hurried the rest of the way to him and slipped in by his side. For a second, she kept a slight distance between them. Mick didn't move, didn't breathe, and then she turned to him and gripped him tight, and all the pent-up tension inside him exploded.

"CHRIST, I'M SORRY, so damn sorry," he murmured into her hair. His hold was tight and infinitely gentle.

Del cuddled closer, comforted by his scent, the warmth of his skin…. "You're not wearing anything?"

He stilled, then said, "I can put something on if you want."

"No." She loved touching him, and she needed the feel of him right now. All of him. The hair on his chest provided a nice cushion for her cheek, and she nuzzled into him. "Just hold me, okay?"

He turned to face her, drew her closer into his body so that he surrounded her, protected her. Always. Del felt a fat tear sting the corner of her eye. God, he was always trying to protect her.

"Does it bother you?" she whispered into the darkness, into the safety of his nearness.

"Hell, yes." His large hand opened on the back of her

head, his rough fingertips sinking in to cradle her scalp, massage, soothe. "When I think of those bastards looking at you, I want to kill them. I *could* kill them."

Del sniffed and laughed and continued to cry softly. She was so damned confused. "No," she chided, wanting to hear him, to borrow some of his strength. "I meant does it bother you that they saw *you*. Your privacy was invaded as much as mine."

"I hadn't thought about it," he said. "At first I was just blind with…"

"Rage? Because you thought I had lied to you?"

He shook his head, then nuzzled her shoulder and squeezed her until she squeaked. "I hate to admit it," he rumbled against her throat, "but you deserve the truth. Ugly as it might be, regardless of how damn asinine I feel about it."

"The truth?"

"It wasn't rage I felt first, but this awful drowning hurt." He pressed his mouth to the skin of her throat, her shoulder. "There aren't many people in this world who could hurt me. But thinking that you'd used me, that you were laughing at me…it knocked my legs out from under me. It was all I could do to get the hell out of Rudy's hospital room without ripping him apart."

Del turned her face to his. "I'm sorry," she said very softly, and meant it.

"Oh God, don't. Don't apologize to me!" He sat up and switched on a light, shocking her, making her blink against the glare of it. "You should slap my face, Delilah. Or curse me or…hell, I don't know what. But don't apologize."

She looked up at him, her eyes welling with emotion, and his expression crumbled.

"Oh, babe, no, don't cry."

That got her laughing again, a wobbly, pathetic laugh. "Don't apologize, don't cry." She sniffed, and gratefully accepted the tissue he handed to her. She blew hard before continuing. "I've thought about it, and I can see why you believed Rudy. We haven't really known each other that long, not long enough for unconditional trust."

She scooted up to sit against the headboard. "Trust doesn't really come easy to me, either."

"Tell me what to do," Mick said, touching her cheek to remove one lingering tear. "Tell me how to prove to you that I *do* trust you."

She blinked. "Do you?"

He settled himself beside her, and their shoulders touched. Del had the sheet to her chin, but Mick barely had it covering his lap. Even now, in a vortex of emotions, he stole her breath away. He folded his hands over his abdomen and stared at the far wall.

"Damn right I trust you," he said. "I think it was myself I didn't trust all along. But you…almost from the minute I saw you, I wanted you. You drew me like no one ever had, and that shook me because I wasn't used to anyone affecting me like that." He glanced down at her. "It's scary the way you make me feel."

Del lifted his left arm over her shoulder and curled into his side again. "Okay?"

His arm tightened. "Better than okay."

"Will you tell me about your childhood?" She felt him stiffen, felt the stillness that came over him, body and mind.

"Why do you want to know?"

"To try to understand. I've gotten the impression it wasn't great, but that kid's a part of you."

"No."

"You can't run away from your past, Mick. All you can do is deal with it."

"I've dealt with it," he muttered.

Del knew she was pushing, but it was important to her to know all of him, the good and the bad. "Then you shouldn't have any problem sharing with me." To force the issue, she added, "Since you trust me."

"That has nothing to do with trust."

"Of course it does!" Again she twisted to look at him, but he pressed her head back to his shoulder. Del grinned. "You know, even Neddie trusted me enough to confide in me. He told me about his past and things he'd done, things he regretted."

This time Mick turned her face up to him. His fingers were hard, firm on her chin. "What things did he tell you?"

"You first."

"Delilah…"

She only raised a brow, waiting.

He sighed, gave a slight shake of his head and then kissed her forehead. He settled back, and though his pose was relaxed, she felt the rigid way he held himself. "Family services took me away from my mother twice. The first time it happened, I was about five. She'd gone out partying and hadn't come back, and a neighbor reported her."

Covering her shock and her sympathy, Del asked, "How long was she gone?"

"All weekend. In those days, other than her disappearing every now and then, it wasn't so bad. The house stayed kinda picked up and she had a regular job and she still seemed to…like me."

Seemed to like me. Del's heart cried out at the hurt he must have felt. She smoothed her hand over his chest and kept quiet.

"They gave me back to her easy enough, and I was glad. Sometimes being with her was rough, but it was nothing compared to not knowing what would happen, or being stuck with strangers. My mother promised to take some classes, to get into rehab for her drinking, and voilà—I was back home."

"Were things any better then?"

He laughed. "They got worse, actually. She was embarrassed that her neighbors knew I'd been taken away, so we moved. She got a new boyfriend and started drinking even more, but she was careful to put on a good show for the folks who checked up on her. It was another couple of years before things really went down the toilet."

Del cringed at the idea of something worse than a mother neglecting her son for an entire weekend, but again she kept silent, wanting him to talk.

"My mother had an affinity for drink first, and men second. She moved them in and out of our house, but none of them ever contributed, and most of them didn't care to see me too often. Until I was about twelve, I tried to just stay out of sight. But then her liver went bad and she got really sick, and the guy who was with her at the time took her to the hospital. She had to stay awhile, and he skipped out, so family services had me again. That was the worst. I mean, at five I probably needed looking after. But at twelve? I'd have been fine on my own, and when they finally let her out of the hospital I knew I had to take over or I'd get taken away from her for good. Not that I'd have missed her much, but…" He shrugged.

"The familiar," Del said, "is almost always easier than the unfamiliar."

"Yeah." He smoothed his fingers up and down her bare arm for a few minutes, thinking. "I was bigger than her by then, so she couldn't close me off in my room anymore or use threats against me. I could outrun her, and smacking me hurt her worse than it did me. So I told her how things were going to be."

Del shivered at the harshness of those words, at the awful reality he'd faced at such a young age. "At twelve years old, you took charge?"

"Damn right. And she listened, and did as I said, because she knew otherwise I could get her arrested."

"How?"

"She had men in the house who were thieves and cons. She'd done a lot of stupid stuff while drunk, including prostituting herself for drinks, gambling with money we didn't have, accepting stolen goods in exchange for a room— usually to someone busy dodging the law. Our television, and for a while our car, were both stolen."

Del wondered if that was why he'd chosen to work Vice, because he'd already seen the other side of it.

"A lot of the men would make big promises, some even to me. They'd talk about taking care of her, buying things, but they all lied. Family services lied, too, always telling me things would get better. And she was the worst of all—she lied every damn time she said she loved me. After that, she'd always tell me not to say anything to anyone because she'd be taken away and I'd be left all alone." He laughed, a rough, humorless sound. "I knew it was bullshit all along. Whatever maternal instincts she'd had got drowned in a bottle early on. By the time I was twelve, she'd already pretty much wiped her hands of me, but my new conditions really finished things off."

He drew a long breath. "She did as I told her, and she hated me in the bargain."

Del hugged him tight. "What, exactly, did you tell her to do, Mick?"

chapter 13

"WE SOLD OUR HOUSE, which we were about to lose anyway, since she missed more and more work from drinking and couldn't make the payments. I didn't want to end up on the street, and neither did she. I checked around and found an apartment building—the one right next door to where you rent. It was a terrible area even then, but I used the money we made off the house to buy it, and the rent from the other apartments was income. I was in charge, taking applications from renters, collecting the rent, running ads when necessary."

"You did all that at twelve?"

"There weren't a lot of choices." He smiled down at her. "But it wasn't bad. Hell, it was the best it had been for a while. She stayed drunk and ran around with every Tom in town, but she knew better than to screw with the bill money. When I got old enough, I got a job and that helped, too."

"When did you meet Angel?"

His gaze brightened with a smile of genuine warmth. "She moved in when I was sixteen. Her first son, Grayson, was just a little-bitty squirt, and she'd been in a car wreck and was barely able to get around herself. I helped her out, and she started tutoring me in the school subjects I had problems with. Angel was…she was the type of woman I hadn't seen before. She didn't lie or make things up. If something needed to be done, she found a way to do it."

Del felt more tears gather and quickly swiped them away. "I know she loves you."

"Yeah. She does. She thinks of herself as a big sister, or a surrogate mother, I guess." Mick reached over and tweaked Del's nose. "Now, you talk about a role model, that's Dane. Alec, too. They're both great guys."

She caught his hand and held it to her cheek. "They say the same about you."

Del kissed his palm, and he asked, "Delilah, will you forgive me?"

She hesitated to be totally honest with him. She knew that she loved Mick, and she'd rather die than hurt him. But the night was quiet, the light low, and he deserved the truth. "I can forgive you, because I understand." *I love you too much not to.* "But I don't know that I'll ever feel the same again."

He went rigid. "What does that mean, Delilah?"

She wished he hadn't turned the light on. She'd have preferred the concealing darkness, which made confessions so much easier. "Since the day I met you, I've seen you as bigger than life, a knight in shining armor, fearless."

He snorted. "That's nonsense. Hell, I just told you, *you* scare the hell out of me."

She shook her head; nothing really scared Mick, she knew. And she certainly didn't have that type of power over him. If she had, he wouldn't have turned on her so easily. "I write about heroes every day, but I didn't know they existed. I didn't think any man would deliberately risk his life to keep someone else safe. I didn't know a stranger would risk his life, not for me."

He frowned over that.

"I saw you as…" she shrugged helplessly "…the best of everything."

Mick shoved away the sheet and stood. Gloriously naked, he stalked to the window and looked out at the black, balmy night. A large oak blocked what little moonlight there might have been. No leaves stirred; all was silent except for the bumping of her heart.

The faint light from the bedside lamp threw a glow along one side of his body, causing shadows to dip and swell over his muscles and bones, exaggerating his strength, which she already knew to be considerable. She wanted to touch him everywhere. She wanted to eat him up. And nothing, not even her hurt, could change that.

"I come from nothing, Delilah." His voice broke the night, harsh and raw. "For most of my life, I was nothing. Despite how they feel about it, I'm like a stray that Angel dragged home and everyone accepted. I owe Angel and Dane and their whole goddamn family for showing me what family is, for letting me know how a real life could be, and for helping me to get that life. I owe them for who I am now. But if you stripped them away and left me with just myself, with just the bare bones of *me*, I'd be back at square one. And that sure as hell isn't a white knight."

"No!" She struggled to her knees, clutching the sheet to her throat. "You are who you are, Mick Dawson, a strong, capable man with or without anyone else."

He whirled around. *"I am not a damn hero."*

He looked livid, his eyes red, his nostrils flaring. Del stared.

"Don't you dare put me on some fucking pedestal," he growled, "because I'm guaranteed to fall off. I'm human, and I blunder my way through life just like everyone else."

When she remained silent, wide-eyed and stunned, he stomped back to the bed, caught her upper arms and lifted her from the mattress, causing her sheet to fall. She worried for his injured shoulder, and his injured soul.

"You thought I was impervious to cold, too, that I had insides made of iron."

Del sputtered. "Don't bring up my coffee now!"

"You don't know what I go through, how I fight every day to make sure I stay deserving."

Deserving of what? she wanted to ask, but she couldn't. "Mick…"

"To a lot of people, right and wrong are clear-cut values. But not to me. I force those ideologies into the front of my mind all the time—that a woman strung out on drugs is wrong, not just desperate. That a young man with a gun is a criminal, not a kid trying to survive. I don't even know what a white knight is, but I know what the rules tell me, and I follow those rules to the letter."

Del swallowed her hurt. Looking at him, seeing his pain, hurt even more. "Did those rules tell you to protect me when you knew it might get you killed?"

His jaw clenched; his entire body tightened. But his hands didn't hurt her. She knew without a doubt that Mick would never, ever physically hurt her.

"An officer has to take action when he sees a civilian threatened."

She barely heard what he said. "Did those rules insist you

turn me in because you thought I was breaking the law? Or did you do that because you thought I'd used you?"

He tipped his head back and groaned. "Both."

"Mick?" She needed to touch him, to soothe him, but his hold didn't allow for that. So she gave him the only words she knew that might help. "I forgive you."

His gaze jerked to hers, hot, burning, filled with relief, with satisfaction, greed, elation.

She saw the pulse racing in his strong throat, saw the muscles in his shoulders quiver, saw the glaze of relief in his eyes.

"I want you," he groaned. "More than I've ever wanted anything. More than I wanted my mother to care, more than I wanted Angel to be safe." He shook her slightly. "More than I want my next breath. But I'm just me, and if you try to make me more than that we'll both be disappointed."

Del licked her lips. It sounded to her like he loved her, though he hadn't quite said so. "Do you want me now?"

He lifted her a few inches more until his mouth ground down on hers, bending her head back. His tongue thrust deep. Her body came into stark contact with his, making her aware of all his hard angles and firm muscles, and the long, hard length of his throbbing erection.

Just as quickly his kiss eased and he gentled his hold. His velvet tongue licked, teased, then slowly withdrew. "I'm sorry," he murmured against her mouth, nibbling on her lips, softening them. *"I need you."*

"Your shoulder," she said in alarm, fearing he'd hurt himself.

And Mick groaned again, a sound of half humor, half awe. "Even when I act like a marauding bastard, you don't put me in my place." His expression was less strained, and a half smile curled his mouth. "You're something else, Delilah Piper, you know that?"

"Something good?" she asked.

He smoothed her hair, stroked her lips with his thumb. "Something wonderful," he whispered, and then he kissed her again, this time with such sweetness, such love, she didn't even need to hear him speak the words. She couldn't resist him. He'd tell her what she wanted to hear sooner or later, but for tonight she had him, she had his confidences, and that was more than enough.

THE SECOND MICK AWOKE, he knew the other side of the bed was empty. He sat up in a rush, panic closing in—and saw Delilah sitting in the chair by the window. He eased back, but his heart continued to stutter and his stomach still cramped. "You couldn't sleep?"

A dark shadow made up her form in the gray, predawn light, and still he sensed her smile. "Watching you is more fun than sleeping."

He realized the sheet was around his ankles, and he cocked a brow at her. It was easier to breathe now, with her so obviously teasing. "Taking advantage of me?"

"Yes."

Mick stretched and yawned. With his initial alarm gone, he realized he felt better today, less frazzled, but not completely satisfied. He didn't think he'd be content until he had Delilah committed to him one hundred percent. And that meant getting a ring on her finger and hearing her say the vows.

When she was officially his wife, then maybe he could relax.

He'd made progress last night, though he hoped like hell

she'd never put him through anything like that again. He hated rehashing the past. It shamed him, reminded him of how weak he'd been, how far he'd struggled. And whether Angel admitted it or not, he always knew he'd never have made it without her. If it hadn't been for Angel, he'd be on the other side of the law right now, the one being arrested for God only knew what, rather than a cop doing the arresting.

It was an emotional struggle he dealt with every day.

He heard Delilah sigh as he stretched his left arm high, and grinned. She was so blatant about enjoying his body, both by touch and sight. He was glad he hadn't spent his life chasing women and screwing around like so many males seemed driven to do. It made their relationship that much more special. She was the only woman who'd ever lived with him.

"I thought you'd be writing," he said as he stood and went to his dresser to get some shorts.

She turned to watch him. He knew his way in the dark, but still he flipped on the wall switch, wanting to see her better.

She looked...dreamy.

"I didn't even think about writing."

He frowned, stepped into his gray boxers and went to her. She wore his shirt, and that turned him on. Of course, if she'd been wearing nothing at all, or the sheet, or her own T-shirt, he'd have still been turned on. She couldn't breathe without making him hard.

He stood looking down at her, dreading the question he had to ask. "Did I interfere with your work?"

"How so?"

He smoothed her glossy dark hair behind her ears, touched her arched brows. "You were so upset, I thought..."

"Oh, no. When I'm upset, I usually work through it at the computer. Same when I'm excited. Or sad."

Mick shook his head. Not much got in the way of her writing.

"It's just that last night was so wonderful. *You* were so wonderful." She sighed again, a sigh of repletion and fulfillment, making him feel like that damn white knight she'd spoken of.

Then she added, "I've been thinking, too, about Neddie, about some of the stories he told me."

Slowly, Mick straightened. "Let's do this over coffee."

"Do this?"

"I have a gut feeling that whatever you're going to tell me will be the clue we've been missing. I need caffeine to digest it all, so I don't miss anything important."

Delilah stood and did her own stretching. His pulse leaped. If this wasn't so important… He eyed the bed. But no, it *was* important, and he had to see to her safety first.

"This gut feeling of yours," she asked, "is it like a cop's sixth sense?"

Mick put his arm around her and led the way to the kitchen, flipping on the lights as he went. It was only five-thirty. It'd be another hour or so before the sun lit the sky. "I just know that somehow all this stuff is related."

She nodded, took a stool at the counter—evidently more than willing to have him wait on her, which he was glad to do. "I think it has to do with the story I'm working on."

"Your newest book?" He measured coffee and turned on the machine.

She nodded. "You got anything I can snack on? I'm starved."

He remembered she'd been too upset to eat much the night before, and guilt washed over him. He scrounged around until he found her a few cookies. "I can put some eggs and bacon on, too," he offered, and she accepted with a mouthful of cookie.

"You talk while I cook," he said.

She waved the second cookie at him. "Neddie was trying to go straight, you know? A condition of his parole was that he continue to be counseled, and part of his counseling was to own up to the things he knew he'd done wrong. So he sometimes talked to me."

"You were supposed to absolve him of guilt?"

"Not even close." She chewed on her cookie, thinking, then shuddered. "He told me some gruesome stories," she admitted. "Stuff I could never use in a book. It was too… real, and you know what they say about truth being stranger than fiction. But in a way, Neddie had this odd code of honor. He didn't hurt anyone that he didn't think needed to be hurt. I mean, he didn't just choose innocent victims."

"He hired himself out, honey. He did what he was paid to do."

"I know." She brushed the remainder of the crumbs from her hands and watched Mick lay bacon in a hot skillet. "But he only took jobs that his conscience would let him take. Like this one guy he snuffed—"

"Snuffed?" Mick eyed her, appalled at the casual way she said that.

She shrugged. "It's part of the lingo."

Didn't he know it. "Go on."

"Anyway, the guy he killed had some huge gambling debts, but Neddie said he took the job because the guy also abused his wife."

Mick made a face. "What a discerning fellow."

Delilah laughed. "That's what I said to him. And he knew it was still wrong, but he said he half enjoyed beating that guy up and then dumping him for dead, because he hated anyone who would hit a woman."

"We're in agreement on that."

In a voice as soft as butter, she said, "I know."

Mick poked at the bacon with a fork. He couldn't take her hero worship on an empty stomach, so he steered her back to the subject at hand. "What does any of this have to do with your story?"

"Well, Neddie told me that these guys tried to hire him to kill a man because the guy knew too much and wanted to come clean. They were afraid he'd turn evidence on them or something, so they wanted Neddie to kill him, then sink his car in the river."

Mick jerked around, staring at her. A limp piece of uncooked bacon dangled from the fork in his hand.

"Neddie refused. Not only because he was out of the business and trying to go straight, but because he said he sympathized with the other guy. He said they were alike, both of them wanting to be legit, and there was no proof the guy would rat. After all, Neddie said he'd never ratted anyone out before."

This is it, Mick thought with a surge of triumph. *This is the link.*

"I told Neddie about how I'd learned to escape a car that had gone into the river, and he said I couldn't have escaped if I'd been dead before it went in." Delilah tilted her head at Mick, her beautiful, light blue eyes filled with a heavy sadness. "Is that what happened to Neddie? You said he was murdered, and I know he drowned. Did someone kill him, then drive his car into the river? The paper didn't give all the details. I didn't know you were a cop, so I didn't think you'd know, either. After all, it was supposed to be confidential stuff for the ongoing investigation."

For the first time that he could remember since becoming an officer of the law, Mick didn't even consider what was right or wrong. He set a cup of coffee in front of Delilah and pulled out the stool next to her. Their bare knees touched, his on the outside of hers. "Neddie's wrists," he explained carefully, "had bruises on them, evidence that he'd been tied up, though there were no ropes or anything on him when his body was found."

Delilah reached for his hand, and Mick squeezed her fingers.

"He had a wound on the back of his head, too. The coroner said he'd been struck with a blunt object, knocked out just before the car went off the bridge—or possibly as the car went over. It'd be impossible to tell for sure, but as you just said, he wasn't given the chance to escape the car and swim to the surface. We're thinking whoever did it hoped the car wouldn't be found until time and the natural effects of water and cold had done enough damage to disguise a deliberate murder."

"He had a suicide note in his pocket?"

Mick nodded. "Yeah."

Her lips quivered, and she drew a ragged breath. "That's exactly what Neddie described, what he said the men wanted him to do." She blinked away a sheen of tears, and whispered raggedly, "I used that whole scenario in my book."

"The book you're working on now?"

"Yes. In the last book, the hero got away by keeping his head and doing the things I'd learned from submerging myself in a car."

Mick shuddered. He could *not* think about that now. Somehow he'd figure out a way to temper Delilah's more dangerous inclinations, without stifling her.

"But in this book," she continued, oblivious to his turmoil, "he was knocked out, a suicide note planted on him, and the heroine had to save him."

Just like Delilah to twist things around, Mick thought. But then, if any woman were capable of a rescue, it'd be Delilah Piper. He wouldn't underestimate her on anything, once she set her mind to it.

It was an enormous long shot, but Mick asked, "That whole scenario is too damn close to the truth to be comfortable. Does anyone know what's in this book?"

She nodded. "Tons of people, I'm sure. Remember I told you I was on the news, discussing my current project? We talked about that whole scene. I…I was laughing about it, bragging that it could happen, and that a woman might indeed be a hero. I never once considered that I could be putting Neddie in danger."

"Neddie didn't know about the interview?"

"I don't know." She covered her face. "He died shortly after that. He…he might have died because of *me*. Someone could have heard that radio program, someone who knew we'd become friends, that Neddie coached me on my research."

"And they might have assumed he'd told you too much, and that you could repeat it." If Mick thought he'd felt fear before, it was nothing to what he felt now. Someone wanted to shut her up, to make certain she couldn't repeat details that might be incriminating. But he didn't know who, and until he did know, until he could get the bastards, her life was at stake.

Delilah rocked slowly back and forth in her seat as the ramifications settled around her. "I'm to blame."

With a new fury, Mick tipped up her chin. "*Wrong*. Don't even go there, babe. When you live the type of life Neddie did, then you run the risks. That's just how it is."

"He was changing."

"Maybe just a little too late." Mick pulled her into his lap. "Did Neddie give you any names, anything that might connect him with the killers?"

She thought hard, staring down at her hands. Slowly her gaze rose to his. "You know, he did say something, but I'm not sure it'll help."

"At this point, it'd have to be more than we've got."

She nodded, her brows drawn. "He said the guys who wanted to hire him should have known better, because they'd been in prison with him in '86, all of them convicted for car theft."

It took several moments for it to sink in, before Mick allowed himself to believe. "Bingo."

"You think?"

"I think it'll be easy enough to check prison records. That might do it, with your testimony. Especially if the fingerprints from the apartment next to yours match up. We should have those today."

"Is that why they tried to kill me? They knew Neddie had been talking to me? They knew he'd...told me things?"

Mick hugged her. God, she was precious to him. And she was also smart, so there was no point in hoping to protect her. Besides, he didn't want her feeling guilty for Neddie's death, not if he could help it.

"The bruises on Neddie's wrists showed that he put up a hell of a fight, that he tried to work himself free. But he didn't make it." Mick kissed her temple, her ear. "Could be they promised to let him go if he named everyone he'd talked to."

She shook her head, adamant in Neddie's defense. "No, Neddie would never have done that, not if he thought they'd hurt me."

Her innocence amazed him. "How long did you know him, sweetheart?"

"A few months. But we were friends, Mick," she said staunchly.

"That's not enough time to really judge."

She leaned back and gave him a level look. "It's longer than I've known you."

Mick scowled, not appreciating that comparison at all. "He was an admitted murderer. A car thief. Those things are not synonymous with ethics, and any man could cave when his life was on the line."

"I won't believe that."

Mick decided to let it go. She'd been hurt enough, and disillusioning her now wouldn't accomplish a thing. "Let's finish up breakfast and shower, then I'll call Faradon. He should be up by then, and if not, well, he'll get up."

"You really think any of this will make a difference?"

"I know it will."

"I hope so," she said. "I want this behind us. I want us to take walks in the park and go to the zoo, and I want to get back to my research."

Mick groaned. He didn't know if he could live through her special brand of daredevil study.

But he knew he didn't want to live without her, so he supposed he'd find a way to get used to it.

chapter 14

THE PHONE RANG while Mick was in the shower. He'd insisted that Del go ahead while he cleaned the kitchen, and when she'd protested, he claimed it had to be that way. If he showered with her, they'd never leave his house.

She accepted that he probably was right.

With her hair still wet and her feet bare, Del picked up the phone. "Dawson residence."

"Faradon here. Is this Ms. Piper?"

"Yes," she said shortly. Detective Faradon still wasn't one of her favorite people, not after the interrogation she'd been through.

"We got the fingerprints back and have some photos to go with them. We'd like you to come to the station and take a look, see if you can ID anyone. How soon can you be here?"

She bristled at his demanding tone. At the very least, she felt the man owed her a few apologies. "Actually, Mick and I were coming in, anyway." She didn't mention her new "evidence" because she wasn't convinced it would help. Mick could explain everything.

There was a pause, then he asked, "How soon?"

"Mick is about done showering now. I'd say we'll leave here in the next fifteen minutes."

"I'll be waiting," he said, and rudely hung up.

A few minutes later Mick came out looking nicely rugged and sexy as sin in faded, well-worn jeans and a soft gray T-shirt. He wore scuffed, lace-up black boots. As Del watched, he checked his gun.

She inched closer. "Can I see?"

He glanced up. "What? My gun?"

Nodding, she said, "A Smith & Wesson, right? Semiautomatic?"

Mick held the gun out of her reach. "No one touches my gun but me."

She rolled her eyes. "I'm not going to fire it. And I do know a little about guns."

"Research, I suppose?"

"Yes."

"Well, then you know enough to understand how dangerous they are." With a dexterity that proved how quickly he was healing, he tucked the gun into a holster at the small of his back, and smoothed his T-shirt over it. "And," he said again, "*no one* touches my gun but me."

"Fine. Whatever."

He caught her before she could turn away, and kissed her neck. It was shameful, but she immediately softened, just as he'd probably known she would.

"Who was on the phone?" he asked against her throat.

Sometimes it was annoying, loving Mick. She couldn't seem to stay angry with him, especially when he kissed her. "Your buddy, Faradon."

"He's not my buddy, he's just the lead investigator on the robbery and shooting." He kissed her again, this time nuzzling beneath her ear. It felt like her toes melted. "What did he want?"

Struggling to get her brain in gear, she succeeded in saying, "He has fingerprints and photos, and he wants us to come take a look for a positive ID."

Stepping back from her, Mick looked at the chunky black watch on his wrist. "Hell, it's barely eight o'clock. He's at it early."

Feeling hopeful for the first time, Del asked, "Do you think that means we're close to having this wrapped up?"

Mick took her arm and headed for the door. "Even with an ID, we'd still have to get hold of them, but it'd sure make it easier to track the bastards down. It's tougher to hide when everyone knows who you are. There's also the possibility that Rudy'll be more willing to talk once we have names."

The sun never did quite rise. Instead, as they stepped outside, they saw that fat purple clouds had rolled in, leaving the air heavy with the scent of rain. In the distance, lightning flickered.

Mick cursed. "Did you want to grab a jacket or umbrella?"

"I won't melt."

She saw his surprise, then his smile, as he opened the car door for her. "I'd forgotten your affinity for rain," he said.

When she raised a brow, he explained, "The day I finally met you, the day of the robbery. Everyone else had an umbrella, but you didn't even seem to notice how soaked you'd gotten." He slid his hand over her waist and squeezed suggestively. "I noticed."

Del smiled at that. It was nice being reminded that the awesome attraction went both ways. If Mick had indeed noticed her when she looked like a used rag mop, then his interest was as keen as hers. Maybe more so, because she hadn't paid him a bit of mind until the shooting.

Once he folded his big body behind the wheel, she told him, "I love running in the drizzling rain. It's peaceful and it stimulates my muse."

He started to make a nasty crack, no doubt about stimulating her, and Del elbowed him. They both laughed and she thought how nice it was, how right, to be with Mick this way. She wondered, once everything was settled, what would happen. When it was no longer necessary for her to stay with him for protection, would he ask her to leave? Would he ask her to stay?

Half an hour later she was still pondering that when the sky opened up. No slight drizzle this, but a raging summer storm full of power. The stuffy, humid air came alive with electricity, crackling and snapping all around them. Trees bent and dipped, leaves and debris danced across the rain-washed roadways.

Del slanted Mick a look. "Rainstorms are sexy," she whispered.

"You're sexy. Rain or no rain," he replied, keeping his gaze on the road.

She grinned, about to tell him how she'd like to spend the afternoon once they finished at the station, when they were blinded by a sudden glare. In the darkness of the morning storm, an approaching car's bright lights reflected off Mick's door. He flinched, throwing up a hand, but it didn't help. The car came from an empty side street, and rather than slowing, it accelerated to a reckless speed across the slick roadway, coming right for them.

Mick glanced out his window, gripped the wheel tightly and muttered with icy calm, "Hold on."

The car struck the back side-panel, throwing them into a spin. Del's seat belt tightened; she yelped in alarm, barely keeping her wits enough to twist around, trying to see what happened.

At the force of impact, Mick first overcompensated, and the car slewed off the road and into the mud before grasping the slick pavement again.

Del, assuming it was an accident—a result of the rainy conditions—wondered why Mick didn't just pull over. She looked over her shoulder, wide-eyed, in time to see the other car straighten and shoot toward them again.

Mick's hand flattened on the top of her head, and he shoved her down in the seat. "Stay there!"

The rear windshield exploded, glass flying everywhere. "Dear God!" Del held Mick's thigh, her face pressed into his side. This couldn't be happening! She tried to sit up, wanting only to protect Mick.

"Keep down," Mick barked, again flattening her in the seat. It suddenly hit her who was after them and why.

Del felt another impact, this time to the rear fender of the car, and there was no way to steer out of it. The car swerved off the road, slinging mud and fishtailing, and finally colliding with a scrawny tree, jarring them both hard.

Mick's head hit the wheel and he slumped.

"Mick!" She screamed his name, scrambling to get her seat belt off, to reach him. Her heart leaped into her throat, her vision clouded with fear. Before she could reach him her door was jerked open. The thunderous roar of the storm intruded, along with a spray of rain and turbulent air. Hard hands grabbed her, yanking her back. She fought them, seeing the trickle of blood on Mick's forehead, the stillness in his body.

He needed help, a hospital! But already her feet were being dragged through the mud, and no matter how she fought, she couldn't escape. The hands holding her only tightened with bruising force.

Someone grabbed her hair and wrenched her head back. "Do you want me to go back and put a bullet in him to make sure he's dead?"

That voice was rough, familiar, and Del froze, choking on her terror. "No."

"Then come along and be quiet."

A hard shove landed her facedown in the front seat of the other car, and she barely had time to right herself before two men squeezed in around her. The battered car had been left running, idling roughly. The interior smelled of smoke and stale liquor. It was dirty, cluttered.

The man on her right pressed a gun to her ribs, hard enough to make her groan, and with enough intent to scare her witless. She recognized them as the same men from the jewelry store—the men who wanted her dead.

"What do you want?" she asked around her fear, wanting, needing Mick. *Dear God, please let him be all right.*

"Shut up."

The car lurched away, tires squealing, zigzagging with a distinct lack of caution for the weather and road conditions. Wet tendrils of hair stuck to Del's face and throat. She swiped them aside and twisted to see Mick's car as they made a screeching U-turn and sped away. Right before he was out of view, she could have sworn she saw him lift his head, but it was hard to tell with the rain streaking the dirty windows and the strobing effects of the electrical storm.

Del closed her eyes on another silent prayer. Mick *had* to be okay. The gun prodded her when they made a sharp turn, keeping her own danger in acute perspective. She felt icy cold inside and out, and couldn't stop the racking shakes that made her teeth chatter and her head hurt.

Keep them talking, she thought. "How did you know where to ambush us?" she asked.

Smirking, the man lifted his hand to his head, finger and thumb extended as if it were a phone. "This is Faradon," he mimicked. "We need you to come to the station."

Her stomach roiled. "You had us bugged again?" Had these disgusting men heard Mick's heartfelt admissions about his past? She couldn't bear it.

"Nope. I didn't overhear the call, I *made* the call. Your protector was rather accommodating, sharing his home number with Faradon and asking him to leave any messages concerning the robbery on his message machine. He didn't want you to know he was a cop, you see, but he still wanted to stick his nose where it didn't belong. The son of a bitch was determined to get hold of us." He shrugged. "He called his house and took his messages that way, and you went on in blissful ignorance, thinking you screwed a PI, not a cop."

Reality sank in. One more lie Mick had told. Strangely enough, she felt more concern for his guilt, if he should find out, than she did for the lie. She understood him. She knew why he hadn't confided in her. She'd meant it when she'd said she forgave him for that. "You got Faradon's name and Mick's number from a call he made at my place."

"That's right. So, no, Faradon isn't expecting you. He won't send out the cavalry."

Del looked through the mud-spattered windshield and saw they were headed toward the river. Not the Ohio—no, that would be too obvious. This was a much smaller, much dirtier river. But it was deep. And fast. Mostly isolated excepted for the occasional fisherman. But not today. Today the river was deserted.

And she knew why they were going there.

Do not get hysterical, she told herself, even as her breath hitched and her lungs constricted. She could smell the two of them in the stuffy, steamy interior of the car. She could smell her own fear and their excitement. Bile rose in her throat.

They pulled off the main road and drove through a patch of weeds and scrub. A ramshackle outbuilding sat to their right, and a long wooden pier, probably private, stretched along the shore, then angled out into deeper water. The car bumped onto it, tires thumping along the uneven, weather-worn boards.

Though they moved slowly now, edging nearer and nearer to the end of the dock, Del felt time speeding past her. A cabin cruiser docked to their right blocked them from view of the road.

Over the river, lightning danced, temporarily illuminating the sky and emphasizing the blackness of the deep, churning water. They meant to drown her, to kill her and sink the awful, dirty car with her inside it.

The driver laughed, reaching for her upper thigh and

giving her a lecherous **squeeze.** "It's a shame we have to end this so quickly," he sneered. "Watching you with that cop makes me want to taste you myself."

Del slugged him.

She didn't think about it, didn't weigh the wisdom with the folly. She simply snapped, then reacted on instinct. Using a technique she'd learned in self-defense classes, she brought her elbow up and back. Hard, fast. Right into his face.

"Fucking bitch." The driver grabbed for his bleeding nose and temporarily lost control of the car. The other man grabbed Del by the neck, squeezing as he shouted orders.

In that single moment of chaos, everything became clear for Del, and she knew what to do.

She ignored the fist clamped around her throat, making it impossible for her to draw air, and instead put her efforts into a hard shove on the driver. He lost his balance, and Del wedged her foot down to the floorboards. She found the gas pedal and jammed down.

With a loud roar of the engine, the car lurched forward. The driver shouted, gripping the wheel, but Del had clamped both hands on it. They wrestled, but he sputtered blood and went blind with panic.

The hand at her throat let go to grab her shoulder. It felt like her arm had been wrenched from the socket—but it was too late. The old car went airborne off the far end of the dock, suspending time and sound and reality, then dumped hard into the icy river with an enormous splash. Hissing and sputtering, the car tipped, engine first, and began sinking.

Both men forgot about Del in their panic. They pounded

at the windows, screamed as the blackness engulfed them and water began rushing in.

Del concentrated on regaining her breath. Her throat felt crushed; it hurt to swallow, even to breathe, but she did it, slow, deep. The gun had dropped onto the seat beside her, forgotten. She tucked it into her pocket. The man to her right got the window open, and a great gush of frigid river water knocked him backward into Del. His elbow caught her shoulder, his foot dug into her thigh as he scrambled frantically to get to the window again, bent only on escaping the car.

On her knees so that her head stayed in the pocket of air inside the car, Del inhaled deeply, then slithered to the back seat. Water closed over her face just as her fingers found the window handle.

She thought of Mick, thought of everything she wanted to tell him, and did what she had to do.

MICK WIPED BLOOD from his face with one shaking hand and maneuvered the slippery, winding road with the other.

After smacking his head on the steering wheel, he'd come to in enough time to see the car leaving with Delilah—but not in enough time to stop them.

Going seventy miles an hour to diminish their lead, he'd called for backup. His actions had been by rote, because both his mind and his heart stalled the second he'd realized what had happened.

He reached the river just in time to see the car sail off the dock and hit the churning water with crunching force. Terror blinded him. He wasn't aware of slamming on his brakes. He wasn't aware of the other police cars pulling up at the same time, sirens blaring and lights flashing.

He threw open his car door and hit the ground running, his only thought to get to Delilah. The storm surrounded him, lashing his face, making his feet slip in the wet weeds and slimy mud. Just before he reached the end of the dock, he got tackled hard and then held down. He fought the restraining hands without thought, hitting someone, kicking another.

"No, goddamn it," Faradon shouted when Mick almost wrenched loose. "Hold him!"

Mick barely heard. Three men gripped him, twisting his arms, making his wounded shoulder burn like fire, but it was nothing compared to the agony in his heart.

They jerked him to his feet, and all around him men shouted orders, while sirens continued to squeal and blue lights competed with the white flashes of the storm.

Numb, Mick continued to strain against the arms holding him. Faradon stepped up close. "We have a team preparing," he said not two inches from Mick's face. "Dawson, do you hear me? They'll be in the water in ten minutes tops."

Mick shook his head. In ten minutes she would be dead.

With renewed strength he lurched forward, taking the men by surprise. They lost their footing on the slippery, weathered boards and their holds loosened. Mick broke free.

He'd taken two running steps when someone shouted, "Look!"

A spotlight searching the surface of the water reflected off Delilah's inky-black hair. She sputtered, coughed. Mick went into the water in a clean dive. With several hard fast strokes, he reached her.

When he closed his hands around her, she at first fought him.

"It's all right, baby," he said, spitting dirty water, "it's me."

"Mick?" She dog-paddled, swallowed some of the water and choked, then cried, *"Mick!"*

She clung to him. Mick felt so weak it was all he could do to drag in air. Then several men surrounded them, catching them both and pulling them to the docks.

He hoisted Delilah up first. Faradon himself leaned down. "Give me your hands, miss," he said, and Delilah reached upward.

Sloshing, shivering, she landed on the dock, and someone rushed to put several blankets around her.

"M-M-Mick?"

He heard the shivering alarm, the need, and helped to drag himself out. Officers tried to cover him, too, but he wanted only Delilah. Weaving on her feet, she reached for him, and then he had her, tight in his arms where she damn well belonged and where she'd damn well stay.

He heard her crying, and his knees went weak. He tangled his hands in her wet hair, knowing he was too rough, but unable to temper his hold. "I've got you," he said gruffly, and crushed her to him.

"Mick, c'mon, man," said a gentle voice. "Let's get her out of the rain."

As if from far away, Mick heard Faradon speaking to him. He wrapped Delilah closer and allowed them both to be led to the outbuilding. It was dry inside, that was the best to be said for it.

Faradon stood there, looking slightly embarrassed. "We're, uh, fetching some dry clothes."

Mick gulped air, swallowed choking emotions and a love so rich he couldn't bear it. Delilah clung to him, and he didn't know if he'd survive the fear of thinking he'd lost her. He lifted his head. "The bastards who took her?"

"We're looking for them. If they surface, we'll fish them out. If not, we'll start diving until we find them."

Delilah struggled for a moment, and Mick loosened his hold.

"Take this," she said, digging a gun out of her baggy jeans pocket. She held it out to Faradon, and he carefully accepted it.

"You disarmed them?" he asked, his voice heavy with awe.

Mick pressed her face to his shoulder. "She can explain to you later."

Faradon didn't look like he wanted to wait until later, but then a cop wearing a slicker stepped into the doorway. He held out a bundle of clothes, wrapped in another slicker, then nodded and excused himself.

Mick said to Faradon, "Get out. And don't let anyone else in."

Half grinning, shaking his head, Faradon said, "Right."

The door shut behind the detective, and Mick forced himself to loosen his arms from around Delilah. The small building was dim, crowded with boat trailers, ski equipment, tools. Mick bent, touched his nose to hers and whispered, "Let me get you dry, okay?"

She nodded. "I'm all right now."

"I know you are." He strangled on the words and had to stop, had to draw in a shaky breath. His hands trembled as he stripped away her sodden blankets and started to work on the fastening of her loose jeans.

"I lost my shoes in the river," she said.

Mick wondered if she was in shock. He needed to get her warm and dry, needed to get her to a hospital.

He needed… Swallowing hard this time didn't help. He hated it, hated himself, but tears clogged his throat. He felt unmanned, vulnerable.

Without the gentleness that he intended, he removed her clothes and turned to rummage through the bundle inside the slicker. He found a loose jacket, two more blankets.

"Lift your arms," he murmured, and she obliged. The jacket, apparently donated by one of the officers milling around outside, hung to her knees. Mick shook out another blanket, this one thankfully dry, and draped it over her.

Delilah clutched the edges together and said, "It's not really cold. I mean, it must be eighty-five outside. I'm just chilled…." Her teeth chattered, making her explanations difficult.

"Shh," Mick said, and stripped off his own shirt so he wouldn't get her wet. There was nothing he could do about his pants. He sure as hell wasn't going to run around bare-assed. He pulled one slicker over Delilah's head, then another over his own. "Let's get you to the hospital so you can be checked over," he said, deliberately concentrating on only one thing at a time.

Her fingers clutched at his arm, gripping the slicker with surprising force. "Mick, I don't…I don't want to go back out there yet."

His heart hit his stomach with her trembling words. He turned to her, opened his arms.

And she launched herself into him. "I was so—so scared," she said on a wail.

Mick wanted to absorb her into himself, to surround her always and keep her from ever being hurt again. Those damn tears got him again, and he squeezed her tighter, assuring himself that he had her, that she was okay.

Rain drummed on the metal roof of the shed and wind howled through every crack and crevice in the aged boards.

Then Delilah said something that made his knees give out. "I thought I'd lost you."

"What?"

She sniffed, shook her head while tears mingled with the wetness on her cheeks. Her words were broken, scattered and rushed. "I saw the blood on your forehead and I thought you might be dead or dying. You've already been hurt so much because of me." She leaned back to gently touch his face. "Are you all right? Truly?"

Mick dropped to his knees and stared up at Delilah, not caring that he cried, having totally forgotten about his own cut head. "*You* almost died," he groaned.

"Oh no. I knew what I was doing." She smoothed his sodden hair, her hand tender, loving. "I was afraid at first. Terrified really. But I kept thinking about you. I kept thinking what if I survived and you didn't? When I realized it was you in the river with me, I went weak. I was…well, I was doing fine until then."

Mick pressed his face into her belly. The chill had left her body and she felt warm, smelled musky and damp, and he knew he couldn't stand it, knew he was going to embarrass himself.

He held her tighter but it didn't help.

Faradon rapped at the door. "You two about done changing?"

"Go away!" Delilah yelled impatiently. "We'll be out in a minute."

Faradon grumbled something, but he didn't open the door.

Mick felt her cool hands cup his face, but he couldn't let her go, couldn't unclench his muscles. He hated feeling like this, powerless and weak and... He opened his hands on her behind and squeezed her closer, grinding his face into her, trying to absorb her.

He heard Delilah's smile as she said, "I love you, Mick Dawson. More than anyone or anything, now and forever."

He drew a shuddering breath and rubbed his face over her belly, on her borrowed blanket, drying his eyes and attempting to regain control. He had to get hold of himself. He had to...

"Tell me you love me, too," she whispered.

"I do," he said without hesitation. Only a trace of tears remained in his raw voice, not that he gave a damn. Delilah deserved to know everything about him.

"You do?" she asked.

"So much it hurts."

"I don't want you to hurt."

"Then don't ever leave me."

"Never." She slipped to her knees in front of him, still cupping his face. She kissed him, then kissed him again. She even smiled. "Will you stop calling me Delilah and call me Del?"

His shoulders shook. "No."

"Oh." She sounded surprised and disgruntled, and that went a long way toward helping him regain his discipline. Even at the worst of times, she amused him.

Finally she asked, "Well then, will you marry me?"

He actually laughed, but it turned into a groan. "I was going to ask you, you know."

"Sorry."

He touched her face, her sodden, tangled hair, her small breasts and narrow hips and long thighs. "God, I love you, every inch of you. I'll always love you, I swear it." When she gave him a brilliant smile, he added with more strength, "You've stolen forty years off my life with that last damn stunt!"

Her smile never wavered. She stood and held out her hand to him. As if *he* needed *her* assistance to stand!

He did.

He still felt wobbly, but as long as he didn't think about the moment that he'd seen that car go into the river...

He shuddered, took her slender hand and let her help haul him to his feet.

She put an arm around him and leaned her head into his shoulder. "I lost fifty years, leaving you behind in that car, bleeding. Nothing has ever scared me like that."

They headed for the door together. Just as Mick opened it, someone shouted, "I've got one of 'em!"

They followed the spotlight, and saw several cops converge on a man trying to crawl onto the muddy, thickly weeded shore. He was promptly handcuffed.

It wasn't until the next day that the police finally found the other man's body and confirmed his death. But they had two of them, Rudy Glasgow and the driver. They also had fingerprints, both from the apartment next to Delilah's and the gun she'd retrieved from the car.

It was over.

DEL FLITTED from one person to the next. She loved being in a large family, even if most of that family was male and not really family at all. They felt like family, treated her as such, and they loved Mick to distraction. That in itself made her more than a little fond of them.

At the moment, Angel and Celia were perusing Mick's new bookcases, now holding her books. Del had pretty much taken over his house. His spare bedroom served as her office, and he'd already had an extra phone line put in.

The kids were all outside playing, but they could be heard through the open windows. Every minute or so one of the adults went to check on them.

Dane and Alec were seated on the couch, Josh and Zack in adjacent chairs, all of them watching a sports channel. Now that Del was used to them, Dane no longer seemed so imposing and Alec was nowhere near as frightening. But they were still fascinating characters.

Grinning, Del dropped down on the seat between them, using each hand to pat a hard masculine thigh. The two men looked at her warily. "Now that I've finally finished my current book and got it all turned in," she said, "I've been thinking of doing a book about two PIs who—"

Mick, who'd sauntered over to stand behind the couch, covered her mouth with a large hand. Del froze.

"If either one of you wants to remain in my good graces you won't tell her anything about anything…dangerous."

Alec saluted Mick with his cola. "Sorry, but Celia knows everything dangerous involved in my job, and she's been chewing Del's ear for the past hour."

True enough, Del thought, appreciating both Celia's forthright information and the way everyone had taken to calling her "Del," once she'd explained that she only used the name "Delilah" for writing.

Everyone except Mick, that is, who swore he loved her name as much as he loved her. The charmer. He even claimed "Delilah Dawson" had a very nice ring to it. Del couldn't wait for that to become her name in fact.

Dane nodded. "Yep, I'm afraid you're preaching to the choir here, Mick. You should have gagged the women, not us."

Mick groaned with heartfelt sincerity. He'd promised to be understanding about her research, though Del knew he wanted to keep her in a cotton-lined box so she didn't so much as stub her baby toe.

Del pulled his hand away and tipped her head back to see him upside down. "How'd you sneak in here behind me?"

Mick rolled his eyes. "Sweetheart, when your brain is plotting, a herd of buffalo could tramp through and you wouldn't notice."

Since that was true, she said instead, "But I thought you were outside playing with the kids."

"They did me in. They're vicious little brutes who keep singing about how I was saved by a woman."

Del frowned, feeling a good dose of jealousy. "What woman?"

Mick leaned down to kiss her. "You."

"Me?" He nodded, and Del said, "But I didn't save you."

The awful nightmare of the car wreck, of Mick's head injury and her dousing in the river was two weeks old now, but she still shivered whenever she thought of how close she'd come to losing him.

Angel sidled up behind the couch, too, and hugged Mick. Celia joined her, resting her hands on Alec's shoulders.

Zack and Josh twisted in their seats to face Del. She felt hemmed in by them all—but now the feeling was nice, sort of comforting.

She was surrounded by friends and family.

Mick smoothed his hand over her hair, something she was now more than familiar with. "Of course you saved me," he said. "You love me, right?"

"Absolutely."

"There, you see?" Alec chimed in, nudging her with his rock-hard shoulder. "You saved Mick from being a cynical fool who didn't believe in love."

Del looked at Mick again. With the way these people adored him, she found that hard to believe. "You didn't believe in love?" she asked skeptically, but at the same time she thought it probably explained his reticence in admitting his feelings to her. Now, of course, he told her how much he cared in a thousand different ways—including the simple words *I love you.*

Mick just smiled.

Dane nudged her next, almost knocking her into Alec's lap. "You saved him from being a control freak, too."

Del righted herself and laughed; Mick was still very much a controlling man, and she doubted that would ever change.

Zack said, "You saved him from living his life like a monk."

With a very slight blush, Del said, "Okay, you got me there." Everyone laughed.

Mick was a voracious lover, and he couldn't seem to keep his hands off her. Which she appreciated because she loved when he touched her. He'd also become a voracious reader. He'd devoured her books and claimed he couldn't wait for the next one. She'd been nearly beside herself with his praise.

Josh tossed back a drink, then asked, "So when is this wedding we're all anticipating?"

Mick frowned at his friend, but said, "I just got the church reserved for the first Saturday of next month."

"You're all invited," Del announced, "as long as you know it won't be too fancy. No tuxes, and definitely no long white lace gowns." She pulled her jeans-clad legs up onto the couch and hugged her knees. "I hate dressing up."

"I'll be lucky to get shoes on her," Mick teased, and Angel promptly corrected him. She'd been with Del when the dress *and* matching shoes were bought.

Del noticed Josh heading for the kitchen, his head down, his hands shoved into his pants pockets. She smiled at Mick, rose from the couch and went to her friend. She found him standing at the sink, watching the children play through the window. "Josh?"

He turned to her, but said nothing.

"You're happy that Mick's marrying me, aren't you?"

He looked surprised, then wary. "Why?"

"Because you're one of his best friends. I don't want to come between you."

That made him laugh. "You belong between us, honey. Mick's a lucky guy, and yeah, I'm happy for you both."

"I hesitate to point this out, but you don't exactly look happy."

"No?" He studied her face, his green eyes dark, his slight smile crooked, chagrined.

She shook her head. "*Morose* might be a better word."

Mick's arms slid around her, lacing over her stomach. "*Defeated* might work, too," he said gently.

Josh snorted.

Mick tightened his hold, surprising Del, then said, "There are plenty of women out there, Josh."

"Yeah?"

Zack stepped up. "That's right, and I intend to find one."

All eyes turned to him. Del grinned. "You're bride hunting?"

"Why is that such a surprise?"

Josh said, "Because you seldom date? Because you're the quintessential bachelor? Because no woman will ever come before Dani?"

Del slugged Josh, making him jump and rub his shoulder while grumbling.

Still frowning, she said, "No *good* woman would want to come before his daughter! Children should always be first. At least until they're self-sufficient. Besides," she added, patting Zack's chest and smiling, "Zack has enough love for a wife and several children."

"One daughter is enough! All I want now is the wife to complete the set. After all, Dani is crazy about you, Del. It made me think about what she's missing."

"Like what?" Mick asked. "You take great care of her."

"I try," Zack admitted, "but she needs a female role model. Someone quiet and intelligent and sincere."

"And sexy?" Mick asked.

Zack shrugged. "I'd rather she was domestic, if you want the truth."

"I wish you luck," Josh said with mock sincerity.

"I don't need luck, because I already have a plan. And I'm starting tomorrow."

Mick and Josh groaned, but Zack just smiled, confident in himself and his eventual success.

The rest of the family filed into the kitchen, including the children. Zack scooped up his daughter, hugged her tight.

"Time for us to go," Dane announced. "Tomorrow is a school day."

There were kisses all around, and everyone gradually left except Zack and Josh. Zack's daughter had fallen asleep on his shoulder, her blond curls disheveled, her mouth smooshed on her daddy's shoulder.

Zack pulled Del close with his free arm and gave her a smacking kiss on the mouth. "Congratulations again on the engagement," he whispered. He patted her cheek and stepped aside.

Josh set down his drink and reached for Del, catching her shoulders in his hands. He gave her the softest look she'd ever seen from him, leaned forward—and Mick's hand was suddenly between them, covering her mouth.

Mick bared his teeth at Josh and said, "Out."

Laughing, Josh pushed him aside and kissed Del on the forehead. "Your future husband is a jealous lout, did you know that?"

She waved his comment away. "Nonsense. He knows I'm crazy about him."

Josh and Mick exchanged a certain look that Del didn't understand in the least.

Shaking his head, Josh gave her a squeeze. "I'm glad you're so happy."

Holding his daughter to his shoulder, Zack grabbed Josh's collar and hauled him toward the door. "Let's go. Dani is starting to snore, and you're pressing your luck."

After they'd gone, Del asked Mick, "Okay, what was that all about?"

"What?" he asked, pretending innocence.

"That business with Josh. What's wrong with him?"

Mick looked briefly harassed. "Nothing that he won't get over," he said, and it almost sounded like a threat.

Before she could ask any more questions, he took her hand and herded her toward the bedroom.

"What do you think about Zack wanting a wife?" she asked.

Mick lightly pushed her down on the bed, then covered her with his body. He touched her cheek, her chin, the corner of her mouth. "I think he's a little jealous, too."

"Too?"

Mick kissed her. "Everyone knows I'm the luckiest man alive. When I think about the fact that you're mine, I almost can't bear it, it's so incredible. I want to tell the whole world." He smiled. "I love you, Delilah Piper."

"I'm lucky, too," she said softly. "I have you. And I did tell the whole world."

Startled, Mick leaned back. "You did?"

"Wait until you see the dedication in my next book. It's to my very own hero, the finest man alive." She cupped his face. "And everyone knows that's you."

Mick frowned for just a moment, then his frown lifted and he shook his head. "Damn, I do feel like a hero. After all, the hero always gets the girl in the end, right?"

Del laughed. "In my books, he sure as heck does."

Who is Gena Showalter?
Gena Showalter is amazing.

What, you want more than that? Okay, fine. (But you asked for it.) Gena Showalter is amazing and she suffers from Writer ADD. She simply cannot write in one genre of romance. She must dabble in all of them. She divides her time between writing about the mythical world of Atlantis (where demons, dragons, vampires and nymphs somehow manage to find eternal love), a futuristic world where aliens stalk the night and elite agents stalk them (and everyone manages to find eternal love), a secret paranormal society of superheroes (you know the drill—eternal love), young adult books (yeah, she's gone there, too, but sadly, no eternal love, just boyfriends) and ultra-sexy contemporary romances with absolutely no supernatural elements (but—gasp—there is eternal love).

Right now she's working on a brand-new paranormal series, Lords of the Underworld. What could be better than immortal warriors, curses, Pandora's box, and—can it be?—eternal love? The first book, *The Darkest Night,* features a man cursed to die every night, only to awaken the next morning knowing he has to die again. Oh, and he happens to be possessed by the spirit of violence. Don't worry, though. He's not evil—he's just very, very naughty....

For more information about Gena (as if you haven't learned enough already!) and her (delicious) books, visit www.genashowalter.com and her blog at www.genashowalter.blogspot.com.

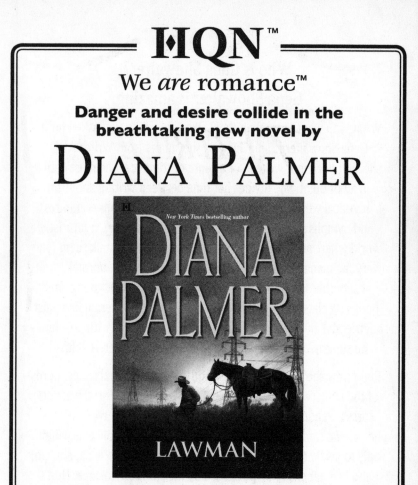